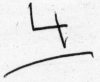

Elsie Silver is a Canadian author of sassy, sexy, small town romance who loves a good book boyfriend and the strong heroines who bring them to their knees. She lives just outside of Vancouver, British Columbia with her husband, son, and three dogs and has been voraciously reading romance books since before she was probably supposed to.

She loves cooking and trying new foods, traveling, and spending time with her boys—especially outdoors. Elsie has also become a big fan of her quiet five o'clock mornings, which is when most of her writing happens. It's during this time that she can sip a cup of hot coffee and dream up a fictional world full of romantic stories to share with her readers.

www.elsiesilver.com

Reckless

ELSIE
SILVER

PIATKUS

PIATKUS

First published in Great Britain in 2023 by Piatkus

9 10

A CIP catalogue record for this book is available from the British Library.

ISBN: 978-0-349-43772-9

Typeset in Fanwood by M Rules

Printed and bound in Great Britain by Clays Ltd, Elcograf S.p.A.

Papers used by Piatkus are from well-managed forests
and other responsible sources.

Piatkus
An imprint of
Little, Brown Book Group
Carmelite House
50 Victoria Embankment
London EC4Y 0DZ

An Hachette UK Company
www.hachette.co.uk

www.littlebrown.co.uk

For all the tired mamas out there. I see you.

Failure is not the falling down, but the staying down.
                                              – Mary Pickford

Reader Note

This book contains discussions about miscarriage and infertility. It is my hope that I've handled these topics with the care they deserve.

1

Winter

"I can't fathom why you feel the need to go work at that dingy little hospital in the country."

I used to think Rob was a nice guy.

Now, I know better.

"Well, Robert," I drawl, using his full name to piss him off as I shove a final sweater into my overfull suitcase. "I'm not sure if you're aware, but there are humans—real live ones—who live in the country who are also in need of medical attention."

I can't figure out why I'm packing so much for a single shift. When I'm in Chestnut Springs, I live in scrubs in the ER and in leggings in my hotel room at night.

"Thanks for clarifying, Winter." There's a biting tone to his voice that might make some people flinch. But not me. A dark part of me takes immense pride in the fact I know exactly how to piss off my husband. My lips twitch as I struggle to contain my satisfied smile.

"But why that hospital? Why Chestnut Springs? You're constantly taking off out there and you don't even tell me you're leaving.

Come to think of it"—he scrubs at his chin in a dramatic fashion while leaning up against the door frame of my bedroom—"you never even considered my opinion on whether I would want my wife taking this job. This isn't a smart career move for you at all."

Every time he whines like a child, I find myself wondering what it is about him I ever found attractive.

I'm not sure when the dimple on his chin became repulsive to me. Only that it is. The way he parts his hair to the side with a little swoop that doesn't even move when it's windy used to make him appear suave and put together to me.

Now it looks fake.

Like so much of my life with him has been.

I'm fairly certain the only reason he styles it that way is because he's too vain to admit he's balding.

And nothing makes a man's masculinity shrivel up and die for me quite like complaining about a woman exercising her professional independence. He might as well stomp his foot and storm out like a tiny chauvinist toddler.

I reach for the zipper and force it together against the bulging contents of my suitcase. "It's funny," I start, ensuring that I keep my tone cool and even. "It's almost like . . . you are the very last person I would ever consult about my life."

With a huff of air, I finally slide the zipper into place and stare down at the hard-shell case, propping my hands on my hips and letting a satisfied smile touch my lips.

"What the hell is that supposed to mean, Winter?"

The way he adds my name to the end of every sentence feels like he's trying to scold me.

Joke's on him. I won't be scolded.

He's blissfully unaware of what it takes to navigate the medical system as a young female doctor. If I let men as weak as Rob steamroll me on the regular, I wouldn't stand a chance.

And this career is the only thing I've ever had that's mine. So, he can fuck all the way off.

Flipping one hand over, I gaze down at my neglected nails, trying to look bored by him. I'm wondering if I can find a good place for a manicure in Chestnut Springs when I reply, "Don't play stupid. It pairs so poorly with whining."

I can't help but ask myself why I'm still married. I know why I thought I was sticking it out. But now? Now, I just need to buck up and get it done. I glance back down at my suitcase, packed like I'm leaving for a long ass time, and wonder if my subconscious knows something I don't.

Maybe that bitch is putting her foot down and breaking me out once and for all.

I'm not averse.

"Watch your fucking tone with me."

My eyes narrow on my cuticles as I struggle to bite down the rage bubbling inside me. Hot molten lava simmering below the cool surface, just waiting to erupt all over the place.

But I've kept that at bay for years now. I will not let Doctor Rob Valentine be the one to make me erupt.

He's not worth the energy.

I shift my eyes to him across the room. My room, because when I told him in no uncertain terms that I wouldn't be sleeping in the same bed as him any longer, he directed me to the guest room rather than moving himself out—like the true gentleman he is.

Even though he's the one at fault.

He's the reason we are where we are.

And the worst part is I loved him once. He was all mine. A safe place for me to land after growing up in what felt like some sort of domestic cold war.

I let my guard down with him. I fell so damn hard.

He broke my heart far worse than I'll ever let anyone know.

I don't respond to him; instead, I grab the handle of my suitcase and shove past his lean frame, heading toward the front door of our sprawling ten-thousand-foot home.

I hear him following. Dress shoes against marble. And of course, he doesn't offer to carry my suitcase.

A wry smile twists my lips, and I shake my head at the thought he'd bother to lift a finger to help. The hardest thing for me to accept with the implosion of my marriage is that I didn't see it coming. That I can be smart, and accomplished, and strategic in everything I do yet still allow this asshole to blindside me is just . . . humiliating.

Being swindled this way irks me to no end.

I can feel the rage radiating off of him as he seethes beside me. And I just carry on serenely, slipping my socked feet into a pair of tall leather boots and wrapping a long, brown wool coat around myself.

"Seriously, Winter? You're not even going to dignify me with an answer?"

I methodically tie the coat belt around my waist, deciding I have zero desire to dignify him at all.

The problem is, Rob knows me well. We've been together for five years, which means he understands how to piss me off too.

His eyes trace over my face, taking on a vicious little slant. "I liked

4

you better with lighter hair." His pointer finger sweeps over my head, judging the darker streaks topped with a warmer tone. He's always been obsessive about me having the silvery blonde hair, telling me how much he loves it. "This new color isn't as appealing. It looks dirty."

But the root touch-ups, the purple shampoo, and the deep conditioner were too much work for an exhausted resident, which is why I requested my stylist put in lowlights.

I blink a couple of times, like I can't quite believe he has the nerve to act like the way I color my hair is a personal slight to him.

Except I can. Because this year he took his mask off and showed me all the entitled ugliness underneath.

"That's funny. I liked you better when I thought you hadn't groomed my little sister and then fucked her over."

He scoffs. *Scoffs*. "That's not how it was. She was obsessed with me."

My nose wrinkles, smelling the bullshit wafting off of him. "A much older doctor saves his underage patient's life. Uses his physical appeal and power over her to get her eating out of his hand. Becomes a hero to her. Then, as soon as she turns eighteen, starts fucking her on the down-low like she's some sort of dirty secret. And when he meets her older, more appropriate sister, he drops her like a stone and marries the one that won't cost him his job for a medical license violation. Oh!"—my finger shoots up in the air—"except, here's the kicker. He doesn't give up on the younger one quite yet. He stalks her and harasses her, sabotaging every new relationship of hers just because he can. Or maybe it makes him feel better about that receding hairline he tries to cover up."

My anger swirls, but I'm the one stirring my pot by giving in to him at all.

5

His arms cross and he glares at me. All golden coiffed hair, bright blue eyes, and Ken-doll good looks. "You know I never loved her."

White-hot rage lances through me. Everything around us blurs as my eyes focus on the asshole I married. I try to keep my voice cool. Years of practicing this facade have carried me through the most heart-rending of moments. I have this act down pat.

But today I struggle.

"You think you never loving her makes it better? That's my baby sister you're talking about. The one who almost died. And you fucked her around for years. And me? I don't think you've ever loved me either."

My words echo in the spacious foyer as we stare each other down.

"I have."

I have. That's his proclamation to me?

I laugh bitterly. "Who the fuck are you kidding, Robert? Do you ever tire of lying? Of trying to keep your stories straight? The jig is up. I see you. You made me believe I had something I never did. You played me."

He doesn't correct me. He just glares. It shouldn't hurt, but it does.

"For what you've done to me? I am indifferent to you. For what you've done to her? I hate you. I wouldn't have touched you with a one-million-foot pole if I'd realized the type of man you really are. Fool me once, never again. That's the new saying."

With that, I tug my suitcase up and spin on my heel, flinging the door open so hard it smashes into the wall behind it. I hate how fired up I am. How out of control I feel. But I hold my chin up, press my shoulders down, and walk out of that house with all the placid, unaffected composure I can muster.

"Does that mean you're leaving me?"

How can someone so educated be so stupid? I almost laugh. I keep walking, patting him on the shoulder like the dog he is as I pass by. "Use that fancy medical degree and figure it out for yourself."

"You don't even like her!" he yells in a whiny tone that scrapes down my neck like nails on a chalkboard. "You gonna run back to her and beg for forgiveness after what a royal cunt you've been to her all these years? Good luck with that. I'll be here when you come crawling back."

But I don't dignify his jabs with a single glance back. Instead, I flip him the finger over my shoulder and take satisfaction in knowing he's wrong.

That he's not as smart as he thinks he is.

And I'm not either. I feel very small and very stupid right now.

Because I love my sister.

I just have a fucked-up way of showing it.

I hope I don't die now that I'm taking some control of my life back.

I want to start fresh. And yet I'm terrified to do it at all.

Chestnut Springs General Hospital is only an hour away from the house I live in, so why does it feel like the longest drive of my life?

I started taking shifts here a few months ago, so I could make the drive with my eyes closed, but today it's snowing hard enough that I'm white-knuckling the steering wheel.

I'm also still stewing over losing my cool.

Rob started that fight by saying he couldn't fathom why I'd want to work at this dingy hospital, and I wasn't inclined to tell him the truth.

One, that working in a hospital where I'm not his wife and my mother's daughter is a relief. I can practice medicine and take pride in my work without having to contend with all the whispers and pitying glances. Without that shit hanging over my head.

Because everyone knows, but no one talks about it, and that approach to life is wearing on my sanity. I know how everyone sees me. I'm not oblivious to it. They might not speak it, but I hear it loud and clear all the same.

A doctor who got her position at the hospital through family connections and marriage.

A woman who is unapproachable, cold, and unhappy.

A wife who is pathetic enough to ignore her husband's betrayal.

And two, because I've never wanted to be around my sister more than I do now. When she was sick, I used to sneak into the hospital and check on her, read her chart so I knew how she was doing even though I was still only in university. And now? Now, I look at my little sister and all I see are the years I missed.

I see a woman who lived in misery to save me a little of my own.

It would seem we're kindred that way.

She's happy now, engaged to a man whose hair is far too long but who loves her in a way that I'll never experience. But I'm also happy for her—god knows she deserves a little peace. She left her law degree and secure job at our father's sports management firm in the rear-view mirror to run a gym and live on a picturesque little country bumpkin ranch.

I admire her.

But I have no idea how to mend the rift between us. So, I took a part-time position in the small town she's living in, hoping I might run into her and fix things organically.

I have this recurring story in my head, one that crops up all the time. I must be trying to manifest it or some shit.

In it, she's strolling down the sidewalk, and I bump straight into her as I exit the adorable little Parisian coffee shop on Main Street. She looks shocked to see me. I offer her a warm smile, and it isn't forced. Then, I hike a thumb over my shoulder and say, "Hey, you, uh . . . wanna grab a coffee?" in a casual and charming way that will make her smile back at me.

Of course, I'd have to spend time somewhere other than the hospital or hotel for that to happen. But I keep slinking between the two safety zones, too scared and too embarrassed to face her.

"Fuck it," I mumble as I sniff and sit up taller, eyes laser-focused on the road. "Siri, call Summer Hamilton."

The beat of heavy silence that greets me is laden with years of anticipation.

"Calling Summer Hamilton," the robotic voice replies. The formality is a jab to the chest. Most sisters would have some cute nickname programmed in their phone. Perhaps I'd call her Sum if we were friends. As it is now, I might as well include her middle name in the contact listing.

The phone rings. Once. Twice.

And then she's there. "Winter?" she asks breathlessly. My name isn't an accusation on her lips though. It's . . . hopeful.

"Hi," I say stupidly. No amount of education or medical textbooks could prepare me for this conversation. Since everything blew up in the hospital that day, I've played out this conversation in my head a million times. I've laid awake at night preparing myself.

And it wasn't enough.

"Hi . . . are you . . . are you okay?"

I nod while the bridge of my nose stings. I've been awful to Summer over the years and her first inclination is to ask if I'm okay.

"Win?"

I suck in a deep breath of air. Win. Fuck. That nickname. She just falls into it so easily. I absently wonder how I'm named in her contacts. I always imagined it was "Evil Half Sister" or something along those lines.

She's just so fucking nice. It almost makes me nauseous that someone could be this nice to me after everything that we've been through, after how cold I've been to her.

I don't deserve Summer. But I want to. And that comes with being honest.

"No. I don't think I'm okay," I say, trying to cover the hitch in my voice by clearing my throat.

"Okay." I can imagine her nodding right now, rolling her lips together, mind whirring as she tries to solve this problem for me. That's just who she is. A fixer.

I might be a doctor, but Summer has always been a healer.

"Where are you? Do you need me to come and get you? Are you hurt?" She pauses. "Oh! Do you need legal help? I'm not practicing anymore, but I could—"

"Can I see you?" I blurt. And now it seems like it's her turn for stunned silence. "I'm on my way to Chestnut Springs already. I could . . . I don't know." A ragged sigh drags its way up my throat. "Buy you a coffee?" I finish lamely, glancing at the digital clock that shows it's already 6 p.m.

Her voice comes through the phone a little thick, a little soft. "I would love that. But could we do wine instead?"

A knot of tension unfurls in my chest, one I didn't even know

10

was there until now. And now that I've noticed it, I can't help but feel like it's been there for years.

"Yeah." My fingers pulse on the steering wheel. "Yeah. Wine. Good."

I sound like a fucking cavewoman.

"We're having a family dinner at the main house tonight. There will be a bunch of people. I'd love if you came too."

My throat clogs uncharacteristically. This brand of kindness feels foreign after living in a sterile bubble with Rob and my mom for so long. This brand of forgiveness … I don't know how to react to it.

So I just roll with it. Seems like the least I can do.

"Can you send me the address?"

In my haste to pick up my package and get the hell out of the city, I ignored my gas tank for as long as I could. No doubt cutting it dangerously close. Which only added to my anxiety the farther away I've gotten from that city limit.

So, I give in and stop for gas in Chestnut Springs before hitting the sketchy back road my phone mapped out to the ranch.

As I stand here, freezing and wishing I'd worn more appropriate outdoor winter clothing, I let all the worry creep in through my carefully erected walls.

Worry over seeing Summer.

Worry over sitting down to dinner with a bunch of people who no doubt think I'm a heinous bitch.

Worry over the snow-packed roads. I've seen too many car accident traumas roll into the ER lately.

Worry over my career and what the hell I'm going to do—where I'm going to land.

Hilariously—albeit a dark hilarious—I feel next to no concern over the thought of leaving Rob for good. I've strung that out for a long time. I've thought about it, analyzed it from every angle.

I kept thinking of divorce as a failure. But leaving tonight didn't feel like failing.

It felt like relief. Like someone has been standing on my chest and I finally got my shit together enough to push them off. My muscles are tired from pushing, and I've got some bumps and bruises from the fight.

Leaving hurt, but I can finally breathe through the pain.

I sigh a deep, heavy sigh and watch my breath puff out from between my lips into a smoky little cloud, more obvious under the neon lights that flood down over the gas bays. The tips of my fingers go from tingling to downright numb in a matter of seconds, where they're wrapped around the red plastic handle. I bounce on the spot and look up when I hear a bell jangle at the door of the gas station.

The man who walks out through the glass door is all swagger and broad shoulders. Dark hair, darker eyes, lashes that make the blonde girl in me a little irritated. He's smirking down at the lotto ticket in his hand, like he thinks he's going to win.

I could tell him he's not going to win. That it's a waste of money. But I get the distinct impression this is the type of man who doesn't care.

He's got unlaced boots, jeans stacked around the tops. A couple of long silver chains adorn his chest, disappearing under a plaid button-down that is open just a little too far, a heavy knit cardigan slung carelessly over the top.

He's sexy without even trying. Even the weather doesn't seem to bother him. I bet he rolls out of bed after sleeping in yesterday's socks and just shoves them back in those worn leather boots.

I bet his hands are rough. I bet he smells like leather. And after the man I've spent the last several years with, I'm unable to tear my eyes away from the rugged appeal of the man before me.

I've stared at him so long, so thoroughly, that the gas pump makes a loud clanking noise as it bumps back into my palm, signaling the tank is full.

The noise of it draws his attention my way, and he turns the full force of his sex appeal on me. The square jaw dusted with the perfect amount of stubble, topped off with lips that are just wasted on a man. The way he looks? It's absurd.

I drop my head quickly, fumbling with the pump to get it latched back in its holder. My tongue swipes at my lips.

I get the distinct sense that the sexy lumberjack is watching me, but I don't glance up to see. There's a flutter in my chest and a heat in my cheeks, one I haven't felt for a very, very long time.

Because I was actually happily married. And now I'm . . . not.

I think.

And this is the first man I've let myself look at inappropriately. A man who can't bother to tie his shoes and plays the lotto.

"Ugh," I groan at myself as I approach my door, suddenly a lot less cold than I was before I saw him.

But as I'm about to slide into my seat, I peek back over my shoulder at the guy.

The one standing at his silver truck.

The one who's still watching me with a knowing smirk on his face.

The one who runs a hand through his perfectly tousled hair and winks at me.

I'm in my car and out onto the dark road like a shot, getting away as quickly as possible.

Because the very last thing I need in my life is someone who makes me feel like there's not enough oxygen in my lungs when I've only just caught my breath.

2
Theo

The blonde woman stared at me like I was some sort of alien. I had to stop and stare back because she was so fucking blatant.

I was ready to crack a joke about how objectified I felt by the way she was ogling me. But then she licked her lips once, blinked, and shot off. Which is a shame, because I liked the way she gawked at me. I wasn't feeling objectified at all. If she'd looked me in the eye, all bets would have been off. I could have given her something to really stare at.

I didn't become a bull rider because I can't stand an audience. The show, the crowd, the recognition—I thrive on it. I was born into it. Gabriel Silva is arguably one of the most famous World Bull Riding Federation riders of all time.

And he isn't just my idol. He's my dad.

Was? I never know how to refer to him. He still feels very present to me even though he died so long ago.

As I swing up into my truck, I chuckle to myself. I know the

15

stunning blonde in the fancy Audi will cross my mind from time to time. Because there was something unusually wholesome about that interaction, like she was a teenager caught gawking and got embarrassed about it. I'd feel bad for her if I didn't feel so bad for myself that she ran off before I could get her number.

I hit the darkened road heading out to Wishing Well Ranch. I've come out here enough times over the years that I know where I'm going, whether it's dark or not. My mentor, Rhett Eaton, lives out here, and with my mom and sister living a province away, his family has become a little like my own over the holidays.

I'd usually head to Mom's place for Christmas, but she took a singles cruise with my little sister so they could both meet *Mister Right*, I think they called it.

And though I might be very, very single, I have zero desire to partake in that shit with my family.

Hard pass.

There are plenty of single buckle bunnies out on the WBRF circuit for me to pass the time with—boring as the endless series of mindless fucks have become—that don't require involving my mom.

Not to mention the whole boat thing freaks me out.

Put me on an angry bull? I'm fine.

Put me on a big boat with no land anywhere in sight? Hard pass. I saw an *Oprah* episode about people who go missing on those, and I'm too young and pretty to die.

Within a few minutes, there are red taillights ahead of me and I'm gaining on them quickly. Really quickly.

"Come onnnn," I groan into the quiet cab of my truck as I tip my head back.

Yeah, it's snowing, but the roads are hard-packed and not icy.

I finally catch up to the car and realize just how slow they're going. Thirty kilometers an hour. In a fifty. And this isn't even a school zone.

It's when I get close enough that I realize it's the smoke show in the Audi. I should have guessed. The heeled boots and the long coat didn't scream country girl.

And neither does the way she drives a back road.

The signal light flicks left. The vehicle slows and then speeds up. The signal light flashes right, and the car swerves a little.

Maybe she's lost? Or drunk? I sometimes zone out like she did staring at me when I've had a few too many.

Then I get close enough to see the light of her cell phone through the back window.

Perfect. Texting and driving. This chick is gonna kill herself. Or me.

Maybe if we shared a hospital room, I could get her number after all. Might be worth it.

When she slams the brakes, I startle and honk.

"Seriously!" I shout, my heart rate ratcheting up. I don't care how hot she is. She's a fucking terrible driver.

She shoots forward but slows again. I back off, not wanting to be too close to someone this erratic.

But dammit, I end up thinking of my mom or my sister lost on a back road. I go back to her being lost instead of driving like an asshole on purpose. A quick glance at my phone in its holster tells me reception is officially gone on this stretch, so she can't possibly be texting anyone.

I flash my high beams, thinking I can help if she pulls over.

I immediately feel like a serial killer.

No woman in her right mind would pull over on a dark road to talk to a strange man who flashed his high beams at her.

So, I settle in, crank my Chris Stapleton, and let my eyes wander out over the snow-covered fields. All crisp and white, reflecting the light of the moon, they make it seem not so dark anymore. Before long, I'm approaching the turnoff into Wishing Well Ranch, which means I can finally bid my terrible driving temptress farewell.

Except she signals. And turns into the ranch.

My mind whirs with what that might mean. She's definitely going to think I'm stalking her. And if we're both heading to the same place, she's someone I know in a roundabout way.

Once the lit house comes into view, her car accelerates right to the front porch. She hits the brakes and flies out of her car, slamming the door and storming in my direction before I can even get out of my truck.

When I make it out, I hear, "Are you fucking insane?"

Okay. She's mad. And she doesn't sound drunk at all. She's got her keys wedged between her fingers like claws and I instantly like this girl.

No preamble. Just comes out swinging. She's tiny and ferocious. I feel like Peter Pan getting reamed by Tinkerbell.

"Easy, Tink." I offer her a smile and lift my hands in surrender, not wanting to make her feel threatened.

"Tink?" Her voice goes even louder.

I wave a hand over her. "Yeah, you've got this whole angry little Tinkerbell vibe happening. I dig it." I let my gaze trace her body for only a moment, not wanting to border on leering. But hey, fair is fair after the way she gawked at the gas station.

"You're fucking nuts, you know that?" She starts back in. "You drive like an asshole behind me for a solid ten minutes, and now you follow me here? To . . . to . . . check me out and compare me to a Disney pixie?" Her arms flap angrily, and her dainty face twists up in fury. A look like that could incinerate a man on the spot.

But not me.

I shouldn't prod her. I know I shouldn't. But I feel like a kid with a crush who mocks the girl he likes to get her attention.

And I like the way this one fires back.

I want more.

"I think she's actually a fairy. And for the record, driving twenty below the speed limit is also dangerous and could kill someone. Mostly me. From boredom," I joke.

Her eyes widen almost comically, a sure sign that I failed to lighten the mood at all. "It's dark and snowy! I don't know the area. There could be wildlife! Driving slowly is safe so long as a back-forty hillbilly isn't riding my ass in his small-dick truck, flashing his high beams at me."

My lips clamp down against each other.

Fuck.

I really like this girl.

I should stop. I should walk away. I should channel my maturity and not flirt with her by infuriating her.

But I've always been a little reckless.

"I hear that if you want your ass ridden, a small dick is the way to go. So maybe I'm your guy."

My dick isn't small. But I'm happy to make sacrifices to land a good joke. Only a small-dicked dude would miss this opportunity.

I shouldn't have said it, but the pure shock that paints her pretty

19

features makes it all worth it. She's so fired up; I just can't help myself. Play with fire and I'll be there to pour gasoline on it for you.

Her hand shoots up between us. "I'm married, you fucking pig. Now leave." Her hand flips out firmly, pointing down the driveway.

Married. I just shrug. "Married for now, maybe."

I'm persistent. And this girl wasn't staring at me like a married woman. Not a happily married one anyway.

It's Rhett's voice that draws our attention to the sprawling wrap-around porch attached to the huge ranch house. "Yeah, don't worry, Winter. We're gonna free you from that husband and bury him in the back field. It'll be like that Dixie Chicks song. Rob is the new Earl."

Winter.

Winter, as in Summer's sister? Fuck, that's a stupid combination of names for two sisters. They should hate their parents instead of each other, if you ask me.

I glance back at the woman before me, about six feet away. Everyone has described her as cold and distant. A real ice-queen.

I've heard the stories. The drama. They've made her sound like some sort of criminal mastermind. But all I see is a firecracker who needs my help to work out some aggression.

And I wouldn't be mad at helping her with that. Not even a little. I'm philanthropic that way.

Winter rubs her temples like she has a headache. I consider offering her an aspirin from my truck, or an orgasm. I hear those help too.

"You're lucky you make my little sister so happy, Eaton," she says, sounding utterly exhausted.

Rhett hums good-naturedly, his eyes taking on that melty, drugged look he gets when people so much as mention Summer.

But he doesn't address that; instead, he says, "Theo's just a baby though. You can't corrupt him, Winter."

I roll my eyes. "I'm not a baby. I'm twenty-six."

Rhett scoffs. "No, you aren't. You're twenty-two."

Good god. Does he think he knows my age better than I do?

"Dude. I was twenty-two when I first met you on the circuit. I've gotten older. You're doing the same thing my mom does with her pets. They hit a certain age and then she says that they're that same age until one day they just die."

He chuckles. "Well, I'll be. You're like that store with the skimpy dresses. Forever 22."

I prop my hands on my hips and sigh with a bemused twist to my mouth. "Yeah. You're definitely getting old. That store is called Forever 21."

Rhett just waves me off. "Whatever. I only know about the skimpy dresses."

"Are you two done? I need a drink if I'm going to stay here all night," Winter cuts in, clearly irritated by the route our conversation has taken. Though Rhett's interruption did successfully put a stop to our little spat.

Sadly, I was enjoying sparring with her. She can hold her own in a way I haven't encountered in any of my relationships.

If that's even what you could call them.

"Ah, yes, Winter, meet my protégé Theo Silva. Theo, meet Doctor Winter Hamilton, my future sister-in-la—"

"Winter Valentine," she interrupts him with a stiff correction.

"For now," I add, winking at her. Because now that I know who she is, I don't feel so bad about making my play. I know who her husband is. And I already know I don't give a fuck about that guy.

I already know Winter can do better.

And I'm a lot better, whether she realizes it yet or not.

She gives me the most dramatic eye roll and walks in my direction. I stick my hand out—because Mama raised a gentleman—but she just walks past, glaring at me with eyes bright blue like the bottom of a flame. I turn my head to hold her gaze as she draws even with me, shoulder to shoulder.

She doesn't take my hand though. So, I roll with it, swiping my hand through my hair with a wink.

The same wink I gave her at the gas station.

Our little secret.

"Call your dog off, Eaton." She keeps walking, only addressing Rhett, like I'm not even here.

But goddamn, I love a challenge.

I turn with a loud, "Woof!" as I watch her petite frame slip into the bright light of the warm, bustling house.

Rhett is laughing. At me. Not with me. "You're an idiot, Theo."

I shake my head. "Dude. I think I'm in love with your sister-in-law. She's so fiery."

Now it's Rhett shaking his head, like he knows something I don't. And I follow him into the house because I want to know more.

I want to know more about Winter Valentine.

Like when that divorce is happening.

3

Winter

Rob: Say hi to Summer for me.

I walk into the big house, more unnerved than when I left the city a couple of hours ago. The prospect of walking in here at all, the shitty roads, that all pales in comparison to the beautiful infuriating man standing outside right now.

I swear I can still feel him staring at me, his eyes roaming over my back appreciatively. It makes me carry myself just a little bit taller.

Pathetic as it sounds, it's nice to have someone look at me that way.

Of late, I've grown more accustomed to looks of disdain and looks of pity. And when Rob looks at me in a way that I know means his dick is hard, it just makes my skin crawl.

This is different. I *want* Theo to admire me, but I also want to kick him in the shins.

The sound of a bustling kitchen draws me down the hallway into the warmly lit living space. Hunter green walls and wide, dark floorboards make the space effortlessly cozy. The voices are all happy, and the laughter isn't forced.

There's no marble, no stark white kitchen, no echo when people talk.

It's weird.

I pause at the threshold, stricken by the enormity of what I'm about to do. It's like getting the hell away from Theo Silva—the sexy bull rider maniac driver—and his perfect bone structure pushed me this far, and now I'm between a rock and a hard place.

My throat works in time with my fingers as they curl and squeeze into my palms. Like the inertia from the small motions will just tip into the room, the spectacle for everyone to see.

The first step toward making things right.

"All good, Winter?" A firm palm lands on my shoulder and I glance up into the scraggly face of my sister's fiancé. It's not that he isn't handsome, he's just so . . . unpolished. He's like a big, happy, manly dog that needs a day spent at the groomer.

I offer him a tentative nod before peeking back around the corner.

I'm not all good though. I'm a fucking mess. But I won't show it. I feel safe when I'm composed. And the second set of footsteps coming up behind Rhett belong to a man who makes me feel distinctly not composed.

"It's gonna be great." Rhett's hand squeezes. "Want me to give you a shove like if we were skydiving?"

Now I shoot him an unimpressed look. "No thanks. I can handle this."

I don't know who I'm saying it to. Him or myself? But either way, I step into the kitchen with my head held high and open with a confident-sounding, "Hi, can I help with anything?"

Heads turn, but eyes don't widen. The buzz doesn't come to a crashing halt. Instead, there are waves. And smiles. And a, "Heyooo, Elsa!" from Willa, who is propped in a chair, sporting a small swell at her stomach.

Summer hustles over to me, her cheeks all rosy. Her smile so sincere.

And she says nothing. She just flings herself at me and wraps her arms around my neck, burying her head in the crook of my neck. So openly affectionate.

I'm not used to it. I didn't expect it. So, I stand a little woodenly before hugging her back. Her body softens and a small sigh leaves her lips when I do.

"I am so happy you're here," she whispers to me.

And I'm glad no one can see my face right now because I'm scrunching it up furiously. Doing everything I can to keep from falling apart in the middle of another family's holiday gathering.

That would be overly dramatic. And I'm not big on dramatics. I just put my head down and get shit done.

Reconciling with my sister needs to get done. So here I am.

"Me too," is all I can say back before she pulls away, one hand on my shoulder while the other wipes at her big brown doe eyes. They're the same shape as mine, but a different color.

We both have our dad's features, but I took after our mom's coloring.

"Hi, Winter!" An older man crosses the kitchen, wiping his hands on his pants, which makes the clean freak in me wince a little. "I'm Harvey Eaton. Rhett's dad. It's a pleasure to meet you."

He sticks a large palm out at me, and try as I might, I don't find a single shred of judgment on his face. I don't know what kind of *Brady Bunch* shit is happening on this homestead, but it throws me off.

"Uh, hi," I reply a little tentatively as I take his hand. "Thank you so much for allowing me to crash your dinner."

The man makes a *pfft* sound and waves me off. "You're not crashing a single thing. This is a family dinner. You're family. And so, if my math is right, you're right where you should be."

I swear my jaw drops open. Who is this guy? Cowboy Ned Flanders?

He smiles. Like . . . a nice, normal smile. Not one that has me second-guessing what the actual intent behind it is. Then he walks away. Back to whatever he was cooking, like having me here is normal and not at all bizarre or monumental.

Family? Maybe this Harvey Eaton fella is already in the sauce. Because Summer and I haven't felt like family in a very long time. And I haven't met a single other person here, except for—

"Here." An elbow nudges at my arm, and I smell him before I even give in and look at him. Oranges, fresh and sweet, mixed with something spicy. Cloves? Ginger? He smells like mulled wine.

It's intoxicating. It's masculine. It's not bright and tart, and it doesn't sting my nostrils.

My eyes shift over before my head turns. And I can see his hands, rough and calloused, like I guessed. Big and warm.

A glass of wine in each of them. One red, one white.

"Double fisting tonight?" I tilt my head, quirking one brow at him. "That tracks. You drive like you already were."

One side of his sinful mouth tips up, and I'm struck by the

realization that Theo Silva knows how good looking he is. He probably practices his angles in the mirror. "We already have so much in common. That's exactly what I thought when I was stuck behind you for the most boring ten minutes of my life."

The smile I give him is flat, intentionally bored, as I lift a hand and inspect my nails. If I could go for a manicure, I'd get a warm brown. I don't care if it's Christmas. Red is too showy. But it doesn't matter because the hospital doesn't allow us to have painted nails anyway.

"Well, now you have a window into how women feel in your presence."

"Is that why they scream *Oh Theo, this is so boring!* when I'm inside them?"

I snort and gaze up at him, blushing a little at the knowing look in his eye.

It's unnerving. He's unnerving. So I volley. Hoping I can wound him enough to make him leave me alone.

"They just tell you that so you'll finish and stop flopping around on top of them."

"Do you think? Maybe we could arrange a time when you can instruct me on how to flop less. I do love to practice."

My eyes narrow into a glare.

Leave it to me to attract the one man in the world who seems to be unoffendable. The one man in the world who won't leave me alone when I feel ready to join Wonder Woman on her women-only island.

"Which one?" He shoves the two glasses of wine in front of me, interrupting my daydream.

"What?"

"Red or white? You said you needed a drink. I wasn't sure which one you like better, so I poured both. I'll drink whatever you don't."

I am struck dumb. I want to make a jab about how I'm not surprised at all that he'll drink whatever he can.

He seems like the type. Cocky. Handsome. Thinks far too highly of himself. It doesn't take a rocket scientist to know a man like him gets around. He reeks of experience, something I am sorely lacking.

Because I had stars in my eyes over Rob—until I didn't.

I eye the wine speculatively. Is this considered having a drink with a man?

Rob would have brought a specific bottle of wine from a specific region and had it chilled to an exact temperature. And then he'd shove a glass of it at me and whisper some ostentatious comment in my ear about how the hosts have the cheapest wine out to share.

I reach forward, tentatively taking the white wine. Red will stain my teeth, and I already feel self-conscious enough being here.

I'm about to say thank you, even though it pains me, but the tips of my fingers brush briefly against his and a static shock passes between us. It has my eyes shooting up. My hand darts back from the wineglass as I cradle it to my chest.

"You okay?" His brows knit together.

Okay? I almost laugh. It's just the dry prairie air. Everything is staticky. It's not like I got shot. But he's genuinely concerned, and that is . . . unnerving.

A word I keep coming back to tonight. Word of the day. My life is now *Sesame Street*, and I am Oscar the Grouch.

Pretty sure Elmo just brought me my wine.

I snag it and walk away, planning to try my hand at mingling. Because much as I hate to mingle, I think I hate standing there staring into Theo Silva's deep, dark eyes while basking in his citrus and ginger scent even more.

"Any news on Beau?" Summer asks from beside me at the huge family-style dining table.

Harvey clears his throat and sits up a little taller. "Yeah, yeah. He's doing well, actually. There are third-degree burns on his feet. They had to do a skin graft and were monitoring pretty closely for infection to flare back up. But the update yesterday is they're impressed with how quickly he's healing."

"Leave it to Beau to be fucking good at everything," Rhett murmurs, shaking his head.

He gets a chorus of laughs for that one. I haven't met this other brother. The gist of what I understand is that he's in the military and something happened during his deployment. He's now in a military hospital.

Burns are nasty business. I've seen my fair share in the emergency room. Wouldn't wish them on my worst enemy.

Well, okay. I would Rob. I'm not *that* nice.

"We're gonna have to get him set up with some docs when he comes back home."

I shrug as I spear a brown sugar-glazed carrot from my plate and the offer leaps from my lips before I even have a chance to shut it down. "I can help with that."

"Yeah?" Harvey's face brightens from across the table, and I wonder if being nice is infectious somehow.

It wasn't covered in med school. But science is always evolving.

My eyes lock onto Theo's. He's sitting right across from me and

I'm finding it hard not to stare. The way the candle between us flickers against his lightly stubbled face is distracting. And blinking away quickly like a child caught peeking is immature.

But I do it anyway. Like I'm reverting back to my teen years with some popular boy who sits across the class from me.

Everything about me tonight is so out of character. I opt not to analyze it with a microscope.

"Sure." I drop my gaze back to my plate. "No problem at all. I'd be happy to help in any way I can."

Summer reaches under the table and gives my knee a reassuring squeeze. I look over at her, wondering how two people raised in the same household could have turned out so differently. Opposites. Winter and Summer. Our names weren't just a stupid gimmick, they actually represented us somehow.

But I know the answer. Our parents never split from each other, they just split up everything around them instead. One team versus another.

I got my mom. Summer got our dad.

Rhett pipes up now, talking about a game of Christmas shinny, and how he and Sloane cleared the ice for it. Sloane, the dainty blonde sitting beside Harvey, launches into a story about a similar time she and Jasper played at some other farm.

And she's talking about NHL superstar Jasper Gervais. One of my dad's clients, and the man who is sitting beside her, staring at her like she can shoot rainbows out of her vagina or something.

I don't even think he's listening. He's just staring at her like she hung the moon. It hurts to see his expression. I hate feeling jealous, but so much of what I see here tonight fills me with that dark, bitter emotion.

I could burst with it.

Not like I begrudge anyone else what they have. It's more that I long to have it too.

It makes me realize what I've missed out on all these years. It makes me realize all the things I don't have.

The things I never will.

For the rest of the night, I observe. I pull back a bit, feeling like an outsider. Everyone is so content. And I'm so . . . not.

It's almost like watching bacteria grow in a Petri dish through a microscope. I can see it happening. I can understand why it's happening. I can get close enough to touch it. But I'm still just looking through the lens. Studying.

We've all retired to the spacious living room area around a roaring fire, and I'm sitting in an impossibly comfortable armchair when Theo saunters up.

Again.

He's fucking relentless.

He's only a few feet away, eyes narrowed in on me, all confident swagger and singular focus. But Willa draws his attention. Her eyes dart momentarily to mine, and I give her a small smile. I like Willa. She's been a sister to Summer in ways that I never could.

And I think I'll always love her for that.

"Theo, lady-killer. How goes the hunt these days?"

His eyes stay fixed on mine for a beat, more focused determination than playful nonchalance. Suddenly, I want to know what the hell he was about to say to me. I've been avoiding him all night, and Willa is perceptive enough to have noticed. But her timing is all wrong.

"Willa. How are you feeling? Has anyone told you lately that

31

you're glowing?" He sidesteps the question so effortlessly. So playfully. Even she can't help but grin and roll her eyes at him.

There is something irresistibly charming about Theo. Something boyish and fun. He's not jaded yet. Perhaps that's the appeal of a man whose outlook on life appears to be "glass half full" when I'm a "glass half empty" kinda gal most days.

It's Cade, the oldest Eaton brother, who stomps up and flops down beside Willa, draping a possessive arm over her shoulders. "Leave it to you to hit on a pregnant woman, Theo."

Everyone laughs, even Theo. But I see the way the back of his neck stiffens, like the joke had some bite that no one expected. Like he's forcing himself to hold his head up high when he doesn't feel like it.

I know because I do that too.

"Jesus, man, she's carrying your baby and living in your house. What do you need? Your name tattooed on her forehead? I'm just being friendly."

Rhett walks in now. "Yeah, buddy. I've seen just how friendly you can be. I'd go so far as to say you're known for being *friendly.*"

Theo smiles and rolls his eyes. "Rich coming from you, Eaton."

"Hey . . ." Rhett's hands come up, his beer held in one. "I was Goldilocks. All the porridge was too hot or too cold. Finally found one that was just—"

Summer cuts him off with a feigned look of exasperation on her face. "Please do not finish that sentence. Any analogy that compares me to mushy cereal is just . . . no, Rhett. No."

"But the maple syrup I like to put in it reminds me of—"

"Rhett Eaton." My sister's eyes widen. "Control yourself."

His lips twist, and his expression drips with sex. It's borderline inappropriate, but based on Rhett's past behavior, I already know him to be impulsive and unfiltered.

I blink away, out the big windows and over the snowy farmland. Snow is *still* falling.

"I'm sorry." Theo is standing over me when I glance up. I swear I look behind myself to see if he just said that to me. There's a deer head with a lot of antlers hanging on the wall.

I point. "Why? Did you kill it?"

His lips lift, and the skin beside his eyes scrunches up just a little bit. "I wasn't talking to the stag, Winter."

Other conversations have begun to flow, and attention is no longer on Theo. Instead, it's just his attention on me. Which is almost stifling.

"I'm sorry I made you uncomfortable on the drive here. It wasn't my intention. Like ..." His hand swipes through his hair, all tight on the sides and just a bit longer on top. Lending him a sort of sex-mussed quality. "At all."

I nod but cross my arms like they might shield me from him. "Okay."

His thick, dark brows pop up on his forehead. "Yeah? Is that like ... apology accepted?"

"What if it's not?" I arch one brow at him in challenge. And I almost don't recognize myself.

Am I flirting with him?

Rob has officially pushed me over the edge. I'm flirting with a younger man at a family gathering, not because I like him, but just because ... it feels good.

His features go almost somber. "That would be cruel because

my self-worth is very tangled up in whether people like me. Being well-liked is my best quality."

I blink. I almost tell him that is *not* his best quality, but that seems cruel, even for me.

"I'll be heartbroken if you don't like me," he adds as he drops to a crouch in front of me. Coming to eye level does nothing but increase the intimacy of this conversation.

I roll my eyes. "I thought you wanted me to accept your apology. Now I have to like you too?"

He shrugs, a playful grin making his dimples pop. "They're basically the same thing."

I snort. *This man.* "They are not the same thing."

The tip of his tongue darts over his bottom lip, and my eyes follow raptly. "Agree to disagree."

I stick my hand out like we're making a business transaction, forcing my features into a cool mask. The same one that has served me so well all these years. "I accept your apology," I say, using the most detached voice I can muster. "But I dislike you."

He chuckles, and it's deep and warm, all amused like I'm just a challenge—and not an intimidating one. "I can work with that for now," is what he responds with before accepting the handshake.

And when our fingertips touch, there's a flash of electricity again.

But this time it has nothing to do with the dry prairie air.

4

Theo

Mom: You should have come on this cruise. The weather is glorious.

Theo: Do you even understand how weird it is to look for dates together as a family? Confined to a boat? I would throw myself over the railing.

Mom: It seems to me that getting along with the family is a pretty important feature when choosing a boyfriend or girlfriend. Not that I'd know. You never introduce me to anyone.

Theo: I don't have any girlfriends to introduce you to.

Mom: I think it's more like you have too many.

I haven't been able to take my eyes off Winter all night. I feel like I'm watching the Discovery Channel, studying the merging of two packs of hyenas or something. The chatter in the house doesn't stop, neither does the laughter.

No one is trying to make her uncomfortable. They don't need to. She does it all on her own.

She watches every movement so closely, and she listens hard, turning over every snippet of conversation in her head. And every time she catches me staring, she looks away so quickly that I'm sure she's going to have a sore neck tomorrow.

"I think I'm going to head back."

I saw her working up to this declaration. Fiddling with her fingers anxiously. Leaning forward a bit when there was a lull in the conversation. Her lips would pop open, but then conversation would surge back up and she'd visibly shrink back in her chair.

The remarkable contrasts of this woman, removed and bordering on insecure in one moment, cool and snippy the next. And to think she started off all fucking fiery and flying off the handle.

She must be exhausted.

"Are you okay to drive?" Summer asks, always doting on everyone.

Winter's gaze darts out the window where snow is still falling. *No.*

"Yeah. I'm all good."

My molars clamp down tightly. She's not all good. She wasn't two hours ago, and she won't have magically become comfortable driving on snowy, dark roads just by eating dinner and having a single glass of wine.

"I can drive you. I'm sure we can get you your car tomorrow."

She scoffs, rolling out the ice princess routine as she shimmies her shoulders and tips her nose up. "That is entirely unnecessary."

I give her my best *you're full of shit, sweetheart* look from where I'm sitting on the leather couch opposite her.

"Don't give me that look."

"What look?" I make my face suitably blank.

Her finger squiggles in the air at me as all eyes in the room volley between us. "That one that says you know better than me."

"In this case, I might."

Her lips purse, so damn prim. "I guarantee you don't. I'm a doctor."

"Oh? Did you take a special winter driving class at med school?"

"Did you at bull riding school?" she snipes with some venom, but I just want to laugh.

"Don't be ridiculous. Bull riders don't go to school. We're lucky if we learn how to tie our shoes and brush our teeth." I give her a flash of my pearly whites, not caring that everyone is watching us.

"I already know you can't tie your shoes. The hygiene part doesn't come as much of a surprise either, if I'm being honest."

"Flattered you looked long enough to notice my boots weren't tied. And I'd be happy to prove you wrong about my hygiene since you're clearly very invested."

Her eyes narrow, and I laugh. Try as she might, she can't get under my skin because this is *way* too fun.

"It's true. Rhett wears mostly pull-on boots," Summer interjects with a slightly awkward laugh, clearly trying to cool the tension.

I wish she wouldn't. I get off on watching Winter thaw.

Everyone laughs as Rhett exclaims, "Rude!"

Winter takes that opportunity to stand. She doles out an awkward hug and back pats to her sister while avoiding even turning her body in my direction. There are quiet whispers exchanged between the two women, and I feel a little tug at the sight.

I've come to love Summer like a sister, and I know from what Rhett has divulged that the distance between her and Winter pains her.

So, I tell myself that what I'm about to offer is for Summer, and not at all because there's something undeniably intriguing about her sister.

"I'm going to leave too."

"Already?" Rhett asks.

"Yeah, meet you at the gym tomorrow? Maybe Summer can make us cry?"

Rhett and Jasper laugh, because they *know* what I'm talking about from working out with her. Summer may be small and sweet, but put her in personal trainer mode and she becomes downright evil. I don't think any of us have been in better shape than since we started working out at Hamilton Athletics.

"It's not my fault you're all so fragile," she volleys, spinning to smirk at us. Yeah, I think she enjoys watching us struggle.

"That's men for you," Winter says tartly as she turns to leave without another word.

Her sister hits me with a pleading look. "Theo—"

I hold up a hand to stop her. "I'll make sure she's alright."

Winter scoffs from down the hall, because of course she has superhuman hearing or something. And I just roll my eyes at Summer.

"Careful, that one's got claws," Cade offers right as Willa shoves a pointy elbow into his ribs.

I grin. "That's okay. I like having my back scratched."

"I'm not driving with you."

Winter flies off the front steps into the storm, flakes swarming her like she's living inside a snow globe.

"Okay."

"I don't even want to talk to you."

"Well then, stop," I tell her with a chuckle as I come to stand at the top of the stairs.

Her mouth opens and then closes. "You are so annoying."

"Is that a medical diagnosis?"

"I . . ." She looks away and I swear I see her lips twitch. "Good lord, you are unbelievable."

I hit her with my best knowing smile. "I get that a lot."

She barks out a harsh, dry laugh as her head tips to face the perfectly dark sky. Snow adorns her lashes when she turns her attention back to me. "You're also confusing. What do you want from me?"

The tone of her voice is different now. It bleeds exhaustion. From where I'm standing, she looks small and tired, like she might laugh or cry but isn't sure which.

I don't even want to keep needling her. What I want to do is give her a hug and tell her everything will be okay. I sense she needs that comfort.

It's what I'd do for my mom or my sister.

But I give her what she can handle, which is cold, hard facts. "I just want you to get back home safe."

She responds with a laugh that borders on a sob and then peers back up at the navy sky. "Home."

I lean against the porch railing and cross my arms over my chest, watching her. Giving her space, but also not wanting to leave her alone.

"I'm staying at the hotel in town. The Rosewood Inn."

"Yeah?" I quirk my head. "Same."

The look she gives me is disbelieving.

"Come on, Winter. I'm not a total dog. Give me some credit. What if I drive in front of you and you follow? That way, if there is any wildlife, I'll hit it first."

Her eyes roll, but her lips reiterate, "Follow?"

I shrug. "Yeah. And when you get into town, you'll be fine. You can watch me walk away and never see me again."

Now her lips do tip up, but it's practiced. "That holds a certain appeal."

"Watching me walk away? Busted you doing that earlier already." I wink as I jog down the stairs and hit the button to unlock my truck.

"You are incorrigible."

"Oooh! Incorrigible! Great word. Very *Bridgerton*. I could role-play the duke if that's something you're into."

I tug her driver-side door open and gesture to usher her in, but she stops in her tracks. Finally looking amused. "You know *Bridgerton*?"

"Yes. They even taught me how to read at bull riding school."

"You read *Bridgerton*?"

She's so impressed by my ability to read that she still doesn't move, so I leave the door open and carry on to my truck. I laugh as I haul myself up into the driver's seat. "Stole them from my mom for teenaged spank bank fodder." Her responding gasp makes me laugh harder and I call out, "Let's go, Tink! We're off to Neverland!" right as I slam my door.

Knowing that now she'll follow me just so she can tell me off about comparing her to a Disney fairy again.

I go slow. Slower than necessary, but it eases the pressure in my chest to see her headlights behind me. She drives like she's never seen snow before, and I'm worried she'll hit the ditch. But at least I'll be here to pull her out and call a tow truck. Better than sitting at Wishing Well Ranch thinking a woman who is far more terrified than she'd ever admit is out on the roads white-knuckling it by herself.

The drive takes twice as long as it should, and I let out a deep sigh when we hit the first stoplight in Chestnut Springs. The roads were ugly, and I swear I can feel her relief from twenty feet away.

When we pull up in front of the Rosewood Inn, I hop out and start to walk away like I promised her I would. I think I've needled her enough for one night. Yet I find myself somewhat disappointed at the idea of never seeing her again.

A good sparring partner is hard to find.

"Hey, Theo?" she calls, chin tucked deep into her coat to keep the snow out, warm honey hair shining under the flood of light from the streetlamp arched over her. "You uh . . ." Her arms cross over her body protectively and she drops my gaze awkwardly. "Thanks for that."

I nod. "Of course. Anytime."

"Anytime the roads are bad, I can just, what? Give you a ring and you'll come running to the rescue?"

"Yeah. Sure. If you ever need help, you can give me a call."

She looks momentarily stunned. "Why?"

I lift my shoulders in a shrug. "I don't know. Why not?"

Her lips roll together as she contemplates for several seconds. "But you don't even know me."

"Don't have to know a person to be nice to them."

The woman seems genuinely confused. "Is this some stupid karma shit?"

"No, it's entirely self-serving. I have this thing where if I'm shitty to someone, it eats me up inside. So, if I'm just nice, it makes me happy. Being negative is exhausting, ya know? And I don't have time to nap."

"Weird."

My head quirks. "Is it? You seem tired, Winter."

"I am."

"Try it then."

"Try what?"

"Doing something nice. Try it on for size. If you hate it, you can be mean to me again and I'll let you."

Her eyes roll, but I can see her biting at the inside of her cheeks like she's mulling it over. "Okay," she finally says on a deep exhale. "Theo, can I buy you a drink to thank you for helping me get back here safely?"

"Depends." I scrub at my chin like I'm turning this offer over carefully, even though I already know I'm going to take it. There's something different about Winter, and I'm not ready to say goodbye. There's a draw I can't explain.

With any other woman I would probably take one look and think *too much work*, but I'm eager to get to know her better. To figure out what's underneath that icy exterior. "Are we drinking more wine?"

Maybe I just feel bad for her, and I'm being extra nice, in the spirit of Christmas or whatever. But I'm drawn to her, and not just because she's beautiful.

"No. I think it's more of a tequila kind of night," she replies, surprising me as I start toward her, inexplicably pulled closer.

"Whatever you want," I say as I come near enough to reach out and touch her cheek. Would she flinch? Or lean into it? I don't get a chance to find out because she turns away toward the hotel lobby.

And this time I don't hesitate to touch her. I press my hand against the small of her back as I usher her through the front door and toward the bar.

Tequila is not my friend.

But for this girl, I'll make an exception.

5
Winter

Marina: I just spoke to Rob.

Winter: Oh, good. I love that he opted to air our marital issues to my mother.

Marina: You can't seriously be thinking about leaving him.

Winter: After what he's done? Yeah, I am.

Marina: I doubt you'll do better. I would tough it out.

Winter: Yeah, I know you would. I got to grow up in that household.

Marina: If you leave him over that mongrel sister of yours, you're just letting her win.

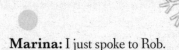

"**M**y mom is a massive, unforgivable bitch. That's where I get it from." I rest the side of my face into my hand, elbow propped on the table. "It's hereditary. That's why Summer is so nice. Her mom, Sofia, was the best.

44

I don't remember her that well, but I remember her being fun. I remember her smiling a lot. Deep down, I can't blame my dad for fucking the nanny."

Theo watches me, riveted by the story of my upbringing. We've resorted to sipping our shots of tequila after tossing two straight back.

"And you know what the worst part is? When she got knocked up, my mom fired her. Like it was her fault alone. And I loved Sofia. The nanny that came after was *mean*. Like my mom wasn't just punishing my dad by hiring her, but punishing me too."

Most people look at me with pity when I tell them this story. But Theo just looks entertained.

"God. I knew Kip was a wild card. But this … he's a pig." He chuckles out the last word, disbelief lacing his tone.

My dad is a top sports agent, and apparently, he represents Theo. A little tidbit I didn't know until tonight. I knew he'd been Rhett's guy, and when Rhett hung up his cowboy hat or whatever you say when a bull rider retires, he got his protégé in with the man who made him famous.

"Yup." I pop the *p* before tipping the tall shot glass back and taking another sip that burns down my throat. A comfortable and unfamiliar heat blooming in my chest.

I can't remember the last time I got properly drunk. Rob would tell me I wasn't "appreciating the flavors" if I drank his wine past a certain volume and I was too damn busy busting my ass professionally to cut loose. Studying. Picking up extra shifts. Being on call.

Trying to keep up with my mom's expectations of me.

"So, Sofia gets pregnant with Summer. Kip tells your mom."

"Marina," I correct, because over the years I've shifted to using her name. Or Doctor Hamilton, since we spend almost every day working together. "Her dream is for me to become an accomplished plastic surgeon like her. If I'd taken that route, maybe I'd still be calling her mom. But the chaos and unpredictability of the ER feels like home."

"Is this all real? It's like you're recounting a soap opera to me. Sometimes my mom tells me about the plot for *The Young and the Restless*, and I swear I've heard this before."

I scoff, wishing my mom would call and talk to me about something as mundane as a soap opera. The alcohol hums through my veins and I just keep going, processing out loud rather than in my head for once.

"I defied her for the very first time in my life, after years of being her puppet, and she turned that cruel side on me without even thinking twice." My head shakes and Theo stares at me with those dark eyes, looking a little stunned. Probably hard to imagine when you have a mom who hugs you and tells you about her favorite trash TV.

"I wonder if that cruel side is as hereditary as Summer's nice side, you know? Like maybe that facet of my personality is just waiting to rear its ugly head. I don't want to be like my mom, but I worry I already am."

"I think the fact that you're even worried about that means you're not like your mom at all."

I take another sip. He's sweet. I'm not *that* reflective though. I'm just drunk and loose-lipped.

"Yeah. I'm a mess. Marina would never allow herself to end up where I am."

His hand slides across the small, circular high top, his strong fingers tapping against my elbow. "Hey, hey. Sitting here with me isn't *that* bad."

My head tilts further as I let my gaze scan him lazily, if a little drunkenly. "No. I agree. You're pretty easy on the eyes."

Under normal circumstances, I'd cringe at myself for saying that out loud. But nothing about sitting in this small-town hotel bar is normal.

"Woah." He rears back a little, holding both hands up, a dramatic expression gracing his perfect features. "I said you should give being nice a try, not excel at it."

My lips curve up slowly. He's funny.

It strikes me I haven't spent time around a lot of funny people in my life.

Smart. Academic. Accomplished.

Funny and nice have been very low on the list of traits I look for in the people I surround myself with.

"Am I a snob?" I wonder out loud, brain hiccupping all over the place.

"If you are, I like it."

My eyes roll and I shift on my stool, feeling like I might slide straight onto the floor if I keep leaning on that hand.

"Why are you rolling your eyes?" He tosses his shot back and signals to the bartender for another. The man's lips purse in disapproval, like he thinks we don't need another round. And I almost laugh.

I'm so tired of everyone's condemnation.

"You don't like me."

"I do." The way he dips his chin is sure. It hedges no room for debate.

I toss back the last of my tequila, a droplet of it spilling out and landing on my lip. For a moment, the world stops when Theo's eyes land on my mouth. On that drop of golden liquor. And when my tongue swipes out to clear it away, to end his attention, his gaze heats in a way that's unfamiliar.

Because men don't look at me like that.

Not the one I'm married to.

And definitely not ones like Theo.

The crash of glasses from behind the bar has all the sounds around us screeching back to life, like someone just jammed down on the play button after hitting pause.

A nervous laugh crests my lips and I glance over at the bar where the tired-looking bartender is cleaning up a mess of broken glassware.

"I like you, Winter. As a person." Theo's eyes are so intent on me. It's unnerving. "Why does that make you so uncomfortable?"

"Do you always just say what you mean all out in the open like this? It's fucking weird." My eyes narrow. "What's your angle?"

"I don't have an angle. I'm just a nice guy having a drink with a likeable girl."

Two more shots of Anejo drop between us, but neither of us glances up. I'm too busy staring at the peculiar man sitting across from me.

"You're a manwhore. Who is younger than me. And you look like *that*." I wave a finger over him.

"And I still like you."

"And I'm an unhappily married twenty-eight-year-old—"

Theo interrupts me with an eye roll. "Mention our *two*-year age difference like it matters again, and I'm going to mock you mercilessly."

I lick my lips. "Fine. I'm an unhappily married *woman* with an entire storage locker full of baggage. I'm just trying to make it through a residency that no one approves of."

"I approve," he replies, without show or flash, just saying it like it's a fact.

"You approve of me. But you don't like me. That makes a lot more sense."

He grins now, taking a swig of the liquor, and my eyes drop to watch his throat work as he swallows. The tawny skin, the dark stubble, the pronounced bump of his Adam's apple.

Who knew a man's thyroid cartilage could attract me?

"No, Winter. I like you. Stop telling me I don't."

A wry laugh twists my lips as I drink and inspect the charming little bar. A sort of old-world Victoria allure graces the space. A perfect fit for the elegant boutique hotel.

"I'm not likeable, Theo. People don't *like* me. Not really." I hold up a finger and give him a wide-eyed look, signaling that now is not the time for him to barge in with his tongue-wagging nice-guy act. "People respect me because I'm smart. Or because I'm accomplished. But they don't *like* me."

The man across from me stares. I can see him turning my words over in his head. It tilts back and forth as though he is considering everything I've just said.

"I think I like you because you are a heart-stopping, jaw-dropping type of beautiful."

My face reveals nothing. No one has ever complimented my looks over my brains and I . . . I don't even know what to make of it.

"Are you fucking with me?" I blurt.

"Nah." He leans back in his stool, biceps bulging in a distracting way as his eyes peruse me with appreciation. "I definitely like you because you're hot. And because you enunciate your swear words so clearly. Did you know that people who curse are more honest and trustworthy than people who don't?"

My jaw unhinges and then I feel it. It's foreign, but there's no stopping me. I drop my head onto my crossed arms on the table and burst out laughing. The laughter hurts my throat as I try to silence it. It leaks from my eyes no matter how hard I try to keep it in. It shakes my shoulders as it overtakes me.

And the deep baritone of Theo's laugh joins me, twisting with mine like a symphony.

"But I've also had a lot of concussions. So my judgment could be off," he adds through the laughter.

I'm just drunk enough, just wrung out enough, that I laugh even harder. "Fuck," I gasp, sitting up and wiping at my eyes.

"Yeah, you need to give less of those."

"What?" I reach for the tequila, needing to lubricate my throat after my laughing fit.

"You need to give less fucks."

I offer an exaggerated shrug and roll my lips together as the alcohol races straight to my bloodstream.

"It's like this." Theo reaches out one toned arm, grabs my stool, and tugs it around the small round table. He turns us both. Bringing us face to face, so the outside of my knees presses up against his inner thighs. That spicy citrus scent wraps around me. The urge to lean forward and nuzzle into his neck hits me like a ton of bricks.

We're too close.

But he doesn't seem to notice. He just turns and lays his hands flat on his well-built thighs, all ten fingers stretched wide. "Pretend you only have ten fucks to give—"

"Oh, I think I remember this math problem from second grade."

He ignores my jibe and forges ahead. "And when you run out of fucks, you're spent. Wrung out. Stretched too thin."

My eyes roll. "Good god."

"But you're out here giving one fuck to your mom about the career you already know you want, giving one to Summer over some slight that she doesn't seem to know exists, giving at least a few to your husband who makes you miserable."

He directs a pointed look at me that says he knows that story too. I shrink a little.

"I just watched you give me a fuck over that story, like I'm judging you when I'm not. So, we're at . . ." We both peer down at his hands. "You have four fucks left to give and then you're burnt out." He's on a roll now. "I'm pretty sure you gave that bartender a fuck when he had that whole judgy, sour expression on his face after we ordered another round. I mean, come on, Winter. That guy? He just dropped an entire tray of glasses. You've only got three now. Why'd you waste one on him?"

I sigh. "This is the stupidest math I've ever encountered. And me giving people *fucks* . . . the way you're saying it makes me sound . . ."

His dark brows rise. "Sound what?"

"It sounds like I'm just out fucking people willy-nilly." I laugh. I have to. "Please don't say anything about me giving my dad fucks for abandoning me. I'll never recover."

"Don't need to. You just admitted it yourself."

He folds another finger under and as I watch him, I realize I'm mirroring him. Hands splayed on the expanse of bare skin between my stockings and the edge of my dress, fingers curling every time he ticks off a fuck.

Two fucks stare back at me, one of which sports a simple gold band. I wear it so the diamond Rob bought me doesn't rip through my medical gloves.

I glance up at Theo. He's watching me so carefully. His skin is so smooth, so tan. His features so dark. His persona so . . . *fun*.

The antithesis of everything in my life.

And suddenly I give a fuck about what he thinks of me too.

I fold another digit down without saying a word. He watches me do it, but his warm hand covers mine, a brush of his calloused fingers on my thigh as he reaches for my ring finger and pulls it out flat.

"Don't give me that, Winter. I don't need it. I'm not judging you. And you're only two fucks away from bottoming out."

Bottoming out. The inanest pairing of words sends a zing of arousal through my body. *Bottoming out.* Said with a light growl in his voice while he leans into me so intimately. I cross my legs and squeeze to dull the ache between them.

"God." I run my hands through my hair, pushing it back tight and away from my face. "Are you telling me you don't give a fuck what people think of you?"

He shrugs and cants his head in my direction. "I try not to."

He's so close, all tequila and tangerines and deep, chocolatey eyes. "I saw you tonight. The way you went rigid when you got called a lady-killer."

His gaze bounces between my eyes, and god, I feel seen. My skin itches under the pressure of his gaze. No one ever looks at me this closely. This discerningly.

"Changing your stripes isn't always easy."

"I think the saying is literally that a tiger *doesn't* change its stripes."

His tongue presses down on his bottom lip as he gives his head a minute shake. "Then let's call it a Dalmatian changing his spots. They're born without them, you know."

"So, you're not a total manwhore?"

His mouth twists. "I'm outgrowing that phase. But people see what they want. Imagine if I gave them all my fucks over that when I know deep down what kind of man I am?"

Man. Yes. Man.

My brain stutter-steps on that. Because Theo is all man, all masculine lines, dark swirling colors, gentle touches—gentlemanly behavior.

Okay, he's charming as hell.

"When I didn't win at the end of this season, I made it a goal to redouble my focus. Grow up a notch. That's why I'm here, training with Rhett and Summer. More workouts, less . . . play. All work and no play makes Theo a dull boy."

Play. Does every word this man says have to sound sexual? I swear he isn't even trying, but his words scrape against my skin like the edge of his teeth might, the way his stubble might. There isn't a single dull thing about Theo Silva.

In fact, he might as well be a gigantic neon sign, flashing at me to back away. Because people have hurt me, my capacity for trust is practically nil. And yet . . .

"I could really use some play." My knee bumps into his as I turn to him, an idea blossoming in my mind.

A *very* bad idea.

"Less fucks and more play. I like this strategy for you."

The way his lips part when he says *fuck* has my stomach clenching and my inhibitions flapping in the wind. What if I let go of them and turned my brain off for a bit? What if I did something just for me? Something that feels good.

God knows Rob has never been effective at making me feel good. Not the way it appears in movies or sounds in books. When the woman's heart races and her skin prickles just because a man is looking at her.

Theo looks at me like that. Like I might be his next meal.

"Maybe what I really need is more fucks?" Oof. That sounded a lot cooler in my tequila brain than it does out loud.

"You only get ten for the purpose of the example."

I bite down on my bottom lip. "That's not what I meant."

He must see it on my face because he rears back, full lips parting even as his eyes smolder. "Are you propositioning me?"

I scoff and blink away. "No."

He says nothing and when I drag my attention back to him, I confess, "Okay, maybe. Just for fun. I want to know what that's like." An image of Rob pops up in my head and I toss it away. He's not allowed here in this moment. I need to be myself. I need to be free of him if I'm going to do this. "I don't think I know what it's like to be properly fucked."

Amusement and shock war on his face. "You've officially had too much to drink."

"I have not. You're just using that as an excuse. If you aren't interested, just be direct. I'm a doctor. I understand how the biology of attraction works. You can't force it. I get it."

When I glance back up, the expression on his face is primal. He's beautiful, and I'm instantly struck by the realization that I'm an idiot. This man is out of my league. He's too good looking. Too experienced.

"You know what? Forget I said anything. I've got this whole uptight spinster thing happening and I don't blame you for—"

"Winter. I'd have properly fucked you in the back room of that gas station if you'd asked me."

I freeze at his words.

"I'm not going to sit here and pretend I haven't been thinking about it all night." His eyes glaze over and peruse my body in a knowing way, like he can see my skin flush and my nipples pebble. His legs squeeze in on mine. Trapping me. "That dress could be so *easily* tugged up. But . . ." His head tilts down at the glass on the table beside us. "We consumed a lot of tequila. I don't want you to regret anything."

Regret? I look him over like I would a patient and wonder if a single woman has ever regretted fucking Theo Silva. It seems highly improbable.

And I want to find out.

For science.

So I toss back the rest of my shot and pull a pen out of my purse. Flipping the coaster over to the blank side, I write:

I, Winter, do legally swear that I am not too drunk to . . .

I glance up at him. "What are you worried about? I don't have orgasms, so alcohol intake won't matter."

He blinks once, slow and methodical, those thick, dark lashes wiping away a flash of annoyance on his perfect bone structure. "Consent, Tink. I'm worried about consent. The rest isn't an issue."

His voice drops to a low growl. "You'd get there with me. I'd make sure of it."

Heat lashes at my cheeks, spills down my throat, and washes over my chest. He's so damn confident. Tequila or not, talking brazenly like this is new to me. So, instead of arguing with him, I use a shaky hand to finish the sentence:

Consent.

When I peek up, our eyes lock. I'm practically panting and he's just sitting there, vibrating with sexual energy, fingers clenched around the edge of the table.

I bite at the inside of my cheek and drop his gaze before I sign my name.

Winter Hamilton.

My maiden name.

He registers it too, because when I look back up at him, his gaze remains fixed on the coaster.

"I thought it was Valentine?"

"It's not. The divorce papers are stashed in my car. On my way out here, I picked them up. I'm a private person. I don't need my messy divorce to be dinner conversation."

He nods, searching my face. Then the tip of his tongue peeks out from between his lips as he stares down at the coaster. "So this is a . . . sex contract?"

"Essentially, yes." I feel like an idiot, but I also feel like, for the first time in a long time, I don't care. Every step I took away from that house today was a domino falling. One after the other. Now, there's only one left, and I'm about to knock it right into Theo Silva's lap.

"Well, this is a first." Theo's fingers dust over where I signed my name and I imagine them on my body. *In* my body.

"I think . . ." I put a hand on my throat, like that will force me to keep using my words when all I can think about right now is him touching me and the heavy rush of pressure between my legs. "It keeps things very clear. For us."

He leans close, his demeanor shifting right before my eyes. Hot, damp breath dances along the shell of my ear as his deep voice rumbles against my skin. "Contractual clarity has never made me harder."

My body flares to life, even though I know he's teasing me. I force myself to swallow and nod as I shift my eyes to meet his.

"I don't know if a sentence on a coaster will hold up in a court of law."

"One night," I reply. "That's all. I'm not equipped for anything else. I'm too fucked-up. Taking you to court would involve seeing you again, and I don't plan to do that."

His throat works once more.

"And we never tell anyone. We shake hands and walk away, like mature adults with a contract."

"Winter . . ." He doesn't love that part.

I push the coaster at him, feeling more laid bare than I have in, well, possibly ever. My voice shakes. "Sign it or I'm going to bed. My ego is too fragile for this right now."

His gaze softens on me, the warmth in those chocolate depths heating my chilly exterior. I watch the veins in his hand bulge as he picks up the pen. The tendons in his forearm ripple as he writes.

One night only. We never tell anyone.
But I'll probably beg you for another shot,
eventually. —Theo Silva

Even his handwriting is beautiful.

He looks smug when he slides the coaster back across the table at me. I lift the piece of cardboard and eye it, like I really am reading over a contract. *Another shot*—as if. But I'll let him get the last word in.

I hold the coaster out and he takes it, his warm fingers wrapping over mine. He lifts my hand to his mouth and presses a firm kiss to the top of it, sending a shiver down my spine.

He smirks, and I want to stomp on his foot. I hate how obvious this is. How unnaturally it's come about. How *knowing* he is.

But I also want it so damn badly.

We hold up one last shot of tequila, and honestly, I need the liquid courage. Our glasses clink as we cheers.

His eyes lock on mine with a level of intensity that screams at me to be careful. And then he says, "I'm going to ruin you tonight."

We toss the liquor back, not dropping each other's gaze. I slam my glass down harder than necessary. It's loud, like the shotgun at a race signaling it's go time.

He cants his head at me. One more silent assurance.

I nod.

He nods.

And without another word, he links his fingers through mine and leads me out of the bar area and onto the elevator.

When the door slides shut, that last tether of control between us snaps. It's an audible ping in the small, private space.

He tugs me into his chest, fingers instantly tangling in my loose hair.

All I can hear is the heavy bass of my heart pumping blood through my veins.

All I can see are his rosy cheeks, and full lips.

All I can feel is the press of his rock-hard length against my stomach.

He looks me straight in the eye and grabs the back of my skull roughly with one hand while the other pulls at my bottom lip. "I can't wait to see how fucking pretty you look when you come with my name on your lips."

6
Theo

Rhett: Did you and Winter get back safe? Summer said
Winter never responded to her.
Theo: Yeah. She was tired and grumpy. I think she went to bed.
Rhett: Yeah. Okay. Gym at 11?
Theo: See you there, old man.

"Theo. You're a sack of shit this morning."

I flop back on the mat and decide I'll just die here
in a pool of my sweat. "Summer, you look sweet, but
you're kind of an asshole."

From the mat beside me, Rhett turns and kicks my sneaker.
"Talk to her like that again. I dare you."

"Rhett, twenty-five burpees for assaulting a client." His fiancée
smiles smugly at him from where she sits on a bench. Or as I've
dubbed it in my head, the *Torture Throne*.

Rhett scoffs like she's joking, but she inclines her head at him and crosses her arms over her Hamilton Athletics hoodie.

"You're evil. What about Theo?"

"What about him?" Summer's voice is all sugary and amused.

"Dude, shut up. Just let me die in peace." Slinging a damp arm over my face, I get a strong whiff of alcohol. I am literally sweating tequila.

"He was clearly out all night," Summer says. "Probably making babies all over North America at this rate."

"Please. I always wrap it up." The truth is, since hitting the road this past fall, there has been no one in my bed at all. I let everyone believe what they want, but I'm changing.

Rhett quirks a brow. "You're not denying being out with someone last night, though, are you?"

I groan in annoyance, but Summer leans forward, eyes sparkling with interest. "Who was it?"

"I had a long romantic evening with my right hand." I don't kiss and tell. Especially where Winter is concerned. I'll be taking this one to the grave. Unless she comes back for more.

"Did you light a candle?" Rhett laughs at his own joke.

"Why are you still lying there, Eaton?" Summer snipes at him. "I said give me twenty-five or I'll make you join a Zumba class."

I snort. "Fuck. I would pay a lot of money to see that happen."

Rhett playfully kicks my foot again as he pushes to stand.

"Who was it really, Theo?" Summer isn't letting this go.

I sit up and sling my elbows over my bent knees, looking her in the eyes. "It wasn't anyone. And if it was, I would never walk around here talking about it. You'll have to get your small-town gossip elsewhere."

"Everything comes out in a town this size. You need to be careful if you plan to spend more time here, Theo." She takes on a more serious tone with me now.

We never tell anyone. I wrote it out myself, and I'd never betray Winter's trust. Too many people in her life have and no matter what we are or if I never see her again—I won't be another person who lets her down or lies to her.

I shrug and hold her gaze because I'm not saying shit. "No one."

Rhett is jumping beside me, huffing and panting. But Summer? Summer is just staring at me. It's *almost* like she knows. But how could she? I don't think a single person would ever guess that Winter and I would end up together.

I'm a bull rider and she's a doctor.

I'm fire and she's ice.

She wants to forget about me, and right now I can't stop thinking about her. Her softer side. The way she opened up with me. The way she whimpered my name when—

"Twenty-five burpees, Silva." Summer's lips stretch into an evil smile.

"Are you kidding me?"

Rhett is too breathless to even mock me, but when I glance at him, I can see his bearded cheeks stretched up into a smile.

"No. Get your ass up."

"I thought I was done?" I whine but do as she says, because I promised myself I'd do my dad proud this season. He may have died riding a bull, but he did it with a couple of championships under his belt.

He mentored Rhett, and Rhett has two.

I want *one.* I want a fraction of his greatness. I'd be happy to have even a sliver of their success so I can be part of that legacy too.

I want to be more than the World Bull Riding Federation wild child and a fantastic lay.

So, I start my burpees.

Summer smiles at me and shakes her head. "Wow. You really must not want anyone to know about last night."

"He's just . . . miffed that he already . . . failed at his goal," Rhett puffs out from beside me as I start my first jump up in the air. My muscles riot against me as I urge my body back into action after what has already been a two-hour workout.

"What was your goal, Theo?"

I ignore them both.

Sure, I stepped out on the goal I shared with Rhett during one of our talks, but I'm not about to explain to them that this was different somehow. This wasn't just another—

"Something about living like a monk for the next season to help with his focus."

Rhett chuckles as he bends over, and I find myself hoping he hurls. The agitation pushes me harder. As I keep going, I feel Summer's eyes on me.

Assessing. She analyzes things way too damn closely. Sees far too much.

"You smell like tequila," she says, clearly opting not to pile on with her fiancé.

Once I join Rhett back on the mat, huffing and puffing and wishing I were dead, he turns and grins at me. "I knew you'd never be able to keep your dick in your pants."

Though they're meant as a joke, his words sting. They're also the nudge I need to get motivated, because I want my mentor's respect. I don't want to be the butt end of a joke or seen as the child who never grows up. I want to chase my dreams and prove to myself I can do the things I set my mind to.

I don't want to be the one-night stand who's used to scratch an itch. I want a woman like Winter Hamilton—beautiful, and smart, and sharp-tongued—to look at me and see a future.

7
Winter

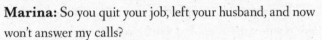

Marina: So you quit your job, left your husband, and now won't answer my calls?

Winter: Seems like you've figured out the gist all on your own.

Marina: Call me back.

Winter: The more I think about it, the less I have to say to you.

Marina: I raised you better than this. Stronger than this. More focused than this.

Winter: I can't remember a single hug.

Marina: What?

Winter: You never hugged me. Never consoled me.

Marina: That's what the nanny was for.

"Well, shit. It looks pretty damn good in here." Sloane has her hands propped on her narrow hips, taking in the small house with a satisfied expression on her face.

My nod feels like a Herculean feat. For the past three weeks, I've experienced a whirlwind of emotions and made life-altering decisions. Because I was too bitchy to hang out with joyful people, I spent Christmas alone in a hotel, dreaming about Theo Silva running his rough hands all over my body and trying to recreate the sensation with my own.

Not that I'd ever admit that last part out loud.

But there's something unforgettable about the way his callouses felt sliding over my skin. The way he touched me like he couldn't get enough. His palms never stopped exploring me, worshipping me.

I clear my throat. "Yeah. It does. Look good."

The blonde woman beside me beams with pride and I can't help but smile back.

It sounds childish, but somehow Sloane has wiggled her way into my life in the past couple of weeks. She's Rhett's cousin, and she says she thinks she met me at exactly the right time. She says she needed someone like me in her life, but the thing is . . . I think I'm the one who needed her.

We've both faced a lot of upheaval in the short time we've known each other. The difference is her upheaval led her to being with her childhood crush—the hockey player who treats her like a goddess—and mine led me to giving Rob divorce papers, quitting my job at the hospital in the city, and moving into a rental house in Chestnut Springs.

Looking at Sloane now, all smiles and messy hair, I suppose it also led me to having a friend.

Possibly my only friend in a life full of acquaintances and co-workers. And that alone makes everything I've been through worth it.

"Should we shift the TV a bit? It might catch too much light there during the day."

I snort and flop down onto the couch behind me. "I work insane hours. I doubt I'll be watching TV in the daytime."

"What about days off?" Sloane follows suit, falling into the cushy new couch beside me.

"Yeah. I guess so."

"Or are you going to be too busy hanging out with your cool new neighbor?" She waggles her eyebrows at me, and I can't help but laugh. She and Jasper live in the bungalow next door. In fact, Jasper owns the entire block, a row of houses on this side and the businesses on the other that face out onto the main drag. Sloane has been carefully restoring each one back to its original glory so they can rent them out.

"Do you think you'll keep both jobs now that you've moved here?"

I shrug and let my head sink into the soft velvety fabric behind me. Except it's not velvet, it's microfiber, because rich as Rob might be as a cardiothoracic surgeon, I'm still just a resident.

Velvet taste, microfiber budget. That's me. Winter *Hamilton*. And I'm alright with it.

Twenty-eight-year-old almost divorcee. Ex-husband who hates my guts because the only thing he's better at than fixing hearts is playing the victim. Mother who is all up in my face because misery loves company and she's chosen to live a miserable life. A dad who is just as fucking awkward around me as he always has been—bless him. And an estranged sister who is feeling less estranged every day.

That's the bright spot in turning my life upside down. I really doused it all in gasoline, dropped the match, and said, "Fuck it."

"I quit today. Having to work in the same hospital as both my mom and Rob? No thanks." I point a finger into my open mouth and make a gagging noise.

And doing that makes me a bit nauseous. A bit light-headed.

Sloane laughs, all light and airy, while I suck in deep breaths, trying to master my roiling stomach. "Good for you."

I nod and she carries on. "We can always hang the decor tomorrow. I'll help you unpack more. We can enlist Jasper when he's back from his road trip. I like the placement of all the furniture though."

"That sounds good," I whisper, licking my lips and letting my eyes flutter shut.

"Wanna grab a drink? A snack? Something? Otherwise, I'll just stay up late working on the other house."

"You need an HGTV show." I give her a wan smile, but don't move. If I sit still and think about the cold air filtering in through my nose, I feel fine.

"Oh my god. I do! That's the dream." Her hand slaps on my knee before she sits up, bursting with energy. "Should we go?"

I do simple math in my head, think about number patterns, not hurling the Chinese takeout from earlier all over my new microfiber couch.

"I think I'll pass." My voice sounds breathy, and my heart thunders against my sternum. It feels so loud I wonder if Sloane can hear it.

"You okay?" Her fingers pulse on my knee as concern laces her voice.

Twenty-eight minus seven equals twenty-one.

Ovulation.

I turn and peek at her. "Just kinda wiped right now. I think I'll bail. Crawl into bed."

Her eyes hold so much concern. Sloane is one of the most genuine people I've ever met. She's sweet, but not sickeningly so. Now and then she says something inappropriate and then giggles to herself about it.

I like that about her. She's relatable.

"You sure?"

Divided by seven equals three.

Cycle starts.

I offer her my most convincing smile, but I'm a terrible actress. I'm quite certain the look I give her is just a scowl with my lips in a slightly upturned shape.

She snorts and pushes to stand. "You look like a serial killer when you do that." She freezes before spinning back to me with a laugh. "Imagine that! I help this nice doctor girl who I think is a new friend move into the house next to mine. But it turns out she's a serial killer and is just playing the long game with planning my murder." She giggles. "Now *that* would be a good story."

I rub at my temples. "Sounds like a Catherine Cowles book."

"What?" Her head quirks.

"Nothing. I'm going to go read in bed."

Three weeks ago was the Saturday before Christmas.

"Okay. Text me when you're up and ready to finish this place off in the morning." Sloane leans down and gives me a breezy kiss on the cheek. "And please don't murder me tonight."

I would laugh, but if I open my mouth, I will barf on the

microfiber couch. The sales guy told me it wipes up easy. I absently wonder *how* easily.

The Saturday before Christmas was dinner at Wishing Well Ranch.

Sloane is laughing as she slides on her UGGs and leaves.

She's happy and carefree, cracking serial killer jokes.

And I'm doing math in my head. Math I'm painfully familiar with because I've spent the last two years desperately trying to get pregnant. Tears, positive ovulation strips, negative pregnancy tests, fertility appointments.

Of all the times I've obsessively run these numbers in my head, my math was right once. That test was positive *once*.

It was the highest high. But it ended in loss, and pain, and the lowest low.

Now, my math is right again.

Wishing Well Ranch is where I met Theo Silva.

Winter: Do you have access to the gym? You dance there after hours sometimes, right?

Sloane: Yeah. Sometimes when I can't sleep. I use the Zumba studio.

Winter: Can I get you to let me in?

Sloane: But it's 10 p.m.

Winter: Yeah, I know. I just got off work.

Sloane: Am I allowed to ask why you need to go into your sister's business after hours?

Winter: You can ask, but I won't tell you.

Sloane: Does it have to do with your murder plot?

Winter: Yes. I'm making you my accessory.
Sloane: New friendship level unlocked! I'll be out
front in five.

"Do you want me to come in with you?" Sloane gives me a worried glance as we stand outside the darkened gym.

The cold air feels good after the unending nausea I lived with through my shift. The smell of antiseptic that I usually find comforting turned on me in the most vicious way. Even finally talking to Marina made me more nauseous than usual. But telling her to stop contacting me felt good too. I felt strong. I felt relieved knowing I wouldn't ever subject another human to her toxicity.

Hilariously, as soon I stopped giving any fucks about what she thought of me, I stopped caring about her opinion—but today I could have hurled all over my phone from the mere sound of her voice.

"No, that's fine."

"I'm coming anyway." Sloane hustles past me, our puffy winter coats brushing against each other and making a little zipping noise as she heads straight for the number pad where she inputs a code.

Sloane turns and stares at me expectantly.

"Are you going to crack some wiseass comment about me coming here to do something mean to my sister?" I ask.

Her brows furrow. "Why would I think that?"

My eyes roll in time with my arms crossing. "Everyone thinks that."

"I think you're a lot more likeable than you realize." I quirk a brow at the other woman, and her head wobbles back and forth as she smiles. "When you want to be."

I huff out a laugh. "*Likeable when I want to be* could be my slogan."

Truthfully, it smarts. As though no one really likes me when I'm at my worst. I'm likeable when I put on a smiley, happy face. But what about when I crumble? Then all I get is criticism and reprimand.

"Okay, well, I just need a few minutes."

"For what?"

"To check something on the computer."

Sloane's eyes go comically wide. "I thought murder was the thing. But are you stalking someone?"

I press my lips together and motion locking them with a key before throwing it away. The truth is . . . this *is* kind of stalkery.

But after confirming what I already knew with a positive pregnancy test this morning, I know I need to talk to Theo. Because our one-night secret isn't so secret anymore.

I think I'm still in shock. After years of trying and failing, I can't find it in me to be upset. I cried in the hospital bathroom while I stared at that tiny pink plus sign.

I cried happy tears.

Because no matter how unplanned this is, I can't help but see it as a blessing. *Something* turning up Winter after getting shoved down so many times.

Something just for me.

And this left me with a whole other issue to face. *Getting in touch.*

Sloane chuckles but turns away, offering me privacy as I sneak over to the front desk and fire up the computer. My hope is that I can find Theo's contact information listed in the gym database.

I could ask Summer, but that would lead to questions. If I contact my dad, who is his agent, that would lead to questions *and* awkward conversation. And I don't want to deal with either.

I barely know Theo, but I know I have to tell him. He deserves to know, and he deserves to know before anyone else. He's a wild card, but there's something deeply caring about him. And no matter what our situation might be, there's a part of me that thinks he would be a great dad.

And if he doesn't want that, I'm okay with it too. But he deserves a choice.

I can't think of anything worse than everyone around you knowing something this personal before you've even had a chance to process.

I know all about needing time to process.

It's why I'm terrified of telling everyone this news and then losing the baby like last time. Having clothes and toys and plans. Everyone thriving on that excitement, only to have them pour on condolences that I couldn't even cope with.

If I'm going to grieve a loss again, I want to do it privately.

Biting down on my lip, I try to navigate the software searching for . . . *members*. There! With a quick click, a list of names fills the page. I navigate to the miniature magnifying glass in the corner and type in *Theo Silva*.

Another window pops up with his information. A home address in Emerald Lake, a college lake town in British Columbia. An emergency contact by the name of Loretta Silva, which sounds like the name of a woman who would live on a ranch and is far more fitting for the wife of a bull rider who was an icon on the circuit. (Thank you, Google.)

And then I see it. His cell number. I swipe a pad of Post-its, and scribble the number down before I exit every window on the computer, wanting to make sure it looks like I was never here.

Within seconds I'm rounding the desk on the tips of my toes, like someone might hear, even though it's completely empty in here.

"Ready. Thank you," I whisper at Sloane as I draw near to her.

She turns now, having been totally respectful. The perfect accomplice, not pushy or nosy.

"Did you wipe down the keyboard?"

My brows knit together. "What?"

"You know. To clean off the fingerprints."

"Are you—"

"Looking out for you? Yes. That's what friends are for."

I snort, because I *think* she's joking. "No crimes were committed here tonight."

"You sure about that?"

My mouth twists as I consider it. "I don't know. I'm a doctor, not a lawyer. It might be a crime *lite*."

She laughs as she resets the alarm. "I like that. Hopefully, the police appreciate your branding."

We walk through the door and it's my turn to laugh. Except my stomach is twisting inside. I'm not worried about the police, but the reality of what I'm about to tell a man I barely know hits me and I can feel the anxiety building in my chest.

I rub my palm there to lessen it. And even as Sloane and I bid each other goodnight, I continue to push against my sternum.

I don't stop until I'm seated on my microfiber couch, staring down at the pale-yellow piece of paper.

What have I done? How did I let this happen? We used condoms. *And condoms break.*

It's a peculiar feeling to have all that you ever wanted, but not in the way you envisioned. I've been that girl since I was a child. The one who carried a doll everywhere and pushed them around in a tiny stroller. I was thrilled about having a baby sister until my mom ruined it for me.

I've wanted a child of my own for as long as I can remember. Desperately, with every fiber of my being. But never in my wildest dreams did I imagine it happening like this. Like some sort of cosmic joke.

Clomid. Legs up the wall. Bladder infections. All to no avail.

It's like my body knew Rob was a piece of shit, even when my brain didn't. *Ha. No. Nice try, honey. We don't want a baby with this man.*

And then I got pregnant. After which, I promptly found out all the ways my husband had betrayed me.

I lost him.

Then I lost the baby.

Then I lost myself.

I've only admitted it once out loud—to my little sister's best friend Willa. I confessed to her that broken as my miscarriage left me, there is a shameful part of me that's relieved I'm not tied to Rob Valentine for the rest of my life.

I get to move on from him with no strings attached. A blessing and a curse. A guilt that eats me alive. One I have to learn to live with, because I *am* relieved to be free of him.

But this is different. The timing is different.

Theo is different.

I lift the phone and dial his number, taking a steadying breath as it rings.

But it keeps ringing and then goes to voicemail. His deep

baritone telling me to leave a message sends a shiver down my spine. The things he said to me that night.

Filthy fucking girl. Just begging for—

"Hi, Theo. This is Winter. From ... well, from the hotel. Or the ranch? From the coaster contract. I tracked your number down and was hoping we could chat, even though I swore I wouldn't ever contact you again. Can you call me back when you have a moment? Thanks. Bye."

I haven't told him yet, but I already feel relieved. I'll face this head on. It's going to be fine.

My hand falls across my still flat stomach and I sigh.

I'm going to be happy.

"Hi, Theo. It's Winter again. I haven't heard from you and it's been a few days. At the risk of sounding totally nuts, I checked the WBRF website and know that you're out on the tour again. I get that you're busy, but I really need to talk to you. I have something really important to tell you.

"Theo. Hi. I hope you're okay. Based on the scores I can see listed online, it would seem you're doing just fine. I'm not trying to be some clingy buckle bunny or whatever the fuck you call it. I just need to share some information with you, and I would like to tell you directly."

Winter: Hi, it's Winter. Is this Theo Silva? Are you getting my voicemails? I've left three now.

Winter: Are you aware that you have read receipts on? I know you've seen my text.

Theo: Yes. I've gotten your voicemails. I'm not interested in talking.

Winter: Listen, I'm trying not to be a full-on bitch to you right now. But can you please call me? I need to tell you something.

Theo: Then tell me.

Winter: Via text?

Theo: Yup.

Winter: Fine. That night in the hotel, a condom must have broken. I'm pregnant. The baby is yours. Thought that might interest you.

Theo: Thanks for letting me know.

8
Winter

Eighteen months later ...

Winter: Is she okay?

Harvey: Yes, my world is her jungle gym. She's going up and down the stairs. Getting pretty fast on the way down now. She even tried to climb the banister. Doesn't stop moving much.

Winter: Harvey. Please don't say things like that.

Harvey: If it wasn't rude, I'd ask if her secret daddy is a monkey.

Winter: You basically just asked that.

Harvey: Where's the question?

Winter: I'm coming back.

Harvey: No. You aren't. If I can keep Rhett alive, then Vivi will be a breeze.

Winter: Somehow that isn't very comforting. Rhett is insane.

"This is going to be fun, Winter. You'll see." Willa pats my shoulder, and I cast her a sidelong glance.

"Vivi is going to have the best time with Harvey." Summer squeezes my knee.

"Did you guys plan this pep talk?" My arms cross and I stare out at the dirt ring in front of us.

Willa shrugs with a slight grin on her lips. "Sloane told us you might need it, but that we had her permission to drag you out of that house kicking and screaming."

"Easy for Sloane to say while she's on a road trip with Jasper. I'm going to FaceTime her later and give her a piece of my mind."

I lick my lips and peer around at the sea of people before me. Summer and Willa don't respond, but I'm sure they roll their eyes at me as they too take in our surroundings.

It's day three of the first annual Chestnut Springs Rodeo and I feel like a sociologist watching it all go down. The actual town is small and charming. But the fairgrounds this weekend?

I don't even know what the fuck this is.

Wranglers, cowboy boots, rhinestone belts.

Even the children are wearing little cowboy and cowgirl outfits. It's like I'm at one of those historical re-enactments where all the dorks dress up like knights and kings.

Except here, all the dorks dress up as cowboys.

"There are children everywhere," I announce. "I can't fathom why I couldn't have brought Vivi with me. You'd hardly notice her in the carrier."

Summer edges closer, pressing her body into mine reassuringly.

I'm not about to admit it, but I like it. No. I love it. Getting to know my sister the way I've always wanted over the past eighteen months has been a bright spot in my life.

"*You* notice her," Willa says. "She's nine months old now. You've pumped enough to feed an orphanage. I saw the freezer, so don't try to tell me otherwise. She's going to have fun and so will you. You need this. The first time I left Emma was hard too, but I . . . Winter, just trust me. You'll feel somewhat like your old self after tonight. You can't do it all alone. You'll have to go back to—"

Summer cuts her off with a stern glance, and I almost roll my eyes. Does she think I don't know what Willa was about to say?

Back to work.

One year. The hospital in Chestnut Springs allowed me one year of maternity leave and that is rapidly drawing to a close. September 21st is the day I have circled in red on the calendar.

I wish someone had told me that once I had a baby, I wouldn't give a flying fuck about anything else. They act like I need this night away, but I don't feel like I do. I already miss her even though I've spent the past couple of weeks saying all I want is for no one to touch me for a few hours.

And I don't want to feel like my old self. My old self was angry and bitter and alone.

Okay, I'm still not a ray of sunshine, but I have turned over a new leaf since moving to Chestnut Springs.

"I'm going to get us all some drinks," Willa announces, slapping her jean-clad thighs and all I can do is nod while Garth Brooks blares from the speakers while men in leather chaps mull around.

They might be dorks, but I'd have to be blind not to appreciate the things this getup does for a man's ass. Everyone is on and on about a man in a suit, but I can't help but wonder if they've ever seen a man in Wranglers and chaps.

Suit who?

Summer bumps her shoulder against mine. "Thanks for coming."

I bump her back. "You're welcome."

"Rhett and Beau have been working so hard on this event. I know they appreciate you being here too." I just nod. "I think your suggestion of something that might give Beau a purpose was helpful. He seems more like himself all the time. Planning this rodeo has been fun for him."

It's true. I said that. Because I've seen it before. A veteran moves into a new phase of their life, and they feel monumentally lost, like everything that was important about them isn't anymore.

I wrinkle my nose and look away. As much as I fight leaving Vivienne, there's a little part of me that can relate. The ER was exciting. Something new happened every day. I worked damn hard to get there, to become the best doctor I could be. And now I've turned all that focus on being the best mom I can be.

I miss it.

I miss that part of myself.

"Oh." Summer brightens and sits up tall beside me. "There they are."

"They?"

"Rhett and Theo."

Theo.

My heart comes to a screeching halt in my chest and my limbs turn to ice. At the same time, my stomach falls fast and hard, like coming straight down off the highest point of a roller coaster. Except the cart goes off the wheels and crashes straight into the pavement.

That's how I feel right now.

"Theo?" My voice doesn't betray me. It comes out perfectly smooth. Perfectly unaffected.

"Yeah. You know . . . Rhett's protégé. I believe you and him got into a screaming match at the ranch a couple of Christmases ago."

I scoff. "Screaming at someone is not my MO."

"It's not, but I could hear you from inside."

My little sister is giving me her know-it-all look. The one I've come to know well over the last year and a half. I don't know what kind of karma was working in my favor to make Summer put all the years of tension behind us so readily. And I still haven't quite found the words to thank her for it.

She was there for me while I was pregnant and alone.

She was in the delivery room holding my hand.

She was at my house, filling my freezer with meals when I got home.

I'm not sure I deserve her, but I'm too selfish not to lap up what she's giving me.

"You must have misheard." I sniff, peering out over the crowd before glancing down at my nails. The ones I still haven't gotten done, even though I swore that was one of the first things I was going to do when I went on maternity leave.

"Why is he here? I thought this was some Podunk rodeo, not the fancy bull riding circuit they do."

Summer elbows me. "You live in this Podunk town now, remember?"

I do. And I love it. Same little house Sloane helped me move into.

"Anyway, he came to do a demo. Rhett thought if he brought in a big name, it might help draw the crowd a bit."

I glance around and can't deny that his plan worked. It's packed. "I thought Theo wasn't that good?" I lie. I've checked his stats.

Summer huffs out a laugh. "He's always been good—a bit injury-prone, maybe. But in the past year he's turned a corner. Changed his focus. Now he's the best, following right in his dad's footsteps. He's already planning for the finals in Vegas. It feels like it's his year, you know?"

My lips purse. What I want to say is *how convenient for him.* I take maternity leave and he levels up his career because he washed his hands clean of any responsibility. Not that I expected him to do anything. But it still stings.

I don't *need* him. I never did. But he hurt me all the same.

Thanks for letting me know.

Sometimes that sentence wakes me up at night. I hoped that even though we were clearly incompatible, he might want to play some part in raising the child we made.

After all, I watched my dad dote on a little girl born of an affair my entire life. There were times I begrudged him for that, but now? Now, I can respect him for how he handled Summer—even if he failed me in the process.

"Cool," is what I respond with. And it's not something I would ever say, which is why Summer turns and eyes me with suspicion.

"Wh—"

"Summer!" Willa calls from the end of the row of stands where she carries three drinks in each hand. I guess all those years spent bartending weren't a total waste. "Did you know they have mimosas in the beer tent?"

My sister rolls her lips together and casts her gaze down. "I might have known, yes." Mimosas are her thing. She often hosts a "Boozy Brunch" as she and Willa call it.

"Man, Rhett can be really romantic sometimes." Willa drops down and shoves the plastic cups in our direction. "Help a girl out."

"Why are there six?" My nose wrinkles, mind still on the too-good-looking asshole bull rider down near the gate. Do I act normal? Kick him in the balls? Ignore him?

"I don't know, Winter. You're the doctor here. How many hands do we have between us?"

I glance down at us, like I need a visual representation of how many hands there are between three humans.

God. Theo Silva has a knack for making me lose my brain. I almost don't think I should drink. Maybe there's something chemical between us, because when I peek at him from beneath my lashes, I see a flash of his white teeth and almost *feel* the rumble of his laugh when he throws his head back. So carefree.

And flashing his Adam's apple. I remember the way it moved up and down when I dropped to my knees in front of him. His head tipped back in a similar fashion when I fisted his length and—

"Winter, stop being such a buzzkill." Willa pushes the two drinks into my hands, the ones that are now clammy and clasped over my jeans.

My fingers fold around the damp plastic cups and I look down at the new boots on my feet. Pale brown cowboy booties with a metal embellished toe. Because, apparently, I can't wear normal shoes to this event without becoming some sort of pariah.

Summer's snakeskin boots are a subtle touch with her white WBRF tee. But Willa has adopted the lifestyle. The boots. The jeans. The sparkly belt with her mane of coppery hair blown out and curled like some sort of rodeo Barbie.

The two of them talk around me about the event. Today's lineup. The final night of the three-day rodeo and what a success it's been.

I take a sip of my mimosa and will myself to remain calm as events pass. Barrels, roping, something where small children try to stay on sheep and everyone laughs when they fall off. Summer and Willa pat my back and try to engage me in conversation. They think I'm worried about Vivi, but all I can think about is that her father is right fucking there.

I've imagined this moment in my head a million times. What I'd do. What I'd say. I've oscillated between hating him and understanding his choice.

But I've never gotten over how his reaction doesn't match the man I thought I met that night. Sure, he was wild and carefree, but he felt like an old soul somehow. There was a gentleness in him.

A roughness too.

Choke on it, Winter. I blink the memory away, not wanting to go there.

"Oh, here goes Theo."

My head snaps up and sure enough, the man holding the microphone in the middle of the ring is talking about Theo. About his dad, Gabriel, and their family legacy. About his accolades and wins.

But my eyes are stuck on Theo, his ass looking way too good in those jeans.

I can resent him and still like his ass. That's perfectly acceptable.

"Fuck. He is hot, isn't he?" Willa takes a sip of her orange drink without sparing Summer or me a glance. Then she carries on with, "What? I'm still allowed to window shop."

My sister snorts, but I feel wooden. Hollowed out. Theo climbs into the chute, bull jostling around between the metal gates. But he's unaffected.

He gives zero fucks.

His stubbled chin tips down as his gloved hand pulls methodically at a rope. I have no idea what's going on. He looks like he's jerking that rope off, and it entrances me how he can come off so tranquil despite the chaos surrounding him.

"You trying to put a curse on him, Win?" Summer nudges me and I offer her a wan smile, trying to cover up how insane I must look staring at the man everyone thinks I hate.

Who I *do* hate.

"Nah, just interested. I haven't seen bull riding live before."

"You watch a lot on TV?" Willa cracks.

No, on my laptop is what I almost reply, but that would raise some eyebrows. The truth is, when I was trying to get a hold of Theo, I would sometimes watch his rides.

"That'll be the day," I reply, forcing myself to scan the ring. But my eyes always come back. The helmet over his head doesn't hide the look of concentration on his face. The way his tongue darts out over his lips as he hunkers down on the bull.

With a swift nod, they tug the gate open and the bull bursts out into the ring, head down to the ground, back hooves up so high they almost kiss the setting sun. My heart thuds loudly enough to rattle my ribs while the crowd around us cheers.

For one brief moment, I hope he falls off. I hope he doesn't hit the eight seconds. It's petty and low, but there's a bitterness in me over the fact he could so easily walk away from me. From her.

But I also don't much like the idea of my child's father being a loser. At least I'll be able to tell her he can ride a bull exceptionally well one day. And that's something, even if it doesn't make up for him not being a part of her life.

Theo pushes his broad shoulders back, his hand held high in the air. He comes off perfectly in control, or as in control as you can be on a thousand-pound animal who wants nothing more than to drive you into the dirt, I suppose.

And drive Theo into the dirt he does.

One dropped shoulder, one hard turn, and Theo's body launches toward the ground like a lawn dart.

I gasp. But so does everyone around us. And when the bull turns to leave, and steps on Theo's shoulder in the process, there is a chorus of "Ooohs," but I'm up and moving before I even have time to make a noise.

I hustle past the people seated on the bench, heading straight toward the fence of the arena. Guilt gurgles in my stomach, like I willed this to happen to him. What the fuck kind of doctor am I?

A bitter one.

I ignore the answer and duck through the fence. The rodeo clown draws the bull toward the exit, and it crosses my mind that Vivienne doesn't need to be left an orphan if that bull decides to turn around.

But all my emergency training kicks in, and I forge ahead anyway. Cowboys surround Theo's body, including Rhett, who looks distraught.

"Move." I physically push a man aside and insert myself into the circle of people around Theo. I drop to my knees at his head, noting his still body. My hands cup the sides of his helmet, holding him in place until the paramedics can get here. I lean down over him and see his chest rising and falling, but I need to hear his breath—I need more proof.

87

The quiet whoosh of air hits my cheek right as his spicy citrus scent hits my nose.

People are too close. Hovering. Pushing in.

"Back up!" I bark sharply.

"It's okay, she's a doctor," I hear Rhett say behind me. "Everybody back it up a bit."

The press of bodies around us recedes. I hear soft feminine sobs and almost feel the vibration of anxiety around me. When I glance over my shoulder, a girl decked out in rodeo gear has makeup streaming down her face.

She's weeping.

And all the possibilities of what that means race through my head. I have to remind myself that I was the one-night entertainment. That's what I asked for, and he probably found someone who wanted more.

I stare down at Theo and am hit with a pang of longing. Not for myself, but for ... everything we missed. After eighteen months apart, he's just as beautiful as I remember. Moreso even.

And fuck, he looks so much like Vivienne. It's almost alarming. How no one has put it together yet is beyond me. It doesn't take a doctor to see she's a dead ringer for him.

Without even noticing, the pad of my blissfully bare ring finger has started stroking along the bare skin of his neck. Tan and warm.

And once I notice that I'm doing it, I don't stop.

"Please be okay," I murmur under my breath.

And then his eyes open, long dark lashes flicking up to reveal those dark onyx eyes. They take a minute to focus in on me and then a small, confused smile touches his lips.

"Hi, Tink."

9
Theo

I hiss out a breath when we hit a pothole. It's not as bad as the dirt road leading out of the fairgrounds, but it's not ideal either.

The other thing that's not ideal is the small blonde stewing in the corner of the ambulance. I can't even turn to look at her properly with my head strapped down onto the board like this. If it didn't hurt to laugh, I'd laugh right now.

I knew I'd see her again at some point, but this isn't quite what I'd pictured.

From the corner of my eye, I watch her stare down at one hand while her opposite arm wraps around her midsection.

The thing that woke me up was her snarky little voice barking at everyone to back off, and the feel of her finger stroking my neck. Before I even opened my eyes, I knew it was her. It's been well over a year, but I still remember how her hands felt on me. The way she felt under my own, all damp and writhing.

I thought we had a good time. A *really* good time.

"Why are you ignoring me?" Just the vibration of my voice in my chest sends shocks of pain through my collarbone.

I know it's broken, because it's sticking out through the skin. I passed out for a second time when I reached up and ran my fingers over the jagged edge.

Winter tilts her head and gives me a thoroughly unimpressed look. "You must be kidding me."

"Listen, I know you said it was a secret, but it's just us here. So you can stop pretending that wasn't the best sex you've ever had. How many times did I make you—"

"Theo. Shut up," she snaps, but it's not her usual Tinkerbell vibe. There's an edge of something I can't quite place.

Pain.

And it silences me.

The minutes filled with silence stretch between us. The hum of the road beneath the ambulance tires and the light rattle of the drawers in the back are our only companions.

Anxiety replaces discomfort as the main thing I'm feeling. There's an unfamiliar heaviness. I didn't expect to see her again, and I for sure didn't expect the cold shoulder—even from her.

"How many concussions have you had, Theo?" Her voice is emotionless, but confident. Very doctor-y.

I sigh. "A lot."

"How many is a lot?"

"We talking diagnosed or suspected?"

Her head flips away. "Jesus Christ."

"Last time I got one, I was told not to get any more."

"How long ago was that?"

"Probably three concussions ago."

Her head taps back against the single seat she's strapped into. "I can't even tell if you're joking right now."

"I'm not joking, just trying to lighten the blow. No pun intended."

I see her shake her head, but she says nothing. I am joking a little bit. It's keeping me from falling into a pit of despair over watching the most epic season circle the drain before my eyes. All my hard work and sacrifice gone up in a puff of smoke because I did a friend a favor and offered to do a demo ride at his small-town rodeo on an "easy" bull.

Epically stupid. Just like many of the decisions I've made in my life.

"When I started out, I didn't think wearing a helmet looked as cool."

"Yeah, brain injuries make you look so cool," she scoffs, jaw popping with tension.

"Have you seen the episode of *Grey's Anatomy* where McDreamy dies?"

Her expression is one you'd use on a child, full of deprecation. But it's a little lighter somehow.

I'll take it. I love watching this woman thaw.

"Are you telling me you watch *Grey's Anatomy*?"

"Every episode of all eighteen seasons."

She looks confused. "Why?"

I go to shrug and instantly regret it. "My mom loves it. When I was younger and lived with her, we watched it together every Thursday. Now, I watch it on my own and then call her so we can talk about it. It's the only reason I still have cable."

"How often?" Winter's eyes are comically wide.

"Every week. Well, while the season is running."

She stares at me like I'm some exotic animal in a zoo. "That's . . ."

"Are you going to say weird? Don't bother. You won't convince me. I never thought it was that weird. Sure, the guys have made fun of me for it along the way. But I don't give a fuck. She's my mom. Seems like the least I can do for her."

Winter almost jolts in her seat before she drops her eyes to her lap. Her voice is hushed when she says, "I wasn't going to say weird."

"You're gonna make sure they do a CT scan so that doesn't happen, right?"

Her head snaps up. "What?"

"Remember? We were talking about the episode where Derek dies. You sure I'm the one with a concussion?"

"I'm not Meredith. And you are certainly no McDreamy."

"They got married on a Post-it note."

Her brows scrunch. "And?"

"And we made a sex contract on a coaster. What was it? One night only. We never tell anyone . . ."

I don't need to ask. I know what's on that coaster, and I'm trying to see if she does too.

The ambulance stops, and she stares at me, not even a twitch of her lips. Blank and icy and thoroughly unimpressed. "That's not funny, Theo."

"I wasn't trying to be funny—"

"Okay, we're here," the paramedic announces as he yanks the doors open.

I see the reflection of flashing red lights bouncing off the hospital.

And the silhouette of Winter escaping the ambulance, getting away from me as fast as possible.

My eyes blink open to take in the hospital room around me. Dim lights. A steady beeping. Dryness in my mouth.

"You must enjoy spending time at the hospital," Rhett quips from beside me.

I squeeze my eyes shut once more to get my bearings and eventually grumble out, "I hope your stupid rodeo was a huge success, asshole. Where's my dog? One of the girls was watching him."

The sound of Rhett shifting in a vinyl hospital chair joins the chorus of beeps. "Don't worry, Summer has him. He might as well be a child, considering she just sent me a photo of him in our bed with her. And it's not my fault you dropped that inside shoulder like a rookie. Right down the well you go."

My eyes open only so that I can shoot him a glare. "Hilarious. The best season of my life is trashed because I did you a solid and you're sitting here telling me what I did wrong. Next time, you ride the fucking bull yourself. You're the one everyone wants to see anyway."

His lips flatten and his arms cross. "People were there to see you, Theo. Don't kid yourself."

I glance away, noting that whatever drugs they gave me after surgery are doing a great job because there's no pain to speak of. "People are there to see me because I'm Gabriel Silva's son and your protégé. Not because I have any accolades of my own."

Rhett's amber eyes narrow on me, his hands steepled beneath his chin. "That's not true."

"Don't bullshit a bullshitter, Eaton. Tell me what I'm known for in the WBRF?"

His lips twitch. "Chasing tail."

I swallow my frustration and focus on the ceiling. I fucking hate that for me.

"Theo, you're gonna bust a tooth grinding your molars like that. Everyone knows who you are because you're piecing together one of the most impressive seasons anyone has seen. A better run than your dad or I ever went on. That's for sure."

"So much for that."

"Don't be a pessimist. It doesn't suit you."

"I'm allowed to have a moment, Rhett. I've seen you brood over shit. I remember how hard you sulked when you first got saddled with Summer as your babysitter. This is ten times worse. I don't have to *always* be in a good mood."

"You'll be back this season. You're far enough ahead that you can pull it off. We'll make sure that you—"

A slightly raised voice cuts in from the hallway through the open door. "You didn't check his head?"

A deeper one responds. "He was perfectly alert. Laughing. Joking. I'm heading in there now. He's already awake."

"Have you not seen the episode of *Grey's Anatomy* where Derek Shepherd dies? It was one little CT scan to double-check the brain of a man who has had multiple head injuries—"

"Winter, relax."

Rhett's eyes widen at me. "If I didn't know any better, I'd say Winter Hamilton likes you. She's been a fucking terror out there, checking your charts and demanding updates."

I'm about to respond to that, but a stout man with gray hair wanders into my room.

He stops near my bed, glasses dropped low on his nose, while he stares down at a clipboard. "Mr. Silva, I'm Dr. Forrester. Nice to see you're awake. Surgery went well—"

Winter storms in behind him, doing her best crabby

Tinkerbell impression, and I can't help but smile. "How's your head?"

"Winter," the older doctor admonishes her.

It annoys me. He introduces himself as *doctor* but calls Winter by her first name.

"Doctor Hamilton," I correct, letting steel seep into my voice.

The man glances at me, head quirking to the side. "Yes? What about her?"

"You keep calling her Winter. But she works here, right? It's Dr. Hamilton, isn't it?"

An awkward hush permeates the space. Three sets of eyes lock on mine. Rhett's amused. Dr. Forrester's taken aback. And Winter's confused.

The man clears his throat and offers me a flat smile. "Right, well, yes. Dr. Hamilton here is concerned about head trauma, but I've assured her that you are most likely concussed. The helmet is what saved you."

"I'll take him for a CT myself, then."

The other doctor lets out a beleaguered sigh and Rhett fails to stifle a laugh.

I have to confess I'm a little lost as to why Winter cares so much about this. I'm not mad about it though. If she wants to play doctor, I'll be the patient.

"I think Dr. Hamilton is right," I pipe up, lasering my eyes in on hers even though I'm addressing the other doctor in the room. "I'd like to go for a CT, just to be safe. I'd hate to pull a McDreamy." Her lips flatten and she looks away. I'm pretty sure that's her version of holding back a laugh. "But first, how did surgery go? All fixed up? When can I get back on?"

"Surgery was a success. You've got a shiny new set of screws to go with the plate along your right clavicle. You're going to need to do physio, though. I'm thinking you'll be back to regularly scheduled activities in about three months. You're young and fit. We'll just have to see how those bones heal up. Could be sooner. Though I can't recommend you getting back on a bull."

Winter scoffs and rolls her eyes, hip cocked out and foot tapping the polished floor.

"Something to add, *Dr. Hamilton*?" He uses the right words this time, but the way he says them is almost worse.

"Yes, actually." Her eyes narrow and she doesn't back down at all. "His job is riding bulls. Telling him not to get back on one isn't helpful. We need to come up with a rehabilitation program that caters to him as an athlete."

"Excellent idea, Dr. Hamilton. I love your youthful exuberance." He smiles and stashes his pen into the top of the clipboard. "If you're so passionate about his rehabilitation plan, I invite you to come back from your maternity leave and take it over."

Maternity leave?

Winter pales, her cheeks losing their angry flush right before my eyes. She bites at her lip and nods, ignoring my gaze in such an unnatural way that it makes me stare at her even harder.

"Maybe I will," she says coolly. And then she spins on her heel and marches out of the room.

Disappointment roils in my gut, because I've been carrying a torch for her since that night. And clearly I covered it well, because Rhett never brought this up. Or her up at all. But I didn't care. I thought when the dust settled for us both, I'd be back, annoying her into giving me more than one night. Maybe into giving me a shot at more. Like maybe if I got myself together enough, I'd be worthy of that shot.

Clearly that ship has sailed. She wanted this. And I should be happy for her.

But in the wake of everything that's gone down today, I don't feel happy at all.

10

Winter

A shrill yap wakes me from what has to be only a single hour of sleep.

Yap. Yap. Yap.

I wonder if the oath I took to protect lives extends to dogs, because after two days in teething hell, I'm ready to murder someone. A dog is just an easy target.

You'd think that after years of residency and late-night study sessions, I'd be prepared for this phase of my life. But this is the most exhausted I have ever been.

I am a walking, talking milk bag and the sole source of comfort for the most precious little human I've ever laid eyes on. You'd think a night away from her would be what I needed, but instead, the rodeo went to shit, and I missed her so badly it hurt.

Yap. Yap. Yap.

I sling an arm over my face and groan, but I cut it off when I remember I gave in and kept Vivienne in the bed with me last night. I know what the baby books say. I know the methods. I know the *rules*.

But no one tells you just how tired you'll be, how thoroughly beaten down. I no longer care about her being independent. I just want to sleep. And if latched on in the crook of my arm is how that happens—then fuck all that advice. I'm a doctor. Ask me how exhaustion wreaks havoc on a body.

Yap. Yap. Yap.

I turn and peek down at the sleeping little person beside me. She's so beautiful it makes my chest ache. Her pert button nose looks like she has a dot of highlighter on the tip. Pudgy cheeks, full and rosy even in her sleep. Perfect skin. Why is perfect skin wasted on a baby? It seems unfair. I'd have taken wrinkles as a baby to have this smooth, soft skin now.

It's her lashes that always get me though. Similar to her dad's. Thick, and dark, and long. Almost like one of those dolls with the heavy lids that flip open and shut.

Except way less creepy.

Yap. Yap. Yap.

Her straight black hair flops over her head when she stirs, and frustration rises in me. I swear if some goddamn dog wakes her up when she's *finally* asleep, I'm going to lose it.

I slide out of bed as seamlessly as possible, doing my best ninja imitation to not move the bed at all. Thank god for memory foam. Once I'm safely off the bed, I turn up the white noise machine on the nightstand and say a small prayer that I can make it out of this room without waking her.

This bungalow is full of charm. And by charm, I mean creaky floors. But I think I mostly have those loose floorboards memorized now. I twist and turn, combine long steps with choppy ones and when my hand wraps around the crystal doorknob, I say another prayer that the door doesn't squeak.

I know the hinges need oiling or whatever, but I keep forgetting. Or feeling too tired to care once I have the time to do it.

This is my new reality.

Yap. Yap. Yap.

But a yappy dog next door is *not* my new reality. I refuse to let it be, so I swipe my cotton robe off the bathroom door and tie it around myself. With my shoulders squared, I march out the front door but hit the brakes to prevent the screen door from slamming behind me in my huff.

"What the hell is—"

I stop in my tracks as my eyes land on the white picket fence that divides my property from the one next door. There are three shirtless men moving furniture out of a box van.

I take an inventory of myself. Bare feet on warm wood boards. Heat already licking at where the belt of my robe is tied around my waist.

What time is it?

The full sun overhead means it must be a lot later than I thought.

Yap. Yap. Yap.

"Morning, Win!" My head snaps to the men and I squint, realizing it's Rhett with his hair tied up in some weird little bun. My gaze zips to the side, recognizing Beau with his close-cropped hair, and then . . .

Him.

It's been seven days since I last saw Theo Silva in the hospital. I don't know how long he stayed there or if he ever got the CT scan I ordered through my favorite nurse before I left. I don't know where he's been, and I sure as shit don't know what he's doing here. Shirtless and looking this goddamn sinful.

It's annoying that I have to remind my brain that he may be hot, but he's also shitty.

Thanks for letting me know.

That's the sentence that will do it.

"Hi, Tink," he says with a smirk. And how dare he smirk at me like that after everything? Knock me up, take off, and then fly back into town, gawking at me like I'm his next meal?

Fuck him.

"Looking forward to being your new neighbor."

My jaw drops and I almost laugh. What the fuck kind of cruel joke is this? He's planning on living next door to Vivienne and pretending she's not his?

"Over my dead body." I cross my arms, and his gaze lowers from my mouth to where my robe undoubtedly gapes open over the flimsy tank top I'm wearing beneath.

"Winter, it's almost noon. Did you just wake up?" Beau asks a little mockingly.

I turn, raking my eyes over his beefy frame, then Rhett's, who is the lankier of the two.

Theo is somewhere in between. I'm like Goldilocks picking a type. Too beefy, too long hair-y, and then there's Theo.

Even with one toned arm in a navy-blue sling, he looks good. And I hate my brain for practically sighing and saying *just right*.

A light brown chihuahua with a graying muzzle runs stupid circles around Theo's sneaker-clad feet. For a moment, I feel like I found a kindred spirit in the animal.

"Winter?" Theo's voice is softer, a little gentler than the other two. "You okay?"

My eyes widen at him. "Okay?" Disbelief bleeds into my voice. "No, Theo. I'm not okay. That dog is yapping nonstop, and you are not allowed to live next to me."

The other men chuckle and get back to unloading the moving van, but Theo's perfectly shaped lips curve up as his head tips, revealing the incision along his collarbone. "Oh, yeah? I guess I'll have to check the by-laws. Find the rule that says I'm not allowed to live next to you. I must have missed it. And Peter?" He motions down at the dog, whose forehead is way too big and whose tongue lolls out of his mouth. It appears to have cataracts, which explains why it's regarding Theo like he hung the moon. "He's deaf and going a little blind. He's just stressed. He'll settle once we move all our stuff in and it feels like home. He doesn't usually bark at all."

Nausea roils in my stomach as I wonder what the hell he's playing at here.

"Theo," my voice cracks. "Why are you doing this?"

All three men look up at the tone in my voice and I realize this isn't the place to have this conversation.

Theo's brows knit together. "Jasper offered me this house. It's close to the gym. I'll train there while I recover, hopefully make it back on the circuit before fall. I won't be here for long."

The knife in my gut twists harder.

"Are you kidding me right now?" I sound breathless, weak. I sound *shocked* and Theo looks forlorn, totally confused by my reaction.

"Winter, suck it up. You barely know the guy," Beau calls out, muscles bulging as he carries an armchair toward the front door. "You don't have to be friends."

I want to pick up a rock and throw it at Beau's stupid GI Joe head. *Friends*. God. We are much more than friends. And nobody knows except us. The shreds of dignity I kept in my grip when I left Rob were all I had and admitting to anyone that Theo didn't want me either was more pain than I was equipped to handle.

So, I told everyone I had a one-night stand and didn't remember who the guy was.

The problem is, I remember that night in vivid detail. And it haunts me.

I shake my head at Theo, for the first time feeling like I might truly hate him. Tears well in my eyes, which is my signal to get the fuck out of here.

Theo steps closer to the fence, his face etched with concern. He lifts his good arm like he's about to stop me. Like there's something he wants to say.

But I don't want to hear anything he has to say. And I don't want to break down here with the guys watching.

So, I turn away and toss out over my shoulder, "Shut your dog up, Theo. If it wakes *my* baby up, I'll castrate you."

Then I slam the door on them in a fit of frustration.

Then I hear Vivienne's startled cry.

Then I sink to the floor and cry too.

11
Theo

"**H**ard to believe Summer came out so nice when her sister came out like *that*." Beau shakes his head as he comes back down the front steps with empty hands.

"Winter is nice." The sentence comes out with more force than intended, more than is appropriate for the situation. But I think I've felt protective of that woman since the first night I laid eyes on her.

I didn't know then how desperately she needed someone to be. That no one had *ever* been that for her. That she's been fending for herself since before she should have needed to.

Beau scoffs. "With those moods I'm surprised she found someone willing to knock her u—"

"Beau, shut up," Rhett cuts him off. "She's done a lot for you. She's family. If we're gonna talk about her moods, maybe it's time we talk about yours, hmm?"

The two brothers stare each other down in the front yard of the house I'll be renting for the next few months. My chest vibrates with tension, partially because if these two go nuts on each other, I will not jump in. I'm smarter than that.

But tension builds in me all the same as I fixate on the *willing to knock her up* part. I don't know how old the baby is, and I don't know the specifics of how long that process takes beyond that nine-month marker, but I suddenly have the urge to pull out a calendar and check.

Beau stares but says nothing. Since going missing in action on an assignment overseas, he hasn't been the same. He's physically healed, but he's different. Darker.

"I'm going to take a walk," he mutters and drops his brother's gaze, shoulders slumping as he edges past us and out the white gate.

Rhett props his hands on his hips and lets out a long breath. "I hate when that version of him pops up."

"Yup," is all I come back with because, well, I don't know what else to say. Although I don't know Beau well, I'm familiar enough with the Eaton family to know Harvey would give him a good shake for disrespecting Winter.

"It's getting better, but now and then I'd just like to deck him. It's like Winter going out of her way to help him with treatment back home has irritated him somehow."

"What did she do?"

"I don't know. Got him in with some doctors to help with the scars. Pretty sure she told him he needed therapy, but in whatever Winter-way she'd have of telling him that, which went over poorly. He's a terrible patient, always has been. But he also doesn't tell anyone shit—that's not new either."

I think of how I've felt, going from capable to injured, and can see it. Watching these two unload the truck while I move lighter things with one hand doesn't exactly have me feeling useful.

"The more I see him now, the more I realize that even when he was home, he wasn't. His head was always off on assignment somewhere. He'd waltz in and be all happy-go-lucky. But I can't help but wonder if that was an act. Ya know?"

Rhett looks down the sidewalk where Beau's outline has now rounded the corner onto the main street of Chestnut Springs. I have a sinking suspicion he won't be back for a while.

"Right, well ... I'll do everything I can to help you with the rest of this."

My friend shrugs and glances back at the truck. "It's okay. I can call Summer, see if she can scoot over from the gym to move the heavy pieces. Let's just do all the rest."

I can't help but smile. He and Summer are so damn good together.

"You think she can squat more than you?"

Rhett cracks a grin. "I don't think. I *know*."

With a chuckle, I scoop Peter up, because as soon as I start walking, he's going to bark at my feet. There's a laundry room in the basement and he'll get set up there with a bed, food, and water. I just hope the concrete walls drown out his annoyed yips at being left behind.

I nuzzle the top of his bubbly little head. "Be quiet, okay? We can't have everyone next door crying, alright? It's not gentlemanly."

He shakes in response. As a chihuahua does. Or so I learned when I rushed him to the vet for shaking all the time.

Then I'm back to all my worldly belongings in the back of that truck. It's not much, because I've never really hunkered down anywhere. Over the past four years, I've spent the better part of my time on the road. I spend a few days here and there with my mom at her place in Emerald Lake, but more often than not, I crash at the small condo I rent in the city. It's practically a storage locker and not very well equipped, but it's all I've needed.

And the thought of living there for a few months while I recover felt depressing. So here I am, being swallowed up by the Eaton family. I don't even know who suggested this living arrangement anymore. Summer? Because I could rehab at her gym? Harvey? Who said I shouldn't be alone? Sloane? Who said she knew the perfect house?

Whoever it was, I wasn't sad about it.

But I didn't know Winter would live next door.

Once we've got the four chairs set around the square table in the dining room, I finally break down and ask, "So what's the deal with Winter?"

Rhett swipes a hand over his forehead. "What do you mean?"

"I don't know. She's living out here now. She has a baby? She—"

He huffs out a laugh. "Don't harass her like you did that night at the Christmas dinner. She's got enough on her plate without you air humping in her direction like that little dog of yours."

My nose scrunches up. "Peter doesn't air hump."

"Why does your dog have a human name? Everything sounds so much weirder when I imagine an accountant or something air humping. Plus, Summer sent me a video of him humping my pillow when we took care of him."

"That's not air humping though. That's him humping your pillow. Don't judge him."

Rhett wheezes out a laugh. "Do you know that dog gets boners randomly sometimes? Like he'll just be sitting there and have his red rocket out."

107

"You'd be in the same boat if you couldn't wear pants."

"Leave it to you to get the world's horniest dog."

I laugh. "He's not horny. Those are stress boners."

"What the fuck is a stress boner?"

Scrubbing a hand over my jaw, I try to keep it together and not burst out laughing. Peter deserves my defense right now. "He just gets nervous, or excited, or overstimulated sometimes and it happens."

Rhett's shoulders shake silently as he crosses his arms and leans back against the wall. "Theo, all you did was describe the different emotions someone feels when they get a normal boner."

"It's different." I look away, biting at the inside of my cheek to keep my grin under wraps. "Stop picking on Peter."

"You even named him after a penis."

"What? His full name is Peter Pan."

"Peter is—" He waves me off. "You know what, never mind. The moral of the story is: keep your stress boners away from Winter."

"Why?"

"Because she's got her plate full enough with Vivi. She doesn't need you making more work for her."

"Does she have help?"

"Is that your way of asking if she's single?"

"Jesus, Rhett. Give me a little credit."

"Right." He grins. "I keep forgetting you're a monk now. But no, she doesn't. She's all on her own. And that woman is an island, so if you figure out a way to help her that isn't with your dick, I'm all for it. Mow her lawn or something, yeah?"

I can't help it. I waggle my eyebrows at Rhett.

"Good lord." His eyes roll.

"What? You just handed me an alley-oop. Only a loser wouldn't take that joke and run."

His head is shaking, but he's all smiles. I know he feels guilty about my injury and he's here playing mentor-on-steroids just to make up for it.

"So . . . who's the dad?" I press further.

Rhett's eyes narrow. "Why?"

"I just want to know what I'm getting into when I mow her lawn. Like if I see a dude lurking around, should I worry?"

Rhett scoffs. "Beats me, man. Like I said, she's an island. That baby girl is nine months old, and no one has a clue who the dad is. She hasn't told a soul. Says she was drunk and doesn't remember."

And just like that, all my jokes turn to stone and land heavy in my gut.

I really need to look at a calendar.

I managed to keep a smile on my face around Rhett while he and Summer finished helping me move in. But even they noticed it was forced.

When Rhett asked me if I was sore, I said, "Yeah." But it wasn't my broken collarbone or bruised body. It was the tight knot constricting my stomach.

I haven't moved off this spot on my couch since they left. First thing I did was pull up the calendar on my phone. Peter is curled up smack dab in the middle of my lap, where he likes to be, snoring like he weighs a lot more than ten pounds.

Don't go too hard on her. She's so tired. She's just doing her best. She needs all the support she can get, whether or not she wants it.

Summer's assessment of her sister's situation didn't make me feel any better. In fact, it made me a bit sick.

Because I have a feeling. A gut instinct.

And I don't want to be right. Because if I am?

God. If I am, I've really fucked up.

A crash of thunder outside startles me, but Peter carries on snoring, just deaf enough not to notice. Blissfully unaware.

Fuck.

Is that what I've been?

I lift the small dog off my lap and squish him into the corner of the couch, covering him in a fuzzy blanket so that only his little head and the dirty glare he's giving me peek back out. The tip of his tongue is pushed out between the huge gap in his teeth where I had to have the rotten ones removed, and gray hairs dot his muzzle.

"I'll be right back. Don't give me that look."

He makes a small grunting noise and shuts his eyes as his dismissal. And then I'm hefting lead feet across the floor, equal parts dreading going next door and feeling pulled in a way that I can't fight or resist.

I need to go there. I need to know.

After shoving my feet into a pair of slip-ons, I open the door and step out into the downpour. Thunder rolls in the distance, and a few seconds later, the sky illuminates. In the summer, it stays light until late on the prairies, but the storm clouds have cast a dark eerie glow over the tree-lined street. My T-shirt and jeans are soaked within seconds as I make my way down the short, narrow sidewalk, out the front gate. I turn and do the reverse up to the white house next to my blue one. The row of four houses all have the same build, but Sloane's attention to detail when she renovated them makes each home unique.

I trudge up the front steps, eyes on my feet, the sense of dread in my chest expanding until it feels like hard labor to even breathe. My hand raises, and a finger extends to press the doorbell, but I hesitate when I think of how exhausted Winter looked today. She seemed irate over the noise earlier, so I consider if ringing the doorbell is my best option.

The truth is, I don't know what to do.

So, I sit on her top step, drop my head into my hands, and wait.

12
Winter

Winter: Why is Theo Silva moving in next door? Who okayed this? You or Jasper?
Sloane: Is it a problem? I didn't even think you'd care. You guys got in that spat, what? A year and a half ago?
Winter: Never mind.
Sloane: Oh, shit.

M y phone vibrates when motion at the front door trips the alarm system. I slide the screen open and pull up the video feed.

And there is Theo, sitting on my front porch with his head in his hands. Not wearing the sling that he still should be.

I'm torn. The bitter she-devil on one shoulder wants to leave him out there getting soaked, but the curious caretaker angel on the opposite shoulder wants to make sure he's okay.

Because I've never seen him look beaten down. Even in the hospital, he was cracking jokes and flying to my defense like I needed that from him.

I pad down the hallway toward Vivi's room and peek in on her. She's flat on her back, arms splayed, with her tiny fingers curled into loose fists.

I want to sleep like that again. Instead, I feel like I'm in this constant state of alertness where, even when I'm exhausted, I find it difficult to relax enough to truly sleep deeply.

After the soft click of her door shutting, I wait with bated breath to see if I've woken the teething monster.

One. Two. Three.

I press my ear to her door and when I hear no signs of movement, a deep sigh lurches from my chest. *Relief.*

Until I remember who is sitting on my front porch. But I approach the front door with a cool level of detachment taught to me in med school. One I've spit-polished into a perfect shine working in the emergency room.

One I mastered as a child, if I'm being honest.

My hand wraps around the knob, and with an aggressive tug, I yank the front door open and stare down into the second most beautiful set of brown eyes I've ever seen.

It's impossible not to gawk for at least a moment. Theo's wet hair hugs his forehead and drops of water cling to the two peaks of his top lip. Rain has plastered his white T-shirt to his body in the most obscene way.

"Why aren't you wearing your sling?"

That is what my brain decides to open with, even as I gaze down into his tortured eyes. He unfolds himself, and when he steps closer, I'm forced to tip my chin up in order to hold his stare.

"Winter, I need you to tell me the truth."

I can feel my heart beating in my throat, and I lift a hand to quell the ache there. "Okay."

"Is the baby mine?"

My face goes slack. *Is the baby mine?* Is he fucking kidding me? The crash of thunder hits me like a slap. "That's not funny, Theo."

"I'm not trying to be funny, Winter."

"We've already talked about this, so I don't know what you're playing at."

"Talked about this?" His face scrunches and his arms gesture open on either side of him.

I'll give it to him. He appears to be genuinely confused. "Yeah. I believe the last text message I received from you was"—my hands gesture beside my head in air quotes—"*Thanks for letting me know.*"

For as long as I live, I don't think I'll forget the look on Theo's face right now. I just watched a heart break right in front of me. And I remember how it feels. I'm familiar with the sensation of everything you thought you knew toppling down around you.

The expression on his face is haunted and my hand moves up from my throat to cover my mouth. "Oh god," I whisper. "You really didn't know."

I feel outside of myself. Above us, observing. Like I'm watching two people interact in a movie or TV show.

This can't be real.

A disbelieving laugh escapes him. "Nah. You can't be serious."

I stare back, not sure what to say.

He paces and lets out another laugh. This time, it sounds a little unhinged. "You gotta be joking." Faster than the lightning streaks across the sky, he turns his back to me and jogs down the steps.

"How did …" He swipes a hand through his hair and glances around the soggy front yard. "How come …" Those usually happy eyes swim with devastation when he turns his gaze back on me. "When did you …"

"Two weeks or so after. I tried contacting you so many times. I don't know …"

His forearm flexes as he wipes his hand over his mouth. "No." He laughs, but it borders on a sob. "You're telling me I have a daughter and I missed it all? The pregnancy? The birth? Everything?"

It strikes me I'm watching a man unravel right before my eyes. A beautiful, *shocked* man. I've spent the past eighteen months assuming the worst about Theo, and here he is, crumbling to pieces, like the rain is disintegrating the clay that holds him together.

My mouth opens, but I don't know what to say to him. I mean, yeah, he missed all those things. And I don't know why, but based on the way he's gone back to pacing and tugging at his hair, I have to assume he didn't do it on purpose.

"Winter. Don't fuck with me. Are you serious?"

He looks downright forlorn. Soaked and bedraggled, he makes his way back up the steps. I can hear his breathing now, not just pants, but a sort of keening sound on each exhale. A fist thumps against his chest.

"Winter." Now my name is him pleading with me.

He's panicking. Truly panicking.

"Theo." My hands shoot out and I hold his cheeks, forcing him to come to a standstill. I grip his skull, his stubble rough on my palms, his damp neck smooth under my fingertips. "Stop. Tell me three things you can hear."

His body heaves as he stares back at me. Moments pass.

"Rain."

I nod.

"Thunder."

I lick my lips.

"Your finger rubbing the back of my head."

I swallow and press my opposite hand to his chest. His heart thunders beneath my palm. "Okay. Now three things you can see."

His eyes rake over me, and I don't let go of his head. "Your white house. The stroller folded by the front door." His voice cracks.

I massage the back of his neck, trying to bring him back down. "You."

My lips press together, my gaze bouncing between his eyes. He seems calmer now. "Yeah. Good." My grip softens, my hands sliding down to his shoulders with the soothing sound of rain falling in the background.

I watch him closely.

His hands hang limply at his sides, but it's the tremor in his voice when he says, "Can I see her?" that has my eyes filling with tears.

I don't know what the fuck is going on right now, but I do know that the man at my door deserves to see his daughter. I nod and turn to open the door, allowing him into our house. His presence is large and consuming when he steps inside.

I point at the shoe rack, trying to ignore the press of his body behind me. Even in a moment like this, the air between us hums. It makes me want to lean back into him and have his arms wrap around me.

It would feel so good to be held by someone.

Instead, I rush ahead, padding quietly down the hallway to grab him a towel. When I return and give it to him, I chance a look at his chiseled face. His normally tan skin is now a perfect match for the white terry cloth in his hands.

I try not to stare as he dries himself off, opting to glower at my fingers instead. Still no manicure.

A sad laugh bubbles up in my throat.

"What?" Theo focuses on toweling off his wet hair now, bicep bulging and flexing as he reaches up over his head.

"I just . . . nothing. It's silly."

"No, tell me."

When the sigh leaves me, my entire body sags in its wake. Heat blooms on my cheeks as I stare down at my outstretched hands. "It sounds ridiculous, but for a long time, I've been telling myself that I'm going to start getting manicures. I don't know why. I just want them. I can't have my nails painted at the hospital and the job is too hard on my hands anyway. I keep meaning to do it while I'm off work, but I just . . . haven't."

When I peek up, Theo is staring at me with an intensity I don't think I've ever seen any man direct at me in my life. Which I suppose makes sense. He's gutted and I'm standing here talking about wanting to get manicures.

I hit him with a watery smile. "Just drop the towel there. Ignore the mess." I wince a little when I gaze out over the kitchen and living room. It could be worse, but there are unfinished dishes in the sink, coffee pods on the counter, and toys all over the living room floor. It's all proof that I am just doing what needs to be done to get through this godforsaken teething phase. "It's been a rough couple of days."

He says nothing and I don't chance a look in his direction before I lead him down the hallway toward Vivienne's room. I know the intrusion might wake her, but this seems like one of those moments where it doesn't matter. If the thunder hasn't done it yet, maybe we're in the clear.

With a gentle click, I open the door to the nursery. It's a beautiful, cozy room that came together with a lot of support from everyone out here in Chestnut Springs. Sloane helped me paint it the softest pink, with high-gloss white on the crown moldings. Lace curtains lay over the blackout drapes behind them. The crib is from my dad—he sent it in the mail. The rocking chair is from Harvey, a family heirloom that I'm sure I don't deserve. He brought it over and placed it in the corner himself. Willa brought all the useful things, a diaper genie, a wipe warmer, loads of spit rags. And Summer still hasn't stopped buying her clothes.

The way everyone rallied around me is still almost more than I can comfortably think about.

I walk across the room and open the blinds, allowing the soft gray light from outside to illuminate the nursery. Theo stands in the doorway, motionless.

I peek down at Vivi, still in the same blissful position as the last time I checked on her. Then, with a deep, centering breath, I march across the room and wrap my hand around Theo's. His palm is damp and clammy as I lead him over to the edge of the white crib.

And then we stand there. Two people who barely know each other.

Staring down at our daughter. Him for the first time. And me for the millionth.

After only a few beats, he shifts his fingers so that they link between mine. His hand squeezes, and it feels like he's squeezing at my heart instead. When I look up at him, his eyes are wide and unblinking.

"Winter." My name is a breath on his lips this time. He reaches down and trails a knuckle over one of her full cheeks. Her little lips make a suckling motion, and she turns her head into his touch.

"Oh god. What's—" His free hand clamps up over his mouth. "Where's the bathroom?"

"Straight across the hall." I barely get the words out before he's gone.

I follow and hear him heaving as I approach the door. He's left it slightly ajar, and I can see a sliver of him hunched over the toilet, hands in his hair, looking utterly defeated.

I step away to give him some privacy. And then I slide down the wall beside the bathroom door and hang my head in my hands before giving myself over to my own feelings of nausea.

Something went wrong along the way. I'm not sure what, or where. All I know is the man in my bathroom would never have sent me that text.

13
Theo

I've missed so much.

It's the sentence that keeps running through my head. The one that hammers at my heart until it hurts. The one that has me heaving as though I could expel the thought from my body.

My head snaps up when I hear a soft knock against the door. "Theo? I, uh . . . I brought you some mouthwash. Can I come in?"

I flush, stand, and open the door the rest of the way. In my haste, I didn't take time to close it and lock it. My vision went blurry at the edges and my stomach turned over on itself as the realization that I have a child struck me down to my knees.

A little girl.

And I've missed *so damn much.*

I take Winter in, really take her in, seeing her in a different light now. Hair tossed up in a messy bun. Face makeup-free with dark circles under the eyes that are fixed on mine and wide as saucers. She looks tired but healthier than the last time I saw her. There's a glow about her, like she spends time outside.

120

I let my eyes trail down her body but snap them back up to her face when I get to her chest. Her loose tank top hides nothing and she's not wearing a bra. Gawking at the outline of her nipples through the thin gray fabric isn't what the moment calls for, so I focus on her icy-blue eyes, swirling with so many questions.

But she doesn't ask them.

She holds out a white plastic cup, halfway filled with a liquid that matches her eyes. "Here."

When I take the cup, our fingers touch. For a minute, I rest the pad of my index finger over the tip of hers. I slide it up to the next knuckle, feeling as though I'm touching the edge of all the ways I need to say sorry. I don't even know where to start.

"Thank you." I toss the minty liquid back, then brace my hands over the sink and stare down the drain as I try to come to grips with all the ways my life has changed today.

A daughter.

Another wave of nausea hits me, so I spit, rinse, and sit on the floor with my back leaned against the tub, ass plunked down on a plush pink bathmat.

"Wanna come sit in the living room?" Winter's voice is smooth, calm. I've heard people call her icy, but I see a strong woman. One I admire even more now.

"I think I should stay close to the toilet." I glance at the pink foamy duck covering the tap and organic baby soap with little ABC blocks on the front label.

Her lips roll together as she regards me. "Listen, it's clean in here but like . . . not *that* clean."

"To be frank, the cleanliness of your bathroom is the last thing I care about right now."

Her lashes flutter in time with the nervous way she nods her head. "Yeah. Okay."

To my surprise, she puts the mouthwash on a shelf and heads in my direction, plopping down onto the bathroom mat right beside me.

Her soft jersey shorts slouch down over her thighs when she props her knees up and her bare leg presses against mine. "Is this okay?"

I nod, eyes still fixed on her smooth tan thigh, her femur so much shorter than mine. I remember how it felt to grip that thigh, how she wrapped them both around my waist and tugged me close.

The round lights above the vanity hum and the only other sounds in the bathroom are the soft splatter of rain against the windows and us breathing in time.

"What's her name?" A watery laugh follows my question. "Please tell me you didn't name her Autumn."

Winter snorts and her head drops. "Fuck. I would never." Then she turns her face up to mine, sadness etched into her beautiful face. "Her name is Vivienne Hamilton. But we all call her Vivi."

We all.

Those two words hit me like a ton of bricks. *We all.* Everyone here knows her. Has seen her grow. Got to be there when she was born.

And I've had no idea.

"Does she have a middle name?"

"No."

I nod. Who cares about a middle name? God, I'm an idiot.

"What day is her birthday?"

"September twenty-second. Would have been stupid to name her Autumn with a birth date like that."

I chuckle, but it's strangled. "How was labor?"

She blinks up at me. "Labor?"

"Yeah. Her birth. How was it?"

"It ... it ..." She pauses. "Sorry, I wasn't expecting you to ask me that question."

"I want to know everything, Winter. Every little detail."

"Okay." Her face scrunches up a little. "Well, not *every* little detail."

"My mom is a midwife. You can't shock me after years of listening to her tell birth stories."

My mom. Another rock lands in my stomach. This will gut her. She'll be excited but heartbroken all at once. I know because that's how I'm feeling right now.

"Honestly, it was incredible. Powerful. And exhausting. But so rewarding. She was healthy and so was I."

I swallow the words *I should have been there* over the lump in my throat.

"Theo?" Her knee nudges mine. "If I wasn't talking to you, who was I talking to? I got your number from the Hamilton Athletics member list."

"It was probably Geoff at Hamilton Elite."

"Wait." She holds a hand up. "At my dad's work?"

I nod, staring at my hands, pressing on the calloused pads. "I refocused after that Christmas and cut out all the noise. All the social media, all the ..." I tip my head back and groan as I look up at the ceiling.

"Women?" Winter provides with no inflection in her voice.

"Yeah. A new phone seemed like the easiest way to disconnect. I handed that one over so Geoff could manage my social media accounts. I told him to tell me if anything important came through."

"Hmm." She nods, long and slow, almost rocking her body with the weight of it.

"Do you still have the messages?"

"Not the voicemails." She sniffs as she fishes her phone out of her pocket. After a few swipes, she hands it to me. *Theo Silva* is the contact at the top, and I double-check the number. I know she sees me do it, because I feel her tense. But I need to know for sure she contacted the correct person.

The number is right, and part of me wishes it wasn't so I could be angry at her for not trying harder to get in touch with me. I want someone other than myself to blame for this colossal fucking mess.

But when I read the messages in the chat, all those feelings evaporate, and in their place comes an oppressive dread. Grief. A sick twisting in my stomach. Because no woman in her right mind would continue trying to track me down after getting messages back like this.

I'm not interested in talking.

Thanks for letting me know.

I'm going to kill Geoff with my bare hands. He might be the only person in the world who would deem these messages "not important."

Anxiety unfurls in my chest. I'm overwhelmed by the instinct to take this jumbled clusterfuck and untangle it. Make things as right as I can.

When I glance back at Winter, she's curled in on herself, her gaze fixated on her fingernails again.

"Winter. Look at me."

Her tongue darts out to take a nervous swipe at her lips, but she doesn't turn her gaze my way.

I reach over, ignoring the sharp bite in my collarbone, and guide her chin gently with my fingers. When she finally gives me her eyes, I let my gaze trace them, wanting to know I have her full attention.

"If I had known, I'd have been here every step of the way. Supporting you in whatever way you needed. And Winter?"

"Yeah?" For the first time tonight, her voice sounds weak.

I catch a stray tear that slides down over the apple of her cheek and brush it away, tamping down the rage in my chest over how this entire thing played out. "Now that I'm here? I'm here. Okay? No expectations, but I want you to let me help you. I want to get to know her if that's okay with you."

She nods, and more tears fall. I bring my other hand up and try to catch them all, but I fail. They come too fast, so I pull her head against my chest and opt to let her soak my already damp shirt.

Seems like the least I can do for this woman after how thoroughly I've let her down.

I don't sleep. Even though we've moved all my furniture into this brand-new house, it doesn't feel like mine. I lie on my back, staring at the ceiling. I've got Peter wedged into my armpit, snoring softly on one side of me, and regret on the other side with one hand on my throat.

Winter has always drawn me to her in some inexplicable way, and knowing she's just a few steps away with *our* daughter? It's shifted something in me.

I didn't want to be disruptive, or overstep my bounds, but I wanted to sit on the floor of that nursery and stare at Vivienne for the entire night.

Knowing you want to have children one day is a lot different from facing one that already exists. I don't know how to wrap my feelings around it.

But I know who will.

Wincing as I shift in bed, I swipe my phone off the bedside table and call my mom.

"What's wrong?" is how she answers the phone. Her instincts are wild.

"Why would something have to be wrong for me to call you? You're my mom."

"Right, but I know you. It's currently six o'clock on a Sunday morning where you are, which means it's five here."

"Shit. Sorry, Mom."

"It's okay. I was just getting set up to do some restorative yoga. I can fix your problems while I make myself some green tea."

I snort. I don't think anyone can fix this problem in the time it takes to make a cup of tea.

"Why don't you just sleep in? It's the weekend."

She scoffs at me, and I hear a cupboard thud shut on the other end of the line. "I'll be sure to tell that to the next mother that goes into labor on a weekend. *Sorry, doll. You're going to have to wait until Monday.*"

I chuckle because I remember having to take care of my sister at odd hours now and then when my mom would have to rush out to a birth. Or when we were younger, getting woken up so that she could drop us off at a friend's house.

She did the best she could after our dad's death. A single mom to two kids wasn't an easy gig. Though when she got a job teaching midwifery at the college, things slowed down a bit.

"Fair enough."

Peter lets out a loud snore beside me, not at all bothered by the phone call.

"Oh, is that little Peter?"

Leave it to Rhett to ruin my dog's name. *Little Peter* does distinctly sound like a penis. But I'm not about to tell my mom th—

"God. Every time I say that dog's name, I think of a dick."

I bark out a laugh and the way it jostles my body is enough to wake *Little Peter*. He gives me a dirty look, like I'm the world's worst pillow, and nuzzles back in. When I picked him up off the street in Mexico, I thought he'd think I was his hero, but the attitude on this dog is insurmountable.

"It's true. I hope you didn't name him after your—"

"Mom." I close my eyes and rub my fingers against my eyebrows.

"Right. We're getting off track." The low rumble of water boiling in the background filters in through the receiver. "Tell me what's wrong."

I sigh. "I don't know if *wrong* is the word I would use."

"Stop beating around the bush, Theo."

"I have a daughter." I feel like I've shouted the words. Somehow, saying them out loud is very different from being told them or just repeating them in my head.

The line is silent.

"I just found out last night."

I wait a few beats. Still silent. I flip the phone to check the screen and make sure I'm still connected.

"Mom?"

"Oh, Theo." She almost sighs it, like I exhaust her. And I'm sure that on some level I do. Choosing to pursue the career that killed

127

my dad might be one of the most thoroughly exhausting things I've ever done to my mother, but she still supports me. She always has. I'm hoping I haven't pushed her too far with this little tidbit though.

"Are you okay?"

A heavy breath I'd been holding leaves me in a whoosh. "I'm . . . yeah. I think I'm just in shock."

"How did this happen?"

"Well, Mom, when two people—"

"Theodore Silva. Don't turn this into a joke to cope with your feelings. Talk to me."

I hear her pouring water into a cup, taking things in her stride like she always has with us kids. The universe blessed her with two handfuls. Julia is just as bad as me.

"What do you want to know?"

"Everything! How old is she? What's her name? Does she look like me? When can I meet her? And how the hell did this happen?"

No one but Loretta Silva would take this so easily. "And you were on *my* case for covering with jokes."

She blows a raspberry, and I can envision her flipping a hand across herself like she's swatting a fly as if we were in the same room.

So, I fill her in on everything I know, noting the happy little sigh she makes when I tell her about Vivienne. I don't miss the strangled sound that catches in her throat when I explain how it all got lost in translation.

"I could kill that Geoff asshole," she mutters.

"No, he's mine to kill."

"Theo! You can't threaten shit like that. You're a father now."

Fuck. I'm a father now.

"Okay, so I need to compose myself before I cross that bridge.

And tell Winter's dad since he's Geoff's boss, and that is all its own massive clusterfuck."

"So, the mom is Rhett's sister-in-law?"

"Well, the wedding isn't until next month. Remember? You're invited."

"Don't be like that, Theo. You know what I'm asking."

My teeth graze along my bottom lip as I stare up at the white popcorn-style ceiling. Since I failed to put up any blinds, morning light has filled the room, and the blue hue gives the space a cool, serene vibe that reminds me of Winter.

"Yeah. It's her."

"Huh. *That* girl, huh? Well, I can't wait to meet her."

"Vivienne?"

"No. Well, yes. But Winter too."

I smile up at the ceiling. "Yeah, I think you'll like her."

"How is she holding up? I was never a single mom with a baby. But I remember your dad going on the road and leaving me home alone with you two. I would practically toss you at him and walk out the door the minute he got back, just so I could have a few minutes by myself."

"I think she's okay. Happy but overwhelmed, if that makes sense?"

"That makes perfect sense. If I wrote a dictionary, that might be the definition I put under motherhood."

I laugh, lighter already for having talked to my mom.

"Theo, honey, the question any good dad would ask himself now is: what are you going to do to make her feel less overwhelmed?"

14
Winter

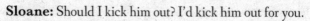

Sloane: Should I kick him out? I'd kick him out for you.

Winter: It's fine.

Sloane: Should I come back from vacation and beat him up?

Winter: I would pay good money to watch you beat someone up.

Sloane: Is that a yes or a no?

Winter: Just don't tell anyone. It's his story to tell.

Sloane: What story? I don't even know what you're talking about.

Sloane: LMAO. See what I did there?

Winter: Did Jasper fuck all the brain cells out of your head with his massive dick?

Sloane: You love me.

Winter: I do.

heo Silva is standing on my front porch at 10 a.m. on the dot. I can see him on the screen of my phone, awkwardly shifting his weight on his feet, with a paper coffee cup in each hand.

I've been ready for this. For him. Yesterday, I got the sense he wouldn't be taking off into the sunset after finding out about Vivi. And I spent the entire night awake thinking about it.

He must hate me deep down. How could he not? But I want him to have a relationship with his daughter. I don't want her to live with the fraught tension that I grew up around. I'm a grown-ass woman. A *doctor*. I know that I'm not warm and fuzzy, but I'm mature.

Ish.

I have my moments, and this needs to be one of them. For Vivi. I won't worry about Theo liking me, and I'll ignore how painfully attractive he is and chalk him up to an excellent specimen.

Vivienne will thank me for those genes one day.

Tugging at the bottom hem, I glance down at my vintage Rainbow Brite T-shirt. I paired it with baggy boyfriend jeans because none of my jeans from before fit that well anymore.

Something I try not to think about too much.

At least my tits look great.

Not that it matters. Because Theo is my … co-parent. We're like business partners. Yes. I like how that feels. Tidy and non-threatening. Like we're a team but can go our separate ways at the end of the day.

With a sure nod, I pocket my phone and open the door.

"Dr. Hamilton, were you waiting for me?" He winks, and all that composure evaporates like it was barely ever there. I'm plunged back to that night at the gas station. His undone boots and cocky grin.

Me staring like a total idiot.

The rush I felt when he hiked my dress up over my thighs like he was unwrapping a present. His fingers hooking inside my panties without even hesitating.

I clear my throat. "Looked more like you were waiting for me from what I could see on the camera."

He glances up, eyes shifting until they land on the little square with a lens in the corner. "Good. I'm glad you have a security system. I was going to offer to put one in."

I nibble at my lip and blink away. Why is he so . . . *nice*?

It's unnerving. People are never this nice unless they want something from you. It's not normal.

"Why don't you just knock or ring the doorbell?"

He shrugs. "I don't want to wake her up again."

"I can give you my number."

"I have it already."

"How do you have it already?"

He clears his throat and then says, "I put it into my phone that night."

I blink. "That night?"

"*That* night." The word drips with innuendo. There's no mistaking what night he's talking about.

"You took my number without asking?"

Pink tinges the top of his ears, and he has the sense to look a little chagrined. "Figured I'd need it someday."

I don't know what to make of his revelation, and truthfully, don't feel equipped to deal with it. I opt to forge ahead, leaving whatever complicated shit that is in the rear-view mirror. "So . . . you were just going to wait out here until I, what? Checked my mail?"

A deep rumble rolls in his chest and he smiles. Fuck, his smile is blinding. "I don't know, Winter. I didn't have a big plan. I grabbed you a coffee and decided to figure it out from there."

He holds one hand out to me, steam wafting up through the hole in the lid. "Got it in town. Thought you might need one as much as me." The corners of his eyes pinch, and I recognize how tired he appears. His golden skin has blue smudges beneath his dark eyes, and the stubble on his jaw has grown a little longer than his usual curated scruff. "It's just an Americano." He gestures the cup to me again.

I take it, realizing I'm staring at him, wondering why he's bringing *me* coffee.

"I didn't know what you like."

I stare down at the lid, almost teary over the fact he's *here*. Even though I dropped a bomb on him last night, he's bringing me coffee.

"Other than tequila and doggy style—fuck." He swipes a hand through his perfectly tousled hair. "Sorry. Can you say something so I stop making awkward jokes to fill the silence?"

I peek up at him through shrink-wrapped eyes. "Why are you being so nice to me?"

His brow furrows and his face shows genuine confusion. It strikes me as unusual how he wears his heart on his sleeve, the way every emotion and thought almost prints itself on his face.

"Winter, I think we've been through this once before. You keep looking for some ulterior motive with me, and there isn't one. Can I come in? I want to see . . ." He pauses and clears his throat, like it's still a struggle to say this out loud. "Vivi. I'd like to spend some time with her and talk to you some more."

With a nod, I step aside and usher him in.

For a normal meeting.
A business meeting.

Watching Theo hold Vivienne for the first time does a lot of things to me. First, it makes me want to hurl in much the same way he did last night. There's something profoundly overwhelming about seeing his eyes latch onto hers while her small hand wraps around his finger. "Hi, baby girl," he murmurs. "It's so nice to meet you."

The sweet cooing noise she makes back at him, like she's an instant goner for this man, makes me want to cry. And I *never* cry. It's just not my thing. It's pointless, and I always feel tired and bereft afterward—not better.

But when I can see *him* getting emotional just looking at her, holding her in his arms so naturally, it hits me in a way I never, ever saw coming. He stands and bounces gently, walking toward the big bay window that overlooks the front street.

He turns them toward his yard. "That's where I live. Right next door. So, if your mom says it's okay, I could come visit now and then."

I sit on a stool at the kitchen island and try to remember the last time I just sat and drank a coffee that was still hot. Not hot out of the microwave, but truly fresh. I feel like I'm in this constant cycle of not having anything specific to do all day, yet the day goes by so damn fast.

Cooking, cleaning, sleeping, entertaining, snuggling, nursing, socializing. It seems like it should be easy. I work in chaos for a living, but this is so much harder.

Which is why I cannot, for the life of me, account for the way my body reacts to the sight before me. Theo was already hot as fuck, and Theo holding a baby is even hotter. If he goes out in public with Vivienne, he's going to get more pussy thrown at him than he already does.

And somehow *that* makes me irrationally jealous.

"Look how beautiful you are." The sun lights Theo and Vivienne's faces in the same warm, golden hue. "You look just like your mom."

Vivienne stares up at him and giggles, small hands reaching for the stubble on his cheeks, squealing when it rasps against her palms.

"Fuck," I mutter, blinking faster than a hummingbird's wings as I try to burn my tongue on the coffee just to give myself something less mushy and unhinged to cry over.

I've seen Rhett hold her a million times, and it's never been like this. No, this is all Theo.

"Did you sleep okay?" he asks as he turns back to face me.

Vivienne laughs and continues running her hands over his face. And gah, I can't even blame her.

"Yeah," I lie. "You?"

"Not especially." His face morphs into a more solemn expression as he glances down at her again. "So, what led you to pick Vivienne?"

I chug back a hot gulp of coffee. Yes, more coffee. *Why am I so emotional?* I need to get this shit on lock before I go back to work in a few months. If I cry while I deliver bad news to people, I might as well quit.

"Um ..." I glance around the room, feeling like I might be stronger if I don't have to look at them. "It means 'alive' and, well ... she made me feel alive again. She made it when my last baby didn't.

And it felt like a good adult name, you know? Like she could be prime minister with a name like that."

Theo hums happily and smiles down at Vivienne. "Prime minister? Good for you, girl. I can't wait to tell people my daughter is the prime minister."

Breathe, Winter.

I laugh to cover the emotion welling at the back of my throat. How dare he be so ... *him*. "Of course, I never considered that feeling alive would also be so exhausting. Or that I'd want nothing more than for no one to touch me, even just for an hour. Or that I'd never bathe alone again." A shrill laugh leaps from my lips, a sad attempt to cover the emotion in my voice.

Theo's dark eyes glance up at me. "Go take a bath, Winter."

"What?"

"Take that coffee and go run yourself a bath. Close the door. Put some music on. Watch some porn. Go have a moment to yourse—"

I bark out a laugh. "You did not just tell me that. In front of a young, impressionable mind, no less."

The grin he hits me with is pure knowing. He knows what he does to me, I'm sure of it. The way his eyes peruse my body is proof. I don't think I'm the only one who vividly remembers *that* night.

"Tink, please. I might not know you all that well, but I have a sinking suspicion that the future prime minister's first word might be *fuck*."

I bite down on my lip to hide the smile. Solo motherhood has turned me into a fucking trucker. I can't even deny it.

"Go. I've got her. We'll stay right here and wait for you."

I glare at him.

"To *finish*."

Asshole. I glare harder, but the desperately touched-out part of me screams, *Do it! Take the bath!*

"You know what? Yes, I'm going to go. I haven't had a bath alone in nine months."

"Good. Enjoy yourself."

"If she cries . . ."

"We will be fine. All my older cousins have a million babies. I used to babysit."

"I just fed her, so she should be fine."

He smiles, all warm and gooey.

"Look. I haven't left her alone with anyone except Harvey and Sloane's mom, Cordelia."

"Not even your parents?"

I glance away. "No. That's complicated."

"Listen, if you're not comfortable, I can leave. I don't want to barge in here and demand time you aren't ready to give. This must be weird for you."

For me. That's the final straw. Tears build in a way that is impossible to stop.

All my life, not a single person has prioritized how things might feel *for me.* And here is this man I barely know, prioritizing me.

I force a watery smile. "I can't think of a single better person to watch her right now."

He nods, eyes scanning me just a little too closely.

I nod back and head to the bathroom to cry in my bath.

And maybe watch some porn.

15
Winter

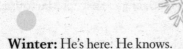

Winter: He's here. He knows.

Sloane: How did he take it? Is that why we did a B&E? To get his number?

Winter: Yup. Except someone else had his phone just to manage social media and never told him.

Sloane: Shit. Are you okay?

Winter: I'm taking a hot bath. Drinking a hot coffee. I'm in shock. But also heaven.

Sloane: You deserve it.

Winter: Do I?

Sloane: Yes. Hot baths and a hot baby daddy. You deserve the world.

Winter: He really is hot.

Sloane: Hotter with a baby I bet.

Winter: You have no idea.

When I walk down the hallway, I expect mayhem. Tears and frustration. A desperate plea for help because he's out of his depth. I stayed in the tub with my noise-canceling headphones on until the water was cold, and it still felt luxurious.

So shit has to be falling apart.

But no.

Theo is laid out on the couch, his good arm slung behind his head, which makes his bicep bulge in a very distracting way. Vivi is sprawled across his chest, looking like a koala who's climbing a tree that is too big for her to reach around. Her red, heart-shaped lips are just a little bit open, and his arm that should be in a sling is folded beside him, one broad palm splayed over her back.

There's some sort of car race playing on the TV, but Theo is staring at Vivi.

Something about the moment feels profoundly special. He's missed a lot of moments, a lot of firsts. And this is her first nap on him.

I yank my phone out of the back pocket of my jeans and snap a photo. The warm light gives it a dusty vintage effect. They look so peaceful.

"Hi," I whisper as I walk over to them.

Theo glances up at me but does a double take.

"What?"

"You just . . ." His lips roll together. "You look beauti—different."

I almost smirk. *Beautidifferent.*

"Well, I put on some makeup. How is she?"

He stares back down at her. "Perfect."

I feel weird hovering, so I sit on the coffee table next to them and hold my phone in front of Theo to show him the photo. "If you give me your number, I'll send it to you."

His thumb swipes over Vivi's back in a soothing arc. "I'd like that. I feel . . ."

I stare down at my phone. "I know. You must hate me. And that's okay. I think deep down I don't blame you. Maybe I should have gone crazy and told everyone. Been more spiteful, ya know? I tried giving less fucks and it backfired kind of spectacularly."

"Winter, I do not hate you." His voice is soft but sure, but I still can't bring myself to look at him. "You did plenty. You did more than enough."

"You have to say that because I'm the mother of your child."

"I—"

I hold a hand up. "I know you wouldn't have signed up for fatherhood. But I . . . *really* wanted this. Not how it came about, maybe. I mean, how cliché is a broken condom? But a baby? Theo," my voice cracks, "I really wanted a baby. I have no regrets."

"What makes you think I don't want this?"

I let my eyes trail over the beautiful man on my couch, with our baby girl laid over his heart. "Not at this point in your life. And not with me. You'll never convince me otherwise."

His features harden, a steely glint flashing in his eyes. "What makes you think I wouldn't want this with you?"

I scoff, wiping away a stray tear again.

Fuck my life and all this crying.

"Sorry, I never cry."

A smile touches his lips. "Yes, I can see that."

"Shut up." I swipe again, turning away to stare out the front window.

"I feel like I've missed a lot of firsts, Winter. That's what I was going to say. I feel like an interloper, but I don't want to. I wish I'd been there to see her grow. To see you grow. To be at the birth."

I sniff. "Willa took a very graphic video. I can show you sometime."

"I would love that."

"It's not sexy." I side-eye him and he scrunches his brow. "It will ruin any splendid memories of my vagina you might have."

"Nah. That's impossible. Those memories are why my right forearm is bigger than my left."

I roll my eyes and bite back my laugh. "You're impossible to deter."

He grins. "Yes."

"I'm happy to have you around, Theo. I would never, ever keep you from her. After what I grew up in, I just want her to be surrounded by so much love. You know?"

"Of course. We're on the same page." His voice, his words—they're like a firm hug. They instantly make me feel better.

Vivi stirs, drawing our attention, and for a few beats we both just . . . baby gaze.

"We're going to have to tell people soon."

"Yeah," he says in a rough voice. "I already told my mom. I hope that's okay."

"What did she say?" Panic seeps in. God, what must this woman think of me?

"That I've got some catching up to do. And that she can't wait to see you."

"Vivi, you mean? Yeah, that will be nice."

He peers up at me. "No, Winter. You. She can't wait to meet *you*." He's being serious again, and I want to squirm under the intensity of his stare.

141

"That should be interesting." I laugh. "Hope she's not too disappointed."

But Theo doesn't follow suit. Instead, he scowls at me. "I could fucking bury whoever made you believe you're as unlovable as you seem to think."

I stand and swipe at the front of my jeans, smoothing invisible wrinkles. "Yes, well, I've had years to bask in this feeling, so I don't think burying anyone will help."

"We'll see," he grumbles, the vibration in his chest enough to make Vivi's eyes flutter open.

"Good nap, Vivi?" I ask, my voice swapping to a softer one.

She yawns, body tensing as she stretches out like a happy cat in a sunbeam. Theo has a way of making a girl feel like that when he turns his attention to her.

I know. I remember.

Her head tilts, and she looks up at Theo.

"Hi, baby girl."

That "baby girl" thing in his deep voice will be my undoing. I just know it.

She smiles, almost bashfully, and reaches for me. And to his credit, Theo doesn't hesitate. He hands her over, and I sigh when I hold her against my chest.

The break was nice, but the relief at having her back in my arms is inexplicable.

Theo pushes to sit, and our knees bump against each other as he moves around, putting his shirt back straight.

"You should still wear the sling."

His eyes roll playfully before landing back on us. "I know, but it sucks. I'd rather hold Vivi. Send me that picture, okay?"

"Okay. Write down your number before you go."

"Oh yeah. I'll just text you first."

He pushes to stand, which puts his crotch right at my face height. My cheeks heat, because I know what's on the other side of that zipper. And I *know* what he can do with it.

I turned porn on in the bathroom, but truthfully, nothing compares to that night. It's the fantasy I go back to every time.

"Why did you take my number?" I peek up at him while Vivi grabs at the neckline of my shirt in the most unsubtle way possible.

Theo smiles down at me. "Told you I was going to come back for another shot, and I meant it."

A thought hits me and steals all the air from my lungs. It's irrational. And it's jealous. And I'm just insecure enough to blurt it straight out. "Oh my god. Do you have other children with other women? You're on the road so much. You're already so good with her. You could have baby mamas all over the place."

His big brown eyes go wide, and then he barks out a disbelieving laugh before he tips my face up to his. Exactly how he did in the elevator that night. He bends down and whispers against my skin, "No, Winter. You're my only baby mama."

And then he swaggers out the door, like that's a perfectly normal thing to say.

I need to clear my head. So, I take Vivi out for a walk in her stroller. We hit the park and I push her in a swing. Once she's had her fill, we stroll down main street.

I'm so zoned out that I end up walking right past Hamilton

Athletics, where I may or may not sneak a peek through the front windows at Theo working out. He's wearing his sling, but it doesn't make him look inept. It's more like he can do lower body and balance exercises with one hand tied behind his back.

Every line on his arms shimmers with perspiration. His body is firm, coiled—a machine.

Who knew bull riders had to be so *fit*.

But I am *not* gawking. I'm just out clearing my head after the shock of the last couple of days, which is why I turn the same shade as a strawberry when he catches me standing in the middle of the sidewalk on Rosewood Street.

Sipping a coffee and gawking at him like a brain-dead bimbo.

I give my head a brief shimmy and turn to keep walking. I'll pretend that little moment didn't happen at all. It's just the baby-brain. I zone out all the time now.

It has nothing to do with Theo Silva.

And definitely nothing to do with *that night*.

And now, I'm irrationally annoyed with him. Because when I sneak a final peek over my shoulder to see if I got away with it, he's still standing there smirking at me.

He *winks* at me.

The absolute gall of this man to come waltzing back into my life and wink at me. Like no time has passed at all between now and when we saw each other last. Like it's not insane to flirt with me openly, as though I'm something more to him.

I storm back home, flustered by his confidence. Rattled by his presence. Annoyed that he's not only a great lay, but a shameless and persistent flirt.

With no boundaries.

The sight of a woman standing at his front door with a gift bag in hand stops me in my tracks. I watch her ring the doorbell and check her teeth for lipstick in the reflection of the front window.

Figures.

As she waits, she shifts the bag between hands, seeming a bit nervous in her painted-on jeans. One hand tucks a loose strand of perfectly blown-out light brown hair behind one ear.

She knocks, then waits again. When he doesn't answer, she tries to peer in through the front bay window, still looking around like he might be hiding from her.

His dog doesn't even bark.

Then she turns and glances back at the front street. I don't even register with her, but she does for me. She's the girl from the rodeo. The one with tears streaming down her face, who was ready to crumble when she saw Theo on the ground.

She's pretty. Really pretty. She's fit, and she doesn't appear exhausted or chaotic like me. Theo and I haven't covered this ground yet, but it makes sense he'd have someone.

I mean, fucking look at him. Of course he would.

Except he winked at me. And he keeps smirking at me like he's replaying when he licked tequila off my—

"Do you know if Theo Silva lives here?" she calls out to me.

"Yup," I reply with a thin smile. For all the hard work I've done on becoming a kinder, less judgmental person, I take one look at this girl and hate her.

"Is he home?"

"Doesn't seem to be." I try to make my voice sound peppy as I unlatch the white picket gate at the front of my house. It's a dumb question though.

Obviously, he's not home. Or doesn't want to see her. Those are her two options, but she's asking a stranger.

Stupid questions get stupid answers.

"Winter, hold up!" Theo calls, coming down the sidewalk from the same direction I just did. When he clears the hedge that was hiding him from the hot girl on his front step, she brightens.

"Theo! Hi!" She rushes down the front steps and toward the front street.

Theo pulls up, blinking. "Cindy. Hey."

She flushes and smiles at him, sparing me a quick glance before going straight to him and wrapping him in a hug.

A very comfortable hug.

Her hand rests on his cheek when she pulls away. "How are you feeling? Sorry I didn't make it to the hospital again for a visit. Got tied up with work in the city."

He steps out of her reach, and her hand falls between them. "Feeling pretty good. And no problem. It was nice to catch up with an old friend."

She visibly winces, and okay, now I feel bad for her. It doesn't seem like *old friend* is what she was going for.

"Well . . ." She straightens, brightening her tone even further. "I couldn't get a hold of you at the number I have for you. But Rhett told me you were staying here for a while, so I figured . . ." She shrugs, lips forming a small curve, making the apples of her cheeks fill. "We could catch up?" She holds the bag up. "I brought you a housewarming present!"

From the bag, she pulls out an expensive-looking bottle of tequila and a set of ornate shot glasses. "We could party like we used to."

Theo laughs politely, taking in the gift and the woman before him.

And once again, I'm gawking at Theo.

Except, this time, I'm not embarrassed. I feel like I want to break something.

Preferably those shot glasses. Because tequila is *our* thing.

I turn away, letting the gate close with a loud, petulant crash as I head up to my front door.

Vivi is asleep, which means I'd be an idiot to move her. Usually I'd get a book, sit in a sunbeam on the porch, and soak up the peace and quiet. But hot Theo is here with his hot fuck buddy and I would rather drink a glass of thumb tacks than watch them interact.

I'm about to reach in and take my chances with moving Vivi when I hear the rumble of Theo's voice. "This is really kind of you, Cindy. Thank you. But I'm in a new place now. Partying like I used to isn't in the cards."

He's kind, but direct.

Bent behind the shade of the stroller, I pause and eavesdrop.

She laughs, but I know that laugh. I use it to cover being disappointed. "Fair enough. It has been a couple of years since I left the circuit. Dinner sometime instead?"

I clench my molars, prepared for him to say yes. Why wouldn't he say yes?

His hand swipes through his hair and he steps away. "Ya know, I'm in the middle of something. Something I have a good feeling about. So it's a no."

My stomach goes hot, like it's melting in on itself.

Her responding laugh is shriller this time, her tone not as sweet. "Oh, my bad. I didn't realize you were with someone."

His eyes slice over to mine, busting me. *Again.* "I'm not. Yet."

16
Theo

Theo: Pick you up at 4.

Winter: For what?

Theo: Dinner at the ranch. We can drive together.

Winter: Don't you think that's kind of obvious?

Theo: We're going there to tell everyone that I'm her dad. I think things are going to be obvious pretty quickly.

Winter: Fine.

Theo: What are you wearing?

Winter: I don't know. Probably a sundress or something. Why? You planning on choosing an outfit that matches like we're going to prom?

Theo: No. I mean, what are you wearing RIGHT NOW?;)

Winter: Seriously?

Theo: Send pics.

Theo: Okay. It's fine. I'll just continue to use my imagination.

"It's annoying how good you are at all things dad-ing."

Vivi babbles in the back seat as she beats on a fabric book that makes loud crinkling noises. We're heading out to the ranch to let the cat out of the bag. Or, rather, let the dad out of the bag.

"Dad-ing?" I arch a brow at Winter from the driver's side of my truck. She looks like an angry Barbie doll, arms tucked tight over her ribs, which does nothing but push her tits up. I'm already distracted by them, so this isn't helping.

"Yeah. Like just now. Doing the car seat? Simple. Feeding her? No problem. Changing a diaper? Immediately faster than me. Bathing her? Like you've done it a million times. Getting her into a carrier? Not a single cuss word while you struggle with a strap. It's *annoying*."

"Gosh, Winter. I didn't know we were competing. Do you have a special trophy for me?" I don't bother hiding the humor in my voice. In the past week, I've come to her house every morning, hot coffee in hand. Despite how badly this whole thing has fucked with my head, I keep a smile on my face and put my best foot forward to learn everything.

I glance at her, waiting for whatever barb she'll fire next. She's fidgeting to cover for her nervousness. But all I see is how the navy dress with a tiny floral print slides over her skin, making the slit on the skirt gape open, giving me a peek of smooth thigh.

My gaze snags there, remembering how her skin felt beneath my hands. I absently wonder if she thinks about that night. She *must*. I did good work that night. I know I did.

"Cindy seems nice."

Ah. There it is. She's stressed. And this is how she copes, by reverting to the ice-queen version of herself.

"She is," I deadpan as I back out of her driveway.

It's time to head to Wishing Well Ranch for a family dinner.

The tip of her nose wiggles as she glances away. "You should have gone out with her."

My lips twitch. "Is that so?"

"Yeah. You two make a cute couple. She's pretty."

"I hadn't noticed."

She scoffs at me. Loudly. "Don't be ridiculous. You've probably already slept with her, which means you noticed."

"Yeah, years ago. She used to stay out on the circuit and travel with us."

When I glance over, Winter's skin has gone all pink and splotchy. She looks ready to blow a gasket.

"Don't tell me things like that," is her hushed reply.

"Why? I'm not going to lie to you about it. I have nothing to hide. I assumed you knew you didn't take my virginity that night."

She snorts and stares out the window, chewing at her nails.

"Why does that bug you, Winter?"

"Because you can't have women traipsing in and out of your house willy-nilly if you're going to have Vivi around!"

"Well, they aren't exactly coming down one hundred strong."

"They fucking better not. You're a dad now. Have your one-night stands somewhere else."

"Like the Rosewood Inn?" I snipe, still unable to keep myself from firing her up. Still getting off on watching her go from cool and unaffected to *this*.

"Rude."

"I seem to remember you enjoying how rude I was to you once."

Her head snaps in my direction, eyes flaring. "Stop. There's a child in the vehicle."

I hum thoughtfully, playing up that I'm mulling over her point when I'm not. "So this is about Vivi?"

She nods, blowing a heavy breath out as she does. "Obviously. Who else would it be about?"

"Do you mean *what* else would it be about?"

Her pouty lips thin and silence descends between us until she finds something else to pick at. "And you live next door. You didn't need to drive over to pick us up."

It's a struggle not to laugh. I shouldn't find this side of her endearing, but I do. "I thought swapping the car seat into my vehicle would be easier that way."

She huffs out a quick breath, shoulders rising and falling as she does. "You're annoyingly gentlemanlike."

"Wow. It sounds like the only constant where I'm concerned is that I'm annoying and rude."

When I peek over, her face softens. The cool veneer slips and her tightly held posture relaxes a little. "Sorry. I'm freaking out."

"I know." I smile as we pass by the gas station where I first laid eyes on her.

"I'm being a bitch."

"No, you aren't. You're just using the coping skills you've got."

"Is this some Tony Robbins shit? Because I hate that guy. Only a man could be that big of a douchebag and still make millions of dollars peddling the most elementary advice."

I bark out a laugh. "He really is a douchebag, isn't he?"

Her lips twitch and she glances out the window to cover. "Yes."

"Okay. I'm no Tony Robbins, but do you know how I deal with freaking out?"

Her blue eyes widen as she turns back my way, elbow resting on the center console like I might give her some profoundly helpful answer. She's mocking me, but that's fine.

I prop my elbow next to hers, basking in the fact that she doesn't move away.

Fuck. I want to touch her so badly. More than just this chaste elbow touch or whatever the fuck I'm doing right now.

I want to grip her hair. Bend her over. Spread her—

I shake my head to clear it. My cock is thickening in my jeans, and it isn't the time or the place.

Clearing my throat, I forge ahead. "When I'm freaking out, I try to make myself as useful as possible. I get busy. I clean. I organize. I get great at changing diapers."

She slumps back in her seat. "Fuck. I'm sorry. I really am—"

"Winter, don't finish that sentence. Instead, promise me when you meet my mom, you will tell her I'm annoyingly gentlemanly. That will make her proud."

She snorts. "Fine. I will."

"I don't think I can hold her back much longer. She is feral to meet Vivi. Pictures aren't cutting it," I admit as we pull into the ranch.

Winter's head tilts in my direction and her brows furrow. "Why are you holding her back?"

Her body jostles as I pull to a stop near the main house. All river rock and stained logs with a tin roof and spacious wrap-around deck.

"I don't know. Just trying to give you and me a second to figure things out."

"You and me." She shakes her head, followed by a scoff.

That can't stand, though, so I hop out and round the truck. Based on the way she's digging through her purse in her lap, I have to assume she expects me to go for Vivi. But I rip her door open and step close enough that my knees butt up against the edge of the truck.

"What are you doing?" Her tone bleeds alarm as she jolts and faces me.

"What's so funny about you and me?"

Her hands flip out in disbelief. "Seriously?"

"Seriously."

"It's ... it's ... you ... you don't need to feel obligated to make this a thing when it's not. You can want her in your life without pretending you want me too. Don't feel obliged to act like you're attracted to me just because I'm her mom." Her eyes are so sparkly, her stubborn chin tipped up so high, her lips so fucking kissable. "Not when you have girls like Cindy."

I interrupt her, leaning across to release her seatbelt and turning her to face me like that night in the bar. Our eyes collide, questions swirling in her blue depths.

With one hand propped above me on the roof of the truck, I lean in, my lips hovering over hers as I whisper, "That's a fascinating assessment, Winter. But I'm not pretending a single fucking thing. Because for a year and a half all I've had to do is *remember* you and me that night to be stuck walking around all day like this."

I cross a line.

My hand darts out and I grip her wrist, pulling her hand down to slide it over my rock-hard cock.

She doesn't pull away. The only thing moving on her are her irises, tracing my face, her expression carefully blank.

153

But then her fingers flex over my dick.

She puffs out a breath and licks her lips as I groan and drop my head. The sliver of space between us crackles as one finger moves, running over the denim that divides us. Her touch is painfully, deliberately slow.

"Oh good! You're here!" Summer's chipper voice and footsteps bounding down the stairs have me lurching back away from Winter. Both of us panting, staring at each other.

"So happy you guys carpooled!" Summer pats my shoulder. "You are such a gentleman, Theo. Opening her door like that!"

Summer is oblivious.

But I don't think Winter is anymore.

17
Winter

Summer: Everyone is good for dinner at the main house tonight?

Sloane: Yup! We just got back.

Willa: I'll bring the mimosas. Cade is cooking.

Winter: Yep.

Summer: I heard you're driving with Theo?

Willa: I like him a lot better than Doctor Douche.

Winter: We're not together.

Willa: But if you were, you'd be trading up.

Summer: Way up.

Willa: Way WAY up.

Sloane: Leave her alone, you guys.

"**H**ow's the physio?" Rhett asks as a lull in conversation around the table hits.

"Good, actually. Got the go-ahead to ditch the sling. Not that I've been wearing it anyway," Theo replies with a chuckle.

Theo, who refused to sit anywhere but next to Vivi. Not that I can blame him, but still. I'm not oblivious to the quick looks people are shooting at him. Shooting at *us*.

"So, when is your mom coming? Summer and I should have her out for dinner. She hasn't seen the new house. Come to think of it, I haven't seen her in quite a while." Rhett leans back in his chair, eyeing Theo up.

It all feels very obvious, especially with Theo winking at me every time I nervously clear my throat. It's like I'm about to say something, and then get washed out into the tide of the conversation.

"Of course. She'd love that. I think she's going to come out a bit early. Stay at my place."

Everyone continues eating the prawn and lemon pasta that Cade whipped up. A heaping bowl of watermelon and mint salad sits in the middle of the table. It's the perfect summer meal and everyone is here to partake.

Willa, whose shrewd eyes jump between Theo and me. Cade, who is managing their daughter Emma and their son Luke, who has barely lifted his head from shoveling the pasta into his mouth like his parents haven't fed him in days.

Sloane and Jasper, who might as well be eating with her on his lap for how close they're sitting.

And Beau, who's doing his best to steal the asshole crown from me, is opposite Harvey at the head of the table, spinning a bottle of beer and peeling the label off. Not saying a word.

Even Sloane's mom, Cordelia, is here. *Still.* She moved in for a safe place to stay after she left her dickwad husband over a year ago and just . . . hasn't left.

And the way she says, "Harvey, you need some salad too. You can't stay healthy only eating meat and carbs," while primly blotting at her lips and glancing away is adorable.

Harvey rolls his eyes and reaches forward, serving himself a few scoops of the fruit.

That everyone keeps looking at Theo and me suspiciously while being so willfully ignorant of what's going on between Harvey and Cordelia blows my fucking mind.

"That's good. I'd like to meet her too." Harvey's gravelly voice cuts in as he stares down at the fruit on his plate like it's his enemy. And then he blurts something out that I shouldn't be surprised by—but I am. "I reckon she'll wanna spend a little extra time getting to know her new grandchild."

The table goes silent, save for the clatter of Summer dropping her fork on her plate.

It feels like time stretches out, accentuated by the thump of my heart in my ears. I was planning on saying something, but I just hadn't found the moment yet. I was still gathering my courage, trying to work it in, not just blurt it out with zero tact.

"What?" Harvey says over a mouthful of watermelon. "It's been a couple of hours now. Are we all just gonna keep sitting here pretending Theo isn't Vivi's dad? I mean, *look at them*."

My lips twitch and my cheeks heat.

Fucking Harvey.

Theo saves me. Like always. "Well, Winter and I spent a lot of time talking about how to bring this up, but I should have known to just leave it to you, Harv."

Sloane is sitting straight across from me, hand on her chest, pretending to be shocked. Bless her.

"Thank you," I mouth to her.

She shakes her head and waves me off.

"Wait." Sweet Jasper looks genuinely confused. I owe Sloane a flat of Buddyz Best lager for keeping this secret as close as she has. "The only thing I remember about you two is that entertaining spat you had in the driveway."

"Yes!" Willa's eyes light up as she jabs her finger in Jasper's direction, her voice full of energy. "That was a good one!" And based on how memorable that altercation seems for everyone else, I must have made a real ass of myself.

Harvey gives a derisive snort. "Come on. Don't you kids know anything? You ever seen a tomcat fight a female?"

Willa's body is taut with barely contained laughter, while Cade groans and scrubs a hand over his beard.

"They start off scratching and screaming at each other—"

"Dad, please stop." Cade braces his forearms against the edge of the table, staring at his place setting.

"And then before you know it …" Harvey carries on, undeterred.

"*Dad.*" Now even Rhett is trying to make him stop.

"Before you know it what, Harv?" It's Jasper who gives the older man the final shove he needs, ignoring the light slap Sloane lands across his chest.

Harvey shrugs matter-of-factly. "Before you know it, they're breeding. Kittens everywhere. That saying about cats in heat didn't come from nowhere."

A chorus of groans ring out around the table.

"Lord, help me," Beau mutters. But miserable as he's been, even he can't keep his lips turned down at his father's antics.

When I glance at Theo on the other side of Vivi's highchair that separates us, he has his palms pressed into the sockets of his eyes, body shaking with silent laughter.

"Seriously, Theo?" I hiss at him, trying to sound menacing, but a giggle slips into my voice.

"Sorry. I just need a minute after that." He looks up at me, wiping tears from his eyes, thick dark lashes clumped together as he shakes his head in disbelief.

I push my shoulders back and meet Harvey's glittering hazel eyes at the end of the table. "Thank you for that explanation, Harvey. When Vivienne gets older and asks how we met, I'll be sure to drop her off with you."

"No," Cade jumps in. "Don't give him any ideas. Young, impressionable minds do not need the Harvey Eaton version of the birds and the bees."

"I think when Grandpa told me about the birds and the bees, he used rabbits instead," Luke adds innocently.

"Yeah." Harvey laughs. "There's a saying about rabbits too, ya know?"

I see him startle a bit as his eyes shoot over to Cordelia, who clearly kicked him under the table.

"But . . ." His eyes gauge the large group of people staring back at him in varying states of amusement. "That's not appropriate dinner conversation."

Luke, all of seven years old, scoffs before saying, "Yeah, Dad will lose it if you say 'fucking like bunnies' in front of me again." His eyes go round as saucers, and he slaps a small hand over his mouth like he might be able to shove the words back in.

Cade's chair screeches as he shoots up to standing. "Lucas Eaton, outside. Now."

Luke drops his eyes and shoots Willa a playful little grin from under the fringe of his new longer hairstyle.

"You too, Harvey."

Willa leans across the table and whispers loudly, "Shit, Harv, you've made Daddy mad now."

Harvey's lips press together to hide a smile as he rises and walks outside to get a "talking-to" from his son.

"I heard that, Red," Cade calls out as he marches out the back door without another glance.

Willa fans herself and pulls Emma out of her highchair and into her arms. "Well, this has been an interesting family dinner, to say the least."

"No shit," Rhett replies, staring hard at Theo, like he can't believe what has come out tonight. "When did you find out about this?"

"About a week ago," Theo replies.

Rhett turns his attention to me. "You didn't tell him? Or anyone? You've known all this time, and you didn't say anything?"

There's disbelief in his voice, but also accusation. Of course, he'd think the worst of me. I might be sitting at the table with this family, but I'm not one of them. No matter what I do, they'll always regard me with a hint of suspicion.

Theo snaps his fingers over the table, drawing his mentor's attention back to himself. He went from looking amused to downright murderous. "Watch your fucking tone when you're talking to the mother of my child."

Rhett's jaw pops and his arms cross. He looks *shocked* by Theo's sharp tone.

Sloane cuts the tension. "You don't owe us an explanation. If you guys are happy, I'm happy. Vivi has so much love, and she's the luckiest girl in the world with two great parents in her life now."

I settle back in my seat as Sloane gives me a brief nod from across the table.

Like a physical reaction to the spike in tension at the table, quiet whimpers start up from beside me, Vivi's eyes suddenly coated with tears.

Before I can react, Theo reaches for her. "Hey, hey, hey, baby girl. It's okay," he coos as he sidles her up against his broad chest.

And it's a shot to my core.

He has no business looking this good and *being* this good. Jumping from defending me to consoling her.

I don't deserve it, and there's a part of me that still feels like I've saddled him with something he can't possibly want.

There's also this little part of me that's more drawn to him with every moment I spend in his company. I felt it that night, a level of comfort I've never known. And now that feeling builds every second I'm around him.

Every time I see him with Vivi.

Every time he shows up at my door with a coffee.

Every time he winks and rakes his eyes over my body like he's replaying that night in his mind.

But sitting here, watching him surrounded by friends and family, consoling our daughter like the sweet man he is—I feel like an outsider.

Like I don't belong. I'm going to be tied to him for the rest of my life, so there's a good chance I'll be forced to watch him date

161

other women. Marry another woman. Have children with another woman. And Vivi will be part of that family too.

And I'll still be the outsider. Because making his dick hard isn't enough to make a relationship last.

"So how is all this . . . going?" Summer inquires carefully.

The ball of anxiety in my chest as I come face-to-face with the reality of my future and this foreign, consuming jealousy keeps me from talking.

"Great. We're still figuring things out." Theo glances my way, wide palm rubbing his daughter's back as she nuzzles into the crook of his neck. Like she just *knows* he's hers somehow.

Hers in a way that he'll never be mine.

"Living next to each other is helpful, actually," he adds in a good-natured way, followed by a wink.

A wink that screams danger to my heart, just like it did the very first time he aimed it my way.

"Yes," I say, fiddling with the napkin in my lap. "It's perfect. It's kind of like we're business partners. You know?" Summer nods slowly, her eyes clouded with confusion. "Like we have the same goal, but can still keep things separate. Professional almost." I say it to lay things out, a nice chain-link fence around myself to keep my battered, untrusting heart safe from harm. Safe from a man like Theo, who would be too damn easy to fall for.

Theo tenses beside me. I know instantly I've landed a blow that hurt him.

When I glance over, I can tell he's avoiding looking at me. I can tell the proud smile on his handsome face has melted away. The corners of his eyes are pinched, and he snuggles Vivi closer to himself, like I might take her away.

And as much as I felt the need to draw that line in the sand to protect myself . . .

I regret saying it at all.

18
Theo

Mom: You're telling everyone tonight?

Theo: The big reveal.

Julia: I'm a little surprised this is the first time this has happened.

Theo: Jules, don't you have some homework to do or something?

Julia: I feel like you could be that guy who has kids cropping up left and right if you ever do one of those ancestry DNA tests.

Theo: It's not my fault I'm so fertile that no barrier can stop me.

Julia: Gross. You're my brother. That's the line.

Mom: Play stupid games, win stupid prizes.

The sun is setting on the sprawling back deck of the ranch house when Rhett catches my eye. He tips his head toward the house, silently gesturing that I follow him inside.

I glance across the table at Winter. She's sitting with her back straight, right beside a large standing heater with Sloane on the opposite side of her. Willa and Summer talk over them about something.

As if she can feel my eyes on her, Winter turns her head at a snail's pace, like she's resisting a force that's overpowering her. Our eyes meet.

Vivi is asleep in my arms, but Winter's attention is on me. I can't quite place the look on her face, and I do my best to keep my features casually blank. Try to put on a smiling face and not give away to a lively group of happy people that being referred to as a business partner makes me want to flip the fucking table.

I stand at the same time as Rhett, and mouth to Winter, "Heading in for a minute."

She nods tightly in response, arms gesturing out in an offer to take Vivi.

I shake my head. No chance am I giving up a single moment with this little girl asleep in my arms.

After following Rhett in, I prop against the island in the kitchen while he leans against the back of the big leather couch that faces into the living room. It's like we're both playing at being casual when we know this conversation is anything but.

He's got a bone to pick.

And frankly, so do I. Winter can call me her business partner all she wants, but no one is going to accuse her of the things Rhett did earlier. I won't allow it.

"How you doing?" His arms cross, and he glances between Vivi's sleeping face and mine.

"Fine," I bite back.

"This must have come as quite the surprise."

"No shit."

"How are you feeling about it?"

I give a single, rigid shrug. "Good."

"No, really, Theo. You can't have wanted this. Obviously, Vivi is amazing, but this isn't what you signed up for, and we both know it. I didn't hurl myself in front of a bull for you to throw everything away."

"Rhett, I'm going to stop you right there. You have been my friend for a long time. My mentor for even longer. My dad loved you, and I do too. But so help me, if you keep talking about this current situation like it's a burden, it will become difficult to stay friends with you."

He flinches, his eyes widening. "Wow. Alright. It's just that Winter is kind of—"

"What?" I cut him off. "Strong? Intelligent? A fantastic fucking mom? Because if you were thinking words about her that are anything less than positive, then you've found the line."

Rhett chuckles. "I've never seen this side of you."

"What side?" I mumble, staring down at Vivi's serene face, studying the way her dark fringe of lashes fans delicately over her full rosy cheeks.

"This . . . this . . ." He waves a hand up and down my frame when I peek up at him. "This papa bear side of you. But you know it doesn't mean you have to like Winter. She's a complicated woman. I mean, she's family, but she's not always easy to—"

"I've always liked Winter. I liked her when you told me stories about her before I met her. I liked her the first time I laid eyes on her at the shitty gas station on the corner of Rosewood and Main. I liked her when she yelled I must have a small dick." Rhett's face is a mix of confusion and disbelief. "And I especially like her now. I'm not sad about Vivi. The only thing I'm sad about is not being there for Winter earlier. But that's my cross to bear. So, if you're looking for a person to commiserate with about how awful she is, you need to find someone else."

With that, I push off the counter, open the back door and wave a hand at the only woman who has ever captured my attention. My new *business partner*.

I interrupt the quiet hum of conversation, done with being around everyone. "Tink, let's go home."

She blinks a couple of times, then says a few polite thank yous and excuses herself. When she gets to Vivienne and me, she grips my bicep and lets me lead her out of the house.

We drive home in strained silence. I tell myself it's because Vivi is asleep in the back seat. But that's a lie.

I know it. And I'm getting the sense Winter knows it too.

"That went better than I expected," she says, her voice a little too bright for her personality.

"What were you expecting?" My hands clamp on the wheel, my voice low and quiet.

Darkness settles around us, and the dull hum of the tires on the back road fills the void of her not responding. I try to keep my eyes on the road, but she's quiet for so long that I can't help but glance

167

over at her. Her posture is straight, but her hands are twisting in her lap, giving away her inner distress.

"I didn't expect you to defend me."

I shake my head, a bit irritated she thinks I wouldn't.

"I'll always defend you, Winter."

My statement must shock her, judging by the way her head snaps in my direction. After a few beats, she clears her throat and relaxes back in her seat.

"I'm not surprised by Rhett's take, because that's mostly what I expected. I can't blame him for painting me as the villain. I can understand why he would perceive me that way."

"Why?"

"Because my relationship with Summer is new. And he holds a grudge better than she does, I guess."

"He's an idiot."

"No." She sighs heavily and her gaze drifts out the window. "I've been brutal to Summer almost my entire life."

"Why? Did she do something to you?"

Winter snorts, like we both know it's out of character for Summer to do something mean. "It sounds stupid when I say it out loud."

"I say lots of stupid stuff."

She focuses on me now. "Well, that's true. I think you barked at me once."

My lips twitch, but I just shake my head. "Continue."

"I think I figured out at a young age that if I mirrored the way Marina treated Summer—and my dad—she sort of ... left them alone? Like if she felt like I was on her *team*, she would care less about what they did because she could turn all her attention to me. On priming me to be the perfect mini-me surgeon version of her.

I leveled the playing field for her. In taking me away from them, she felt like she won and, in turn, didn't terrorize my little sister."

"Have you told Summer this?"

Winter's body heaves under a weighty sigh. "No. We just started fresh. Hashing this out will only hurt her. And I don't want to hurt her more than I already have."

"You should tell her."

"Why?"

"It would make you feel better."

"And her worse. She'll feel like she needs to fix me. That's just how she is."

"You don't need fixing, Winter." I swallow the ache in my throat. That seems like too much for a child to process, let alone bear. "But what about you?"

She waves me off. "I'll survive."

"And what about the child you once were?"

Her tongue darts across her lips, covering for whatever anxiety she feels right now. "I was fine. They fed me, watered me, and clothed me in designer everything and I did any extra-curricular activity I wanted." She shrugs. "I wanted for nothing."

"But what about love?"

She twists to look over her shoulder at Vivi, her voice taking on a thicker quality when she says, "What about it?"

"Did you have it?"

I watch her throat work as her attention stays fixed on our sleeping daughter. "No. I don't think I ever had it until her."

Without thinking, I press the heel of my hand to my chest, willing the ache away. I wish my mom were here. She'd know what to do or say.

"It's funny," Winter continues, as though she's in a trance. "I took an oath as a doctor. It's my job to save people's lives. And somehow, that doesn't feel heavy or oppressive. It's more of a challenge I can rise to. But with her? God. It's consuming. Sometimes, I'm so consumed with loving her I can't even sleep. I'd use an innocent stranger as a shield for her if there was gunfire. I'd shove others into the flames to get her out of a burning building. I'd swim through boiling water for her. I wouldn't even blink, Theo."

"So, you love her? That's normal. I mean, your descriptions are a bit . . . dark. But I follow," I say, as I pull into her driveway.

"Is it?" She turns her crystal blue eyes on me. They twinkle in the dark cab of the truck, reflecting every speck of light around us. "I've never loved anyone like this before. And no one has loved me like Vivi does. It feels so foreign."

Jesus Christ. This woman.

I itch to touch her, to soothe her. So I reach out and cup her head, combing my fingers through her hair like I did in the elevator. I lean across the console and she holds my gaze. "Yeah, Winter." Her irises drop to my lips. "That's normal. And you shouldn't settle for anything less."

Her breath fans across my cheek when she sighs. I could so easily turn my fingers into a fist in her hair and kiss her. Give her a taste of not settling. But she pulls away before I can, one hand coming up to give my forearm a platonic squeeze.

I can't tell if this is a one-sided attraction sometimes. Can't tell if I spend every day in the shower jerking off while thinking about a woman who doesn't think of me at all. Winter is almost impossible to get a steady read on.

And tonight is no different.

She gives me a flat smile before we part ways, without another word exchanged between us. I watch her carry Vivi's bucket seat up into the dark house before I pull out and drive to the one right next door.

When I go inside, it feels like I'm entering the wrong house.

19
Theo

Winter: Thank you for tonight.

Theo: I didn't do anything special.

Winter: You did.

Theo: Want me to come over and do something truly special that will have you thanking me profusely?

Winter: Are you always this horny?

Theo: I was going to say clean your house. Get your mind out of the gutter, Dr. Hamilton.

"Out you go, Peter."

If looks could kill, I'd be dead now. Peter glares up at me—back rounded and one front paw lifted—while his tiny body shakes. Some people might think he's cold, but I know better. That's his small-man rage.

"I know. How dare I make you get off the couch and go pee?"

172

He trembles again.

"I am officially the worst person in the world."

The dog's ears flatten and his usually buggy eyes narrow.

I sigh, tired after one of the weirdest fucking nights of my life, and bend down to scoop him up. "Let's go, asshole. I won't have you waking me up in the middle of the night."

We head out the back door, and Peter makes unimpressed grunting noises. I place him on the grass and take a seat on the back porch step. He turns and shoots me a disapproving scowl over his shoulder.

"Is that what I get for rescuing you? I don't even like small dogs. You're an exception."

He gingerly walks across the grass like its mere existence is a personal affront to his sensitive little legs. I decide I'll mow the grass shorter tomorrow. I'll do Winter's lawn too.

That's when I hear it.

Vivi's angry cries filter into the night from next door. These older homes have a lot of character, but terrible soundproofing.

I'm torn about what to do. I hate that Winter does everything by herself.

I can't believe I said something about not wanting my dog to wake me up at night when Winter has been doing *that* for months.

Alone.

Peter sniffs and spins like he's going to pee. For whatever reason, he decides the patch of grass in the corner is trash and unworthy of his gift. So, he goes back to sniffing to find the *perfect* spot.

Vivi wails, and the more I hear her cries, the more agitated I feel. I stand and watch Peter glance around like he's looking for the ideal location to build his dream home, not take a piss.

"Come on, Pete. You used to live in the street. You're not this fancy. Pick a spot." I snap my fingers before twirling them in an agitated "let's go" motion. Because I can't just sit here, or crawl into bed for a full night's sleep, knowing they're struggling a few feet away.

So, when Peter finally relieves himself, I march across the lawn and scoop him up to the chorus of more agitated grumbles. I take the narrow sidewalk between the houses, step over the low picket fence, and walk straight across the neighboring lawn to the front door. Based on the crying coming from inside, I will not be waking anyone up, so I knock three times. Hard.

It takes a bit, but the door opens. Winter's still in her dress, and she's washed her face, but only one side.

"I'm sorry. I'll try to keep it down."

I stare at her. She has no idea how to ask for help.

And then it hits me. She's had no one to ask.

"I thought I could just transfer her from the car seat to her crib." A sigh that could also pass as a sob escapes her as tears spring up in her eyes. "But that stupid fucking creaky hinge that I keep meaning to fix woke her up and now she is *pissed*. I tried bouncing her and she doesn't want to nurse. And I can't handle listening to her cry, but I also don't want to sleep with my makeup on or without brushing my teeth. So I just need a minute and then I'll keep it—"

I put a hand on her shoulder and ease her back into the house, kicking the door shut behind me. Then I hold Peter out to her. "Here. Take my dog and go to bed."

She takes him, even though she looks down at his spindly body like he might be diseased. I nearly smile as the realization hits me. Peter and Winter have a lot in common. Prickly on the outside, a little broken on the inside, and in desperate need of someone to hold them.

"I don't need your help, Theo."

This is the part where she lashes out, but I expected that from her. She's fiercely independent.

I give her a soft smile while she and my dog glare at me. "I know you don't, Winter. But I want to help anyway. Let me help tonight, okay?"

Her eyes go round as saucers. She's so used to people walking away when she gets snappy that I confuse her when I don't back off.

So, I press a hand to the small of her back and lead her down the hallway.

"Am I supposed to let your dog sleep in my bed?"

"Yes."

"But he—"

"Will be good for you. He likes to snuggle, and he sleeps like the dead. Go finish taking off your makeup and brush your teeth."

With a gentle push, I send Winter into the bathroom and then turn around and enter Vivi's nursery, her angry wails filling the air.

"Baby girl, what is the commotion?" I coo as her tiny arms reach up for me. "You can't be partying this late. Your poor mama needs some rest."

I lift her into my arms, and her wet cheek nuzzles into my neck. Tiny fists grip at my shirt, and . . . she just cries harder.

"Okay, you're really mad. I get it. It seems like everyone is tonight, so you aren't being original at all."

Bouncing her, I walk out to the kitchen and pull out all the bits and pieces I need to warm some milk from the freezer for her. "You know when I get crabby? When I'm hungry. So you get that from me. Let's try this again."

She gasps for air, body heaving under the weight of trying to catch her breath. "My mom calls it hangry. Hungry and angry together. My sister gets that way too. Probably why she's always making fun of me. She's just hangry. I'm pretty sure it's a Silva trait."

By the time her bottle is ready, Vivi's cries have slowed and I head down the hallway toward her room. I plan to sit in the rocking chair with my daughter and watch her drift off to sleep.

My head snaps up when I hear the squeak of door hinges. Winter stands at the entrance to her room, directly across the hall from Vivi's, looking tired and wide-eyed all at once. Like she doesn't know what to do or say when someone swoops in to help her.

She nibbles at her lip as I draw closer, and my gaze drops to trace over her flimsy cotton nightgown. I wonder if she's wearing anything underneath. Images flash through my mind of me flipping it up and taking her.

"Go to bed, Winter."

"Are you sure? What are you going to do?"

I place Vivi in her crib and put the warm bottle into her grabby hands before turning to face the woman who has occupied all the space in my brain since the first moment I laid eyes on her—since before that probably.

Every time Rhett brought up what happened between her and Summer, I couldn't help but think that we weren't getting the entire story. That people aren't cruel for no good reason. That two siblings shouldn't be so at odds. That parents shouldn't fuck their kids around as badly as what he described. My childhood wasn't perfect, but I never doubted how much my parents loved me.

It's true I didn't know Winter, but I wondered about her all the same.

"I'm going to take care of our daughter so that you can get the rest you need."

"That's okay. I don't need your help—"

My hand shoots out, wrapping around hers gruffly as I march her back into her bedroom. It's like mine, with crown moldings and polished hardwoods, but hers has a feminine touch. She has a beautiful, antique-style brass bed frame. It's dainty and polished, probably cool to the touch—just like her.

But if you hold that metal long enough, it will heat. Take on the temperature of its surroundings.

Winter just needs a little heat to warm herself.

Peter has already curled himself onto the pristine white bed sheets, approving of the extravagant room.

"Get in bed, Winter. Or I will put you there myself."

Her body is close enough to mine that when she turns to face me, the tips of her nipples brush against my chest.

"What part of I don't need your help isn't registering?" Her shoulders rotate back, but that only presses her breasts further into my chest.

Vivi is blissfully happy with a bottle in her crib, and Winter has her claws out just the way I like.

Two can play this game.

Times are changing.

"All of it, Winter." I run my hand down the side of her body, palm shaping her hip. No hemline of panties at all. I groan right as she sucks in a breath, both our chins dropping to look at my hand splayed over her possessively. So small beneath my palm.

Memories filter in of me flipping her over and lifting her hips just the way I wanted them. Her ass arched back toward me, legs spread wide in offering, while I reached under her body to strum at her clit. She whimpered my name and came on my cock, even though she swore she never could.

I drop my mouth to her ear, not missing the way she shivers. "You're going to accept my help. And you're going to like it. You might even thank me for it." I nip her earlobe and lower my voice to add, "Like you did the last time I gave you a hand."

With a few gentle steps, I move ahead, pushing her toward the bed until the backs of her bare legs butt up against the edge. With a soft nudge at her hip, her tired body folds and she sits on the mattress with me towering above her.

I softly grip her jaw as I bend down to come eye to eye with her. Her pale blue irises race over my face like she's trying to guess what I might do next.

There's no resistance in her right now, only curiosity. Possibly even some of the same memories I've been obsessing over, based on the way her hard nipples strain against her nightgown.

"We're a team, Winter."

Her breath fans out over my damp lips in short, harsh pants as she stares at me. "A team."

I nod. "Yes. A team. So we're going to have to work together sometimes. You can't fight me all the time."

The column of her throat works as she swallows, and I pull away, needing some space. Needing to get away from her before I fuck up this sliver of trust I've worked on earning with her.

"Yes." Her voice is an unsteady whisper. "We're like business partners."

Business partners.

That term still makes me want to break something.

We are not that.

My grip is back on her chin, a little firmer this time, as I angle her face up to mine. "Winter," I rasp. "I have sponsors. And agents.

Doctors and trainers. Those are business relationships. You and I are a lot of things, but *business partners* is not one of them."

She licks her lips—licks her fucking lips—gaze bouncing between my eyes while her hands grip the edge of the mattress.

"Why not? We could be."

This woman never backs down. It's fucking infuriating, and I love that about her.

"Because the things I dream about doing to you are horribly unprofessional."

I throw all my restraint out of the goddamn window and take her mouth.

I'm hard and unyielding, one hand at her jaw while the other slides into her hair. And she doesn't miss a beat. Her mouth opens, and she welcomes the kiss. Her hands latch onto my shirt and she steps in close.

Like a precious metal, she warms.

Soft lips and hungry moans take me back to our night in a dimly lit elevator. To a hallway where I shoved her up against a wall.

I swipe my tongue into her mouth, deepening the kiss. She pulls me closer, over her. Until she's laid back on the mattress and I'm straining to keep from falling straight into the bed with the woman who doesn't seem to comprehend how tempting she is.

Her kisses are wild and frantic, edged in desperation. Her nails dig into my back as I nip at her bottom lip. My cock strains at the front of my jeans, but I force myself to hold back.

One of her legs wraps around my hips, tugging me close. Lining us up.

I grind into her, knowing I shouldn't.

Knowing these jeans are so easily discarded.

Knowing how long it's been.

Knowing she'll regret this in the morning. Or worse, hold it against me and think I pounced on her in a moment of weakness when she wasn't sure.

I want her to be as sure as I am.

I draw back, and for several seconds, we stare at each other. Much like eighteen months ago, I think we realize there's a fervor between us that neither of us can explain or resist.

A pull. A connection. A *longing*.

Or maybe that's just me. After all, she just announced me as the father of her child and also her business partner to our closest group of friends and family.

"I'm sorry. I . . . you need rest."

As I pull away, her hands tighten momentarily, like she might give me a sign that I shouldn't leave. That she wants me as badly as I want her.

But nothing comes.

When I stand and stare down at her, she is deliciously disheveled. Puffy lips, chaotic eyes . . . and her nightgown has shifted up, baring her to me. Pussy spread, looking so damn pink and wet and inviting.

I often daydream about spending long, lazy hours with my head between those thighs.

Tearing my gaze away is nearly impossible, but continuing to stare at her with no response feels like an invasion.

I scrub a hand over my stubble and force myself to look away, seeking control in whatever corner I might find a shred of it. Then, with a pained groan, I reach forward and gently lower the light cotton to cover her while her eyes stay fixed on mine.

A deep flush creeps down her throat and over her chest, but she makes no move to stop me. Her chest rises and falls heavily as she watches with vibrant blue eyes and bright pink cheeks.

"Goodnight, Winter," I whisper, clinging to the thread of control that doesn't feel strong enough to drag me away from her.

That cool mask slips back over her dainty features as she replies with, "Goodnight, Theo."

There's a bite in her words. She wields my name like a whip, and I feel the sting of it.

"Sleep." My voice comes out scratchy and unsure. "And don't get out of bed until it's light out."

Peter peeks one eye open at me in dismissal before I walk away, forcing my joints to carry me toward the hallway.

And when I go to close the door behind me, the hinges squeak and Vivi's cries come roaring back to life.

I'm happy to take over tonight. I want to spend quality time with Vivi.

That's why I'm here.

But fuck. I can't keep pretending either.

I want to spend quality time with Winter too.

20

Winter

Summer: You okay after last night? I'm sorry it got awkward.

Winter: I have a special knack for making things awkward. So does Rhett.

Summer: You do not. I think Rhett was being protective in his own way.

Winter: Wow. Lucky me. The macho big brother I never wanted.

Summer: Lol. You're stuck with him though. And Theo, apparently. That was . . . news.

Winter: Yep. Sorry.

Summer: Don't be. Do you like him?

Winter: He's fine. Except I just had a dream that he married a really annoying and hot buckle bunny with a super high-pitched porn voice. I had to spend every holiday with her so I could also be with Vivi.

Winter: And they were into PDA. Like lap-sitting and making out.

Summer: You make it sound like he got a lap dance at Christmas dinner.

Winter: That's what it was like! Brutal. It woke me up, and I'm irrationally annoyed at him now for bringing a fictional person to a fictional dinner set far ahead in the future.

Summer: So the dream made you jealous?

Winter: No. I'm not jealous. It was just a dream.

Summer: There's only one way to make sure a hot, high-pitched voice buckle bunny doesn't take over all your holidays.

Winter: How?

Summer: Marry Theo yourself.

Winter: Ha. That'll be the day.

Gray light filters into the room when I pry my eyes open. I can't tell what time it is and there's a part of me that doesn't care. It isn't technically still dark, so I've done what Theo asked.

Annoying Theo, and his annoying nightmare wife.

I brush the memory away, refusing to let dream Theo ruin my first full night's sleep in who knows how long. For the first time in recent memory, I didn't wake up dog-tired. With a smile, I stretch lightly, and my bare legs press up against ... fur. It takes me a moment to realize Peter the dog has wedged himself between my ankles, under the covers.

And I'm not even mad about it.

We never had pets growing up. Marina wasn't a fan, and I don't think Kip wanted to die on that hill. Now I'm wondering if

I'd have liked a pet. A cat? A hamster? I lift the duvet and peek down at Peter.

His head lifts slowly, but he doesn't turn it to look at me. Only his eyes shift over in my direction, like I've pissed him off.

A small chuckle escapes me as the dog's ears flatten against his bobble head.

I like him. I'm pretty sure I've given people this look before. Peter is relatable, and I decide to ignore the fact he's getting his little chihuahua hairs all over my fresh bed.

When I drop the cover and flop back down, his head goes down with it, satisfied that I'm no longer disturbing his peace. He's happy to use my legs for warmth, but not especially grateful about it.

Which makes me think of Theo. Again.

Last night took me through a whole range of emotions. From an unexpected kindred feeling at dinner all the way through to desperation.

Because the things I dream about doing to you are horribly unprofessional.

With that one sentence, he blasted through every wall I've worked at assembling. And when he pulled away? Stared down at my body and then stopped?

I'd been vulnerable for a beat, and he gutted me without even trying. As if he didn't like what he saw. Hence, the nightmare wife.

I hate being this self-conscious. But the truth of the matter is that my body has changed since Vivi. Yeah, I grew a human. It's amazing. *Blah, blah, blah.*

But it's hard to avoid the thought that I wasted my best years on Rob Valentine. I worked out. I ran. Made sure you could bounce a dime off my ass. I spent hours at the salon. All so I could hold up the facade of us being a storybook couple everyone would regard with envy.

I looked my best and felt my worst.

I can't blame Theo for taking one long look at me and backing away slowly. Maybe it wasn't the changes in my body, but the truth of who I *am*. A little petty. A little bitter. A lot closed off.

Where's the appeal?

I snort and roll over to sit up. Theo is here for his daughter, which is all I've wanted for her from the beginning. So I need to gather my wits about me and put on a happy face.

Last night, when she cried, I listened to the deep rumble of his voice as he talked to her. Heard the floor creaking as he rocked her.

I laid awake, thinking I should march out there and take her back. Not saddle him with her when she's tired and teething, probably wanting me. But my body failed me. I was so tired I couldn't move.

And my pride wouldn't let me face him after he kissed me and apologized like it was a mistake. So, I drifted off to the sounds of her soft cries and Theo's patient words.

The little lump between my feet moves toward the top of the covers, and those buggy eyes pop out. He shakes the sheet off, ears flapping as he does. He sits and stares at me.

"Don't pee in my bed."

He just blinks.

"Am I supposed to take you out?"

Another blink.

"I went to med school, but they didn't teach me how to speak dog."

Blank look.

"Are you hungry?"

Peter stands up, his tail waving like windshield wipers on a rainy day as his enormous eyes go even wider.

"I thought you were deaf," I say as I rub my eyes and push to stand.

I pull my robe on, and when I turn around, he's still standing there at the edge of my bed looking expectant.

My gaze drops to the floor before lifting back to the small beige dog. "I guess that looks like a real death drop to you, huh?"

With a couple of steps back, I scoop him up and head into the hallway while muttering, "I can't believe I'm talking to a fucking dog."

After setting Peter on the back step so he can do his business, I head into the house, fully expecting to find Theo crashed out on the couch after his first night of solo dad-ing. The man must have a breaking point. Him being this natural at parenting just cannot stand.

But he isn't on the couch or on the chair. My heart rate spikes instantly, my brain spiraling into panic. I barely know the man and I left my baby with him? We haven't talked about custody. What if he's just . . .

My hand flattens on my chest as I force myself to breathe. Then my eyes catch on his shoes at the front door, and my body relaxes a smidgeon.

Maybe they're up already? That's what I tell myself as I walk toward the nursery, forcing myself to take calm, even steps. Panicking is never the answer. I never feel better or think clearer when I panic.

I push it all down, wrap my hand around the doorknob, and peek into the room while telling myself everything is fine.

And it is. Except for the fact that I can't breathe again.

Because it seems Theo did, in fact, reach his parenting breaking point. But of course, it had to be the most precious, heart-twisting, ovary-bursting breaking point in the world.

God. I fucking hate Theo Silva.

I move into the room to get a closer look and can't keep from smiling.

Theo is asleep *inside* the crib. His muscular frame curls around the little girl tucked tightly into the crook of his arm with a peaceful, pleased expression on her face.

And who could blame her? She's known her dad for all of a couple of weeks, and she's got him wrapped around her little finger. He risked it all to test the weight limits of her crib and looks stupidly delicious doing it.

I wish I didn't feel such a powerful attraction to Theo, but he makes it really, really hard. All that mussed dark hair, the dark lashes fanned down in a thick fringe—just like Vivi's—and his broad palm splayed protectively over her back.

And he's so damn *good*. Down to the marrow. I've spent enough time around shit men to recognize the caliber of the man before me.

Some nightmare wife is going to be very lucky to tie him down one day. My job means I'm trained to let people go, but I have a sinking suspicion that letting Theo go will hurt more than it has any right to.

My eyes sting at the sight and I blink rapidly. I *really* need to stop crying.

But this?

It stirs the mom-arazzo in me, so I pull my phone out of my pocket and take a few steps closer to document this moment.

For Theo. He'll want this picture.

And for Vivi. I imagine she'll want this one day too.

I snap the photo and leave. As I stare down at the image, I rub my chest, feeling like I have heartburn just from looking at them.

But I understand the body's inner workings, so I should know better.

This isn't heartburn. It's just me thawing out for the man lying in my daughter's crib.

21
Winter

"What are you doing?" My sister's dark brows knit.

"I don't have a leash."

Peter takes another bite of blueberry muffin from my fingers.

"But why do you have the dog standing *on* my front desk?"

"He's so small. I don't want him to get stepped on. And I don't have a bowl. I'm not going to make him eat off the floor. That's gross. This is a gym." I wave a hand toward the main part of Summer's fitness center. "There are gross, sweaty dudes everywhere."

"Right. But that's a dog. I bet he's eaten literal shit in his lifetime. Why is he getting a blueberry muffin?"

My lip curls as I watch Peter daintily eat a cooked blueberry. "Please don't ruin this newfound canine friendship for me, Sum. I let him sleep in my bed last night."

"Theo?"

I start. "What? No. The dog."

"Oh. Yeah, I've slept with Peter too."

189

I can't help but snort. "How very on brand for us."

Summer's eyes go wide, and I wish I could take back the joke. "It was a joke," I blurt, internally berating myself because I came here to work more at mending my friendship with her and instead, I inadvertently insulted her. "I swear it was a joke. God. Fuck." I scrub a hand over my face. "I'm sorry. I'm still so awkward around you."

My hand is over my eyes when I hear a small chuckle. "I feel like being able to crack rude jokes about Rob is us leveling up, to be honest."

I peek at Summer from between my fingers. "Yeah?"

Her lips roll together as she nods. "Yeah."

I square my shoulders, emboldened by her softness. Sometimes, I still can't believe she doesn't hate me.

With that thought in my head, I blurt out what I came here to say this morning. "I've always loved you and I want you to know that. Even when it hasn't seemed like it. I know you've told me you don't need me to explain myself, but *I* need to explain myself."

My out-of-left-field statement catches her off guard, so I take a sip of my coffee to give my sister a moment.

"Of course. Do you want to go"—she glances around the public gym—"somewhere more private?"

It's still early, so it's quiet except for the clank of metal plates over the low beats that play through the speakers. Some guy who looks like he's doing his best Drax imitation grunts while lifting heavy weights. He's ridiculous.

"No. Here is good. If we go somewhere more private, I'll cry."

Summer's brow furrows. "But you never cry."

"Pfft. Apparently, it's my new thing. It has to be some medical condition I don't know about."

I'm still staring at the man whose biceps must be as big as my head. His veins bulge, and his handsome face is all red as he struggles with the weight.

Theo is so much hotter.

I clear my throat and turn back to my sister, prepared to deliver this update in my I'm-a-doctor-with-bad-news way. "I vaguely remember when you were born. I was three, and I remember feeling excited. I wanted you to be a girl so we could play together. Especially with my dollhouse. I loved that dollhouse."

Summer's eyes twinkle and she crosses her arms over her torso, drawing my eye to the scar running down her chest.

"But it was never quite like I wanted it to be. Marina kept me away from you before I could even understand why, and then Kip was always busy tending to you on his own, so he didn't truly have time for me. It felt like he chose you over me sometimes, but I think I know better now." I wave a hand, not wanting to get into our dad right now. "One time, he had to run to the office while you were napping. Except you woke up and cried. And god . . ." I run a hand through my hair, frustrated at myself because this isn't the delivery I planned. "I must have been four at that point, but I couldn't handle listening to you cry. And Marina planned to just leave you there. She said you were safe in your crib, but I . . ."

I gaze out the window, making a mental note to research crying for no good fucking reason. If I wasn't living the celibate life, I'd worry I'm pregnant again. "You didn't sound safe. You sounded *distraught*. So, when she took a call and left me alone, I snuck into your room. I didn't know what to do, so I crawled into your crib with you and held you. You still cried, but I felt like I was there for you all the same."

Summer is crying again now, right out in the front of her business. Fat, silent tears slide down her cheeks as she stares into my eyes, listening intently. She doesn't look away, no matter how badly it hurts.

I take a deep breath and forge ahead. "When Da—Kip—home, he found us like that, and it turned into this big fight between him and Marina." I sniffle, turning to give Peter more muffin. "I don't remember all the details. Only that Marina took my dollhouse away as a punishment and it never came back because I"—I hold my fingers up in air quotes—"made her look bad."

"Winter, you don't need to go back and relive this. It's okay." Summer steps closer and places her hand on my bicep, squeezing gently.

"No, I do. Because that day, I learned being close with you wouldn't end well for me. And that once you were old enough, it wouldn't end well for you either. I mean, I don't think I *knew* the lesson at the time, but I learned it all the same. Learned we both could fly under the radar best that way. That Marina paid you less attention when I made her look good." I can't help but roll my eyes. "I think I always protected you in my own way. I got comfortable in my role as the evil stepsister, and it just didn't feel worth changing."

Summer nods, the tip of her nose pink from crying. "You're not evil. I wish you'd stop thinking of yourself that way." Her voice breaks and my throat thickens, stupid eyes stinging as they fill.

"Ah, fuck. Come here, Sum." I toss the rest of the muffin down in front of Peter and wrap my arms around my little sister. "I'm just so sorry. I don't know how I'll ever repay you for being here for me and Vivi. I don't know if I deserve all the support, but I've taken it anyway. And you haven't badgered me or asked questions."

"That's not how family works, Winter," she whispers tearfully in my ear. "Plus, Willa told me she caught you sneaking into my hospital room during those years while I was asleep to read my chart and check on me."

I sniff. "Willa has such a big fucking mouth. But yeah, I did that all the time." Then I pull back and look my sister right in the eye. "I love you, Sum."

More tears slide down over the apples of her cheeks, and I peer up at the ceiling like I can use gravity to my advantage and push mine back in.

"I love you too, Win. You really should get this crying thing checked out though."

A laugh lurches from my chest, and it squeezes the tears from my eyes. "Fuck my life. I'm so soft now. What happened to me?"

Summer giggles, and she's joined by another chuckle. One I know well. When I glance back, Sloane has emerged wearing leggings and ballet slippers. I didn't realize she was here, but I should have known. She and Jasper might live at their new house on the ranch, but she still comes in to dance in the back studio. Even when she's around, she and Jasper are constantly taking little vacations and road trips. I feel like I hardly see her these days.

"You're happy." She smiles. "Is it Theo? Does he make you happy?"

Summer smiles, still holding me. "Just don't ask her about dream Theo. He's the worst."

"I'm melting." I wipe my cheeks. "I'm like Frosty the Snowman."

Summer presses her head back down on my shoulder. "Thanks for visiting."

The door jangles, and Willa walks in, fiery mane glowing in the morning sunlight. "Why the fuck is everyone crying? Mondays aren't *that* bad."

"Sloane's not crying." But when I turn to my friend, I notice there is, in fact, a tear rolling down her face. "Jesus. I think my disease is infectious." I continue to swipe at my face. "Everyone stop."

"Yeah, seriously." Willa looks between the three of us. "You're supposed to make grown men cry at this gym, not have some weird *Yaya Sisterhood* cryfest at the front door. And why is there a dog on the front desk?"

Leave it to Willa to lighten the mood without trying.

"That's Theo's dog, Peter."

She steps up to the desk and scratches Peter behind the ears. He licks his lips, small belly all round and full when he sits. "Like Peter North? Nice."

"Willa. Please. No." Summer scrubs at her face.

"What? It's just that with the way he's sitting, I can see that for his body size he has a pretty big—"

"Attitude," I cut her off and let out a watery laugh. "He's got a big attitude."

My sister glances up at me, still pressed close. "Thank. You."

"Willa, what are you doing here?" Sloane asks, trying to redirect the conversation.

"Cade told me to take the morning to myself. So here I am, ready to work out."

"Work out?" I arch a brow.

"Yeah," Summer says. "Willa has decided she wants me to train her."

Willa gestures her chin in my direction. "Winter, you should join us. Summer is vicious. I'm ready for her to hurt me and come out with a killer bubble butt."

I smile politely, but I don't know if I'm ready to add that dynamic to Summer and me yet. I'm not sure if it's what we need.

She must agree, because my sister says, "I could set you up with a different trainer. Might be good for you. I'll watch Vivi and give you a break. If you do it at the end of the day, I can put her to bed."

Relief washes over me because it does appeal. Maybe I could make the time.

"That might be good. I could ask Theo to watch Vivi too," I say, stepping away from Summer to give her a grateful glance. She's intuitive. She knows.

"Where *is* Vivi?" Sloane asks, and I sigh, sounding a bit like a lovesick teenager.

"She's with Theo. We traded for the night. Actually ..." I pull out my phone and hold it up so they can see the photo of Theo and Vivi in her crib.

There is a communal intake of breath before a resounding chorus of "Aww."

"Yeah, you should definitely bang him again," Willa says.

Summer reaches for my free hand, squeezing tight and staring up at me, even though I don't look back.

Did seeing Theo in the crib this morning take me back? Yes.

Did my conversation with him last night make me want to talk to her? Yes.

Do Theo and Vivi make me want to be a better person? Also, yes.

I swing by Le Pamplemousse, my favorite coffee shop in Chestnut Springs, and grab Theo a coffee. After days on end of him bringing me coffee with a smile on his face, I should return the favor.

But when I walk up to our matching bungalows, a flurry of butterflies erupts in my stomach. Last night we kissed. I yanked him down on me. He got an eyeful and walked away.

This is fine. Perfectly normal. I repeat positive sentences. I manifest that shit.

"Theo is a mature man. This is fine. We will be fine. It was just a pussy. He's seen lots of pussies."

The last part doesn't actually make me feel better, so I bite down on my inner cheek to shut myself up. Peter trembles under my arm like he thinks I'm full of shit.

"Shut up, Peter," I mumble as I open the gate into my front yard. From here, I can hear music coming from the house. The nearer I draw, the more the song takes shape. "Mystify" by INXS blares from inside, and I'm pretty sure I can hear Theo's deep voice singing along.

With a shake of my head, I place Peter on the ground and unlock the front door. I step in and stop in my tracks.

Theo has on the same clothes he wore last night. A smiling Vivi is strapped to his chest in the floral-patterned Tula baby carrier I bought.

He's singing to our daughter. And dancing. And *cleaning*.

One hand rubs the back of her head like she's some sort of crystal ball, while the other wipes at the white cabinets in the cottage-style kitchen.

The house smells like lemon Lysol. He's cracked the windows, letting the summer morning breeze waft through. I've been out sipping a coffee while reading the newspaper and then visiting my sister and friends. A part of me feels guilty I haven't been here helping.

Vivi stares up at him like he's the most impressive man in the world. And fuck, she might be right.

But me? I'm just slack-jawed.

Frozen.

But Peter isn't.

He trots right into the kitchen and yaps at Theo's feet, surprising him right as he belts out another, "Mistifyyyyyy."

Theo spins to take us in as he pulls his phone out of a back pocket to drop the volume. "Jesus, Peter. Warn a guy."

"What are you doing?" My voice is full to the brim with disbelief as I look around my sparkling clean house.

Theo rolls his eyes at me. "Cleaning."

"Why?"

He grins, gives me a wink, and blesses the side of my ass with a playful slap. "I just felt like it. That coffee for me, Tink?"

I glance down at the cup in my hand. "Yeah. I figured you'd need it after last night." I'm acutely aware of the way his eyes blatantly rake over my body, trailing down and back up.

My cheeks heat as I wonder if he's thinking about how I don't look like I did the last time he saw me naked. I push those thoughts away, because none of that matters. We are just ... not business partners, apparently.

Teammates? Co-parents?

Co-parents could work.

"Here." I shove the coffee at him. Up close, he's even hotter. His stubble has grown a little longer than the perfectly groomed shadow he usually sports, but it suits him. Even with a bit of darkness under his eyes ... he's just more rugged somehow. More masculine.

It's annoying that I look like trash when I'm tired and he looks like *this*.

The fact that he's got our child strapped to his chest enhances the appeal by a million. But it doesn't matter in the least what Theo looks like. I could see him carrying Vivi, singing a song, cleaning my goddamn house, and I wouldn't notice his physicality at all.

I'd just see a man so deeply dependable that I'd want to rip my clothes off and suck his dick in thanks. It's a biological loophole, I swear. Because for the life of me, I can't hold a grudge against Theo when he's done nothing but show up for me, no matter how much I've snarled at him.

When he takes the coffee, I try to pull away, but his hand is too big. Too sure. His fingers wrap over mine and he gently guides me closer to them.

"Vivi, look how sweet your mom is, bringing me a coffee."

I glance down at her and a sudden surge of longing hits me. I haven't been away from her overnight before. And suddenly I want nothing more than to pull her out of the carrier and nuzzle into her neck where there are still traces of baby smell.

I drop my forehead against hers. "Good morning, sweet baby," I say as I press a kiss to her soft, pudgy cheek.

When I glance up, Theo points at a familiar stack of envelopes. "Those from your ex? I wasn't snooping. I just found them underneath a pile of magazines."

I swallow, deciding how to play this off. For some reason, I don't want Theo and Rob intersecting. Rob isn't welcome here, sullying this happy little bubble.

Looking around my house, I can't help but feel like Theo has already stepped into a colossal mess. I don't need to add to that burden with drama from my ex.

"Yeah. Don't worry about it. He keeps sending bills for things like our wedding or house, as though I owe him something when

I don't." I swipe a hand between us like it doesn't bother me at all. But it does. Rob did this same thing with Summer. He could never let her go. Her disinterest became some sort of slight to him, and now I'm getting the same treatment.

The man won't give me peace, even though I specifically took *nothing* in our divorce to get rid of him. But it still wasn't enough.

"There's no postage on them though. Is he dropping them off here? Is that why you have the cameras up?"

It is, but not because I think he'd do anything violent. Just because if I see him at the door, I don't want to answer.

"Mama."

That one word instantly changes the subject.

I freeze and stare down at my daughter, and then I glance up at Theo. "Did she just say . . ."

"Mama?" Theo quirks a brow at me and slides a palm down the center of my back, stopping when he hits the waistline of my yoga pants. Then he . . . leaves it there. His big, warm palm at the small of my back. Sure, and steady, and supportive.

"That's her first word." I stare at her in wonder.

"Of course it is. What else would it be? And she's been saying it all morning." He turns his gaze back to Vivi. "Haven't you, baby girl? Been talking about your mama nonstop. And who could blame you? Look at her." They both turn their big brown eyes on me, and suddenly I'm aware of how close we're standing. My hand on Vivi. Vivi's hand on Theo. Theo's hand on me.

Connected.

We will always be connected.

"She's beautiful, isn't she?" Theo carries on, blissfully unaware of the turmoil this moment stirs in me. "Just like you. Imagine how beautiful she'll look when she gets back from getting her nails done."

"What?" My brows knit and my head flips toward Theo.

He removes his hand from my back to check his watch. "Yeah. I booked you a manicure for ten."

"But you've been with Vivi all night. All morning."

He shrugs, a gentle smile stretching over his too-handsome features. "I don't need a special trophy for parenting. I love it, Winter. Don't worry. Go enjoy your manicure while you can still get one."

His hand returns to my back as he nudges me toward the door. "But I—"

"No buts. You go. I'll be here. I got this."

I turn and give him a stern stare, one finger up. "I'll be back before lunch."

He chuckles and *winks*. "No, you won't. I booked your massage right after the manicure. Sloane is meeting you there and for lunch. See you later, Mama."

He leans forward, maneuvering around my hand to drop a light, *friendly* kiss right beside my mouth. I'm pushed out the door before I can even speak. The music cranks back up before I've even moved off the front step.

At the salon, my nails finally have their day. I select a pretty shade of pink and Sloane picks a bright purple. After our massages, we fill our faces at our favorite spot in town, chat, and laugh until our cheeks hurt. It is truly the perfect girls' day out.

I feel more myself than I have in months. I feel more relaxed than I have in years.

And when I get back that afternoon—all pampered, and rested, and sane—I walk into a spotless house. A happy little girl plays with wooden blocks on the carpet. Theo builds them up, and she knocks them down, laughing hysterically while he acts offended that she could do that to him. On the stove, a delicious aroma wafts from a large pot. Theo calls it "Brazilian Stroganoff" and says it's something his dad used to make for his mom.

And when I go to bed that night, the hinges on my door don't squeak at all.

22
Theo

Winter: I'm going to go work out tonight. Summer offered to watch Vivi, but if you aren't working, you can have her instead.

Theo: Unfortunately, I'm working tonight. I close the gym. Are you working out alone? I could help you.

Winter: No, you don't need to do that. Summer booked me a session with another trainer. Max, I think?

Theo: You could have asked me.

Winter: I don't want to work out with you.

Theo: Is it because you're going to wear tight pants you know will give me a boner?

Winter: This job must be hard on you with your uncontrollable erections.

Theo: The gym is fine. It's living next to you that's the issue.

"**N**o." Winter's arms cross under her breasts, propping them up in the most appealing way.

I've spent the past twenty-four hours thinking about her new pink nails and how good they'd look wrapped around my dick. And now she's gotta create a shelf under her tits and put them on perfect display for me.

I'm going to have to deep-clean my own house to keep my hormones in check. My mom used to bug me and say the Virgo in me would stress clean. I laughed her off, but the older I get, the more I wonder if she was onto something.

Is horny cleaning a Virgo thing? Cause that's where I'm at right now. I could clean this whole fucking gym and it wouldn't sate me.

"Yes," I deadpan back at Winter while Summer shifts awkwardly on the spot, Vivi babbling happily in her arms.

"I had my session booked with some Max guy."

I groan and roll my eyes. No chance that was happening.

Summer shoots me a look, and I give her my best puppy dog eyes. "Somehow, the schedule got changed around. It'll be fine. Theo knows this stuff inside and out."

"I'm not paying for him to work out with me. He's not even certified."

I stifle a laugh. Tink is *mad*. "I am. Did the course during my off-season. But you don't have to pay. I'll do it for free."

Summer's eyes volley between us. Amusement and nerves war on her face as she bounces on the spot, clearly not sure what to do with herself. "Theo insisted that it be him—"

"Summer," I cut her off. "You can go. I'll talk to Winter."

"Don't tell her what to do. This is *her* gym. I'm *her* sister. And this is supposed to be *my* free time."

"Okay! On that note, Vivi and I have a date with the bathtub and her rubber duckies." Summer's tone is altogether too bright, smile too forced.

Winter turns on her. "You're taking his side?"

Summer's head tilts and her eyes roam over Winter's face. "No, Win. I'm taking *your* side. This will be good for you. Go take care of yourself. I've got your girl."

She looks at us both when she says *your girl* and makes a show of waving at both Winter and me before turning around and leaving the gym.

"I don't want to work out with you," Winter announces without glancing my way.

"Something else you'd rather do instead?"

Winter's eyes roll as if I exhaust her, but her tone has no malice when she says, "I hate you."

A chuckle rumbles from the back of my throat, and a knowing smile touches my lips. She didn't hate me when she tugged me down on top of her. "Haven't you figured out that doesn't deter me at all?"

She scoffs, turning away to scan the gym floor. Various machines and weights litter the space in a sort of organized chaos, but in a town this size, it's quiet at this time of night. The group classes have filtered out and only a few stragglers remain.

"I could take you for tequila again."

Her shoulders stiffen. "Yeah. That ended so well last time."

I step closer to her, admiring the elegant column of her neck. She always holds her head so high. I admire that about her. No shame, like the opinions of those around her don't matter to her—even though I know they do. She's *strong*.

"I think it ended pretty well." I trail a finger up the indent that runs through the center of her back, right over her spine. She shivers but makes no move to pull away. I lean forward and whisper in her ear. "I still think about pressing you up against that window. The way you trembled when I—"

"That's not what I meant." She swallows, eyes full of pride. I see the tip of her tongue dart out over lips.

"Did you mean Vivi? Because I thought nothing would be sexier than that night. Until I saw you with her."

A small whimper escapes from her lips, and she steps away. "Yeah, sure. Until you decide you want to trade me in and shack up with some bimbo buckle bunny with a porn voice and give Vivi a new stepmom."

"What?" My brows knit as she finally turns to me, glancing around to see if anyone is watching us.

She snorts. "I had a dream about it. She was hot. I mean, good for you. It just made me realize things might get complicated. I'll have to share Christmas morning—"

"With me and my bimbo wife?" I roll my lips in to stifle a laugh.

"Yes!" Her hands shoot out, annoyance billowing from her in waves.

"Can you give me a demo of this porn voice?"

Winter swaps her facial expression, batting her eyelashes so fast it looks like something is stuck in her eye. "Oh, Theo, there aren't any chairs left. Can I rub my ass all over your lap for Christmas?" she mocks, and I don't bother holding back the laughter anymore.

"Is that what she said?"

"Basically. Before grinding herself all over you."

"That sounds like a pretty great Christmas gift."

Her lips twitch. This conversation is ridiculous, and she knows it. "You're the fucking worst."

"You're the one who's mad at me for something I did in a dream."

"I'm not mad at you." Her arms cross. "I'm mad at the future."

"Don't be. I promise you that's not what the future holds."

"Okay, I'm mad at you for torpedoing my training session with someone who doesn't constantly hit on me. Why did you do that?"

I shake my head as I breeze past her, through the turnstile and onto the gym floor. Might as well be honest with her, so she isn't confused about what I want. "Because I'm the only one who's going to be putting his hands on you in those tight fucking pants, Tink."

Winter is lying on a bench in front of a long bank of mirrors. Racks of dumbbells line the lower part of the wall in front of her. She has her knees bent, her sneakers resting against the end of the gray pleather seat, and her palms covering her forehead as she stares up at the ceiling.

I'd worry I worked her too hard, but we kept things light. I showed her the machines she can use in her free time to get back into things slowly. It was on the turf floor that everything went to shit.

I started her in plank pose, set a slider under each foot, and had her use her core to drag her feet toward herself, piking up into a V-shape. Then she'd walk her hands back out and start over.

At first, she seemed unsteady and struggled with the exercise. But she wasn't a quitter, and I supported her where I could. A hand on her hip. One flat on her bare back where her tank top had ridden up.

It was why I went into the computer system and changed her session to be with me. Not a fucking chance would I sit at home while some Roid Monkey ran his hands all over her under the guise of helping her work out.

When I tugged the fabric back down to cover her, she snapped. In a flash, she dropped to her knees and rolled up into standing.

"Yeah. My core sucks after pregnancy. No need to rub it in. I'm done now. I'm going to go stretch."

And with that, she marched off without a backward glance. If she'd bothered to look, she'd have seen me staring at her ass.

I decided not to push her and started tidying the gym for closing. Putting away the plates people left all over the place. Wiping down touch points. Bidding patrons farewell as they head out the door.

And through it all, Winter has laid there on the weight bench, not moving. And definitely not stretching.

I decide to wait her out and let her have whatever moment she needs. As I slip behind the front desk and turn the music down, the last guy here walks out of the dressing room. His head snaps in Winter's direction and he hesitates before walking over to where she's still laid out.

He hikes his bag up on his meaty shoulder and tips his head down over her. I don't like the way he's leering at her. And I hate the way he says, "Hi," with that dorky, bashful smile, like he hasn't been eyeing her up all night.

"You okay?"

"No," Winter replies, making my stomach drop.

He crouches beside her head as if she invited him to talk to her some more. "I saw you here yesterday."

My feet move before I realize what I'm doing. All I know is I don't want him towering over her while she's laid out like that. I don't want his eyes on her body. Not today, not yesterday. I want him *out*.

"Thought that sometime we could—"

Winter doesn't even turn her head to look at the guy. "Goddamn, I wish I had your confidence. My life would be so different."

I come to a screeching halt several feet away from where his massive back stretches against his tank top.

"Pardon me?"

"I just told you I'm not okay, so you ask me out? If I didn't want so desperately for you to leave me alone, I'd ask what leap of logic brought you to the conclusion that this was the way to go."

He pushes to stand, ears a little pink, like she embarrassed him. "I . . . I just thought—"

"Hey, pal. We're closed. Time to head out." Maybe he deserves a chance to defend himself. Winter can be harsh, but I'm also irrationally happy to watch him fail.

He can't handle her claws.

Not like I can.

His thick brows pull together over his pronounced forehead. "I think there might be something wrong with her." He points at Winter, who still hasn't moved, and to his credit, he looks concerned.

"Yeah." My lips twitch as I stare past him at Winter, who glares at me for agreeing with him. "I know there is. That's what I like about her."

His eyes go wide as understanding blooms on his face. "Sorry, man. See ya tomorrow."

I give him a nod and prop my hands on my hips, eyes latched

onto Winter. She's intentionally avoiding my gaze now. I can tell by the tense set of her jaw and the vein throbbing in her neck.

When the door slams shut, Winter flinches, and I watch a subtle pink flush dust her high cheekbones.

"Winter. Look at me."

"No, thank you." Her jaw pops. So stubborn. Reminds me of getting Vivi to settle down the other night. Must get that from her mom.

"Should I turn the lights off and leave you here?"

"Well, you've got the leaving me alone part down pat. Why stop now?"

With only a couple of steps, I'm behind her, crouching at the head of the bench, one hand gently cupping her throat as I stare down at her face. "It's almost like you've forgotten I like when you hiss at me, Winter."

Her wide blue eyes snap to mine.

"Tell me what you're doing."

"Lying here." She fires the words from between her lips like projectiles.

"Why?" My hand tightens, fingers gripping her chin to tip her head back and have her look at me.

"Gravity."

"Gravity?"

"Because if I sit up straight, the tears will fall out. And I don't cry." I notice it then, the sheen to her eyes, the way they fill as I watch. My chest seizes at the sight. Her face is a window into all her feelings. "I'm not at my best right now, Theo. I'm in a bad mood. I'm angry, and it doesn't even make sense. You should leave me alone."

"You know what I think, Winter?" My thumb strokes over her pulse point.

"No, but I bet you're going to tell me anyway."

"I think people mistake you being in a bad mood when you're just overwhelmed. I think you needed to lie here for a few minutes with no one *needing* you. I think you're overstimulated and even the best of us require some time to collect ourselves."

She nods, lips rolling together, and one lone tear slips down her cheek, my thumb brushing it away almost instantly.

"I don't—"

"I know." I nod solemnly. "I'm pretty sure it's a leak in the ceiling."

She snorts now, head shaking as her hands cover her face. "Why are you so nice to me?"

"We've been over this. It's because I like you."

"That was a year and a half ago." Her hands drop to my arm, but not to push me away. They rest there.

"Well, you're hard to forget. And the thing is, I like you even more now."

"Is that why you keep putting my clothes back on me?"

I still. "What?"

"The other night you took one look at me and pulled my nightgown back down. Today you covered me up again. It feels like you don't like what you see."

With a growl, I push her up to sitting, swing a leg over the bench and straddle the seat behind her. One arm around her ribs tugs her straight back into me and I see her shocked expression in the mirror's reflection.

"Don't like what I see?" Her back is pressed up against my chest, pulse vibrating through her body. "Winter, you have no fucking idea what I see. No fucking clue how hard I'm trying not to be another person who needs something from you. I'm prioritizing what life has thrown at us in the past few weeks. I'm trying to give *you* what you *need*. But if you think I don't like what I see, then I'm not the one who needs his head checked." I swipe her ponytail to the side of her neck and drop a kiss on the top of her slender shoulder. "Because your wellbeing has quickly become my number one priority."

"Why?" Her ragged breathing echoes in the otherwise quiet gym.

"Because I fucking adore you. Haven't you been paying attention?"

She shivers and I watch the fine hairs at the back of her neck stand on end when I breathe against her skin.

"Why?"

"Why do I fucking adore you?"

"Yeah. And if you say it's because my body performed miracles growing and birthing a baby or some shit like that, I swear I will get up and walk out of here."

I grin at the image of us in the mirror, her all fierce and flushed but also relaxing back into me. A small sign of trust from a woman who doesn't trust easily.

One I won't squander.

I trail a finger up the side of her slender neck. "This line right here. You carry yourself like royalty. There's something about this curve, the little hairs." I pinch the hairs and give them a gentle tug, eliciting a gasp from her. "Sometimes, when it's sunny in the morning, the light through the front living room window catches all these little flyaways that end up looking like a halo."

She stares at me in the mirror.

"Can I keep touching you?" I rub my stubble against her shoulder before dotting a kiss on the bump where her collarbone attaches.

She nods while swallowing. Her responding, "Yes," is a whisper.

"I like your collarbones." My left hand grips her hip while my right one dips under her arm and over her chest so I can trace the line of bones framing it. "Mine will always look a little crooked now. But if that's the price I had to pay to get your attention . . . I'd break the other one myself."

"Weird. But okay."

My hand shoots up, and I press my pointer finger to her plush mouth while gently cupping her jaw. "I love your lips. This smart fucking mouth. I like the venom it spews. I especially like the way it looked wrapped around my cock."

She moans.

"You liked that too, didn't you?" Her body clenches and I squeeze her thigh before trailing the tips of my fingers over the inside seam of her leggings. "I know you did."

"I—"

I cover her mouth with my free hand. "Don't bother arguing with me. It makes me hard, and I'm not above flipping you over and fucking you right here and now." I grind into her lower back, my dick already straining at the front of my shorts.

I watch her eyes change in the mirror. Instead of tears, they fill with heat. *Longing.*

With one hand still over her mouth, I slide the other under the loose tank top she's wearing. She makes no effort to escape my hold. Her sports bra is tight, but it doesn't stop me.

"I love your breasts." I palm one and then the other before

tweaking a nipple. "Your nipples get hard so easily. They're so sensitive." I tweak again, and her eyes drift closed. "I know that waste of space you married didn't know how to make you come. But I do. And I bet I can do it by playing with these alone."

Her head tips back onto my shoulder, her back arching as she presses her breast into my hand. It's like I can feel her coming back to life. *For me.*

I release her nipple and slide my hand down her stomach, into her stretchy pants. I go straight for her core, running my finger through her soaked flesh before shoving it in. She clamps down on my digit and tries to cry out, but the sound is muffled by my palm.

"And this." I work it in and out of her a couple of times. "You. I love how you look impaled on my cock. Open your eyes. Look in the mirror."

I add a second finger and plunge into her wet heat, watching her lashes flicker open to meet my gaze. "Look at us. How could I not fucking adore this? I love the face you make when you fall apart for me. Am I still the only man who's been able to fuck you right, Winter?"

Her head moves in a shallow nodding motion, her legs spreading wider to grant me deeper access.

"I bet I could make you come on my fingers just describing how beautiful you are to me right now. How fucking perfect you are." I rasp my stubble against the shell of her ear and drop my voice. "But that would be a shame when you have such a pretty pussy for me to eat, don't you think?"

She pants, her chest heaving and rosy. And just like before, her icy exterior melts away and leaves *this* woman. This confident, amazing woman, who's occupied my brain and my body for well over a year now.

I drop my hand from her mouth, and we stare at each other in the mirror for several beats. My eyes are nearly black, while hers appear almost lighter. Brighter. More vibrant.

"You don't have t—"

"You're still not listening." I stand and step around the bench, coming to kneel at the foot with a knowing grin. Winter looks flustered as she glances around. "I like everything I see. I want *you*."

Her throat works, and she drops my gaze. I know there's a cruel voice inside her, filling her head with shit that isn't true. "What if someone comes in?"

"As long as I'm the one with my head between your legs, I don't care who watches."

Her mouth pops open in shock. "I don't know what kind of weird shit you get up to on the circuit but—"

"What kind of *weird shit*?" I quirk a brow at her. "The only 'weird shit' I've been up to is abstaining from touching anyone at all. And you sitting here in these tight fucking clothes"—I reach for the waistband of her pants and tug—"giving me those tortured fuck-me eyes is shredding my self-control. Like you're begging me to be inside you."

Her leggings and underwear hit the point where she'll need to lift her hips for me to pull them down any further. But Winter's ass stays planted on the bench, hands propped behind her. "What do you mean, abstaining from touching anyone at all?"

Cat's out of the bag, I guess. Might as well come clean.

"I mean, I cleaned up my act."

"Why?"

I huff out a breath and hold her gaze, wanting her to really hear this. "Because I wanted to be the type of guy who could land you for more than one night."

Her gaze bounces around my face. "You mean someone *like* me?"

"No, Winter. I mean *you*. That's why I gave up my old phone. That's why I have your number on my new one. I intended to call you. You needed time to rebuild, and I needed time to grow into someone who deserves you. I was biding my time, being patient."

Her breath falls faster, stronger—choppier—as she regards me. It's like I can see the pieces of the puzzle snapping into place, see her mind whirring. Which is why I reach for her hips and haul her toward me, taking the waistline of her pants as I go. Her hands fall to my shoulders when I look up at her and grin, tugging roughly at the stretchy pants that are now nothing more than flimsy fabric getting in my way.

"I'm done being patient, Tink. I'm coming for what I want. Right now."

23
Winter

I've often thought about that night with Theo. Okay, I've obsessed over it. And I was certain I imagined how much he enjoyed going down on me. At first, I felt guilty.

"It's okay, you don't need to," I said, while grabbing at his hair, trying to pull him back up.

He laughed, a deep rumble that I felt against my core. Eyes sparking, he stared up at me from between my legs. "I know I don't need to, Tink. But I really, really want to."

I'd never felt as naked as I did with his eyes fixed on the most private part of me.

I haven't been with many men. I was too busy with school and then work.

And I definitely haven't been with any men who ate my pussy with a smile. Which is what he did.

I had my first orgasm that night, with Theo Silva's manicured stubble rasping against my inner thighs. I should be sad it took me twenty-eight years to have that moment, and yet, I'm not.

There was something poetic about it. Unforgettable. And right now, I'm taken back to that exact spot as Theo yanks my leggings from my body like he can't wait another second.

"I just worked out," I huff out before I internally berate myself for trying to sabotage this moment when I know how good it feels. How badly I want it.

Theo's deep, amused chuckle is what I get in return. He spreads my legs and stares down at me. The bright halogen lights leave me nowhere to hide. "You barely broke a sweat. Which means I didn't work you hard enough. But I will now."

The pads of his fingers trail over the inside of my thighs, leaving gooseflesh in their wake.

"Someone could walk in," I say again.

I hate myself. Why can't I just shut up and enjoy good things?

He nods as he leans forward and drags his tongue over the length of my pussy. A deep, satisfied, "Mmm," crests his lips. "I hope they do, Winter. I hope we have a whole fucking audience to watch how hard I'm going to make you come."

My heart beats so fast I swear I can feel my sternum vibrating. Why does that sound so good? Why is this man so feral in so many ways? And then so fucking sweet? I can't keep up with it.

There's nothing polite or clinical about the way he lifts my legs and props one foot on each of his shoulders. "The only way I'm not eating this pussy is if you tell me to stop, Winter."

I stare at him. Pulse thrumming. Chest heaving. Lips parted.

And I don't say a single thing.

I nod.

And just like all those months ago, he grins against my core and then latches on like he needs me more than the air he breathes.

There are no tentative tongue strokes, no holding back. He devours me, and the edges of my vision go blurry. My hands reach above my head, gripping the bench to hold myself back.

Theo suffers from no such concern. His hands roam all over my body. Stroking. Squeezing. He doesn't hold back with me. Doesn't treat me like I'm breakable, or like I need breaking.

He treats me like I'm perfect. Irresistible. *Worthy.*

With one hand clamped around my shaking thigh, he brings the other to my center and guides two fingers into me with an aching slowness. His tongue makes unhurried swipes at my clit, like he has nowhere else to be. Like his mind isn't in a million other places.

I'm anticipating the slow stretch, the fullness that drives me wild. The patient kisses he presses to my thighs, to my stomach.

"Fuck, Theo."

"How does that feel, Winter?"

I respond with a whimpery hum as I dig my fingers into the tacky seat. I'm holding on for dear life, like I'm on the precipice of something that terrifies me. My brain is too full, my heart too confused. All this sensation muddles me. It pulls me apart until I'm just a puddle for Theo to play with.

His fingers drag out and I can feel my wetness as he spreads it over my lips. "Not good enough?" he murmurs. "Guess I need to step up my game."

My back arches and I cry out as he pushes back in with a third finger, or a fourth. I don't even know, and I'm not about to look. All I know is it feels like a lot.

"How does it feel now?"

"So fucking good." The words rush from my lips. "Don't stop."

I hear his pleased growl but keep my eyes fixed on the ceiling beams and the hanging industrial lights. Making eye contact with him right now might make me combust.

"How could I stop when I'm loving the way you look with my fingers stuffed inside you?"

Heat scorches my cheeks, and my hips buck toward him. Involuntarily. Or at least that's what I tell myself.

My brain has left the building. It's only my body now. And my body wants Theo Silva. I give in and let go of the bench, reaching for him. My fingers tangle in his thick hair.

And just like before, my body lights up for him. I grind into his mouth, and he meets my thrusts with equal fervor.

He spears me with his tongue, fucks me with his fingers, and takes the odd bite of my oversensitive flesh any time I get close to tipping over the edge. My body soars when he takes a long, firm pull on my clit while shoving his fingers into me roughly.

"Theo." I tug his hair. "Theo, I'm going to come."

He pulls back for a beat, and I finally meet his dark, wild eyes, full of lust. "Nah. You don't come, remember?"

He looks so *smug*.

"Keep going." I ignore his jab, whining and trying to pull his face down. Acting as desperate as I feel.

"Admit it." His fingers move again.

My head lowers back down on the bench. "Admit wh-what?" I stutter when he curls his fingers inside me and hits a spot that makes me see stars.

"That you only come for me. And that you fucking love it. All that snarling. All that unaffected nail-gazing. All those scowls. They all disappear when you have my face between your legs. I can fuck you happy, can't I, Winter?"

"I hate you." I glare at him, but there's no malice. How can there be when he's right?

His fingers push and twist and my body bows toward him like the deceitful little hussy it is.

"Admit it. Then I'll let you come. Tell me what I need to hear."

What he needs to hear? I'm panting, body pulled tight. I'm wound up to the point where I could burst.

So I admit it, as much to him as to myself.

"Theo, I only come for you and—"

He doesn't let me finish before he's back to devouring me, and within seconds, I burst. Just like I predicted.

A hot wave rolls through my body, and I give myself over to it. Thrashing in the heat. Relishing in the feel of a man who likes making me come, likes watching me fall apart for him.

He doesn't push me too far. He doesn't pull away too soon. He is so damn good at this.

So damn good to me.

I don't just come. I come apart. I feel like I could break forever, over and over again, under the worshipping hands of Theo Silva.

Which is a terrifying prospect, because I've broken before.

And no one has ever helped me pick up the pieces.

I expected more after he went down on me. But he picked up my pants and carefully bunched them up over my ankles like he was dressing a child. I watched him, deft hands, veined forearms—one that should probably still be in a sling—and a look of satisfied concentration on his face.

"Don't you want me to . . ." I trail off, rolling my wrist to explain

220

my train of thought and realizing I feel a little shy. A little lost for words. A little out of my element.

What he did? The things he said? They shouldn't have felt so momentous, but they did. And it terrified me. He isn't just some hot one-night stand anymore. He's the father of our little girl. I'll be connected to him for the rest of my life, whether or not I want to be.

Whether or not he wants me.

This could be everything. Or it could be the biggest disaster of my life.

So when he smirks, rakes his eyes over me as I fix my fucked-up ponytail, and says, "Nah. I'm good," my mind goes crazy.

He grips my chin and presses a hard kiss to my mouth before turning away to finish closing the gym. I taste myself, but all I can focus on are those two words echoing in my head.

I'm good.

As in, it satisfied him too?

Or like *Ew, no thanks*?

He spent countless minutes divulging all the things he likes about me. It seems unlikely he wouldn't want to do more. And yet, that's where my brain is trained to go.

My dad chose someone else.

My husband chose someone else. He chose my sister.

And I don't resent her for it. I resent myself, because what is it about me that is so profoundly unlovable? I feel like I'm on a constant mission to figure that one thing out. I'm not offended by it. I just need to know what it is so I can fix it.

"Ready?" Theo's voice startles me. My head snaps up to him from where I sit on the bench, lost in thought. His eyes lick up and down over me and my traitor body shivers in response.

I offer back a nod, which makes the annoying dimple pop up on Theo's cheek. He's biting back the smirk, but he still winks.

My stomach flips. Every time he does that, I remember him pumping gas the night I met him. He was hot then, but with another couple of years on him, he's changed again. At twenty-eight he's more man than boy. His shoulders seem wider. He's more angular, more chiseled, more ... overwhelming. And he's got a maturity about him, a wise streak I find comforting. He's playful but not flighty. Fun but dependable.

If I had to fuck a stranger and get knocked up, I picked a good one. If nothing else, Vivienne will have a great dad in her life.

"Did I kill some brain cells, Doctor Hamilton?"

I realize I'm just standing in the now darkened gym, staring at Theo like it's my default mode.

Theo reaches for my hand, and I take it. My body moves toward him without me even thinking about it. Without me even admitting I want to.

His warm palm is calloused, proof of the years spent hanging on to a bull rope every weekend and lifting weights during the week. His thumb grazes the top of my hand as he sets the alarm system and leads me into the warm summer night.

With only the crunching of our feet on the loose gravel in the back lane, I finally say what I've been thinking. "I feel like I owe you."

"Owe me what?" His voice is smooth and velvety tonight, and it brushes up against my skin. It soothes me.

"Sex, or something."

"Or something? Now that part has me interested. What *is* the 'or something'?" He cracks the joke, not realizing the way my mind can take it, spin it, and twist into something he never meant for it to be. Like he wouldn't want the sex.

"Funny." I glance down at our hands as he takes his fingers and threads them through mine.

"Hey." His tone is less playful now, and I can't meet his eyes. "Don't drop your head like that. Stop thinking whatever you're thinking, because I guarantee it's wrong."

He stops, tugging me to face him, and lifts my chin with a bent knuckle. "Winter."

Inky eyes and hair, golden skin; the darkness of the night gives him an edge.

I lick my lips. "Theo."

"Yeah, Tink?"

"I don't understand what's happening here. The things you say. The things you do. Everything that's happened. It doesn't make sense. I can't figure it out."

He tilts his head, as if he's trying to figure me out from a different perspective. "What's happening is Miss Independent met the treat-her-like-a-princess guy, and she's freaking out."

I roll my eyes. "That's ridiculous."

"You only think you owe me something because you've spent too long dating assholes who are terrible lays. Just sit back and enjoy the ride. Stop overthinking it. Plus, my face is the ride." His lips twitch and I mirror the motion.

"You're insane." I pull away, trying to hide my laughter. But I don't let go of his hand as we round the end of the block, heading back toward our respective houses.

"But it's a nice face, isn't it? If you had to ride one?"

Laughter bubbles up in me. It fills my chest and clogs my throat.

It bursts from me like a song I can't resist singing. It sounds foreign to me, light and musical.

God. Am I *giggling*?

His fingers pulse in mine, and then he tugs me back and kisses me. His mouth slants over mine and he swallows my laughter like he wants to keep it for himself.

He created it, so I suppose it's only fair I give it back to him. Our fingers stay linked and his opposite hand dusts over my jaw with a light tremor.

Soft lips. Soft hair. Soft sighs. It's not a long kiss, but it's a heart-rending one. Natural, as though he couldn't help himself.

And not for the first time tonight, I feel *wanted*.

When he pulls away, I leave my eyes shut for a moment, letting this feeling warm me. Because it's fleeting and I want to remember it.

My eyes are still closed when he leans in and says, "Next time, you ride my face. You're going to ask for it. Beg for it. Work for it even. You will tell me *exactly* what you want, and I will give it to you. But this isn't happening again until that time. Until you know what you want. Because I want you, Winter. And not just for one night."

With that, he takes my breath and pulls me along with him down the quiet, tree-lined street. My brain goes from freaking out about Theo to freaking out about the woman sitting on his front step.

I know I shouldn't.

He says I've been part of his plan. But I'm terrified to believe it.

24
Theo

Theo: I need to ask you a favor.

Summer: Sure!

Theo: But you can't ask questions.

Summer: Suspicious. But okay.

Theo: I need to delete some of your security cam footage at the gym. Can you show me how?

Summer: Uhhhh. Okay. Can I do it for you?

Theo: No.

Summer: Was a crime committed?

Theo: No.

Summer: Do I even want to know?

Theo: I said no questions and so far, you've asked three.

Winter goes from soft and giddy to all locked up. When I glance down, I see her tight jaw and narrowed eyes. I follow her gaze to a woman sitting on my front step, scrolling through her phone.

A woman I'd know anywhere.

"Mom? What are you doing here?"

Winter jolts, yanking her hand from mine like we're two teenagers caught doing something we shouldn't, rather than two adults who share a child.

I could let her rebuff sting, but I don't. She's not accustomed to a warm welcome from people who only know stories about her.

Based on what happened tonight, she's not accustomed to people simply liking her for the woman she is. That makes me want to burn the world down around us to right the wrongs people have laid at her feet over the years.

Instead of arson, I'm settling for showing her how good it could be. Showing her what she deserves.

"Came to visit you. Told you I was going to come early."

"Right, but you didn't say today. Or give me any specific day at all." Dropping in unannounced is not out of the norm for my mom. If her schedule changes, she'll randomly show up at an event of mine, screaming louder than anyone else in the stands.

"I reserve the right to be overbearing. You're my only boy."

"Do you do this to Julia?"

"No. But her life isn't nearly as interesting. She won't even tell me about whoever she met on the cruise. But I know she did because I caught her sneaking in and out at night." My mom winks at me, cheeks rounding out into full circles with her closed-mouth smile.

"Is that how I get rid of you, then? By not telling you anything?" I'm joking, and we both know it. That's why she laughs and glances around.

"At first, it pissed me off I couldn't find a spare key somewhere obvious. You know, under your doormat like a normal person. But then I decided I raised you smarter than I thought because I have looked for a key everywhere and couldn't find one."

I give my mom a sheepish grin as I plant a hand on Winter's back to guide her stunned form through the front gate and up the sidewalk.

"Well, Ma, the truth is, I don't have a spare key hidden anywhere at all."

Her head tips back against the siding of the house, inky black hair falling behind her. "Yep. I raised you stupid."

"It might be hereditary." I step up to my mom with a grin and take her hand in mine, pulling her to standing.

"That smart mouth." She grips my chin and squeezes my face hard enough to make my lips pucker, then shifts her head to address Winter. "Does he give you this kind of attitude too? He's always been wild and unruly, but it's hard to fault that heart of gold."

Winter says nothing as my mom pulls me in for a hug. "My sweet, sweet boy. I missed you."

"Is that what all the insults mean? That you missed me?"

Over my shoulder, she addresses Winter again. "He's needy too. Requires a lot of hair petting. I think I told him he was handsome too much as a child."

A soft snort sounds from behind me. "He did just finish telling me what a nice face he has."

"Okay, wow." I pull away from my mom and step back to give her and Winter a clear view of each other. "I haven't even introduced you and you're already mocking me."

"You must be Winter. I've heard so much about you." My mom steps forward, smiling with crinkles around her eyes—the only tell for her age. She says she smiles so much there's no getting around them, so she's embracing them. "I like you already."

Winter blinks at my mom's incredibly timely comment. "Likewise. It's nice to meet you."

She sticks her hand out to shake, but my mom waves her off. "We're not business partners, and I'm a hugger."

Mom wraps herself around a stunned-looking Winter, whose arms hang limp at her sides. I can't keep my lips from twitching. *Business partners.* That fucking phrase will haunt her.

Like always, Winter's eyes find mine. I widen mine as if to say *don't be a dick to my mom, hug her back!*

I get an eye roll, but she has a small smirk on her face when she lifts her arms and hugs my mom back. The sight hits me in the chest. It makes me wonder how many hugs Winter has gotten over the years—as a child. Even on the days my mom thought I was an idiot, she hugged me.

Winter barely mentions her mom. I know the relationship is fraught. With her dad too. And like a lightning strike to grass, I immediately and irrationally hate them both.

My mom is here within weeks of finding out about Vivi, and she lives a province away. Winter's parents live a little over an hour away and I've not seen hide nor hair of them.

I've been so fixated on jumping into this whole scenario that I haven't taken a step back to see the full picture beyond Winter, Vivi, and me.

I don't like what I see. It makes me feel protective in a new way. My palms itch with the urge to make this better for her. To make someone pay for the way they've treated her.

Winter's head tilts as she pulls away from my mom, like she can see the internal struggle playing out on my face.

"Well, Theo told me you were a smart and amazing mom."

My mom's hands stay on Winter's shoulders as she steps back to appraise her. "But he failed to mention just *how* thoroughly he overachieved with you."

"Jesus. Mom, stop." I scrub at my chin and shake my head. This is so on brand for her. She lives to rib me.

"I was drunk," Winter deadpans. The only giveaway that she's joking is the twinkle in her eye. "He looked better with my tequila goggles on."

I sputter out a laugh. If it means watching her be this comfortable with my mom, I don't mind getting dragged. I've seen the way she eye-fucks the hell out of me with not a single drop of tequila in her system.

I know she wants me. I'm just waiting for her to stop freaking out and realize it.

"You weren't so drunk that you didn't write out a contract on a coaster."

Two can play this game, Tink.

A sly grin spreads across her full lips. For a beat, I dream about them parting as I fit myself inside her. Every time she moves them, even to snarl at me, all I can think about is fucking her.

"Prove it." Her arms cross.

My mom steps back, head swiveling between us as we volley back and forth.

She looks pleased.

I shrug. "Okay, I will. Mom, let's get you settled in here. You can meet Vivi in the morning." I stride up the stairs, unlock the front door, and roll her suitcase into the entryway. Because I know my mom, and she's not above barging over there right now to lay eyes on her granddaughter. I'm setting boundaries before she thinks she has free rein.

"Winter, I'm so excited to get to know you better. If you need anything, just ask. I'm happy to help. I've done this gig twice myself, and while the end product might not be perfect, it could be worse. I take that as a win."

Winter's big blue eyes stay laser-focused on my mom. If I didn't know better, I'd say there's a flash of confusion there. "It's nice to meet you too, Loretta. Though I have to disagree. Your end product is pretty damn great." Her eyes slide over to mine. "Obnoxiously gentlemanlike in my experience."

My mother hums and gives Winter an appreciative glance. "Goodnight, kids," she says as she turns and disappears into the house.

I point at Winter. "You. Wait."

"I'm not Peter." She gives me a snarky quirk of her brow.

I chuckle. "Actually, you are. Neither of you listens to me and you both give me dirty looks." I swear I hear a small laugh from her as I turn and step into the house. After I direct my mom to the guest room, I grab my shoulder bag and reach into the small, zipped pocket. My fingertips brush up against the soft cardboard and I turn back to the entryway.

When I hit the front porch, Winter is standing at the bottom of the stairs, staring at her nails. That cotton-candy color gives her something to admire when she pulls this move, at least. It's her signature *I'm pretending to be bored* move.

It's a defense mechanism for when she feels vulnerable. And if I've learned anything about Winter over the past several weeks, it's that she *hates* feeling vulnerable. So it's become the ultimate prize for me.

I don't want to change who she is. I want to earn that side of her.

"Your mom seems nice." She doesn't glance up.

"Does she?" I tease. "I feel like hanging out around you two will be signing up to attend my own personal roast."

Her body heaves with a laugh, and she grins at her nails.

"Are you thinking about how good your pink nails will look wrapped around my cock? Because that's what I keep thinking about when I see them."

Now her eyes dart up to mine. "Seriously?"

"Yeah. You just need matching lipstick so I can imagine how your lips will look—"

She rushes forward, pressing a finger to my lips to stop me. Her eyes catch there, flaring slightly. Winter hasn't initiated any physical contact between us, and I wonder if she's realizing that now.

That she reached for me so easily.

Her finger moves, but not away. Instead, the rest of them join to stroke gently over my stubble. She never meets my gaze, just watches her fingertips trail over me. The shell of my ear. The line of my jawbone. Over my Adam's apple.

There's a reverence in the way she touches me, and I'm not ashamed to admit I savor it. The hair on my arms stands on end. My heart rails against my ribs, reaching for her.

She has the most confusing and consuming effect on me.

Her eyes drop to the front of my shorts. The stretchy material does nothing to hide the way my cock bulges when she touches me.

"Do you think about me when you jerk off?"

Coming from her, the question catches me off guard. She's rarely this direct, usually opting for a more discreet delivery.

I take her hand, pulling her fingers away from where they fiddle with the V at the front of my T-shirt. Pressing a kiss to the center of her palm, I admit, "I think about you all the time." Her breathing grows heavier when my tongue darts out over her skin. I pull away and look her in the eye. "But *especially* when I jerk off."

She laughs in response, but it's breathy.

I lift my opposite hand and press the coaster from so many months ago into her palm.

When she sees it, her body stiffens. "Is that . . ."

I give her a casual smile as I lean in close to whisper in her ear. "I told you I'd be back to beg for another shot."

Then I kiss her cheek, doing that little tongue thing she likes so much. She turns and nuzzles into me.

So, I hug her.

Her arms fold in front of her chest as I press her into me, the coaster with our contract crushed between us.

And I just hold her.

A woman who needs to be held so damn badly. And I'm the lucky one who gets to do it.

She fits her face right over the indent at the base of my throat and presses a soft kiss there.

"Goodnight, Theo."

She doesn't say anything else, and as much as I want to get into her head and sort through all the thoughts running rampant in there, I'm happy with a hug and a goodnight.

"Goodnight, Winter."

Her lips tip up as she turns away, avoiding my gaze. Like our interaction makes her bashful. Like we're two giddy teenagers saying goodnight after a first date.

Being loved is uncomfortable for her. God, I want to change that, but she'll be the one to tell me when the time is right. I have it in my head that after spending her life behaving in a way that suits everyone around her, she might need a minute to figure out what suits *her*.

She walks away, and I resist the urge to follow her. Her sneakered feet pad quietly down my walkway, across the front sidewalk, and up her own walkway. I step onto the porch so she can't see me watching.

Her eyes stay on her toes as she approaches her house. But she doesn't go inside.

She takes a seat on the front step and lifts the coaster, staring at it. Her fingers trace over it, much like they trailed over my face moments ago.

Her features are soft, and she looks younger in this moment. Her eyes aren't pinched, her lips aren't in a pout. This is how she looks when she's with Vivi.

Happy.

After a couple of minutes, she rises and steps into her house. Warm light spills onto the porch for a moment, and the inaudible murmurs of her and Summer talking filter into the night. Through the front window, I see them hug.

Three hugs in one night. Not bad.

I walk into my house with a goofy smile on my face. My mom catches it from where she's sitting on the couch with an episode of *Grey's Anatomy* queued up and ready to go.

"You do know you're in love with that girl, don't you?"

I flop down beside her and sling an arm over her shoulder, ready to get lost in the very best medical drama while sitting beside one of my favorite women in the world.

"Yeah, Mom. I know."

25

Winter

Theo: What if I stayed here as my home base?

Winter: In Chestnut Springs?

Theo: Yeah.

Winter: In your house?

Theo: I could pitch a tent in your backyard if you prefer. Invite you over for a campfire and tequila. ☺

Winter: Not ideal. Someone shitty could move in next door. I could end up with an even worse neighbor than you.

Theo: And who knows if he'd mow your lawn for you the way I do. Pretending to garden would be boring and pointless without me to watch.

Winter: I do not watch you.

Theo: You only ever garden when I'm mowing the lawn.

Winter: How do you know?

Theo: Because I'm watching you back.

235

A loud squeal pierces my ears as Peter slides across the hardwood floor like he's Tom Cruise in *Risky Business*. Vivi has an alarmingly strong arm on her. From her spot on the floor, she wails on the rubber chicken, whipping it across the living room while Peter gives chase.

When he rushes back and drops the squeaky toy at her feet, she slaps her chubby hands together and laughs. Peter's tongue lolls out the side of his mouth from where he's had teeth removed. He's so excited his eyes seem ready to roll right out of his head.

"He really is horrific if you look at him for too long," Loretta murmurs, before taking a sip of coffee. "Theo found him on the street while on vacation in Mexico. Fed him some taco meat, and the rest is history. Refused to leave the country without him. Rescheduled his flight and everything."

I snort. The man has a thing for strays.

From my sitting position on the floor of the living room, I watch Theo walk across the room in a way that should be illegal. He's wearing light-wash jeans and a white T-shirt while carrying a plate of oatmeal cookies. Ones he baked fresh—because of course he did.

His outfit couldn't be plainer, but I can't take my eyes off him. I'm taken back to the days he shows up to mow my lawn, without a shirt. While he taunts me with his muscles, I pretend to garden and creep on him from behind my sunglasses.

It's been a week since he laid me out on the gym bench and made a meal of me. I've worked out alone since our escapade, but he always swings by at the end when I'm stretching.

He crouches beside me and whispers, "Excuse me, ma'am. Did you sanitize that bench right there?" while pointing at *The Bench*.

I scowl.

He winks.

And we part ways.

We've fallen into a rhythm, even though we haven't expanded upon that night at all. There's a lot going on. His mom is here. He's working at the gym while he rehabs. I'm barreling toward my little sister's wedding, where I'm not a bridesmaid. I'm a fucking maid of honor.

A role I keep trying to give to Willa, but that bitch only laughs at me.

So, Theo and I continue to circle each other. We've developed a sort of kinship. My place, his place. We go between them, and so does Vivi. So does his mom, who's taken it upon herself to be the warmest, most helpful human I've ever met. Theo definitely inherited his infallible brand of kindness—the easy smile and gentle touches—from her.

So why do I hold back?

It's because he told me there hasn't been anyone else since that night. It's that fucking coaster tucked in my bedside table. Sometimes, I pull it out just to stare at it.

It's physical proof he liked me even then. Proof that he isn't full of shit, like every other man in my life. That he's thought of me since that night. That Vivi and I aren't the burden in his life I seem to think we are.

Who knew a shitty, stained coaster with both our scrawling signatures scribbled across it could upend my carefully curated boundaries so thoroughly?

I'm not sure how to act around him anymore.

I want him almost obsessively. Things are so good between us right now, but I'm terrified of it all blowing up in my face. I've been the pawn between two parents who hate each other, and subjecting my daughter to the same complications keeps me up at night.

Regardless, I can't keep my eyes from drifting to him. My body from drawing closer to him. My hand from trailing between my legs in the bath while I think about him. My feelings for him have become more than lust.

Vivi chucks the chicken again and Peter scuttles across the floor like a geriatric cannon, narrowly avoiding the wall—and Theo's feet. When he gets the toy, he does his best imitation of a lion killing a gazelle. Eyes wild, head whipping it from side to side. Vivi squeals with joy because this is her and Peter's new favorite game.

"Peter, pull yourself together and bring that back." I use my this-ER-is-going-to-shit voice, drawing Peter's attention for a moment. With a scowl at me, he begrudgingly brings the toy back and spits it out in front of Vivi.

"That dog isn't deaf, Theo. He just doesn't listen to you," I say as Theo places the plate of cookies on the coffee table in front of me with a gentle squeeze to my shoulder.

"How do you know?" he replies as he takes one cookie over to his mom, who is relaxing in the armchair.

"Because he listens to me. And I'm a doctor." He grabs a cookie and hands it to me, before taking one for himself and sitting on the couch directly behind me. I can feel one of his bare feet against the side of my ass.

I blush.

He's sitting so close, and his mom is right there. Plus, he ate me out and we haven't even talked about it.

I feel like a fucking teenager around him.

"But are you a vet?" he says from behind me as he chews.

"No, but—"

"Okay. I'll trust a vet on this then."

"Has a vet confirmed that he's deaf?"

"No."

"So, your only proof is that he doesn't listen to you?"

"Exactly. Just like you."

"What's that supposed to mean?"

His knee nudges playfully at my back as Vivi turns and crawls toward her grandmother with big, sparkly brown eyes.

Her dad's eyes.

"That I need to take you both to the vet."

It's Loretta who snorts this time as she reaches for Vivi, grinning wide as she pulls her in for snuggles. "Maybe you just don't have anything interesting to say and that's why they don't listen to you. Did you ever think about that, Theo Dale Silva?"

My head snaps around to face Theo and I mouth, "Dale?"

He's got a super sexy name and then . . . *Dale?*

He knees me again, but this time, he reaches under my hair and gives the nape of my neck a firm squeeze that has my entire body clenching. His head drops next to mine, and his stubble scrapes against the shell of my ear as he whispers, "Stop being so mean to me. It gets me hard when you're mouthy. Makes me think of all the fun ways I could put that mouth to work instead. And I don't need a boner right now."

My cheeks flame again as he releases me and lounges back on the couch like nothing at all just transpired between us.

Perhaps I should move away from him after that toe-curling warring, but my body follows him instead. I lean back against his legs and revel in his heat and sturdiness.

He and his mom start talking about *Grey's Anatomy*, and even though I could join in, my brain is stuck on how good it feels to lean on someone. To trust someone.

And I realize it then.

Theo Dale Silva has wormed his way into my heart, and I never stood a chance at keeping him out.

"Can I come in?" Loretta requests after a soft knock on my opened bedroom door.

"Of course." I fiddle with the guard for the back of my earring, head tilted in front of the mirror as I watch her walk into the room, Vivi cradled in her arms. "Thank you so much for watching her while I got ready. You're a lifesaver."

"You're the maid of honor today. You need some time to get ready. I'm just a plain old guest. Plus, spending time with my granddaughter isn't a job."

I nod, not sure what to say since my parents make zero attempt to spend time with her. Or me, for that matter. And my gut is twisted in knots today. Seeing people. Not hiding Vivi's paternity anymore.

Speaking of my parents, I still haven't told them about Theo.

"Do your parents come around much?" She sits on the edge of the bed, hunkering down for what I can tell is going to be a gentle inquisition. I can't blame her. I'd do the same if my son was in this complicated mess with someone.

With a heavy sigh, I turn to the older woman. Shiny dark hair to go with shiny dark eyes. There is no doubt where Vivi gets her looks from, and as much as it niggles at me sometimes, I'm relieved she doesn't take after my mom.

"No. When I announced my pregnancy, shit hit the fan." Loretta's brows rise in question, and I can't help but chuckle. "My life is a soap opera."

"I love a good soap opera," she replies with a mischievous grin.

Not wanting to wrinkle the pink silk dress, I rest my butt against the windowsill facing the bed and get ready to explain some things. "What has Theo told you?"

"Well, when I asked him, he said it wasn't his story to tell. He said there was a lot he still didn't know, but he didn't want to push you to divulge. I don't share his restraint."

She grins and I grin back. I swear anyone else barging in on my business would set me right off, but something about Loretta makes her just . . . inherently not annoying.

"The short version is that twenty-six or so years ago, my dad knocked up our nanny. She left the baby with him and that started the new Cold War in our house. So, he spent all his time protecting my sister from my bitter mom. Don't ask me why they didn't split because I don't fucking—sorry, freaking—know. Instead, they stayed together and made everyone around them miserable. So, I grew up estranged from my dad and sister because I got assigned to my mom when they picked their teams."

"Oof," is all Loretta says.

"Yeah, oof. But I'm a survivor, so I kept my head down, did my schooling, and went to med school like my mom always wanted me to. At the hospital, I met a doctor, the doctor who treated my sister as a teenager when she had some health issues. I thought he was handsome and accomplished and couldn't believe he was interested in *me*. After years of not having things for myself, it felt like he was mine. My mom was *all* about me being with a fancy doctor because it made her look good. Like I was doing better than my sister, who was eternally single and 'only' went to law school."

"Ah." Loretta nods, glancing down at Vivi, who is dozing to the sounds of our voices after whatever rigorous playtime her grandmother just put her through. "Law school is where all the underachievers go."

I point a finger at her as if to say, *Yeah, you get it*, then I carry on.

"Except it turned out Dr. Dreamy was a Dr. Douche. A creepy predator who groomed my teenage sister and was hooking up with her as soon as she was legal. But my relationship with her was so fraught that she never told me, even when I married him, because she didn't want to cause any more ripples in our already turbulent family. She didn't want to hurt me."

"Yeah, we definitely don't want to compare this guy to McDreamy."

My god, Theo and his mom with the McDreamy stuff.

With a laugh, I continue, feeling proud that I can find humor in this at all now. "So, Rhett found out from Summer, and one day at the hospital Dr. Douche took it a little too far with talking down to them, so Rhett blew up and spilled the beans in front of my entire family and a good chunk of my colleagues. I mean, not all of them, but the ones who were there played a game of telephone about it. So that sucked."

"That definitely sucks. This sounds a bit like a storyline that belongs in *Grey's Anatomy*."

"Right? I was also pregnant when that happened. After trying for so long. Fertility consults. Fertility drugs. I'm certain I was single-handedly keeping First Response pregnancy tests in business. So, you might say it gutted me. That little corner I was carving out for myself crumbled in a spectacular way that day."

Loretta is still now.

I can tell this isn't where she expected our conversation to go. But she's just easy to talk to, non-judgmental and supportive all at once. I can totally imagine having her in the room with me while delivering. I've never seen her work at all, but I already know she must be an incredible midwife.

I study my nails, a paler pearlescent pink this time to match my bridesmaid dress. "Then I miscarried, and that's when I started considering my options. The way no one showed up for me in the aftermath of that shit show was a wake-up call. Without that baby, I had *nothing*. I had a husband who cared more about me telling the medical board about his misconduct than my wellbeing. A mom who cared more about the optics of the entire situation than how I was doing. And a dad who just stared at me awkwardly, too chickenshit to say anything to me."

"Oh, Winter." Her eyes water, but I refuse to follow suit. Saying this out loud is cathartic. And it doesn't make me sad at all. It's freeing. Maybe I've finally gotten over the trauma. I feel like I want to poke the wound even harder to find out if it's truly healed.

"The *only* person who cared about *me* and how *I* was doing was my baby sister. The one I spent literal decades of my life treating like shit. She never stopped messaging me, never stopped trying, and I felt so, *so* unworthy. And somehow that was the straw that broke the camel's back. I wanted to burn it all down. My life, my job, my house, my marriage. The only two things I wanted to leave standing were Summer and me. So, that's what I did. Except I had a one-night stand with your son, and apparently condoms truly are only 98 percent effective. So, here I am. Or I guess I should say . . . here *we* are."

I straighten and smile. Because this story finally doesn't make me feel weak or sad. I feel stronger for having told it out loud. I feel proud of how far I've come.

"I think his version of events included an inappropriate comment about being too fertile for any barrier."

A laugh bursts from me. "That absolutely sounds like the way Theo would see it."

"Thank you for sharing that story with me, Winter. I can see why you've enchanted my boy."

I give her a wry grin. "That story is not enchanting."

"No, but you are. Your ability for reflection shows a type of maturity and strength that not all adults possess."

I wave her off and drop her gaze, still not comfortable with that level of compliment. Though I can't help but think of my parents, of Rob. Reflective is not the word I would use for them.

"I brought you this. I packed it and knew I wanted to give it to you. I just wasn't sure when the right time would be. I think today is perfect."

I glance down at her outstretched hand as her fingers unfurl from a fist. A thin string of dainty misshapen pearls with a golden clasp rests on her palm.

"This was from my mom. She passed it down to me. They're river pearls. That's why they're all a little asymmetrical and the colors are a bit different. I saw you in this dress and thought it would be the perfect touch."

I reach out and run the pad of my fingers over the lumpy edges. Soft whites, creams, and pale pinks reflect over the satiny smooth beads. It's gorgeous, but I'm not sure I feel right taking it from her.

"What about your daughter? Surely, you'd rather keep it in the family."

Loretta's head tilts as she assesses me. "Winter, doll. You *are* the family. Whatever happens between you and Theo? This little girl right here"—she trails a finger over the bridge of Vivi's nose—"is a gift. She's part of us all. As far as I'm concerned, you and Vivi are a two-for-one deal. I see your connection, how much of yourself you've given to her, and I just . . . it reminds me of myself in those early days."

I haven't cried in weeks. With all the people rallying around me, all the effortless support, tears haven't sprung up out of nowhere anymore. The urge to climb Theo like a tree has replaced the urge to cry.

That's what keeps me up at night instead of my mistakes in life.

If his mom wasn't living with him, I would have broken into his house in the middle of the night and begged him to fuck me by now.

"I think—"

Loretta doesn't let me finish. "I think you should pass it down to Vivi at an equally important time in her life."

My eyes water, and I try to blink the moisture away. "Maybe I spoke too soon," I say as I finally take the necklace. It's short and will fit like a choker. It's dainty, but also sexy and unique. "I love it. Though I'm not sure this could be considered an important time in my life."

She smiles at me, kind and wise, like she knows something I don't. "I was thinking I could bring Vivi home and put her to bed when the timing is right. Let you kids have some fun tonight. You could let your hair down a bit. Maybe that's important for you right now."

"I could." I'm still running my fingers over the pearls. "I'm not good at letting my hair down though."

She huffs out a laugh. "Spend more time around Theo, and he'll show you how."

"That's what worries me," I whisper, confessing one of the anxieties I have about Theo Silva. "He just . . . I have a hard time trusting anyone." I snort and glance up at her. "I'm like a walking, talking daddy issue. And no matter how hard I try not to let my head go back to that place . . . it does."

Loretta nods, her mouth curling into a smile. "As the person who has known him the longest in this life, I'm going to tell you what I know about Theo."

"Okay."

"Theo loves easily. That's just his nature. But he doesn't often love *hard*. He keeps that part of himself, the one that's seen loss too, locked up tight where it can't get hurt. But you, girl? He loves you hard."

I blink, trying to absorb what she's just told me.

"Okay?" She pushes to stand.

"Okay," I reply again.

It's when she's almost at the door with a sleeping Vivi in her arms that she turns back to me on a soft chuckle. "I just remembered that he called me the morning after you two first got together. And do you know what he said to me?

I shake my head. It's all I can manage.

"He said, 'Mom, I met her.' And I said, 'Who?'" Loretta's lips curve up, her eyes taking on a faraway look. "He said, 'The woman I'm going to marry one day.'"

I'm frozen in place. How could he possibly know that? Think that? Why would a one-night stand with me be more impactful that a one-night stand with one of the bajillions of random women I'm sure he's slept with over the years?

"I asked him if she knew about this and he laughed and said, 'Not yet.'"

26
Theo

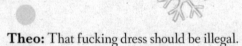

Theo: That fucking dress should be illegal.

Winter: Is that why you're glaring at me from across the room? It's a wedding. Act happy.

Theo: I'm undressing you with my eyes.

Winter: Cheesy.

Theo: Fine. I'm trying to decide if I should rip those thin straps or even bother taking the dress off at all.

Winter: Who told you that you'd be taking my dress off?

Theo: You haven't yet, but you will.

Winter: Rude.

Theo: Rude is me telling you that if you wanted a pearl necklace, I could have given you one.

Winter: Extra rude.

Theo: I'll stop being rude when it stops making you turn that pretty pink color.

Every person in the vintage-style barn has their eyes on Summer as she and Rhett exchange vows at the front of the aisle.

Except me.

I have mine on Winter. And I can't take them off.

Partly because of her clingy silky dress, held up by such dainty straps. Everything about the delicate garment is so easily lifted or ripped. And then she's wearing this pretty choker-style pearl necklace, and I can't help but wonder if she did it to test my control *and* my maturity. I can't wait to whisper something dirty in her ear about pearl necklaces and watch her squirm.

But most of all, my eyes are stuck on her because every time her gaze meets mine, her skin turns this tulip-pink color, and she acts like she's found something interesting in the rows of people watching the ceremony. Her lips will press together, her lashes will flutter, and her gaze will find its way back to me.

I shouldn't eye-fuck her so blatantly at the front of her sister's wedding, but I have been since we all met up in the back room. I couldn't be more clichéd, the best man drooling over the maid of honor at a wedding. Especially since I'm only the best man because Rhett didn't want to pick one of his brothers over the others.

Before I know it, the justice of the peace announces they can kiss and everyone in attendance cheers. When I hear a loud whistle, I turn and see Kip, Winter and Summer's dad. I should find it endearing he's here fervently supporting his daughter, but I saw the pain that flashed over Winter's face when he walked Summer down the aisle to us.

Glancing over at Winter, I find her eyes on me. This time, I toss her a wink. Her cheeks flame and her lips purse as she looks away, trying to hide her smile.

The rest of the day passes in a blur of much of the same. Stolen glances. Posed photographs. A hand on her back, just a little too low. Family speeches. My foot pressed against hers under the head table. The first dance. Me wiping the icing off her lip from the cake.

The tension is so thick between us, I could cut it with a butter knife.

It's when the dancing starts that my cheeky, happy little bubble bursts and I have my first run-in with a feeling I'm not well acquainted with at all.

Jealousy.

Beau Eaton snags Winter for an upbeat two-step and all I can see is his hand on the small of her back. His fingers wrapped around where mine should be. And I hate it.

As the song changes into a slow dance and he doesn't let her go, my agitation builds. I shift my weight on the spot. Her eyes search for me, and when she finds me, she smiles. I lean against the bar, bottle of beer in hand, burning lasers into a guy I generally like for daring to dance with the woman I'm in love with while I wait for her to decide if she might like to be in love with me too.

It's when I feel an elbow against my side that I realize Harvey Eaton has moved in beside me. "Gonna tell you what I told Rhett a couple of years ago when Beau was putting moves on Summer right in front of him."

I snort. "Brave."

Harvey chuckles and takes a swig of his beer, watching them too. "Doesn't much matter who she's dancing with when her eyes are on you."

"Yeah." I scrub at my stubble, hoping to loosen some of the tension in my jaw.

"Plus, it's not what it looks like. I told Beau to stop being a moody asshole and apologize to Winter. See how awkward they are? Was kinda getting a kick out of it myself, like two virginal teenagers at their first dance. Straight-arming each other's shoulders. Not like you two feral cats on the procreation prowl."

"Sorry, the procreation prowl?"

"I googled it after you lot made fun of my analogy. But I was right. You're the tom and she's the queen. Ya'll were blowing shit up like Americans on the fourth of July and then going at it like it's mating season."

"This is truly the analogy that never ends."

"I'm not wrong. Our southern neighbors love to celebrate their independence by blowing off their fingers with excessive fireworks. There are statistics."

"On Google, I presume?"

He scoffs. "Yes."

"You are a national treasure, Harvey Eaton." I chuckle and take a sip of my drink, eyes still plastered to the dance floor. Now that he mentions it . . . there is a leaden quality to the way they're moving. "What'd he do to her?"

Harvey shakes his head, his humor leeching away now. "Bah. Acted like a sullen dickhead when she tried to help him. I'm sure she wasn't warm and fuzzy about it. But still. This is the new normal for Beau, unfortunately."

It's been a tough road for Beau. I don't know him well, but I know he's not the same. Not after he spent days on end hiding in enemy territory with a hostage he freed. A Canadian journalist who'd been missing forever. It was plastered all over the evening news. The hero who walked through fire and knowingly missed his transport out to save a fellow Canadian.

The only person who doesn't seem impressed by Beau is, well, Beau.

Harvey clears his throat. "He's getting better though. Ya know? Takes time to adjust to civilian life. Ah—" Harvey gestures at the dance floor with his beer. "There he goes. Still a good boy at heart."

And sure enough, between the two songs, he steps away from Winter, drops his eyes, and his lips move. I can't make out what he's saying, but Winter nods, looking more like the medical professional she is than the woman who keeps making fun of my middle name.

They shake hands and part ways. Winter turns and saunters toward me, that pink silk slipping against the outer curve of her hips. Beau crosses to the opposite side of the dance floor and leans against the bar where a pretty brunette is slinging drinks. She barely glances his way, but hands him a soda before he even says a word.

"And would you look at that. The queen coming back to her tom. Must be mating season." Harvey cackles to himself as he moves into the crowd, presumably to make jokes that toe the line of appropriate to someone else.

I'm grinning like a fool when Winter finally gets to me.

"Hi." She smiles back, instantly flushed again.

"Hi. Drink?" I tip my head toward the bar.

"Sure. Champagne."

Winter takes a spot beside me while I turn and order her a champagne. With her drink in hand, we both stand and stare out at the crowd. The sun is dropping outside, but inside it feels like things are just turning up. The reception is being held in another outbuilding on the same farm, this one set up for events with a large dance floor, family-style tables down one side, two bars, and a DJ booth. Basically, everything you might need on one property to host a country wedding.

"What were you and Harvey talking about?" I glance down at Winter, lips on the rim of the glass as she tips the champagne into her mouth. Pink lipstick kisses the edge when her mouth comes away.

"The procreation prowl."

Her brows knit together. "The what?"

"You don't want to know. What were you and Beau talking about?"

Her nose wrinkles slightly, and I can tell she's weighing her words. "Basically, he cornered me at a family dinner a while back, asking me to write him a script. I said no. He blew up, and I told him to watch his tone. Now he treats me like I'm the Grinch who stole his sleeping pills. I guess after several months of cooling down, he decided to apologize. Though I'm pretty sure his dad told him t—"

"I think it might be a good time to get this girl home." My mom walks up, pushing a stroller with a passed out Vivi. "She's partied hard for a ten-month-old. I told Winter I'd go on grandma duty so you guys could stay out. I'll just watch *Grey's* reruns at your house until you're back."

Ten months? God. She was nine months when I met her. It seems impossible that a month has passed. There's a part of me that wants to say no and take her home myself. I want to watch her fall asleep and be there when she wakes up.

But Winter jumps at the opportunity. "Thank you, Loretta. That would be lovely." She bends down to the stroller and presses a kiss to Vivi's cheek. And I decide, fuck it, I'm doing the same. So, I place my beer onto the bar and with one hand on the small of Winter's back, I bend into the stroller and give my daughter's soft, pudgy cheek a goodnight kiss.

When I straighten, I'm immediately faced with Kip's stare on me from the opposite side of the dance floor. His dark eyes bore into me as they narrow.

I glare back at him, my hand still firmly pressed to his forgotten daughter's back. I graze my thumb over the silky pink fabric. This dress looks far too much like some sort of sexy nightgown. It really should be illegal.

"Bye, Mom," is my absent acknowledgment of her departure.

I'm sure the stare down is obvious, but I don't give a fuck. Kip might be her dad, he might even be a nice enough guy, but he hurt Winter and hasn't done shit to show up for her.

Which puts him in the asshole column as far as I'm concerned.

"Wow. This champagne is great." Winter sidles closer to me, turning her body toward mine as she holds the glass up to assess it. "Like not too fizzy, you know?"

I'm sure she's aware of who I'm watching, but I wonder if she understands how territorial I'm feeling. "I'm glad. You okay?"

She nods, top teeth sinking into her bottom lip. Finally, she gives me her eyes for more than a few seconds for the first time today. "Yeah." Her teeth go back to working at her lip, like she's trying to clamp down on words she wants to say.

I ghost a finger over her lip and it sends a jolt of lust to my groin. "If you want to be bitten, I can help you with that."

Her eyes widen and she quickly covers by taking a sip of champagne.

Then the questions come.

"Why did you keep that coaster? My phone number?"

"Because I knew I was coming back. You were a mess—respectfully—and I was out of control. We both needed time."

A thin laugh spills from her lips. "I'm still a mess now."

I splay my fingers lower on her back, trailing them over the top seam of her underwear as I gaze out over the packed dance floor. "Maybe I don't care. Maybe I want to be messy with you forever."

Her body jolts, and I smile before taking a swig of my beer. It feels like several minutes before she says another word.

And they aren't the words I want.

"Truly, this champagne is superb. Like not too sweet. Not too dry. I'll have to ask Summer for the name so I can get a bottle."

"I'll buy you literal cases of it if you stop avoiding the conversation at hand."

She sighs and follows my gaze out onto the dance floor where Rhett is spinning Summer. Her full dress trails around behind her, cast almost as wide as the grin on her face. Jasper has Sloane pressed against him like every person in their vicinity might try to remove her from his grip. And Willa is dancing with Luke, doing the most insane moves until they both laugh uncontrollably.

"I don't know how to react to you when you talk like that, Theo," Winter says in a soft voice. "Like . . . what was it then? Love at first sight? I just . . . that makes me uncomfortable. That's a movie thing, not a real-life thing."

"When you saw Vivi for the first time, did you know you loved her? Did you need time and space to come around to the idea? Or did you take one look at her and just *know*?"

A deep sigh lifts her shoulders. "I just knew."

I pull her closer, feeling her stomach press against my hip, her breast against my ribs, as I drop my voice and splay my fingers over her ass. "When I saw you . . . I don't know. I don't want to call it love at first sight. Maybe *need* at first sight? *Want* at first sight? A connection. It was knowing I'd never get sick of your eyes wandering over my body with that slack-jawed feral look on your face."

"You should really try this champagne. I think you'd like it."

"Winter, seriously with the champagne again?"

Her body melts against mine even as her words stay conflicted. "I just . . . That's crazy. That makes no sense."

A laugh rumbles in my chest. "I ride bulls for a living, so it's not the first time I've been called crazy. I guess I'm just crazy enough to want my eight seconds on the frigid ice-queen sister too."

Winter stiffens for several beats and then yanks herself away with a violence that clashes with the peacefulness we had moments ago.

"Are you kidding me?" she hisses right as her eyes go dark and turn glassy.

"Winter . . ."

It was a joke.

A bad one.

"You are the *only* person in my life who has never referred to me that way. Sorry, you *were* the only person." Her mouth pops open and I can see the way I've hurt her; it's written all over her face.

She transforms from raging to heartbroken right before my eyes. A shaking hand places the champagne glass on the bar top, and her quivering lips try to form a polite smile. Her voice comes out watery when she says, "Thank you for the drink."

Then she's practically jogging in her high heels across the

wooden floor, skirt fisted to keep it from tangling in her legs. I'm too stunned to move for a few beats.

We were just talking, laughing. Heading in a good direction. And she's going to run away from me now? After everything?

Nah. Not today, Tink.

I stride after her.

Agitated.

Frustrated.

And fucking done with Winter Hamilton running from me.

27
Theo

I sense the weight of people's gazes as I practically chase Winter through the room. My long, assertive strides gain ground behind her short, choppy ones.

She turns down a narrow wood-paneled hallway. It's quieter here, even with my heartbeat in my ears and her heels clacking on the floor.

At the very end of the corridor, she goes left and wrenches on the door handle, wild eyes meeting mine over her shoulder. "Theo. Go away. I want to be alone." A tear streaks down her face.

I know she hates to cry. Hates having big feelings and big conversations. Hates to feel weak or out of control.

But . . .

"That's too bad, because today, I don't give a fuck what you want," I growl as I yank the door open wider to accommodate my width. "Get in." I push her gently into the washroom, my hand between her shoulder blades as we step into the large space with a butcher-block vanity and bowl sink.

"I don't want you here!" she hisses, wiping furiously at her face as she turns away from me to face the mirror that runs all the way to the ceiling. "Would hate for happy, lovable fucking Theo Silva to get his legendary dick frostbitten by *the ice-queen*."

"Winter, that was a *joke*." I lock the door while she stares at us in the mirror. Flushed cheeks, wide eyes, one hand on her heaving chest. "It was a dumb fucking joke."

"It wasn't funny."

"No shit!" My arms fly out and my voice booms. "I made a mistake. One little mistake after everything and you treat me like I'm just another asshole and take off!"

"It wasn't a mistake! It's a way of thinking about Summer and me that *everyone* does! I'll always be the cold, heartless bitch because Summer gets to be the sweet, agreeable one. And of course, you see me the same way as everyone else. Why wouldn't you?"

Her words stun me. The heat in my cheeks creeps down my throat, a perfect mirror to the tears rolling down her cheeks. Both signs of our frustration.

"You know what, Winter?" My voice is low, but it vibrates with an unfamiliar fury. "I am fucking tired. I am tired of you not seeing what I see. Tired of you talking shit about yourself. I am tired of you not realizing what's right here"—my palm lands heavy on my chest—"right in front of you. What more do I have to fucking do for you to trust me? For you to give me the benefit of the doubt just once!"

She doesn't flinch at my outburst. Silent tears mar her makeup as they flow freely down her face.

But she says nothing. So I keep going. Stepping close enough to trail my fingers over the line of her jaw.

"I am not your dad. I am not your ex. I am here doing my best for you. And it seems like the more I give, the less I get back. Why is that?"

Her jaw trembles as she opens it, like she's about to respond. But then she shuts down. Slams it shut and looks away.

I huff out a frustrated breath, dropping my hand from her cheek as I turn to leave. But the loss of my touch has her spinning on her heel to face me.

"Because I want you!" she shouts, stopping me in my tracks. "And I want this!" Her hand gestures frantically between us. "I want us! And that terrifies me! Because what if it doesn't work and Vivi is stuck with two parents who hate each other? I know how that goes and it fucking *sucks*. We like each other right now. I'm finally happy. It feels safe here. I can't handle another person who hates me."

The tears continue flowing, and she makes no move to stop them. She just stares at me after that brutally honest, raw outburst. She still holds her chin high, defiantly, no matter how vulnerable she's just been.

"That's all you had to say."

She blinks, but otherwise doesn't react.

But I can't handle staying away from her anymore. Can't stand this distance between us. All it takes is two long steps for me to tower over her. One step for me to push her back against the closed door. And a few inches for me to crush my lips against hers.

She doesn't miss a beat, arching into me and wrapping her arms around my neck, moaning into my mouth.

Clinging to me.

"I promise I could never hate you," I murmur against her mouth, hand skimming her jaw.

Her eyes flash to mine. "Don't make promises you can't keep."

We kiss again. Frantically. Like she's still trying to push through this conversation. Hands roaming, she grabs the lapels of my suit jacket, giving them a hard tug.

"I promise I'll never hate you." I drag my lips over her cheek, my teeth back down along her jaw.

"You can't know that," she whispers, a sharp intake of breath hissing from between her lips as I spin her and face us toward the mirror. Forcing her to look at us.

My hands trail over the silk, tracing every curve, thumbs detouring down into that little dip beneath her hips. "I can. I'll be too busy loving you."

All she does is breathe and watch us. Watch my hands sliding everywhere, taking all the ground I've been desperate to cover for so damn long.

Then her hands cover mine, moving as I move. Her eyes now full of awe, she raptly follows the trail my touch blazes over her body. Hips. Stomach. Breasts. Inner thighs.

I'm rock hard, my cock bulging against the swell of her ass.

She grinds back on me, and I groan.

"Tell me what you want, Tink."

Her lips pop open and I watch her thinking, deciding what to say next.

"I don't want any more of those pity orgasms you gave me in the gym."

"Pity orgasms?"

"Yeah. Like you just did it because you were trying to make me feel better. Like you feel bad for me."

This is not what I expected her to say.

"I wasn't just doing it to—"

"I want you to fuck me like you did that night in the hotel. Like you can't stand to keep your hands off me. Like . . ." She trails off, back to biting her bottom lip. "It's like you respect me too much now. I get pity orgasms and pretty words. I want to be more than that. I want . . ." I observe the way she's working this out. She's not used to asking for what *she* wants. "I want you unhinged for me. Just . . . disrespect me. Just for a bit."

That night.

My lips drag over the shell of her ear, and she shivers. "You'd like to be my pretty little slut tonight?"

My teeth sink into the lobe of her ear as the words echo around us. When she doesn't respond, I quirk a brow at her.

She lifts her chin like she refuses to feel any shame about her request. "Yes."

Flames lash at my spine, and I will myself to take this slowly. I don't give a fuck where we are right now. I'm going to savor the hell out of this woman.

"You've been a real cock-tease, strutting around in this dress all day. I think it's time you pay for that, don't you?" I flick one flimsy strap off her shoulder.

Her tongue darts out over her plush lips. Every move she makes drives me crazy. Just being this close to her, inhaling her vanilla body lotion, makes me unbearably hard.

She nods.

I spin her and press down on her shoulders, guiding her to the hardwood floor. "Good. Now get on your fucking knees and suck my cock like it'll end in a mouth full of that champagne you keep talking about."

As she hits the ground, she lifts her baby blues up at me for a beat, and then her hands attack my belt and pants with a needy fervor.

She's too impatient to do more than tug my slacks down far enough to get what she's after. I groan when my cock springs free, head brushing her lips as she wraps her fist around the base. Her eyes flit up to mine as she kneels before me, rubbing the thick head of my cock over her lush mouth.

The teasing drives me insane, so I grip her hair and thrust.

Her lips open and her tongue swirls, cheeks hollowing out as she sucks me.

My hands stay on her head, but they're just there for the ride. I don't need to push or pull. She's eager enough all on her own.

Hot. Wet. Hungry.

Just the way I like her.

"Is this what you needed, Winter?" My fingers stroke her hair.

She hums her response around my length, one hand firm around my dick while the other gently squeezes my balls.

"Fuck." My head tips back and I close my eyes as my hips move, fucking her greedy little mouth. "Winter. It's too good. You're too good."

She doubles her efforts, going deep enough that I feel the back of her throat butting up against the head of my cock. I hear the little gagging noise she makes as she struggles to take it all, and it pushes me to the edge.

"Winter, if you don't stop soon, I'm going to . . ." I trail off as I gaze down at her. Hair mussed. Pearl necklace against the column of her throat. Eyes on me.

"Oh, that's what you want? Of course, you do." I smirk and toss her a wink. Then I take her head, hold her still, and fuck her mouth.

Her gaze remains plastered on me, her hands braced against my quads, holding on for dear life. After a few furious thrusts, I give in and spill myself down her throat.

She doesn't look away. She doesn't pull back.

"Lapping up every last drop, aren't you?" I ask as she holds me there, swallowing it all before sliding off my length.

I'm panting, hands still in her hair, when she peeks up at me. "The champagne was still better," she says with a demure smile as she licks her lips like the little liar she is.

I work on catching my breath for a moment after the hottest blow job of my life before I fix my pants and give a shake of my head at her. "I'll get you more once I've had my turn," I reply, taking her hand and helping her to stand.

Then I kiss her. Because I can. Because she wants me to.

I press that one hard, frenzied kiss to her mouth and then swiftly push her away, flipping her around so we're back to facing the mirror.

We look so good together. Her eyes all sparkly and bright. Her lips all puffy and freshly fucked. But I don't stand around watching for long.

"Don't much like the idea of you not having a turn." I reach down, lifting her dress. My cock already moving again as I expose each inch of smooth skin.

"You seemed fine with it the other day."

"That's different."

Her brow quirks as the silk slides up to her waist, giving me a view of the pale pink thong beneath. I groan at the sight.

"How do you figure?"

I step back to get a good view of her ass before tapping her elbow as a sign to lift her arms. Within seconds, the dress is gone. I'm not a total savage, and I know we need to get out of here eventually, so I hang it carefully on the hook attached to the door.

"Because eating your pussy is one of my favorite things to do."

I flick the clasps of her bra and watch the waste of fabric fall.

My hands cover her breasts, cupping the bare skin in my palms.

Her head tilts. "Who said sucking your cock isn't one of *my* favorite things to do?"

My mouth follows the curve of her neck, planting kisses, until I decide to take a bite of her shoulder. She gasps.

"Say that again," I murmur, pressing a hand to the middle of her back to bend her forward, propping her hands on the countertop.

"Say what?" She's panting now, still watching me in the reflective glass.

I give the left cheek of her ass a bite as I drop to my knees, pulling the thong with me. I'm met by smooth, toned legs propped up in the most alluring way above the three-inch heels she's wearing.

"That sucking my cock is your favorite thing to do."

"Jesus," she rasps, right as I run my fingers over her core, discovering how ready she is for me.

I slide two fingers into her, thoroughly enjoying the view of her body bent over like this for me, enjoying her eagerness. How honest she's been.

"Sucking your cock is my favorite thing to do," she finally gets out in a breathy voice.

My fingers glide in and pull back out, covered in her wetness. "I can tell. You're fucking soaked."

I shove them back in and drop my mouth to her. Licking, sucking, working her with my fingers until she rocks back on me.

Elsie Silver

"Theo." She moans as her legs shake, but I don't let up. I keep a steady rhythm, swiping her clit with my tongue the way she likes.

"Theo." My fingers move harder, rocking her body on unsteady heels. "Theo! If you don't fuck me soon, I'm going to scream!" Her tone is demanding and breathless all at once.

I grin as I withdraw my fingers and come to stand above her. She looks unhinged. Just like that night we shared.

And I love it.

I wedge a dress shoe between her heels and kick her feet apart. "Spread, Winter. Ass up so I can disrespect you the way you want me to."

She moans in response. And I just go to work on my pants again. Pulled down is good enough for now. I can take my time with her later.

"You're going to scream, huh?" I run the head of my cock through her slick center.

She nods, elbows propped on the counter, pink fingernails clawing the wooden countertop as her back arches, pussy tipped up in offering.

"Yes. Loud."

"Begging for it like the good little slut you are." My hand lands flat and firm against her ass cheek. The breath hissing from between her lips rings out in the quiet bathroom. "Just like I said you would."

And then I thrust inside. To the hilt, holding nothing back.

"Fuck." I glance down at where I'm buried inside her and take a moment to appreciate the sight of her stretched around my girth. "You feel so good," I murmur, sliding in and out slowly. "So fucking good."

When I look up, she's watching me in the mirror. "Enjoying the view?"

266

"You've said that to me before," she whispers.

I take one hand and run it up the column of her spine, trailing my fingers along the indent there. "That night when you showed me how you touch yourself, and I made some . . . tweaks." I give her hair a tug, holding her gaze in the mirror. "You gonna look me in the eye and tell me you can't come again?"

"No, Theo." Her tongue darts out between her lips to wet them. "We both know I only come for you."

I hover over her, pulling her hair to tilt her face. My mouth crashes against hers, tongues clashing, teeth nipping. And for a few moments, I let myself focus on taking her mouth, but she wiggles her ass in a desperate plea for more of my cock.

So I give it to her.

My hips slap against her, and she pushes back to meet every motion.

"Is this what you wanted?"

"Yes," she breathes, voice hitching as she grips the spout over the sink.

I reach around and play with her clit.

"Fuck, yes." Her eyes flutter shut, and her knuckles turn white on the faucet.

I pick up the pace, and her legs falter, her body propped against the vanity now as her heels slip and lose purchase.

But I don't stop. Not when she's chanting my name and squirming like she might come apart at any moment.

"You look perfect like this, Winter. Bent over. Cunt full. Only wearing these pretty pink heels."

"Theo . . ."

My finger works more swiftly, rubbing rough circles between her legs. My opposite hand grips her shoulder, her hair. Some tendrils have come loose and stick to the perspiration on the back of her neck.

I fuck her hard.

"Take it, Winter. Come on my cock."

"Theo!" Her voice is loud now.

I hope someone hears us.

"I'm going—"

She doesn't finish the sentence before she shatters. I feel it everywhere. Her body pulsing. Her head dropping. One stiletto-clad foot pops up off the floor as she topples over the edge and lays herself out on the counter like she's finally surrendered. And that flush from before sweeps down her back right before my eyes.

I ease off, pressing my fingers rather than rubbing, taking long, even strokes rather than fast ones. Until her body has gone completely soft, and I've wrung every whimper from her lungs.

She looks beautiful. Wrung out. And all it takes is a few rough thrusts into her body for me to get there too.

I pull out, fist my cock, and blow on her back. Shot after shot lands on her smooth skin, marking her.

It's more satisfying than it should be.

Several moments pass as we catch our breath, and then a spent chuckle leaves her, jostling her body. It's like we were entirely different people just now. Animalistic and passionate and so fucking hungry. As we both come back down, the mood lightens.

"Wow."

"Wow, what?" I reply, propping a hand against the wall to get my own bearings.

"I don't think I can walk anymore. Pretty sure my entire post-secondary education just evaporated right out of my head."

I trail a finger through the mess on her back and watch her shiver. "Just stay like this. I can go again."

Her head flips over her shoulder to me, eyes wide. "What?"

"What? You look good with a pearl belt." My chin juts out at her. "Matches your pearl necklace."

Her head drops, and she laughs. It sounds so good on her, airy and carefree.

"I can't believe I just fucked a bull rider at my sister's wedding."

With a smile, I pull my pants up and turn to gather a handful of paper towels to clean her off. "Rude. You fucked your baby daddy at your sister's wedding, and you know you'd do it again."

Her back shakes on another laugh as I dab her off with steady hands. I toss the messy handful and grab another, reaching over her prone body to wet it with warm water.

With a gentle squeeze of my hand, water droplets fall across her back, little dots that land and roll along the slender slope of her body.

"And now he's giving me a sponge bath."

"Yeah. But this is the slut version. No sponges or fancy soap in a bathtub. Just paper towels and lukewarm tap water in a public washroom."

Her face drops into her hands, and she laughs harder. "Theo, stop."

I smile down at her back as I move the paper towel over her carefully, not wanting to miss a spot. Drunk on the sound of laughter flowing from a woman who has spent far too long feeling sad.

I take my time, reveling in being able to touch her so freely.

"Are you done?"

A sigh leaves me. "I guess so. I want to do this again. The princess version of a sponge bath though."

She peeks up at me through the mirror. "Yeah." She nods. "Okay."

"Okay," I agree, with a wink that *still* makes her blush.

I toss the paper towel away and she straightens. We turn to face each other, and I get sucked in again. My eyes roam her body.

"I could sit you back on that counter and fuck you again. This time, with your legs wrapped around my waist."

"Or we could get out of here and do that somewhere else."

"Yeah." I lick my lips, mind racing with all the ways I could have her. "But I kind of like doing it where we could get caught."

"Well, we can do that again too." She shrugs, looking momentarily innocent. "Sometime. Somewhere."

I grin and quirk my head. "Anytime, anywhere?"

Her head shakes now, and she blinks away, lips pressed together to hide a smile. "You're a machine."

My hands reach for her, and I gather her against my chest. Naked and wearing heels. I thought not having a full-length view would help my erection, but the feel of her pressed against me is almost worse. She smells like cinnamon sugar, and I can't keep my mouth off her. I kiss her hair. Her cheek. Her neck. My hands slide all over before gripping her ass.

"Has there really been no one else since that night?"

Her question stops me in my tracks.

"It just seems very unlikely. That's all. Like borderline not normal. I don't care. I'd just rather have it all laid out. It's the secrets that kill me."

"You calling me weird, Tink?" I squeeze her tighter and drop a kiss on her forehead as her head tips up to look me in the eye.

"I don't know. Am I?"

I reach for her bra, slip it on her, and struggle like an idiot to fasten the stupid hooks. "Yeah. You are."

"Not even a blow job?"

I reach around her and grab her slip of a dress off the hook. I carefully arrange it over her head to drop it down over her body.

"No, the quality of yours ruined me. Nobody else swallows my cum like it's Dom Perignon."

Her eyes roll as I work her arms through the straps. "Not even a kiss?"

"Nobody has the smart mouth that you do. Makes me a lot less interested in kissing them."

The dress cascades down over her body.

"What about my panties?"

"Oh, yeah. You won't be needing those anymore." I swipe them off the ground and toss them in the garbage with all the paper towels.

We regard each other for a beat. She always has a look of wonder on her face when I do or say something playful. It pisses me off and thrills me all at once. It's like no one has even attempted to make this woman laugh.

"Aren't you going to ask me if I've been with anyone else?"

"No."

Her brows draw together. "Why not?"

I reach for her hand and tug her along with me toward the door. "Because I don't care."

"Okay, well, I haven't."

I turn the lock and smirk at her over my shoulder. "I know."

She stomps her foot in faux outrage. "How do you know? Maybe I've had *so much sex.*"

"Nah," I say, as we head into the darkened hallway, "Cadillac Ranch" filtering to my ears from the dance floor. "There'd be no point since I'm the only one who can make you come."

28
Winter

Winter: I've never seen a more beautiful, vibrant bride in my life. I love you, Summer. Congratulations.
Summer: Is this your way of explaining why I saw you sneaking out, holding a certain bull rider's hand?
Winter: I just needed a break. I'll be back!
Summer: Are you crazy? Don't come back. Take Theo and go be happy. Make some more cute babies. Rhett says he'll kick his ass if he's not good to you.

Theo's hand is warm and strong. It swallows mine. He doesn't grip me hard, but I feel the callouses of his palms. I feel his thumb rubbing against me.

The fact I only recently made amends with my sister and now want to duck out of her wedding to get more dick seems bad . . . but is it?

At the end of the hallway, I see a flash of her spinning on the dance floor and get the distinct impression that she wouldn't miss me if I left.

Leaving with Theo and spending a leisurely night with his hands on me sounds like a dream. Waking up with him sounds like a dream too.

But my dreams have a way of crashing down around me, which is what happens when we hit the end of the walkway.

We run into my dad.

He steps across the mouth of the hall, arms crossed, eyes narrowed.

And my stomach drops. I'm a goddamn adult. His opinion shouldn't mean shit to me after the absentee role he's played in my life.

But it *does*.

Because I've seen how he is with Summer. And it hurts. Because I'm his too. I've been here all along, and he pretends I haven't.

"Care to explain yourself, Silva?" His voice is cool and accusatory.

But the one Theo responds with is pure ice, one I've *never* heard him use with anyone. "Not to you I don't."

"Are you fucking kidding me, boy? You've had my daughter back there for far too long to be giving me that kind of attitude. And the baby? Clearly, you have some things to tell me."

Theo straightens, taking an incremental step in front of me, shielding me with his body. He chuckles, but it's not his usual warm laughter that makes my tummy flip.

This is more like a growl.

"Actually, Kip, I do have a few things to tell you. First, refer to my daughter again as *the baby*, like she doesn't have a name, and I'll fucking lay you out. Second, I'll be at your office on Monday morning. Bring Geoff. I don't want to fire you at your daughter's wedding. It would be in poor taste. Lastly, if you think you deserve to stake some sort of claim on this woman as your daughter, you have some serious soul-searching to do. The girl on the dance floor?" He points over Kip's shoulder at Summer, who is watching us now. "That's your daughter. This woman here? She's Dr. Hamilton until you tuck that scaly fucking tail between your legs and come make amends with her."

For the first time in my life, my father appears to be at a loss for words.

For the first time in my life, someone has come to my defense.

"Now get out of my way, Kip. I want to go home and be with my girls."

Home. My girls.

My heart plunges into my stomach. It floats and flips, rolling around in every warm, mushy feeling I've never felt.

I wish I knew what to say to my dad, but I don't. And for once, I decide leaning on someone else to take care of me might be okay.

I give my dad my best icy glare as I pass by him.

And I have another first because my icy exterior isn't reflecting the way I'm feeling inside.

With Theo, I feel the same way I feel with Vivi—in love. But it's too soon. Too fast. I'm still too raw. So, I set the terrifying thought aside and leave it for later when I'm thinking more clearly. When my legs aren't still shaking from the way I just fell apart for him.

"Dr. Hamilton, huh?" I murmur as we clear the doors and head into the gravel parking lot.

Theo pulls me up to him and slings an arm over my shoulder as he leads us to his truck. All swagger and confidence. All protective and loyal. His mouth drops to my ear and he whispers, "Dr. Hamilton in the streets, filthy slut in the sheets."

And I laugh.

No one can make me laugh the way Theo Dale Silva does.

"You're being quiet. Did I go too far? It takes a lot to make me mad. But when I get there? I blow a gasket."

The drive back to our houses is short, but he's right. I haven't been talking. The only sound in the truck's cab has been the muted sound of country music filtering from the radio. Because I've been thinking.

Overthinking.

"You didn't go too far. You . . ." I shake my head as I stare out the window at the darkened side streets of Chestnut Springs. "You were what I've always needed and never had."

When I glance over at him, he seems pensive. His brows have lowered in concentration, like he's really turning my statement over.

And while he does, I blurt out the other thing I've been thinking about. "I don't want you to stay next door anymore."

"What?" He looks gutted.

"No." I hold a hand up. "I've been wording this a million different ways in my head for the past ten minutes. Trying not to sound too bold, but also not wanting to come off indifferent, while worrying about seeming needy. What I meant to say is, I want you to stay with us."

"You do?"

I straighten, rolling my shoulders back as I suck in a centering breath. It's important I'm as honest with Theo as he is with me. "Yes. I've grown to hate you being next door when I wish you were next to me. We should try this thing out."

"Winter." The cheeky grin I've come to love graces his beautiful face. The one that comes right before some punchy little remark. The one that makes me smile before he's even said a thing. "Do you like me?"

I bark out a laugh in the quiet truck and then stare down at my hands, twisting my fingers together. "I think I more than like you."

"Because I'm your baby daddy?"

"No." I meet his eyes at the final red light before we pull up to the house. "Because you make me like *myself* . . . and you're the only one who ever has." I glance away, because staring at him feels like too much. Too heavy.

Butterflies flutter in my stomach as I stress about how he might respond to my vulnerability. But in typical Theo fashion, he does the exact right thing at the exact right time.

He takes my hand and rubs circles with his thumb until we pull up in front of my house. When he hops out, I stay seated. He never responded to staying with me.

Maybe with his mom here, he'd rather be more subtle.

He said he wanted to get messy with me, but it's possible he forgot what a huge mess I really am.

But when he tugs my door open and says, "Let's go, Tink," I know the only reason he didn't respond is because he didn't need to. I should *know*. He's told me enough times.

I get the sense he'll give me everything if I want it. I just need the nervous voice inside my head to shut the hell up. She sabotages me.

And I don't want to sabotage this relationship.

As Theo lifts me out of the truck like I'm a princess and walks me up the front steps to our daughter, I realize that I really, really want this.

He doesn't treat me like a child or placate me. He doesn't play stupid, passive-aggressive mind games or gaslight me into agreeing with him the way Rob always did.

He let me struggle in the deep end with figuring out what I want and was *there*. There to lend a hand. There to step in when I was too tired to keep myself afloat.

Theo hasn't overstepped or tried to control me. He fit himself into my chaotic dynamic without complaint. I'm not sure if he did that on purpose, or if it just happened naturally, like it always has with us.

His thumb never stops brushing against mine, even as we enter the house. Even when we come face to face with his mom watching her *Grey's* reruns on the couch.

"You two wanna sit down and watch an episode?"

He doesn't make a show of what he says next. It comes out so easily. "Thanks, Ma. But I think we're going to head to bed. Want me to walk you home?"

Loretta grins at us, borderline maniacally as her eyes land on our linked fingers. "Nope." She slaps her thighs as she pushes to stand. "I think I can find my way, seeing as how it's right next door."

After a couple of quick hugs, through which Theo keeps a grip on my hand, she sees herself out.

Then he's dragging me down the hallway. We go straight into my room, where he shoves me up against the door, slamming it shut as he drops his mouth to mine. His ability to go from joking around to stealing my breath is unmatched.

I wrap my arms around his neck and kiss him back, smiling against his lips while his hands slide over my ass.

But only for a moment. Because we both hear it and freeze.

My head tips back on a groan. "Why is she so mellow all day and then so sensitive at night?"

Theo pecks my mouth quickly and smiles. "To intentionally terrorize you, most likely."

"I'm going to get her back when she's older."

He lets out a low chuckle. "Petty. I like it. I'll grab her and take some milk out of the freezer. You get ready for bed."

"Sexy bed or regular bed?" I ask as he opens the door and heads across the hall.

"You could wear a nun's habit and it wouldn't stop me," is what he tosses back before disappearing into Vivi's darkened room.

I stand still, like my feet have grown roots to the floor. Theo's deep murmurs filter back to me, along with Vivi's cries that soften and come to a halt as he speaks to her.

Is this what it should be like?

Kisses and jokes?

An extra set of hands?

I'm struck by the moment because it's so pedestrian. So *normal.* It's not even movie worthy.

"Yes, there she is. Your mama." His lips press against our daughter's dark hair as he moves back into our room, holding her.

"Mama," she garbles the word, but we still understand it. My arms reach out automatically as hers stretch toward me.

"Hi, Vivi baby." I dust my nose over hers a few times as I gather her against my chest, basking in that baby scent I know won't last.

"Here, Mama, get some snuggles. I'll grab a bottle."

My hand shoots out to capture Theo's wrist, stopping him. "It's okay. I can just feed her. We're all tired."

It's not lost on me as we sit down next to each other on the edge of the bed that I haven't breastfed in front of Theo. I haven't pumped in front of Theo. That's felt intensely personal. Like something I should hide from him, even though Loretta walked in the other day and didn't give me a second glance when she asked, "Doll, do you have any gardening tools? I'm tackling the front beds at both houses today, but I can't find one of those little handheld shovels."

I told her to try the shed, and she gave me a thumbs up before walking back out.

Bodies don't make me uncomfortable, and I don't generally feel shy about my own. It's just ... Vivi's nursing has been solely ours since the day she was born. Something we did in the middle of the night while it was quiet, or pulled over in a random parking lot when she wouldn't stop crying. Sometimes, in a carrier while I attempted to make myself something to eat, so my breast milk was nutritious and not just glorified coffee.

I pull down the strap of my dress and glance over at Theo, but he's not gawking at my body. Instead, his eyes linger on my face.

"What was it like when she was born? Did she nurse right away?"

My heart twists and I take this as my turn to trace my thumb over the pulse point in his wrist. "Yeah, from day one. It fucking hurt at first too. I cried when she latched for the first bit."

"But you don't cry." He winks at me, and I roll my eyes. Those two motions are like our secret handshake at this point.

"What else?"

"Hmm. It was such a blur. I was so tired but couldn't sleep. I'd wake myself up even when she was still sleeping to check if she was still breathing. My left breast produced so much milk that it squirted her in the eye once."

He huffs out a laugh. "Really?"

We glance down at her, now straddling me, latched on, holding my breast like it's a bottle. "I think I could have fed an entire village of babies off my left side alone. It's the real MVP."

"Is that why the freezer is full of breastmilk?"

I snort. "Yeah, and I've donated over half to the hospital."

"Really?"

I nod, watching Vivi's thick lashes get heavy, her blinks getting slow and languid.

"I wish I'd been there."

God. My chest caves in on itself in a Theo-shaped hole.

"I feel like I've missed so many moments that I'll never get back."

My hand squeezes in a pulse on his wrist. "You won't, but you'll get new ones."

"I'm trying hard not to overstep with her or be overbearing. You two feel so established, like this tight little duo. Teammates."

"You might even say . . . business partners?"

Theo snickers, bumping his shoulder against mine.

"You and your damn business partners." He gives her knee a soft rub before turning thoughtful again. "No, I just I don't want to come between you two. I feel like an interloper in this private world you've created. But I just . . . I could stare at her forever. You know? I keep going back to my place at the end of every day, but I feel like I'm in the wrong house."

When I peek down at Vivi again, she's nursed herself to sleep. Her tiny hands have gone soft, fingers falling open.

"I feel the same way," I whisper. "Here." I lift her carefully as I turn to Theo and gently put his daughter into his arms. "I have an idea."

His head quirks, but he doesn't argue. Instead, he sits on the edge of my bed, holding our daughter, wearing a suit, looking so damn good it hurts. Literally, the back of my throat, my chest, my stomach—they all ache.

I head to the en suite bathroom where I wash my face, brush my teeth, pull out a spare toothbrush for Theo, and change into a pair of gray jersey Calvin Klein shorts with an oversized matching crewneck.

When I come back to the bedroom, my body thrums at the sight of Theo. I get up on the bed and kneel behind him, hands on his broad shoulders as I stare down at Vivi's perfect little doll face.

On the one hand, I feel like I barely know Theo. On the other, there's this comfort with him. This sense of knowing. I can't explain it. All I know is I've never felt it. Maybe it's because we made a whole new human being together, but I think it's more.

I think even without Vivi, we might have ended up back in each other's lives.

I think he would have made sure of it.

And that thought warms me from the tips of my toes to the little fizzy sensation behind my ears. Theo Silva barely knew me but never forgot me. He never gave up on me. He was coming for me with a single-mindedness that I can't understand.

And maybe I don't need to.

Maybe now it's my turn to let him in.

"She's perfect, right?" I rest my chin on his shoulder.

"Perfect." His finger traces her nose, over her pudgy cheek, and around the shell of her ear.

"I put a toothbrush out for you in the bathroom."

"Okay," is his quiet reply, but he makes no move to leave his spot on the bed. We stare at her for I don't know how long. Then I watch him lift her and get a close-up view of him dusting a soft kiss to her forehead.

My mouth goes dry, because an hour ago he bent me over and made me blush harder than I ever have. And now he's all bulging muscles and sweet kisses while he dotes on our daughter.

And it is *the* most intoxicating combination.

He twists, handing her over to me, not failing to kiss my forehead. And then he pads away quietly, appearing introspective.

Sad and happy.

I keep thinking this entire thing *has* to feel overwhelming to him, but he's given no sign of that being the case. He just keeps showing up with a smirk and a wink. Every damn day.

Carefully, I turn on the bed, lying Vivi down in the center before putting my head down on the pillow with a deep sigh.

Today was . . . a lot.

My eyes grow heavy as soon as I go horizontal, but the click of Theo flicking the bathroom light off draws me back to waking.

He just stands there—untucked dress shirt, chiseled jaw, furrowed brow—staring at the bed like he's confused about what to do next.

"Theo. Come to bed."

"Really? With both of you?" Insecurity flashes on his face.

"Yeah." I pat the pillow. "She's probably going to kick you all night. It's not as adorable as you think."

With a nod, he removes what's left of his suit, and I try not to eye-fuck him in his boxers during what should be a wholesome family moment.

I fail.

"You're looking at me the same way you did that night at the gas station."

"No, right now is worse. That night I was guessing how you'd look under your clothes. Tonight, I know."

His lips twist as he approaches the bed, the light from the bedside lamp playing over every line in his chiseled body. He's more cut than I remember. His abs, the line of his quad muscle down the front of his thigh as he places a knee on the bed. The long hours spent at Hamilton Athletics have somehow made him even more mouth-watering. His fists push into the mattress as he hovers over Vivi, muscles rippling on his forearms.

With a soft expression on his face, his dark eyes, deep like the darkest chocolate, flit to mine. "Thank you, Winter."

Part of me wants to ask if he means for letting him sleep here, but I'd be playing dumb. I know he's thanking me for so much more. I feel it in the way my heart pounds under the weight of his gaze.

Saying you're welcome doesn't seem right either, so I say what I've been thinking since the moment he showed up and made it his mission to make my life better. "Thank you, Theo."

My tongue traces my lips as I stare back at him. "Get in and stare at your girl all night if you want to."

I turn and click the light off before he responds. Only a silver-blue light filters in through the window, and slowly my eyes adjust to the darkened room. Theo's on his side, hands folded under his cheek.

But I get the sense he isn't only staring at Vivi. He's staring at me too. His girls.

"Hey, Theo?" I whisper, reaching across to dust my fingers over his forehead and into his hair.

"Yeah?"

"You're not an interloper. You're her dad."

When I wake up, sunlight streams through the windows. Theo is out cold on his back, that square jawline dusted in just the right amount of stubble. He sleeps peacefully with his lips parted gently, his dark lashes fanned down over golden skin.

My gaze traces the apex of his Adam's apple, down over his toned chest, to where our little girl has full-on starfished over her dad's chest. His broad palms encase her tiny ribcage, and her head rests right where I know she must be able to hear his heart beating.

I laid my head there once, almost two years ago. I remember trying to catch my breath, trying to wrap my head around how someone I barely knew could make me feel so good. So relaxed.

But this is different.

This is better.

I just lie here in a happy sunny bubble, letting my head and my heart work around it.

It feels good.

It feels like home.

29
Theo

Winter: Please don't do something that will land you in prison.

Theo: Can't make any promises.

Winter: Please? I'd still bail you out, but I'd be mad at you.

Theo: You being mad at me gets me hard. Angry sex is fun. This is not a deterrent.

Winter: Maybe I wouldn't bail you out at all.

Theo: Nah. You'd miss my dick too much.

Winter: No. I'd miss *you*.

"Phone?" I place my hand on the conference room table where Kip and Geoff sit across from me. Kip is stone-faced and his employee is nervous—as he should be—when he places the phone in my palm.

"What did I tell you to do with my phone, Geoff?" I ask, voice clipped as I swipe into the phone and pull up the text messages without even glancing in his direction.

I search "T" and there they are. *Tink*. I glance through them, but they're hard to look at. They gut me. Knowing Winter like I do now, I can't help but think about how badly this must have hurt her.

Yesterday we spent the day in bed and really dug into those early days. We talked about her parents and her childhood. I cooked. We laughed. She and Vivi napped, and I lay next to them, watching them sleep.

For one day, we lived in the most perfect bubble.

And now I'm out for blood.

"To, uh, respond to your messages? Post some pictures on your socials?"

"And what about any important or personal messages that came through?"

"Forward them to you." He gives me eager nods, like he's proud of his work.

I slide the phone across the table to the two men and lean back in the chair, knitting my hands behind my head and crossing a booted foot over my knee as I wait for them to read.

It's fascinating to watch. As they scroll, it's like all the color that drains out of Geoff's face is transferred into Kip's by osmosis.

One turns white while the other turns red.

"That seems like a pretty important set of messages to pass along, wouldn't you say, Geoff?"

"I thought—"

"You thought you'd respond as me? To a woman telling me she's pregnant with *my* baby? And *that's* how you responded?"

"I thought—"

"Nah." I sit forward abruptly, my elbows hitting the table loudly enough to startle him. "You didn't think at all."

"I did you a favor! You wanted to clean up your image. You get all sorts of crass messages on that thing. Women asking you for stuff, sending you things I'd rather not see. This was no different."

"This was *my daughter*," I hiss, swiping the phone back from his incapable hands. "And I missed her birth along with the first nine months of her life because you're a judgmental piece of shit who overstepped his boundaries."

Geoff swallows and drops my gaze.

"You didn't *know*?" Kip's voice sounds hollow, his jaw popping as he looks between Geoff and me.

"Of course I didn't know. What kind of asshole do you take me for?"

"Winter never told me."

"She never told *anyone* because everyone always treats her like shit!" My fist slams down hard enough to rattle the table as I let them have it. "Her mom. You. Her shitty fucking ex, who is *still* harassing her. She's convinced she needs to do everything alone because that's what *you* showed her all her life. That no one will show up for her. That everyone always abandons her."

The boardroom is quiet as I suck air in through my nostrils, trying to calm myself down. "Except me. I'm going to show up for her. Every goddamn time. So Kip, you're fired. I used to like you, but I no longer respect you. And Geoff, if I could fire you twice, I would. You fucking suck."

It was an immature final blow. But man, Geoff fucking sucks.

When I stand, Kip does too.

He meets me at the door and shakes my hand. Hard. "Theo, you may not respect me, but I respect the hell out of you, and I wish you the best. And I'm . . . I'm going to make this right."

I don't think he's trying to make me feel bad, but he does. Bad for him. I don't think Kip is a shitty person at heart, but he's a flawed one. We all are. His best wasn't good enough. Maybe he tried to be a good father to them both. I can't say for sure. But what I do know is he failed. Monumentally.

And I think he just realized it. I can see the devastation on his face.

"Thank you, sir," is all I give back before turning to leave.

As I go, I hear him say, "Geoff, pack your shit up and get the hell out of my office. I never want to see your face again."

I smile to myself as I head to the elevator, because Geoff got fired twice today after all. And that makes me happy.

When I pull up into the driveway of Winter's house, there's a fancy car parked on the street, lined right up with the front gate. In my truck, I watch the vehicle through the rear-view mirror. I see movement, but the tinted windows on the car obscure any further detail.

Not that I need much more to make a guess. Winter has been tight-lipped about her ex, aside from mentioning he never went down on her. Which is enough to let me know he's useless, no matter what the piece of paper hanging in a gaudy gold frame behind his desk might say.

I'm already fired up from my meeting with Kip, so I decide to roll with that energy. I grab my empty paper coffee cup and step down from my pickup to approach the car.

Three loud knocks on the window are how I announce myself.

When the glass finally rolls down, I'm met with the face of a man who looks like he's doing his best impression of the douchey trust fund baby ex-boyfriend in *Legally Blonde*.

I bet this guy has "the third" tacked onto the end of his legal name.

"Hey, man. You lost? Something I can help you find?"

His smile is greasy and terse. Not real at all. "Yeah, *buddy*." He's also condescending, but I'm not surprised. "Just here to see my wife."

Wife. That word makes me want to break something.

I prop a hand on the top of his car, pulling my sunglasses off to look him in the eye. "No married women live here. But if you're here to harass your *ex*-wife by hand-delivering bills, she'll never pay. I'll take that envelope right there on the passenger seat and save you a trip to the mailbox. Cause I promise you . . ." I lean in and lower my voice. "If you keep showing up here like a fucking stalker, all you're gonna do is make it real easy to get a restraining order."

He glares at me, teeth clenched tight. Too much of a coward to respond. So I needle him where I know it'll hurt. "Wouldn't be hard to consult my lawyer friend about it. You know Summer Hamilton, don't you?"

"Who the fuck do you think you are?" he bites out, hands twisting on his steering wheel.

I smirk. "Just a guy who knows the medical board would have questions about why someone had to take a restraining order out against you."

He scoffs, giving me an exaggerated once-over with an almost impressive level of fake bravado. "I get it now. Enjoy my leftovers." He tosses the envelope out the window, and it sails past me.

I make no move to pick it up. I'm too busy smiling at Dr. Rob

Valentine. "She's no one's leftovers, and I've been enjoying her since before you ever saw the divorce papers, *buddy*."

I shouldn't have said it, but my patience for assholes is shot today.

His only response is to rev the engine while still in park, like we're gonna race or something. But the joke's on him, because I already won.

Winter isn't his leftovers. She's the gem too precious for him to keep.

"You drive safe now," I call out over the sound of his engine as I knock on his roof.

As he pulls away, I toss my empty coffee cup in through his front window. Just to be petty.

Then I stand there, arms crossed over my chest, watching him gun it to the end of the street. He rolls through the stop sign like the rules don't apply to him. His license plate reads *DRHEART* and I grimace at the sight.

So lame.

"Did you throw a piece of garbage into his car?" Winter shouts on a laugh from the front porch.

"Just putting it in the trash, Tink!" I turn, swiping the envelope off the grass boulevard, and grin at her. She has Vivi slung on her hip. Blonde hair pulled back in a loose braid, little wisps sneaking out to frame her face like a halo.

The face I spend an inordinate amount of time staring at because I can never get enough.

"So, now you've met Rob . . ." she utters.

"Yes. Such a pleasure."

Truthfully, I hate him more than he deserves. What I want to feel is indifferent. But I'm not there yet.

I hate him because he almost had all of this instead of me, and the circumstances that led me here still feel so fraught and fragile. I'm not an insecure person, but now and then a thought pops up. A thought like . . .

Without Vivi, would Winter be interested in me?

I do well, but I don't drive a McLaren or own a massive McMansion and I didn't go to university.

But I brush those thoughts off. This is new. These feelings are normal. Plus, I'm the one walking up the front sidewalk to the woman who's been stuck in my head for almost two years.

"I can't believe you married a guy with a personalized license plate. That might be the worst part of it all."

"He thought it was so witty."

"I can think of a lot of words for him, but after that exchange, witty is not one of them."

"Sorry." Winter nibbles at her bottom lip as I take a couple of stairs at a time to stand before her.

"Winter, apologize for him again, and I'll take you over my knee."

Her eyes widen, and I reach for Vivi. I need a hug after the last few hours and something about a squishy baby just hits different. The way she rakes her fingers through my stubble. The way she smells. The way she babbles away at me like I understand her happy little nonsense language.

"I thought he'd have given up by now. He did this to Summer too."

Cupping the back of Winter's head, I press a rough kiss to her forehead, brushing my stubble against her temple as I tug her into me.

The three of us.

Just because I can.

"Well, what happened when he got reported for all that? I mean, Summer was his patient. A minor."

She stills. "I never reported him."

I draw away. "What?"

Winter sighs, and it's a heavy, exhausted sigh. "I was going to, but he trapped me in a place where I can't, and he knows it."

"Why can't you?"

Vivi fusses, getting sick of being carried. She wants to crawl and cruise and climb and channel her inner daredevil. So, I bounce on the spot, hoping that entertains her.

"Because if I do, it will drag Summer into it. That's what's always held me back. She's finally happy. Finally free of all that shit. And I don't want to do that to her. He knows I won't. That's the only reason he feels secure enough to keep showing up here."

I grit my teeth. I hate this, especially for Winter. But I also hate it for myself because I hate the feelings it stirs up. Jealousy and insecurity and anxiety.

I don't like Rob Valentine, and more than that, I don't trust him.

"Well, I told him he's making a great case for a restraining order today." Winter nods, twisting her lips together. "What?"

"I don't know. He's just so . . . prideful. I hoped he would eventually get bored and fuck off. I've thought about the things I could do, the action I could take. But the truth is, I just want to be so inconsequential that he gets bored with me and moves on."

I reach for the screen door and open it for her to walk through. "I don't think he's moving on."

"No, I don't think he is," she says, as she ducks back inside. "But I'll deal with it. I don't want you to worry."

I snort and lock the door behind us.

How can I not worry when two of the most important people in my life are living under this roof and I'm weeks away from going on the road again?

"How'd it go with my dad?"

"Very satisfying. I am officially agentless, and Geoff is jobless," I reply, kicking my lace-up boots off. "How about here?"

Winter is standing in the middle of the house, wearing ripped denim shorts and a baggy Hamilton Athletics T-shirt. Looking all tanned and luminous and tiny in the open space.

She shrugs and glances away, not able to meet my eyes. "Honestly, we kind of missed you."

"We?" I quirk a brow as I approach her. "Did Vivi tell you that?"

She rolls her eyes at me. "No."

"So, how do you know?" I tower over her now, waiting for her to turn her face up to mine. I'm trying not to get my hopes up that she might give me a little something today.

On a day when I need it.

Her chin tips up, blue eyes so crystal clear, a light shimmer of gloss on her lips.

"Okay. Fine. *I* missed you," she confesses.

And then she hugs me.

30
Winter

Summer: What. The. Fuck. Is this a wedding gift?

Winter: Lmao. It's the reason I was pissed you weren't doing a formal gift opening. I wanted to see your face.

Summer: Where did you get this?

Winter: I found it in a box a long time ago and took it.

Summer: THIS IS THE ORIGINAL PAGE?

Winter: No. It's the exact ad you had of Rhett taped to your wall, but blown up, printed, and stretched on canvas. The original is in an envelope taped to the back along with a travel voucher.

Summer: We can't stop laughing! It's so big! I don't even know where I'm going to put this. This is the best gift ever!

Winter: Hahaha. I'm so happy you both love it. I'd like to suggest above your bed. For old time's sake.

Summer: I am dead. You killed me. Best ever.

Summer: *photo of Rhett standing beside the print grinning and giving a thumbs up*

"**O**kay, Vivi. Say *Dada*."

Sitting in her highchair, Vivi picks up tiny pieces of banana and stuffs them in her mouth. Watching me. But not babbling. Lately, when Theo is out, I've started trying to get her to pick up the word. Theo missed milestones during the time he didn't know about us, and I know that makes him sad. Melancholy. He won't allow himself to feel that though. He's perpetually happy, and that shit is going to catch up with him one day.

It's not normal.

"*Da. Da,*" I try again.

She smiles and points at me. "Mama."

My responding grin is automatic. *Mama.* Sometimes I feel like I need to pinch myself. I wanted this so badly for so long that it hardly feels real.

"Where is Dada?" I turn slowly, taking in the whole room, which has Vivi responding in kind. Her little fingers grip the sides of her tray as her tiny body rotates in place.

She says a bunch of words, but they don't mean shit. I've strung more coherent sentences together after way too much tequila.

But I go along with it anyway.

"Oh, you think so?"

Happy babbling is her response.

"He's at work right now, just across the back lane at Aunty Summer's gym."

A tiny hooting sound.

"You miss him? Honestly, same. It's weird. And confusing."

A hum.

295

"Well, because he's so handsome, my brain stops working when he's around. And he's so sweet my heart forgets it's been broken so badly in the past."

She tosses a piece of banana on the floor and the wet slapping noise it makes has Peter skidding out from wherever he was sleeping to hoover it up.

Deaf my ass.

"Da!"

My head whips back to Vivi, but she's pointing at Peter.

I decide I will *never* tell Theo that I'm fairly certain she said *dog* before Dad.

"Dada? We should go visit him? Vivi, that's such a marvelous idea."

So, that's what I do. I grab my gym bag and our baby, taking along my broken brain and mended heart, and head out the back door to see Theo.

"Why right now?"

"Because I need to work out." I tighten the straps of the carrier on Summer's shoulders. "But . . . right now?"

"Yes, right now."

I wasn't lying when I said I missed Theo this morning. And then things became awkward with Rob and my dad, so we barely talked. And quite frankly, I'm feeling a little sensitive where Theo Dale Silva is concerned.

"I'm training right now." She gestures over to Rhett and Jasper, who are chatting in front of a bunch of stackable boxes that I know she makes them jump on to.

"Pfft." I snap the clip shut over her shoulders. "They don't count. Plus, Vivi told me she wants to hang out with you for a while."

Summer looks down at her niece and smiles, her voice changing to this sweet baby tone she only uses with Vivienne. "Oh, well, why didn't she just say that first? There is no one I'd rather hang out with."

Vivi grins, her two bottom teeth jutting up like a jack-o'-lantern mouth, and she lets out a bubbly laugh.

"Even Theo is booked up though. We're always busy from now until around dinnertime. You just . . ."

I zone her out and scope the place for Theo. I know he comes here in the afternoons to work. I've never thought twice about it, but he seemed on edge when he walked out of my house today.

He didn't kiss me. He just said, "I have clients. I'll be back to make you ladies dinner." He winked, but then he left. And my mind did that thing it does where it imagined all the places he might go, and who he might be with, and what if he meets someone less complicated and insecure than me?

And who could blame him for wanting that?

So, I decided the best way to ease my mind was to come see for myself that he was at the gym. Working. And not banging some hot twenty-year-old with symmetrical breasts.

"Are you looking for Theo?"

"Yes."

"He's over there." Summer tilts her head toward the opposite corner of the turf area where Theo is staring at his watch as some hot twenty-year-old with very big, very even breasts pushes a metal sled with heavy plates across the floor.

"Do you train playboy bunnies here too?"

297

Summer snorts. "No, but with all the athletes who train here now, I'd be lying if I said the female clientele hasn't taken on a different vibe. It used to be the old ladies at their Zumba classes gawking. Now, I have girls who drive out from the city to train here several times a week."

"Well, huh." I glance down at my fingernails, trying to decide what color I'll do next. Perhaps green, to go with how I'm feeling right now. "I'm sure that's great for business."

"Winter ..." There's a warmth to my little sister's voice. "Are you—"

"Jealous?" I whisper-shout. "Insanely. Are all his clients so hot?"

Summer laughs. She straight out *laughs* at me and my spiral. "Win, I've never seen you so fired up over ... anything. This is adorable."

"Shut up." My lips twitch.

"I'm just so happy!"

"Summer, go be sentimental somewhere else. It makes me uncomfortable."

Her head tips back and she barks out an even louder laugh, not at all offended by me, before she goes back to torturing her new husband and their family friend with her niece in her arms.

And me? I do the routine Theo set up for me. Today might not be proof of it, but I feel better every time I come here. A little calmer. A little more confident. A little more in control of my life.

From the leg press, I peek at him, wondering if I should have said hi. I decide that seems more insane than this already is.

When I complete another set, I give another glance around the edge of the plate I press my feet on. He hasn't noticed me, which is fine. He looks focused. Perfectly professional. I take a break from spying when his hands touch the woman's shoulders to adjust her position.

That's how my entire workout goes—rap blaring in my earbuds, eyes wandering to Theo Silva and then wishing they hadn't.

I find myself tired of my covert operation and give up on being discreet. I'm laid out on *The Bench* doing my final set of crunches when Theo approaches.

He crouches beside my body, one warm hand over my knee, hot breath against the shell of my ear as I keep my gaze fixed on the ceiling. "Excuse me, ma'am? I'd like to remind you to sanitize this bench. Last time you used it"—his voice drops lower—"you came so hard that you soaked my face."

My cheeks redden. "That joke gets less funny every time."

"No. It doesn't." His stubble brushes against my ear.

"What are you doing? Aren't you working?"

"Yeah, but then I saw you. Didn't know you were here. And I wasn't going to keep going without coming over to say hi to my girl."

I turn and finally make eye contact. "Am I?"

"Are you what?"

"Your girl?"

"That's what I keep trying to tell you. I need to get your hearing checked. Take you and Peter to the vet once and for all."

"I just didn't know if we were like . . . a *thing* thing. Like in public and stuff." My hand waves around nervously as I completely skip over his joke.

"Oh. Hmm . . ." He settles back, peering around the gym. And I look away, that mean little voice in my head saying *See? I told you.*

His firm fingers grip my chin and turn my face back to him. "Winter, we are a thing. We are *the* thing. We are *it*."

And then he kisses me. In the middle of the gym. When he should be paying attention to the girl with the even boobs.

He finds *me*.

He kisses *me*.

He belongs to *me*.

I thought I had that once when I didn't.

But the man who is kissing me now? Out in the open for longer than is appropriate?

He is not the same man.

He's a better one.

His tongue takes one final swipe through my mouth before he pulls away, glittering onyx eyes hyper-focused on my face. "I'm off at seven. Then we're going out."

"Out?"

"Yeah. Dinner. A bar. Something. A date."

"A date?"

He smiles, pushing to stand over me. "Yeah. We haven't done one of those yet, have we? Wear a slutty dress for me."

"Are we having tequila again?"

He turns away with a rumbling chuckle. "Sure, Tink. I'll lick it off you when we get home," is what he calls back.

Loud enough that people stare. And I don't even mind.

"One dance."

How did I let him talk me into coming here after our beautiful steak dinner? The Railspur is a big country bar in town. It has elevated western vibes with industrial fixtures and warm wood finishings. It's also packed.

300

"Theo."

He said he wanted to show me off. That's how. And I fell for it. Hook, line, and sinker.

"Winter."

"It's a country bar. I don't know how to"—I point at the busy dance floor—"whatever that is. Do you?"

"Two-step?"

"Yeah. You don't even seem that country to me."

His face scrunches up. "I grew up on a ranch. I ride bulls for a living. What more do you want from me?"

"I don't know. You've always got combat boots and a tight T-shirt on. And flannel or whatever. Where are the Wranglers? Where is the cowboy hat?"

"That's my uniform at work. Part of the sport. I don't have to dress that way all the time. Should I pick up a twangy Texas accent and start keeping a piece of hay between my teeth? Should I learn to play the banjo?"

I shudder. "No. Please don't. That kid from *Deliverance* really ruined the instrument for me."

He shoves his hand out at me. "Let's go."

He's already dragging me toward the crowd of people. I know our friends are here too, because they just "happened" to be at the bar when we came after dinner. Summer, Willa, Sloane. All the boys. Apparently, Mondays are the new Friday.

"Okay, fine. *One dance*. But only because you refused to let me pay for dinner."

He scoffs, flipping me to face him. One hand lands at my waist and the other gently grips my fingers. He's so effortless. So soothing.

"Hold up. I paid for dinner so you'd have sex with me later."

So ridiculous that he makes me laugh.

So fucking charming that we stay for more than one dance. We stay until I'm breathless and giddy, and my hair feels damp at the nape of my neck.

He pinned me, he dipped me, he kissed me. He showed me off.

I've never felt as cherished as I do in the middle of a busy dance floor surrounded by people I don't know with Theo's hands all over me.

I've also never felt so horny, because Theo can *dance*. His skills on the dance floor are so impressive they make me seem like I can dance too.

"Where did you learn to dance like this?"

He smiles, a faraway look in his eyes. "My parents. They were always dancing. My dad was a great dancer."

"Yeah? You don't talk about him much."

He pulls me closer. "He died riding bulls. I still plan to win a championship like he did—that's my goal. But I think if I let myself talk about him too much, I'll start wondering what the fuck I'm doing getting on a bull who wants to kill me dozens of times every year."

I suspect it's more layered than that. I suspect Theo has his own set of daddy issues, has markers to hit to feel worthy of his father's legacy. Because based on all the internet research I did after I found out about the pregnancy, his dad was one of the best. A legend. One of the first Brazilian riders to really make a mark on the North American circuit.

"Is he why you became a bull rider?"

"Yeah. I was like his shadow. I always wanted to do everything he did."

"How close are you to making it to the finals this year? After this time off, are you too far behind in points?"

His head tips down as he tries to get a good look at my face. "Tink, why does it sound like you know a thing or two about the WBRF?"

My lips curve up against his chest. "There may have been some Google research performed at one point or another."

I feel the deep rumble in his chest. "So . . . internet stalking."

"Research."

"Right. Sure. That sounds far more academic, way less deranged."

"I'm not deranged."

"Is that why you were stalking me from behind the leg press today?"

Oh my god. Cringe.

"Shut up, Theo."

"Saw a little flash of blonde hair and blue eyes from between all those metal machines. It was adorable. Are we going to call that research too?" I groan against his chest. "Smart, pretty, but not stealthy."

I straighten. "New rule, you only train people who are less pretty than me."

His eyes do a dramatic roll. "That's everyone, Tink. You've ruined me. Don't you get it? I only see you. You've got all my attention. Every last bit of it."

"Me?"

"Yeah. You and your snarky one-liners. And the way you're grumbly in the morning until I bring you a coffee. And that goofy voice you use when you talk to Vivi. How sweet you are under all that professional indifference. I even like it when you stalk me. Makes me feel special." He winks.

I roll my eyes and try to bite down on a smile. "I'm not sweet."

"You are. I've tasted you. And now I want to again. Let's get the fuck out of here."

31
Winter

Summer: MORE BABIES!

Willa: Is this in reference to Theo just dragging Winter out of here like a horny caveman?

Summer: Shit. I didn't mean to put this in the group chat.

Willa: Aww. You guys have a sister chat?

Summer: *salute emoji*

Sloane: What even is that emoji? It always looks like a dick to the forehead to me.

Willa: Sorry, come again?

Sloane: Or a side profile of Pinocchio.

Summer: Sloane . . . it's a hand. Saluting. Like YES, SIR!

Sloane: Seriously? I'm looking closer now. *salute emoji*

Willa: A fucking dick to the face? Pinocchio? There are tiny bumps that show the fingers. Somebody needs to take away your beer.

Sloane: Anyway, I hope Winter is taking a dick to the face right now.

Willa: Way to change the subject.
Sloane:

———

Theo tugs the passenger side door of his truck open, but rather than letting me get in, he pushes ahead and steps up into the truck himself.

"What are you—"

Before I can finish my question, he hauls me up like I weigh nothing, positions me straddling his lap, and slams the truck door.

"What are you—" I try again, fingers already sliding up the back of his neck, tickling the base of his close-cropped hair. But he kisses me, stealing any words or coherent thoughts right out of my mouth.

"There's no way I'm going to make it home without getting inside you first. This dress has been making me hard all night."

"You told me to wear something slutty." I giggle against his lips, going back in for more. "But this is a busy parking lot."

"And?" His mouth drags down the side of my neck, toward the line of my jaw, while his hands travel under the loose baby doll dress I chose for tonight. It's flowy with lace details. Each bodice strap ties in a bow at the crest of my shoulders.

It looks really cute with my cowboy boots.

"Someone could see us."

His hand tugs my panties to the side, stroking me. And I'm already wet.

"Good. Haven't you figured out I have a thing for that? Go ahead. Get loud." His mouth works across my collarbones. "I hope someone sees you riding my cock. Screaming my name. I hope they tell everyone. Print it in whatever shitty little newspaper they have in this town. Take out a roadside billboard."

"Rude." I huff out a laugh as he tugs down one strap and pulls my nipple into his mouth, licking and circling it. My hips rock when he bites the sensitive peak before pulling the opposite strap down to give both sides equal attention.

He leans back to admire me, breasts bare and heaving. "So fucking pretty."

And with his eyes on me, I feel beautiful. I don't wish it was darker. I don't wish he'd hurry up and shift his eyes somewhere else. I could lie naked in front of him and luxuriate in the way he appreciates my body.

Suddenly, the need to feel him inside me is overwhelming. My hands are at his jeans. His belt. He's lifting his hips. I'm tugging them down. He's fisting his length and running the thick head of it through my wet core.

I'm impatient though. With one hand on each of his shoulders, I sink down an inch. He's notched inside me, and my head falls back in relief.

"Yes," I breathe.

"So fucking tight." He doesn't move, but he groans.

I move down another inch and his hands grip my ass. A light tremor moves through them as he caresses me. "You trying to kill me, Tink?"

I don't respond, opting to drop my lips to his neck, to kiss him the way he kissed me.

The dip at the base of his throat.

The bump and scar on his collarbone.

Back up to his ear, where I nip at him and then whisper, "No one has ever made me feel so good. Like I don't need changing or fixing. Like I don't need saving. Everything is so rushed with us sometimes. I just want to savor you for a minute."

I kiss his stubble. Beside his mouth. He doesn't respond, but I don't give him a chance, because I press my mouth to his in a searing kiss as I lower myself slowly. My hands move over his pecs and shoulders while his roam my back, always returning to squeeze my ass.

He groans into my mouth when I finally drop onto his full length. I feel him swell inside me, filling every bit of space. Like he was made for me.

"Theo." I nuzzle into his neck, arching my back to push my ass into his grip as I rotate my hips.

"Have you figured out how to make yourself come since that night?"

"Yes."

Over and over again while I thought of you and the way you made me see stars.

"Show me." He gathers the skirt of my dress and bunches it at my hips. "Lean back. Play with your pussy and come on my cock. I want to watch you again."

My entire body flushes with heat, and I don't hesitate.

The glove compartment isn't far behind me, and I straighten until I feel it cool and smooth against my back. Theo slouches slightly in the seat to accommodate.

He feels even thicker inside me, stretching me to my limits. A rush of wetness seeps from me, and I drop my hand down, spreading it on us.

I trace a finger over where my skin meets his. Soft and hard. His hips move and I feel him. I feel myself.

The way we fit.

"Fuck, Winter. You have no idea what you do to me." His eyes glow on me, leaving a trail of sparks in their wake.

I move my fingers over the base of his shaft while he fucks me slow and shallow. It's hot. It's unhurried. I feel like I'm allowed to explore him. Explore us.

I feel like I have all the time in the world, because I'm suspecting we are doing more than just trying this out.

We're seeming pretty damn permanent. The sex is new, but learning to need him has been in the making all summer.

I slide my fingers up to my clit and press hard, chin tipped down, while I watch Theo's hips flex as he slides himself in and out of me. I can't look away. It's . . . fucking hot watching him push into my body.

Without shame, I rub my clit in firm circles, using one finger and then two. Then back and forth, more rapidly.

"You like the way you look taking a cock, Winter?"

I don't even glance at him, still watching his veined length thrusting in a slow, even rhythm. I rub my clit, more frantic now. "I like the way I look taking *your* cock."

His hips buck and he hits me deep, shoving me back against the dash. One hand on my inner thigh presses me open wider while the other grips my hip hard.

"Good. Cause it's the only cock you're ever going to take."

Then we both lose it. We're a tangle of limbs. Curse words. Moans. Whispered names and jerky movements. It all feels like the perfect symphony. The perfect crescendo.

Sweet meets filthy.

Slow meets hard.

His mouth slants over mine, and he whispers, "I hope you're on birth control this time cause you're going to be dripping my cum the entire way home."

And that's all it takes. His words. His cock. My fingers. We explode together. A flash of light. A rush of heat. Tremors and sweat and heavy breathing.

I feel my body clamp down hard on him. I feel him pulse inside me. My body tingles in parts I've never even noticed.

I feel *everything*.

And when he gathers me against his chest, I feel loved.

He holds me, our breathing erratic, as he carefully lays my skirt over where we're joined right as I hear . . .

Voices.

"Theo—"

"Winter, ignore it. Just shut up and kiss me. You're safe with me."

He sits up straight, combs his fingers through the side of my hair closest to the window, and claims my mouth with heart-rending passion. I hear people beside us, but I don't look. I'm all eyes on Theo, body attuned so perfectly to his.

I hear giggles followed by, "Those people are making out!"

And I smile into the kiss.

They don't know we're doing so much more than making out.

Or that what happened between us here tonight felt like so much more than sex.

32
Theo

Theo: How's your bath?
Winter: Good.
Theo: Just good?
Winter: It was peaceful until you texted me.
Theo: What are you doing?
Winter: Enjoying myself. Go away.
Theo: Send me a pic and I'll leave you alone.
Winter: What will you do with it?
Theo: Frame it.

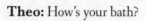

I hand Winter her morning coffee where's she leaned against the kitchen island and press a soft kiss against her plush mouth. I feel her smile even though we both know I'm going back on the road today. "How was your bath?"

Peter sits at her feet, gazing up at her like he's the lovesick one. I don't know how she went from regarding him like he was diseased, to taking him everywhere with her and feeding him all the things a dog shouldn't eat. Over the past several weeks of living together full time, he and Winter have become inseparable.

She already looks rosy from sitting in the hot water, so it's hard to tell if she's blushing. But judging by the way her eyes drop to the coffee mug in her hands and the way she takes a deep sip to avoid answering me, her bath was *good*.

I have the photo to prove it.

"If you'd given me some warning, I could have dropped Vivi off with my mom and come to watch the show."

"Theo . . ." Her eyes dart to Vivi, who has one hand propped against my knee while she takes tiny steps away from me, testing the limits of her cruising. "Young ears. And you got a show last night."

"*Winter.*" I imitate her voice, chuckling when she rolls her eyes at me. "I didn't say a thing. We both know the one guilty of talking like a trucker in front of her is you. And today is a new day, that show was *yesterday*. I have needs."

"You're such a horndo—" She stops short, her eyes fixed on the ground.

When I follow her gaze, I freeze too.

Vivi is *walking*. Like a tiny drunk person with her arms outstretched to her mom's legs. For weeks now, she's been cruising from chair to couch, to table, along the wall. I've urged her to take that one little step without holding my finger, but she just hasn't been *quite* there.

In what looks like a motion that is almost falling into Winter, she makes it, tipping her face up to stare at us. Her dark eyes widen in shock at the same time her mouth opens in the most hysterical "O" shape, like she can't believe it.

"You did it!" Winter squeals, turning to put her coffee down.

Vivi giggles and claps, looking so, so damn proud of herself.

I crouch down to her and hold up my hand. "High five, baby girl! Next up, bull riding."

She slaps my hand and laughs harder. The urge to pick her up is real, but that feels like the wrong way to celebrate this milestone. Like clipping her wings the minute she's learned how to use them. So, I get to my knees and squeeze her in a hug. She squirms when I blow a raspberry on her neck.

"Oh my god." Winter is staring down, pride and horror warring on her face.

"What?"

"I've been so excited for her to walk. It's like I failed to realize how fucked I'm going to be when she can. Like ... how do you control a human with no sense of self-preservation who can *walk*? Run? Let alone ride a bull."

I can't help it. I laugh.

"It's not funny, Theo! She's already got this nutso Silva streak in her. Did you not see her the other day? I turned around for like ten seconds and she used a chair to climb up onto the counter."

"I know. I was watching her figure out how to get up there to get a cookie. She was fine. Really kind of impressive if you think about it. Got her mama's brains."

"What's going to be impressive is me keeping her alive with you away. I've gotten soft having you around. I have to keep her from taking up toddler parkour *and* I'll have to get my own coffee. It's total bullshit if you think about it."

She's joking, but there's a thread of truth in there. We've been living in a blissful world since I made it clear to Winter we were together.

There wasn't a lot of conversation about it. We sort of sank into the warmth of this new normal. My mom is still living next door for a couple of weeks before she needs to get back to Emerald Lake, which is a blessing *and* a curse. And slowly but surely, I've moved my things over to this house.

Winter is funny. Now and then, she empties a drawer and leaves it open. A silent invite to move more of my stuff. It's like she still can't bring herself to believe that this whole thing with us is real, that this is something bigger. Though I can tell she does by the way she clings to me all night. The way she casually swings by the gym while I'm working just to say hi—and glare at my clients.

But we're on the cusp of change today.

"Maybe I'll take one more week off," I announce as I stare down into my daughter's eyes. She's still standing here, listening to us, head swiveling back and forth like she's part of the conversation.

"You will not."

I start at the bite in Winter's voice. "Pardon?"

She lifts her finger to point at me. "Not a chance. You listen to me, Theo Dale Silva. And you listen carefully. You are going to go to whatever shitty little town you need to go to—"

"It's Billings, Montana, Tink."

"The only thing I know about Montana is *Yellowstone*."

"The National Park?"

She scoffs. "No, the show. So you're going to go to Dutton Ranch or wherever the hell it is, and you are going to kick all their hillbilly asses."

I cross my arms and shift over to prop a hip against the counter and face her. "Is that so?"

"Yeah, that is so. Because you can wipe the floor with them. And you want it bad enough to make it happen. And I don't want to tell Vivi someday that her dad gave up on his dreams because her mom became terribly needy and codependent."

I huff out a laugh. "You have the strangest way of telling me you 'more than like me,' Dr. Hamilton. Aren't you worried I'll get hurt?"

She waves me off and takes a sip of her coffee. "No. You're too stubborn. Manifest that shit, Theo. I want you to win. I'll patch you up myself if you get hurt, and then I'll tie you onto a bull myself if I have to."

My lips twitch. "That sounds kind of hot, if I'm being honest. Like a sexy doctor with a bondage ki—"

She points down at Vivi, who is staring up at me with impossibly big brown eyes, facial expression awed like I hung the moon.

It hits me in the chest like a battering ram.

The reason I don't want to leave isn't only because I don't want to leave Winter.

It's because I'm head over heels in love with this little girl. This little girl who I barely knew a couple of months ago. This little girl who has become my entire world without even trying.

The reason I don't want to leave is that I don't want to miss anything.

A first step.

A first word.

A first injury.

I don't want to miss a single thing because I've already missed so many.

"Theo . . ." Winter's voice is soft now, and her soft, slender fingers slide between mine, squeezing gently. "We're going to be good. We're going to be so happy when you get back. But we'll survive without you. You need to do this. You'll regret not doing this."

I blink. "What if I don't win this year? Then I'll be gone next year too."

"Then we'll be here waiting for you to get home next year too. I'm dreading going back to work too. But the world doesn't stop. Dreams don't evaporate. We're going to figure this out."

She swallows, her throat working. I can tell she's not done but is having an internal pep talk with herself to get the words out. "As a family."

That battering ram strikes again. Winter's tied up so tight, sometimes these comments feel like a knot in her mind has tugged free. That she's straightening things out in her head as she goes too.

All I can do is nod.

"But Theo?" She tugs me closer, hand sliding up my chest.

"Yes?"

"I really think the plan should be for you to win this year *and* next year."

Winter hasn't told me she loves me, but this comment tells me she does. That she wants me to do things that are important to me. That she'll be here when I do them. That she's not here to hold me back. That she doesn't just need me around to help with Vivi—she understands that I need to feel accomplished.

Vivi tugs on my jeans with some garbled sentence.

I crouch back down to her instantly. "Is that so? I'm going to miss you too. Very much."

It doesn't matter that it's only a couple of weeks. It's going to feel like a lifetime. I bet she'll be bigger when I get back. Walking around with no problem, not just for a few steps between her mom and me.

One of her tiny hands pats my cheek in response.

I'm an emotional mess. These last two months have put me through the fucking ringer, and I'm not sure I've completely processed it all. I dove into the deep end and started swimming.

So, I cup my daughter's cherub cheeks and tell her what my dad used to tell me before he'd leave. The last words he ever said to me.

"*Te vivo*, baby girl."

She bats her eyelashes and studies me, her little bow-shaped lips turned up in a smile that strikes me as wise beyond her years. Months?

Then she blows a raspberry on the inside of my arm and the moment evaporates. Amused, she turns the other way and blows one on Winter's bare leg. She goes on practicing like she's learning a new instrument.

When I glance up at Winter, her head tilts. "What does that mean?"

"What?" I ruffle Vivi's hair and push back up to standing.

"What you just said to her."

"*Te vivo?*" Winter nods. "It's Portuguese. My dad used to say it to my sister and me. Sadly, it's some of the only Portuguese I know. It means 'I live you' or something along those lines."

"You mean I love you?"

"No." I scrub at my stubble and glance down at our daughter, who is now amusing herself by playing her favorite game of fetch with Peter and his miniature rubber chicken. "It means . . . I *live* you. Like I see you everywhere, you are in everything. Our connection is more than physical."

"Hmm." Winter sighs, glancing down at our daughter. "I love that. But also . . . why is English the least romantic language in the world? Tell me more things in Portuguese."

"I wish I knew more. My dad was so focused on immersing himself in North American culture that we really didn't get a lot of his heritage."

A small frown touches Winter's face. "That's a shame. Maybe we can go one day."

"Where?"

"To Brazil. Teach Vivi about her grandpa."

No, Winter may not say the words, but she expresses her love in different ways. She embodies it so effortlessly.

When I finally pack up to head to the airport that afternoon, I fold her in my arms, kiss her hard, and whisper against her ear, "*Te vivo*, Winter Hamilton."

I push away all the instincts that want to drag me back into the house to be with my girls and make my way down the front steps. I told myself I wouldn't look back at them. I already know Winter has Vivi propped on her hip. I already know she's waving one tiny hand while Winter leans against the door frame, looking too fucking good with her toned, bare legs on display in a soft T-shirt dress.

I told myself I wouldn't look back.

But when I hear Winter's voice, all thick and raspy, say, "*Te vivo*, Theo Dale Silva. Kick some ass this weekend," I fail miserably.

Haven't been able to keep my eyes off that woman from day one, not sure who I was kidding thinking I'd be strong enough to start now.

33
Winter

Winter: Good luck tonight. Break a leg.

Theo: That's not always the best thing to say to a bull rider, Tink.

Winter: I didn't say break a clavicle.

Theo: Hilarious.

Winter: If you win, I'll give you road head next time we go out.

Theo: This brand of motivation REALLY works for me.

Winter: Lol. Awesome. And Theo?

Theo: Yeah?

Winter: I miss you.

"**G**ood," I say as a man I don't know gets bucked into the dirt like a lawn dart.

"Winter, you scare me." Sloane laughs.

Theo has been gone for two days and I've been playing it cool. But I'm a barrel of nerves over his first competition back. My ability to turn anything into a competition has really come out to play by dating an athlete.

"Come on. Tell me you don't curse at every guy that gets the puck past Jasper."

"Fair."

"Aren't you nervous?" Summer asks from the opposite end of the couch.

"Yes. I want him to win so badly I can barely sit still."

"No, like about him getting hurt," my sister clarifies. "I could barely watch Rhett get on a bull without feeling like I was going to barf. Him coaching now is perfect. Maybe Theo could coach."

"No chance." He can't win it all if he falls back into coaching.

"Why not?"

"Because he's not old and washed up yet. Let the man live, Summer. He doesn't need another mom," Willa pipes up.

She's sitting on the carpet with Vivi and Emma, who are busy playing with a full set of My Little Ponies. Apparently, Cade can't stop buying them for Emma, which means there is an alarming number scattered across the floor.

A whole fucking herd of rainbows and sparkles.

Loretta laughs, sitting in the armchair that has become hers. Peter is curled in her lap. The thought of her leaving soon makes my chest hurt. I know she has her own life in Emerald Lake, but she's filled a gap in my heart these past weeks.

She feels like the mom I should have had.

I've decided I'll soak up all the time I can with her while Theo is away. She's helping me plan Vivi's first birthday, but she's leaving the next day. She says it will be a fun and celebratory way to mark her departure.

But I'm not so sure it will work for me.

"Theo is very capable. He knows his body." Loretta's eyes fall to mine. "He's grown up a lot in recent years. I think he'll make smart choices up there; he's got a lot of reasons to come home safe."

My throat feels tight. I assume her husband had a lot of reasons to come home safe too.

But he didn't.

"There he is!" Sloane leans forward in her chair, and I follow suit, my eyes raking over the big screen in our living room.

I see Theo climbing up the metal panels. The cream shirt he's wearing does nothing but good things for his tan skin and alluring dark features. He's wearing a black cowboy hat, but he has a black helmet in hand.

He trades them off with Rhett, who is propped up on the gate beside him. I can see them exchanging words, but I'm too taken aback by the sight of Theo to attempt to lip-read.

He looks fucking hot, like an entirely different person. Like ... an entirely different experience than I've been getting at home.

Theo's chaps are a creamy blue with black stars on them, and his protective vest is black to match his boots. His face is pure focus—with a tinge of vicious.

Like I'd lie naked in the dirt for this version of him.

"Okay, it's my turn to say *good* now that Emmett didn't stay on." Summer pulls my attention away from Theo and Rhett in the background to the blonde cowboy stomping out of the ring.

"Why?"

"Cause Emmett Bush is a douchebag."

"Emmett, who you almost let take body shots off your tits?" Willa asks right as she pops a chip into her mouth from the bowl on the table.

Summer turns bright pink. "I was pissed off that night."

We all laugh because we've heard the story. Pissed off is code for: she was trying to make Rhett jealous. Based on the way she blushes every time it comes up, I'm going to assume it worked.

I turn my attention back to the TV and end up kneeling on the floor behind Vivi. "Look." I point to the TV. "There's Daddy."

Her head turns, and I swear she peers a little closer.

I rub her shoulders just to give my hands something to do as I watch them load up a rather ugly white bull with pink skin around its eyes and a black splatter pattern all over its coat. It looks mean.

The harder they buck, the better chance he has at getting a good score, so I decide it's a positive thing.

My palms sweat. I bite my inner cheek hard enough to make it bleed as Theo lowers the helmet over his handsome face. The cage obscures most of his features, but I see those onyx eyes glaring around until they feel like they're right on the camera.

I can't help but wonder if he's searching for me. I want him to be. I wanted to be there, but two weeks on the road living in hotel rooms with a toddler, eating out for every meal—it just wasn't in the cards. It wasn't the focused setting he needed, and that didn't offend me.

If it means him succeeding, I'll do it. So, I kneel on our living room floor, twisting my hands and watching the live stream.

The people around me chat and laugh like nothing important is happening right now, but my stomach is in my throat.

Willa blabs to Loretta about how she met Cade when she dropped her panties in public. "Shh!"

"Okay, *Mom*."

322

I ignore the dig. She can run her mouth after this is over. Right now, Theo is lowering himself onto the broad back of the bull, running his gloved hand over a rope methodically, in time with whatever heavy drumbeat must be playing in the arena.

Or maybe it's just my heart thumping in my ears.

He wraps his hand. Tugs a couple times. His shoulders rise and fall on a heavy exhale.

Then he nods.

The gates fly open and the bull lurches into motion from a standstill. The timer at the top of the screen flicks through the seconds. He only needs to stay on for eight.

But seconds have never gone by so slowly.

I push up to stand above Vivi. Even she seems to feel my tension because she's watching the screen raptly after ignoring it for the past hour.

Hands gripped on my knees, I don't know what to do with myself as I watch the bull spin and leap and try to kill the man I want to spend the rest of my life with.

He better not fucking die on me.

The thought jolts me for a minute. It came so easily. So naturally. Like being with Theo is the most obvious thing in the world. Like, *of course*, we'll be together. Who the hell else would I be with?

Who would put up with my moody ass?

Who would love Vivi the way he does?

Who would love *me* the way he does?

The answer is no one. Not a single other person would ever love me the way Theo does. No one will ever show up for me the way he has—protect me the way he has. I know it because it's taken me thirty-one years to find someone who will.

What more proof do I need?

323

He's artistry on the back of the bull, and I can't take my eyes off them. My hands cover my mouth as the seconds tick down.

Left.

Spin.

Right.

Dip.

Buzzer.

"Yes!" I jump up and shout, hands in the air. I don't even care if I look like a lovesick idiot.

I am.

Loretta lets out a relieved laugh and claps her hands.

Willa and Sloane seem interested, but not all that excited. So, fuck them. In a friendly way, of course. I'm too excited. No one can ruin this night for me.

"What a ride!" Summer humors me by joining in with my cheering as Theo easily leaps from the bull and pumps his fist in the air. He doesn't take his helmet off, and he doesn't take his eyes off the bull. He beelines it for the fencing and immediately climbs up. Once he's safely over, he gets some hearty back pats from Rhett.

When his score flashes on the screen, I know it's a good one from the internet stalking I did. Ninety-five point seventy-five is not just good. It's *great*. It's what he needed.

And goddamn, I am so proud. I don't even know how to react. So I pace, biting my thumbnail while I watch him.

Helmet off, eyes on the camera again.

He *winks*.

I roll my eyes as I blush. As my stomach flips and butterflies erupt in my chest. Maybe he was winking for the fans, but it feels like he was winking for me.

I glance at Loretta. She saw it too.

"He did good," she says.

I nod and grin at her, feeling antsy. Right now, I could walk around the neighborhood or go for a workout. "He really did."

When the doorbell rings, my head snaps up. I have no idea who would be here on a Friday night.

Summer leans over the arm of the couch to peek out the window. "Looks like a flower delivery!"

She leaps up to follow me to the door, clearly living for the level of mushy happiness in my life right now.

"Hi," I say breathlessly as I open the door and take in the man in street clothes, holding a bouquet of roses and an envelope.

"Winter Hamilton?"

"Yes!" I beam.

"Great." He holds the flowers out to me and the minute my fingers wrap around the vase, he says, "You've been served."

My smile freezes and my blood runs cold. "What? Is this even a thing that happens outside of movies?"

"'Fraid so." The man's mouth twists. "You have a good night now." He jogs down the stairs and takes off to his car.

"What. The. Fuck." I stare down at the blood-red roses, confused. Shocked.

"Give me this." Summer swipes the envelope off from where it's taped to the side of the vase and rips it open. She unfolds the papers, and I watch her chocolate-brown irises move back and forth over the lines of typeface.

Her eyes burn with fury when she looks at me again. "Rob wants a paternity test."

34
Theo

Winter: Congrats! You look hot in your chaps. Let me know when you're at your hotel so I can call.
Theo: You can call me anytime. And also send nudes anytime.

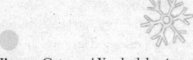

Rhett walks into the empty dressing room and tosses me a beer. "You hiding out in here?"

The can hisses when I open it. "Just taking a second to soak it all in. It's weird being back."

"You know what isn't weird? Watching you kick Emmett's ass. You're coming for him, and he knows it. Spent the last couple months feeling a little more comfortable than he should have. Sleazy fuck that he is."

"You still mad at him for hitting on Summer?"

Rhett nods and takes a sip of his beer. "For the rest of my life."

We're alike in that regard, but we're different in a lot of other ways. He wears his cowboy hat and jeans like it's a second skin. Me, I love the sport. I love the rush. I love the competition. But it feels like a uniform to me.

Rhett loves being on the road. I don't think he misses riding, but he loves coaching. He's still got his hands in the pot.

Me ... I can't see myself staying here once I hit the top. I don't know what I'll do, but it won't be settling down as a lifer in the WBRF.

I'll want to be at home. Close to Winter and Vivi.

"You going out tonight?"

"Nah."

Rhett points at me like that question was a test for how focused I am right now. "Good answer."

"Gonna head back to my room and see if Winter is still up."

Rhett waggles his brows at me.

"Fuck off."

"You've come a long way, you know."

"Well, I've been told I have an excellent mentor."

"No, I mean as a person. As a man. I know I was hard on you, and maybe that came off as hard on Winter. I just ... I've seen you sow some wild oats over the years. I wasn't sure you had it in you to be what she needed."

I nod, not offended by what he's saying—because it's true. "I know you mean well, but you're still a total prick."

He scoffs at me and then my phone rings on the bench beside me, lighting up with a photo I snapped of Winter and Vivi snuggling together in a sunny bed surrounded by white linens.

It makes me smile.

"There she is." I swipe a finger across to answer the phone. "Tink," I say and take my first swig of beer.

"Hi. Congratulations! Pretty good tonight, huh? We watched you." Her voice is soft, but there's tension there too. A tightness like she's holding something back.

"Yeah, felt good to shake the cobwebs off."

"And beat Emmett!" Rhett calls out loud enough that she can hear.

"Summer shared that sentiment too." Winter laughs, but it feels forced.

"Everything alright?" I ask, not wanting to ignore that troublesome tone in her voice any longer.

What I get back is a loud, tired sigh.

"What's wrong?" Panic edges into my voice.

"Nothing, nothing. I'm good. Vivi is good. Where are you right now? I wasn't sure where you'd be. Maybe call me when you get back to the hotel?"

"How about you tell me now so I don't freak out? It's just Rhett and me in the changing room, having a beer. There's nothing going on."

"Okay ..." she whispers, and my heart thumps wildly against my ribcage. When I glance over at Rhett, his brows are drawn, body held taut.

"Okay, so I'm just going to come out and say it. Because you need to know. But you do *not* need to freak out. I've got this. Okay?"

"I'm not going to promise not to freak out over something you haven't told me yet."

She doesn't respond to that, she just forges ahead. "Tonight, my ex served me with papers requiring me to take Vivi for DNA testing."

328

I feel like every noise in the stadium shuts off at once, replaced by a whoosh of shocked and confused white noise.

"What?"

"Rob is contesting her paternity."

"Why?"

"I don't know. He was too big of a coward to deliver the letter himself. But if I had to guess? Just to stir shit up. Just to insert himself where he doesn't belong."

I can hear quiet murmuring.

"He did the same thing to Summer. He'd just pop up out of the blue. Call her, show up to see her. It wasn't until Rhett dropped that bomb on him that he stopped."

"Is Summer there with you?"

"Yeah. She's been looking over the papers. We've been having a long overdue conversation."

"What's going on?" Rhett steps closer at the sound of his wife's name.

I wave him off. "Report him. Drop your own bomb."

The line is quiet for a few beats. "You know that's complicated. I just . . . I don't want to drag everyone into this. They set the court date for next week. Summer is going to track me down a good family lawyer."

"Us, Winter. Track *us* down a good family lawyer."

"No."

"I'm coming back—"

"Theo, no. You are staying on the road. You are getting those fucking points. And you are not fixing another messy thing in my life. One of my favorite things about you is that you don't treat me like I need saving. And I don't. I'm the one who married him. I'm the one who's played into his hand at every turn. *I* will fix this. You didn't ask for any of this."

"No. I chose it."

She's quiet for a beat. And then another. Then a thought I hate with every fiber of my being pops up in my mind. One that I maybe should have had a long time ago. One that got pushed to the wayside while I rolled my sleeves up and got to work righting the wrongs I'd put into motion.

One I never asked straight out.

"I—"

I'm so caught off guard, so angry at Rob, that I snap. I say it. "She's my daughter, Winter. Right?"

A pin could drop and everyone in a ten-mile radius would hear it. That's how silent it is now. Even Rhett is motionless, his face drawn in alarm as he stares back at me.

It's quiet for so long that I pull my phone away from my face to see if the call is still connected. The seconds tick along, like my phone is counting the moments that follow the nuke I just dropped. The devastation worse with every second that passes.

"Well, I guess we're about to find out," is what she says back in a hard voice. It doesn't sound like the woman I know at all.

Then the seconds stop ticking, and the screen fades out to columns of cubes. Colorful squares that mean nothing to me as I stare down at them.

I'm choked. I'm hurt. I'm angry. Weeks of emotions come tumbling down around me. Weeks of emotions that I've pushed away in the name of being responsible and grown up. Weeks of taking care of the people around me, but failing to take care of myself.

And I lashed out at the wrong fucking person.

I want to crawl into the phone and pluck out those five words one by one. Undo ever saying them. I just thought the worst of a woman who has spent her life feeling like everyone always thinks the worst of her.

And I spat those words right in her face.

"That wasn't the right thing to say, Theo." Rhett's rough voice meets my ears as I lean back against the cold metal lockers behind me and close my eyes, my stomach flipping with instant nausea.

"I know."

Mom: Theo, please answer your phone. I've tried calling multiple times now.
Rhett: Text me when you're back safe.
Summer: I'm going to fix this.

"What?"

I flop back on one of the two queen-sized beds in my sad, boring hotel room, phone held up to my ear, and a towel wrapped around my waist.

"Back safe?" It's quiet wherever Rhett is. Clearly, he didn't go out either.

"Yup." I'm not sure why he's calling me when we just saw each other and are staying in the same hotel. "What's up?"

"Just checking on you."

"I saw the text. You gonna come rub my back to sleep too?"

I hear him huff out a laugh. "I can if you want me to."

"Nah. I'm fine."

"You sure?"

"No. But I will be."

"You should call her."

I groan. "I know."

"Are you going to?"

"In the morning. I need a sec to get my head straight. From the day I found out about Vivi, I literally dropped everything I was doing and jumped straight in without even thinking twice. I've just been in survival mode and today . . . today fucked me up."

"Dude. That kid is yours. She's practically your doppelgänger. I don't know how none of us put it together."

"I know. I *know*. But there's this nagging voice that keeps asking me, *What if she's not?* What if there was some mistake? The night we hooked up, she hadn't given him divorce papers yet, so it's not like it's impossible. I wouldn't judge her. And it wouldn't make a difference."

Rhett is silent for a few moments. "If Vivi wasn't yours you'd still want to be with Winter?"

"*Of course* I'd still want to be with Winter. I've wanted Winter from the first night I laid eyes on her. I'd still want Vivi too. But I'd be gutted. Winter may have been the one trying to get pregnant for a long time, and I might be the one who stumbled into fatherhood by accident, but I love it, Rhett. I love *them*."

"Then you should call her and tell her that."

I feel like I have, but she's so fucking gun shy it gets me nowhere. I don't want to rush her, to push her, to wonder if she's putting up with me to appease some perceived insecurity of mine.

But I don't share that with Rhett. That feels personal. It's something that's unfolding between Winter and I, and no one else needs to be privy to that part of us.

"Yeah, I will," is what I say instead, having already settled on licking my wounds and having a pity party tonight. Because tonight, when she told me she didn't want me there for something that concerns *my* daughter? It felt like a slap in the face. My mom told me once that acts of service are my love language—how I show I care.

And Winter doesn't want that from me.

Sometimes I worry that Winter will never love me *quite* the way I love her. Or maybe it's me being greedy. I want to hear her say it so bad it hurts.

"Get some rest, okay? I wanna see you up on the podium tomorrow while Emmett sulks back in the locker room."

"You got it, coach."

I click my phone off and lie here, staring at the ceiling.

Hating myself. Hating what I said. Hating I'm here instead of there, with them.

I call Winter, but she doesn't answer. I call her again. And again. All to no avail. Before I give up and sink into the numbness of the night, eyes latched on the fan above me until I feel dizzy.

My phone buzzes in my hand, and I jump, hoping it's her.

But it's my mom calling. Again.

I press the button on the side to ignore the call. I love my mom, love that she cares enough to call, but I need to figure my shit out alone. I haven't been alone in what feels like a very long time.

Within minutes it vibrates again. This time, Summer is calling me. I ignore it again.

Over the years, I've grown accustomed to fending for myself. I haven't been accountable to anyone.

Now it's like I'm stretched thin. I'm too many things to too many people. My goals and my needs seem to clash with this new perspective on life, with these new people in my life.

I've spent years wanting nothing more than to be my dad. To win a WBRF championship so I can say I followed in his footsteps. Now, what I want even more is to be the dad he could never be because he couldn't give up on his dream. It was never enough.

I still want to win, but there are other things I want too.

I feel like Winter when she needed that time alone in the bath. Time alone getting her nails done.

It's my turn. I'm sick over tonight. My heart is heavy with regret. But I need a moment alone to let shitty thoughts consume me, so I can wake up prepared to go back to Chestnut Springs and dig Rob Valentine a nice deep hole to live in.

One he can't crawl out of and upend my family again.

But at midnight on a Friday, there isn't much I can do. So, I turn my phone off, plug it in across the room, and fall into a fitful sleep where I dream about Winter and Vivi and how much I miss them.

Then I dream about *that* night.

35
Winter

"**M**a."

I wake up to Vivi sticking her finger up my nostril in a darkened room. "Viv, what are you doing?"

I roll toward her, hoping she'll doze back off, but she fights my hugs like I'm an assailant she needs to escape, so I let her go.

The first thing she does is honk my boobs, like she wants to know the milk is there and it's an option. Then she crawls under the covers, and I know what she's seeking.

Peter.

He's curled between my feet in my bed, where I clearly crashed while putting Vivi to sleep. I haven't tried to put her in her crib since Theo left. I've grown attached to having the firm heat of him next to me, and I'm basically using Vivi as the world's tiniest body pillow.

One who picks my nose and grabs my boobs in the middle of the night.

"Why do you love being awake so much?" I groan, scrubbing at my face and checking my phone for the time.

Midnight.

Memories trickle in as my awareness returns. The rodeo. The paternity test. Theo and his bitchy attitude.

He's going to get an earful for that stupid little dig.

"Hey?" The door cracks open, and I see Summer's petite figure silhouetted in the doorway. "Are you awake now?"

"Apparently," I mumble from behind my hands.

"Okay, cool." My sister sounds wide awake.

When the bed sinks down beside me, my hands fall away from my face.

Summer crawls right under the covers—without asking—and I can't do anything but stare at her. It's something I wished we did as children.

She lies down and faces me, hands folded under her cheek. Vivi giggles from under the covers.

"At least she's in a good mood. That's something."

"She's always in a good mood. She's like her dad."

Summer rolls her lips together and stares at me. "Do you think that's why—"

"He said what he said tonight?" Tattling to his mom felt terribly immature, so I stewed until everyone but Summer left. Then I ranted and raved to her about what he said on the phone.

"Yeah. Are you mad at him?"

"Maybe. But not like you might think. I'm also relieved, because I've been waiting for this shoe to drop. His patient and unwavering commitment is superhuman. It's not normal. For the first time, I got a flash of him being a regular insecure human and I find that relatable. I know how to react. This happy, sunny, constantly upbeat person is lovely, but I feel like it's . . . a facade."

"Has he asked you that before?"

"Not since the first night when he kept asking if I was sure. But never a direct question about the paternity or the timing. And that's the first thing I'd have asked."

"So you've been waiting for this to come up?"

I nod. "Yeah, I think so. It seems like a natural progression for how we were thrust into this. I think the Rob news was a threat to this new normal we've created. He just . . . fuck, Sum. He just rolled up out of nowhere acting like this big hot Boss Daddy who swooped in to fix all my shit. He didn't even bat an eyelash."

"Please tell me you don't call him daddy."

A laugh rushes out from between my lips. "Only when I talk to Vivi. I've been trying to get her to say it as a surprise for him. So far, the closest I've gotten is her pointing at Peter and saying, *Da!* So, I'm pretty sure she said dog first. Please take that to the grave. It devastated Theo he missed those early days with her and I'm sure he'd chalk it up to that."

"Well, it's not like Peter was around then either."

I roll my eyes and feel Vivi's tiny hands as she crawls back up my body.

"Hey, Win? I'm gonna tell you something and I want you not to shut down."

I nod, my cheek rustling against the pillow as I shift to mirror Summer's position. "Okay."

"I've been sitting up and doing some reading. Going over

the letter. Doing some soul-searching. And I think it's time we report Rob to the medical board for what happened with me. Even if nothing comes of it, it will give us both the freedom to truly move on."

Vivi is at my stomach now, and I pull her up. This time, she doesn't resist my hug. She nuzzles into my neck as though she knows I need it.

"I just never wanted to drag you back into his orbit. He's so . . . inescapable, and you finally did. I want to do it too."

She raises her shoulder in a slight shrug. "Yeah, but now he's picking on my sister, so he's put himself in *my* orbit. Let me help you get rid of him."

My eyes sting. "I'm sorry."

"No, don't apologize. Let's do it together. Sisters. Yeah?"

"Yeah. Sisters." The room is softly lit from the light of the hallway, and I see white teeth as her lips stretch into a pleased smile.

It strikes me I'm not very collaborative. That I never would have asked her to do this if she hadn't offered. It feels good, not being alone in this.

And suddenly, all I want is Theo.

Theo's voice. Theo's arms. Theo's cocky wink. I want him back here, holding us. Going to that court date.

I don't want to do any of it alone. I don't *need* to do it alone because, for the first time in my life, I have people who want to be there with me.

Everything and everyone around me has changed.

But more than that, *I've* changed.

"I'm going to go call Theo. Feed the hellion and then we—"

"Can I sleep over?" Summer blurts. "I don't want to drive back to the ranch. The house is lonely without Rhett, and the gym is right across the alley."

I can't help it. A small giggle bubbles out of me. I officially feel like a little kid. "Yeah, Sum. I'd love to have a sleepover. I'll be back."

I scoop Vivi up and head to the living room where the TV is still paused on a shot of Theo, sitting up on the fence panels. I stare at the playful grin on his handsome face, the hand swiping through his hair.

Vivi points. "Dada!"

I search her face. "Seriously? Now you say it?" She blinks. I point at the TV. "Who is that, Vivi?"

"Dadadadada."

With a grin, I flop onto the couch, lift my shirt for her, and call Theo back. "We should tell Daddy about this, shouldn't we? Give him some happy news this time."

Except it goes straight to voicemail. I gaze at the phone with a small frown.

Ten past twelve.

He could be sleeping. I should do the same. Once Vivi is suitably dozy, I head back to bed, where Summer has crashed out, snoring softly.

I climb in, but all I do is worry. Vivi falls asleep between us, but I don't.

I get up and call Theo again.

No answer.

I try not to let my head go back to how we started. Those days of calling and texting to tell him something—all to no avail.

I beat myself up for not being more understanding in his one and only moment of frustration.

I worry that I've driven him to do something that will ruin everything we've created.

My mind is a beast that has run away with all my rational thoughts. Every insecurity. Every petty concern. They all filter to the forefront until they're all I can see.

And every time I get up to call Theo . . .

It goes straight to voicemail.

I toss. I turn. I eventually move to the couch where I finally find sleep.

But I don't rest, not really. Instead, I dream of *that* night and how good it felt to be with him.

36
Winter

That night ...

The elevator doors have barely shut before Theo opens his mouth and makes me blush.

"I can't wait to see how fucking pretty you look when you come with my name on your lips."

The words cause me to suck in a sudden breath. But it doesn't help me catch my breath because Theo is *on* me. His fingers are in my hair, palms gripping my head. His lips work over mine, the perfect mix of soft and hard. The perfect tempo for me to find my way and catch up with him.

When I feel his tongue swipe across mine, I whimper. It's not slobbery, he doesn't shove it in like he's conquering my mouth without a thought. He coaxes me into it, makes me want more by tormenting me with never giving enough.

"More," is all I can verbalize—all I'm comfortable saying.

All I know is I want more. More of this. More of him. More of this feeling.

A growl rumbles from his chest in response, and he pushes his thigh between my legs and shoves me up against the wall. My body jostles, but he doesn't stop.

He kisses me roughly now, and I kiss him back. His stubble rasps against my skin, abrading my cheeks. My fingers grip his shirt, fisting the fabric and tugging him closer. I want him so much closer.

He smells like tequila, and oranges, and spice. I want to dive headfirst into a pool of that scent. Of *him*.

I grind against his thigh, not caring if it makes me seem desperate. Base. Shameless.

Tonight, I'm all of those things and I'm shedding all the parts of myself that tell me I should care.

The soft white sweater fabric rides up my thighs as I press myself against him.

"Fuck, Winter." He pulls away and glances down at where I'm riding his leg. Bare skin stretches between the top of the thigh-high socks peeking out from my boots and the disheveled hemline of my sweater dress. "Do that again."

"What?" I huff, feeling the hot rush of my flaring nerves stain my cheeks.

He doesn't look at my face. He has one hand fisting my hair while the other toys with the top of my stocking. "That thing with your hips. Ride my leg."

"Why?"

A knowing grin graces his shapely lips. "Because you look good doing it, and I bet it feels good. Doesn't it?" His hand slides up the bare stretch of my thigh, going right under the boundary of my dress. A warm, calloused hand grips my ass.

I don't move. Actually, my lips turn down. My body screams at me to do it because the way I'm holding my hips back from moving is almost painful. But my head is judging me, telling me this isn't a proper way for me to conduct myself.

And Theo reads me like a fucking book.

"You gonna shed this prissy rich-bitch persona tonight and enjoy yourself? Or do you want me to fuck you politely, like you're used to? Turn the lights out. Pat you on the head and thank you when I've finished, but you haven't?"

"Fuck you," I bite out, right as my hips swivel, my clit dragging against the fabric that separates us.

He chuckles, all deep and warm. "Atta girl. Take it. Take what you want, and who gives a fuck what anyone thinks." His fingers dig into my glute as he moves his forearms, forcing me back and forth on his leg.

I'm panting when the elevator dings. My head flips to the opening doors, like I might get caught with my skirt up, grinding myself on the leg of a man who looks like a god and talks like a porn star.

But then both of his hands are on my ass, and he's hoisted me up. I squeak as my arms find his neck and he strides out of the elevator, carrying me. Past the table with fake flowers. Past the chair I'm sure no one ever sits in.

"Someone might see us," I whisper, even though I seriously doubt this small-town hotel is very lively at this time of night.

"Yeah?" He turns, roughly pressing me into a door, jostling the hinges as he plunders my mouth again.

My legs wrap around his waist, and I grind on him again. "Is this you?"

He smiles against my mouth, grinding back into me and rattling the door. "No."

"Theo!" I hiss, pushing at him.

He swipes my wrists with one hand, pressing them above my head. Another knocking sound as he does.

"Who's there?" The voice on the other side of the door freezes me, but Theo only chuckles. His lips and tongue still move against me. It's like he's feeding me his laughter, because I giggle. And this is *insane*.

Suddenly, he lifts and turns us. We head across the hallway and one slot down where I'm pressed up against a whole new door. The closer we get to his room, each tether that's kept me tied down snaps.

"Sorry, Tink." His teeth drag over my neck. He bites and sucks. "Those socks are driving me wild. Couldn't make it all the way to my room without a quick pit stop."

The door across the hallway opens and over Theo's shoulder I see a middle-aged man in his boxers, holding a TV remote. It takes him a minute to register what we're doing.

I bury my head in Theo's neck to avoid his eyes. "Shit," I whisper.

"Get a room!" he calls out.

"We're trying!" Theo says back, turning his head to smirk at the guy.

I stay hidden in the crook of his neck, basking in the feel of his body wrapped protectively around mine.

The only response we get from the guy is the slamming of a door. Then, in a flurry of motion and kisses and desperate hands, we fall into Theo's room. Only a lamp in the corner lights the space, giving it a warm, dim glow.

Theo sets me down at the foot of the king-sized bed and says, "Strip."

With a deep breath, I give myself an internal pep talk.

I am doing this. And I'm going to enjoy it. It's going to feel good.

Before I know it, I'm pulling the long-sleeved dress over my head. I toss it onto the desk and stand before him in my white bra and panties, topped off with a pair of high socks. Even though his eyes are devouring me, I keep my attention on the desk, too shy to meet Theo's gaze.

"Fuck. Look at you." He tugs my bra straps off my shoulders before reaching behind me and releasing the clasp almost better than I can.

I try not to think about how many bras he's removed.

How many times he's done this with other random women.

"Eyes on me, Winter." His fingers press at my chin to turn my head. "What are you thinking?"

"That you've probably removed a lot of bras."

"I've immediately forgotten about any of them. All I can think about is how perfect you look like this." He drops to his knees and presses a kiss to my stomach. "All the ways I'm going to ruin you tonight. All I see is you, Winter."

Fingers hook into the waistline of my thong, tugging it down until it's mid-thigh, stretched between my legs. Theo Silva is eye level with my pussy.

"Like I said." He licks his lips. "Perfect."

"I bet you always say that."

His cheek twitches, gaze still fixed between my legs. "Trust me, I don't." His eyes turn up to mine. "What should I do now?"

"I don't know." My breaths come hard and fast, heart rate accelerating. "Why do we need to talk about it? Can't you just do it?"

"Oh, because I like to hear you say it. The tone of your voice. The way you're all pink right now, panting over the thought of having to ask for what you want."

My brain fails me. My mouth doesn't move. All I can do is stare down at this insanely sexual man kneeling in front of me, asking me to say things I never have.

His mouth is curled in a knowing smirk. I'm so far out of my depth, it's not even funny.

"Should I finger-fuck it?" His thumb slides through my pussy, spinning a circle on my clit. "Or lick it?" His head drops, the pointed tip of his tongue mirroring the motion.

My head falls back, hands to his dark hair. I moan.

"Use your words, Winter. Which one?"

"I don't know," I repeat breathlessly, turning into a puddle for this man. I can feel myself leaking even though he's barely touched me.

"Okay then, you can show me how you do it to yourself, and we'll figure out what you really like together."

My head snaps down. "What?"

But he's already standing, pushing me back against the bed. The back of my knees hit the edge, and I fall onto my back. He peels the panties from my body and glides his palms up the insides of my thighs to spread me.

His hands grip the top of my socks as he stares at my core, eyes alight.

"What about the socks?" I ask stupidly.

"Leave the socks. I like the socks. Now touch yourself. Show me how you do it." He pushes me farther up the bed until he's peering down over my splayed body.

"Fuck," I mutter, taking one shaking hand and running it over myself. I'm already wet, when I'm usually not.

He says nothing, just presses my thighs open and watches my pointer finger trail through my inner lips. I squeeze my eyes shut, trying not to think how I must look to him.

"You're fucking beautiful, you know that?" His voice is harsh now, rough.

I add my middle finger, rubbing absently, but it's his hands I want. Not my own.

My own are nervous and uninspired. His are rough and adept.

"Is this really how you touch yourself?"

I open my eyes to meet his. "I . . . I mean, yeah? I don't do it a lot. I'm busy and it never really seems like a great use of my time. And it just never . . . does it for me."

He groans and drops to his knees. "You feeling good is the best use of my time. Push a finger in. Let's see it."

I moan and do as he says, curling my finger into myself. Just knowing he's watching makes it different—better somehow.

I'm slick and all I do is pull more wetness out with every slow thrust.

"How is that?"

My nipples ache, and I can barely breathe, but it's . . . "Not enough," I murmur, honestly.

One hand moves off my thigh and he leans down slightly, still towering above me.

I suck in a breath when I feel his finger join mine. "Okay, let's try together."

Elsie Silver

I don't even bother trying to talk. There's no point. All my words disappear when his thick finger slides in beneath mine. Our hands bump as he works me.

After a few gentle thrusts, he adds a second finger. My back arches off the bed in a silent plea for more.

I want more, more, *more*.

"Better? Is that closer to being enough?"

"Yes."

He groans when I clench around us.

"Use that free hand. Let's see you play with your tits while I play with your pussy."

"Oh my god." I told this man I don't come, but he might make me a liar. Because as I fondle my breast and roll my nipple between my finger and thumb, I writhe on the bed.

"Do you know what I think, Winter?"

My eyes glaze over as I peer up at the dark, dangerous man above me. I shake my head.

"I'm watching you. Watching your back arch while your nipples go hard, feeling you make a mess of my hand before I've even really started." He smirks, dropping his gaze to where we're both still wedged between my legs. "I think the only reason you don't come is because you've been fucking a man who doesn't know what you need. A man who is lazy in bed. Who doesn't know how to take care of you. But that's okay, because I'll show you how that feels tonight."

I nod, still working at my breast, watching as Theo drops to his knees at the end of the bed. "Now get your fingers out of my way. I'm hungry."

"It's okay, you don't need to," I say, grabbing at his hair, trying to pull him back up.

"Yeah, but I want to," is all he says.

Then his mouth is on me and I'm having an out-of-body experience. Rob has never, *ever* done this for me. And I never had the urge to ask him to. Even if I had, I'm positive it wouldn't have felt like *this*.

Like I'm being consumed. Like he can't get enough.

Theo's teeth graze my clit and I jolt on the bed, vision blurring. "Fuck!"

He pushes a finger in to work with his tongue and I'm a writhing, whimpering mass of limbs:

"Theo. I . . . oh my god. Fuck. That's . . ." I can't string a coherent sentence together. The only thing I keep asking for is, "More."

And when he adds a second finger, mouth suctioned onto my clit while he impales me roughly, more is what I get.

More than I've ever gotten.

Within a matter of minutes, I have an orgasm at the hands of the most infuriating and persistent man I've ever met.

And not a single part of me regrets it.

In fact, I want more.

37
Theo

That night . . .

She doesn't say anything when she comes, but her legs shake on my shoulders. Her pussy pulses on my fingers and she covers her face with her hands like she can't believe what just happened.

"Hard to see you scream my name when you cover your face like that, Tink." Her head shakes and I hear a soft laugh as I pull away from her body, watching her chest heave and her dusky nipples point up. I undo my belt before she's even come out from hiding. "Guess that means I'll have to make you come again."

That has her hands dropping. "Again?"

My brows drop like I'm unimpressed with her surprise. "And again. And again. Until you can't move."

"I already feel like I can't move." Her hands flop down beside her, and she stares at the ceiling.

"You're going to have to, because I'm not done yet." With that,

I grab her ankles and pull her down to the edge of the bed, so her legs are spread while I stand between them. I strip off my clothes. Shirt, jeans, socks, boxers. All gone.

The only thing left is the shocked, horny look on Winter's usually prim face.

"Enjoying the view?"

She swallows, the column of her throat bobbing. "Yeah. You're . . ."

I quirk my head, curious about where she's going with this.

Her hand reaches up, and trembling fingers gently trail over my stomach, tracing my abs, tracking the V-line that runs down to my groin.

"Stupid hot. Like what in the actual fuck?"

I press my lips together, not wanting to laugh right now. Not because it's funny, but because she finally said something unfiltered.

My dick is already rock hard from finger-fucking her. But I pump it a few times. Liking the way her eyes latch on to the motion. "Open your mouth, Winter."

Her wide eyes turn up to me, and her lips part. I trace them with the head, watching the drop of pre-cum smear over her top lip. Watching her tongue dart out, like she's dying to taste me, before opening her mouth wide again.

I don't think she meant for it to be so sensual, but it undoes me. My control snaps. I take two fistfuls of her hair and push my cock between her lips.

She hums in satisfaction, and the sound vibrates through me. My body clenches as I withdraw and plunge in again. It's heaven having her warm mouth all around me, her tongue swirling, hands roaming over my torso as I control her head.

Her gaze flits up to mine, full of fire. Want. Desire. Not a trace of ice as far as the eye can see.

Her head goes down farther and farther, hands gripping my ass. She's swallowing me like she can't get enough. When she goes too far, she draws back a bit, eyes glassy as she works around that reflex.

Then she goes back down for more.

"That's it." I groan. "Choke on it, Winter." She does, taking me as far back as she can.

She's driving me insane, pushing me to the end. I don't want to be there yet, so I pull out. "I'm not ready to come yet, Tink. Not before I fuck you." I swipe a thumb over her swollen lips to clear the saliva, then I lean down and whisper in her ear, "How should I take you first?"

She licks her lips, a nervous flutter taking over her lashes. I don't expect her to say anything, but she says in a quiet voice, "From behind."

"That's what you like?" My thumb brushes her cheek as she nods up at me. "Good."

I land a nip on her ear and flip her on the bed, lifting her hips so her ass is in the air.

"Condom?" she asks over her shoulder.

I'm already pulling my wallet out of my discarded jeans. The only response I give her is the sound of foil ripping, and a muttered, "Fuck," as I roll the rubber over myself.

I swipe through her wetness, watching the way her back arches, her knees slipping wider on the bedspread. She's soaked for me.

I swipe again. A shiver races down her spine. Her pussy throbs. Her hips rotate and she pushes herself at me.

"Theo, please." She glances over her shoulder at me, pink lips damp, eyes glazed. "I need—"

"This?" I slide in an inch, and her lips pop open into a little "O" shape.

"Yes."

Her body vibrates with need. I can feel it. My body does it too.

"And this?" I push in a bit further. Her head drops, fingers clutching the sheets like she's holding on for dear life.

"How about all of it?" I take her all the way, so I'm seated fully inside her tight body.

"Fuck, yes," she hisses, dropping to her elbows while I take a hold of her hips. "Move, please move."

"Move? Or fuck you? I wanna hear you say it."

Her pants come even like a drumbeat. "Fuck me, Theo. Fuck me so hard I forget my name."

Yeah, that's what she needs. To forget her name and get a new one.

"Happily," I growl as I pull out and slam myself back in.

Her body bows, and her moans turn to screams as I hit a steady rhythm. My groans mix with the wet sound of our bodies crashing against each other.

I tug her hair. She spreads her legs further.

I push her head into the bed. She chants my name.

I can feel her start to crumble, and slow my assault when she gets too frantic, too close.

"More," she murmurs as I draw back to admire her splayed out for me, so snug around my cock.

"More?" She's a glutton for punishment. "I can do more."

I lift her, slipping out as I walk us over to the floor-to-ceiling windows that face out over the quiet town. Snow swirls like a snow globe outside.

"Hands on the window and don't move them." I place them on the glass above her head.

"And if someone down there sees?"

I grip her ass cheeks and spread her before stepping up behind her and gliding back in slowly. "Then I guess they're going to see how pretty this tight cunt looks stuffed full of my cock."

"God," is her hushed reply, right as she grinds her ass back onto me.

Her breath puffs out on the cold window as I ravage her, the fog waxing and waning with each heavy pant spilling from her lips.

I squeeze her throat. I kiss her neck. I bite her back. She takes it all, chanting my name.

Her hips, her back, her legs—every move she makes is designed to get closer to me. To take it deeper. Harder. It's never *quite* enough.

"More. I need more."

My chest slides against her back, our perspiration mingling as I lean into her, sliding my hand around her body to play with her clit. "Like this? You going to come on my cock if I do this?"

Her head shakes. She's delirious. Unhinged. Lost to it all. Alive in a way that must be new to her.

I continue using her pussy while working my fingers over her clit.

"Still more."

"Filthy fucking girl, begging for more," I rasp against her ear as my hand moves up her throat. I press my thumb between her lips. "Suck."

She does instantly, our bodies slowing slightly as she hollows her cheeks out and sucks. "Get it nice and wet, Winter." Her tongue moves now, saliva swirling.

I pull out from her mouth with a pop. She gasps for breath when

I place my hand on her ass and circle the entrance. "You going to bend over and beg me for more again?" I press lightly.

She folds at the hips, stares back at me over her shoulder, and says, "Yes. More."

I move again, sliding my dick in and out of her pussy while slowly working my thumb into her ass. "Like this, Winter? I wanna hear you say it."

"Yes. Like that."

"More?"

"More." She moans right as I slip all the way in.

"You have no idea how fucking hot you look. How fucking good you feel. Best fuck of my life," I grind out as I thrust again. She bucks beneath me while I play her body like an expert.

"Theo. Fuck. That feels . . ."

Her hands slide on the glass, and her legs shake.

"I think I . . ."

I can see the way her eyes widen when she realizes she's about to come again, so I don't let up.

"Theo!" she calls my name as she topples, and I don't hold myself off any longer.

Everything tightens, and I tumble off the same cliff. My cock pulses inside her as she grips me tight before her legs give out and we both crumble to the floor. A mess of sweat, weak limbs, and breathless touches.

I tilt her head and kiss her. "Just as pretty as I knew you'd be."

38
Winter

Present . . .

I'm lying on the couch, wishing I could teleport myself back to the filthy simplicity of that night. Summer's presence draws me from the dream I can't escape to, no matter how many times I wake up and fall back asleep. The dream where I want more—and I take it.

"I woke with a dog curled up between my feet and your kid trying to take my shirt off. It's only five a.m."

"Sorry," I say flatly, in too much of a daze to react.

Summer approaches with Vivi slung on her hip. "What is happening with you this morning? You look terrible. Don't worry about Dr. Douche, as Rhett calls him. His tantrum will end soon. Hard to argue with a DNA test."

"It's not him. It's Theo. I can't get a hold of him. I've been trying all night."

"He's not answering?" She pads across the room and joins me on the couch.

356

"It's going straight to voicemail."

"Weird."

I scrub at my eyes. "Yeah, it is. At first, I thought he was banging some buckle bunny, but I know that he wouldn't, so that fear has morphed into there being something really, really wrong. Like a car accident or something. I even googled to see if there are any active serial killers in Billings."

Summer covers her mouth, pretending to conceal a yawn, but I know it was a laugh. "There isn't a chance in the world that man so much as looked at a buckle bunny. Are you really oblivious to how gone he is for you?"

"I see it, but I don't trust it. It feels too . . . perfect. Any time something feels perfect, it blows up in my face. A sister. A husband. A baby." I drop my head back and close my eyes. "I don't want Theo to blow up. I'll never recover."

"Ma." Vivi reaches for me, and I take her. The squishy feel of her in my arms never fails to comfort me.

"I'll call Rhett and see—"

"Yeah, could you call Rhett and ask him which hotel and room?"

"What?"

"Right after I looked up serial killers, I booked an eight a.m. flight to Billings so I could ream Theo out in person. Because over the phone just isn't going to cut it after this shit."

Summer's eyes widen, but she recovers quickly. "Alright, I'll pawn my clients off for the morning and drive you to the airport."

Theo never backed down when I snarled at him.

And now I'm going to return the favor.

Because he and I? We're more.

39
Theo

Rhett: You alive?
Theo: Yeah. Why?
Rhett: It's been nice knowing you.
Theo: What's that supposed to mean?

I'm pacing my room, phone in my hand, practicing what I'm going to say when I call Winter. *Sorry* won't cut it, so I need to figure out how I can apologize for the way I doubted her.

Because I didn't just toss out a question about the paternity. I questioned her integrity. And that is one thing I've never doubted about Winter, no matter how prickly or unapproachable she was.

A knock at my door startles me, and it must be Rhett. He's probably gotten an earful from his wife by now. I bet he's coming to knock some sense into me.

"What?" I growl as I fling the hotel room door open. The entire world stills around me and I stop in my tracks.

Winter is standing in the hallway, with a duffel bag slung over her shoulder, eyes narrowed like she might strangle me with her gaze alone.

In contrast, Vivi is smiling at me from her stroller, Peter's rubber chicken in her hand.

And when I look lower, Peter is attached to the end of a leash, trembling, like always.

"Da!" My head snaps back to Vivi, who is pointing at me. "Dadadadada."

"Did she just say 'dad'?"

Winter's hip cocks out, her pearly-white fingernails tapping on her bicep. "She did, Theo. She said it last night for the first time when she saw you on the TV. And when I tried to call you and tell you about it, do you know what happened?"

I swallow, but it doesn't help the lump of dread forming in my throat. It feels stuck there, like it's growing the longer I stand here putting things together.

"It went straight to fucking voicemail, Theo. All. Night. Long." Her lips thin as she sucks in a deep breath through her nostrils. She reminds me of a dragon.

"Is that why you're here?"

"No, I'm here because I wanted to kick your ass in person. I haven't slept because I stayed up all night worrying about you, your stupid handsome face, and your big, talented dick." One hand waves over the length of my body. "And just your stupid general wellbeing because you fucking *consume* me."

My stomach sinks, but I'm frozen in place, hand gripping the door. "Winter, come in."

"No."

"You came all the way here, and you're not going to come in?"

"I came here to see that you were in one piece and alone. And I have seen it."

Alone. Fuck. My fingers itch to grab her and yank her in here with me.

"Why did you bring Peter?"

"Because he's part of our family, no matter how much he reminds me of the weird squirrel from *Ice Age*. And I like it when he sleeps between my feet, so he's stuck with me now. Just like you."

"The squirrel from *Ice Age*?"

"Tell me why your phone went straight to voicemail."

I swipe a hand through my hair and blow out a breath. "I had a moment, okay? A weak, petty, insecure one. I needed a pity party. You said you didn't need me. Everyone else was blowing me up. It didn't feel like I could fix anything, and all I did was make things worse. And I knew you were angry at me, so I figured I'd shut it down for the night."

"You don't get to shut it down for a night, Theo!" she shouts. "You got to ditch your phone once before and that really fucking sucked for me. I should have showed up then and demanded you pay attention to me. But I didn't. So I'm here now, demanding you pay attention to me."

"Winter, I am so fucking sorry."

"There are people who need you now. We're stronger than this. And yeah, I was angry with you. That was a dumb thing to say. But guess what? I'm going to get mad at you from time to time. People who are together get mad at each other. They say shitty things they regret. It's *normal*. Being happy-go-lucky Theo, who ticks no one off

360

and never has a bad day, is not normal. You're allowed to freak out." She pauses, breathing heavily. "But you have to freak out *with* me."

My nose burns. Even Vivi looks serious now.

"I'm sorry." My voice cracks when I drop my head.

"You have to freak out with me because I *need* you. And I love you. I love you so much it paralyzes me to think of carrying on without you. You're not allowed to shut me out. Because you made me need you, and now you have to deal with the consequences."

I don't ignore the ache in my hands this time. I reach for the woman standing across from me and crush her to my chest. A surprised yelp leaves her mouth at how quickly I move, but she doesn't resist. My arms wrap around her tiny frame, and I suck in a deep inhale of her warm cinnamon sugar scent as I cradle her head against my heart and close my eyes, sinking into her.

"I'm really mad at you, Theo."

"Understandable." I glance down at the stroller beside us. Vivi's wide dark eyes gaze up at me. "I'm mad at me too."

"Really, really fucking mad," she amends.

I dust my lips back and forth over her hair. "But you love me?"

She doesn't hesitate. "So much it hurts."

I squeeze her tighter, soaking up how well she fits against me. Warm and soft. "Welcome to the club, Tink."

She tips her head back and holds my gaze. Although she looks tired, her eyes are sparking like they were the first time she tore a strip off me. "I love you." She says the words again like they're unfamiliar in her mouth, like she's getting used to how they feel on her lips. Like it's a new language to her entirely.

My hands comb through the warm golden strands of her hair. "I love you too. Now would you come in here so we can all be together while you're being really, really fucking mad at me and I freak out because I love you and want to kill your ex?"

She pulls away and dusts off her perfectly clean clothes. "Yeah. That sounds perfect."

I glance down at Peter, who is now sitting and shaking. "I don't think this is a dog-friendly hotel."

Winter scoffs. "He's barely a dog, more like a rat or a squirrel." She pushes past me. Bag. Stroller. Baby. Dog.

My entire life in one room. And she's right. I'm still freaking out.

But somehow, I feel better with them here.

"No sluts in here, right?" she quips, glancing around the room, looking for evidence of something I would never, ever do to her.

"Only one," I reply as I hug her from behind and rub my stubble over her cheek.

And Winter Hamilton rolling her eyes at me has never felt so good.

"Okay, Theo." Rhett snaps his fingers in front of my face while we sit atop the fence.

I should be listening. I should be watching. I should have my head in the game.

Except my girls are in the stands.

The one who has been saying the same syllables over and over again all day. And the one who napped in my bed and scowled at me the minute I came back to my room with Peter and Vivi in hand.

"Still mad at me?" I asked.

"No, I'm mad at myself."

"Why?"

"Because I'm supposed to be mad at you, but watching you roll around with a toddler and a chihuahua makes me want to ..." She wobbled her head and rolled her hand around as a way of explanation.

"Drop to your knees and put that snarky mouth to good use?"

She glared, but her lips twitched. The tiniest twitch. "Never mind. I'm still mad at you."

But now she's in the stands, holding our daughter. And wearing a pair of cowboy boots with an ornate steel toe, tight fucking jeans, and a tank top that does nothing but show off her breasts. I swear there's oil on them, judging by the way the lights reflect off the round tops.

"Dude, wake the fuck up. Get your head in the game." Rhett pokes me in the ribs and I recoil.

"Ow. That hurt."

"Thank me later when Winter wants to give you a congratulatory blow job for winning."

I rub at the spot where he jammed his fingers. "Rude."

"Fast Fire doesn't care about who's in the stands. He just wants you dead. You drew a good bull. Unless you fall off, then you drew a mean fucker. Don't let him win."

That comment snaps me out of my horny stupor.

"You're the last rider to go. That worm Emmett came back with a good score today. Better than you scored last night. He won't give up the championship easily, so buckle up, Buttercup. You're gonna need to hit the spurs hard tonight."

I nod. He's right. I'm going to have to make this bull madder than he already will be. And he's already known to be wrathful. That's why he's got a spot on the circuit.

"Shoulders back. Chin down. And get ready for the direction change so you don't go straight down the well. I'm only going to be your hero once in this lifetime. Got it?"

"Got it." I feel it then. The focus. The calm. The sense I'm sitting exactly where my dad once was. Doing what he did.

Every time I step up here, every time I sit on a bull, I feel closer to my dad than I do anywhere else.

We watch Jude. He lasts the eight seconds, but it was a simple ride. Nothing the judges will love.

"Heads up! Fast Fire!" someone calls.

The black bull trots down the chute straight into the pen, eyes wild, a string of saliva already dripping from his mouth.

Some people might think now is when the nerves kick in, but for me, it's the opposite.

Now is when everything other than a stupid level of confidence in myself melts away. My heart rate evens out. Every rational thought in my head grows wings and takes flight.

I'm the fucking best at this. And I'm about to prove it.

I drop onto Fast Fire's back and he jostles me around, pitching a fit. I ignore him, tug the bull rope, and stroke it to warm the rosin.

It's second nature, steps I could do with my eyes closed. I thrive with the dependability of the process.

As my hand works over the rope, I peek up to where Winter and Vivi are seated.

Correction: where they're standing.

Winter is on her feet, body swaying back and forth. She has Vivi propped on her arm like it's a seat, facing out over the ring.

I think someone behind her tells her to sit down because her lips clearly say *fuck off*.

A grin twists my lips, and I turn my focus back to my hand. Wrapping the rope. Testing the tightness. Shifting my seat on the bull's back. Giving him one roll of the spur to piss him off more.

Rhett says something to me, but I block him out.

And I nod.

Fast Fire rockets into the ring, bucking hard enough that the clumps of dirt flying from his hooves hit my helmet. He spins left viciously. With my core engaged, arm held in the perfect L, I don't let him shift me.

I keep my chin down, but don't look at the ground. That's not where I want to end up.

My feet slide back. My spurs hit again.

He drops a shoulder. He turns.

I expect it and smile when I keep centered through the change in direction.

"Got you, fucker," I grit out, having the time of my life.

It is both the fastest and slowest eight seconds of my life. The buzzer sounds and I get the hell out of there. A cowboy rides up beside me and I reach for him, taking the lift down and away from the bull. My days of tempting fate by doing a showy dismount are done.

The rodeo clown distracts Fast Fire, and I beeline it for the side closest to Winter. I climb the fence, rip my helmet off, and look for her immediately.

Vivi is getting jostled in her arms, because she's jumping and screaming. Hooting like a mad woman.

"Get 'em, baby!" she shouts as she waves at me.

And when they announce a 96.25 score, she starts all over again. I care a lot less about the score than I do about laughing. My chest cracks wide open for the blonde who is "really fucking mad" at me but is here cheering her ass off like I'm her favorite person in the world while holding our daughter.

It's crazy. It's unbelievable. It's unlikely.

The woman everyone told me was cold, mean, and unavailable is so thoroughly *mine*.

And that's special. That's everything.

"Winter!" I call up at least ten rows. "Get your fine ass down here!"

Her cheeks turn pink, blue eyes glittering like sapphires. With a wide grin, she shoves past people in her row to hit the stairs.

When she gets to me, she climbs up a couple of rungs and breathlessly blurts, "I'm not mad at you anymore. I'm just really, really horny after that ride."

She says it loud enough that the trill of chuckles filters in from around us.

I kiss Vivi's crown and give Winter my most knowing smirk before whispering in her ear, "Am I fucking you like a princess or a slut later?"

And just before she kisses me, she chuckles and responds with, "I don't care as long as you fuck me like I'm yours."

I kiss her back and then leap from the panels with a cocky wink in her direction before turning and striding toward the podium they've moved into place. Emmett is waiting on the lower side.

"Don't get used to it, Silva. You're not as talented as your dad."

"Charming, Bush." I slap him on the shoulder. Even this douche can't ruin my good mood tonight.

I step up above him, using his shoulder like a banister to get into place. "I might not be talented like him, but I am nice like him. So, congrats on your season so far."

He gives me a stunned expression.

I grin before adding, "It's a shame I'm about to ruin it."

The suits come out and talk about the night—the sport, the thrill—but my gaze keeps shifting back to Winter. Rhett has moved over to join her on the fence and they're both watching.

I'm snapped out of gawking at her when the announcer asks me to talk about my first weekend back after an injury.

"Break down your win for us tonight."

I take the microphone from his hand but look back over at Winter, all shiny and glowing. All smiles and excitement.

All mine.

"Well, my time off went different than expected," I start. "The rehab was fairly straightforward. I don't think I'll have any lasting effects to worry about, which is great. But the real highlight was getting to spend some quality time with my family." I tip my chin toward the fence. "Got my baby girl and my future wife here with me tonight. They make this win extra special."

The announcer chuckles and a collective chorus of *aww* sounds from the audience, but my gaze stays locked on Winter.

She doesn't roll her eyes at my showboating.

She winks at me.

"Anything you want to say to this future wife of yours tonight, Silva?"

I don't need to think twice.

I hold the mic up to my lips and murmur, "*Te vivo.*"

It's better than "I love you".

It's more accurate.

It's us.

40
Winter

Kip: I know I haven't been there for you, but I want to change that. I want to help. Summer told me about Rob. Please let me put you in touch with my family lawyer. She's the best.

Winter: Of course Summer did. Why do you have a family lawyer?

Kip: Have you not spoken to your mom?

Winter: Ha. Seriously? I stopped speaking to Marina the day she suggested I pass Vivi off as Rob's. Did she not tell you?

Kip: Well, we're not on speaking terms either. Asking for a divorce went over poorly.

Winter: You're getting a divorce?

Kip: Yes.

Winter: Finally.

Winter: And yeah, I'll take that contact.

"**D**o you want me to throw these flowers out?"

Theo eyes the vase of red roses in the middle of the counter like he wants to pulverize them, not just throw them out.

"No. I'm keeping them."

He scowls at me. He's been in a bit of a funk since getting home. I know he planned to stay on the road between the two events, to immerse himself in the back-to-back weekend competitions.

But I told him I needed him, and he came back without batting an eyelash.

"For what reason?"

"They're pretty." I shrug. "Seems a shame to waste them, you know?" I point at him. "Is that what you're wearing to court?"

He looks down at himself. Dark jeans hug his muscular thighs, and a white shirt with a deep V shows the chain that hangs over a light dusting of chest hair. He's pulled the brim of his cap down low, but I see his brows knitted together and his expression of genuine confusion.

"What do you mean?"

I wave a hand over my sapphire blue pantsuit, feeling more like pre-baby Winter than I have in a long time. "Is that what you're wearing in the courthouse? I mean, if you wear those unlaced boots with that, I'll maul you after we leave. But I was just wondering."

"I wasn't planning to go in."

My hand freezes over the glass of water I was about to pick up. "What?"

"I mean, the summons was for you, right? And Vivi?"

"Yes." I say the word slowly.

"So why would I come too? Isn't family court kind of small?

369

Wouldn't it be frowned upon if I walked over and beat the shit out of Doctor Douche? I'm trying not to be overbearing, but the truth is, Winter, I'm feeling really fucking overbearing about this. I'm not sure I'll be able to keep my cool in there."

My chest goes cold even as my heart accelerates. I'm nervous about coming face to face with Rob. I know he'll be wearing some smug, condescending smirk, all pleased with himself for drumming this shit up.

I admit the truth, because there's no way in hell I can do this without Theo at my side. "I'm scared. I don't want to go alone."

It's his turn to go still, to stare back at me and turn my words over. Because it's one thing for me to tell him I need him and another thing for me to *show* him. And today, I really need him. His presence beside me, his hand wrapped around mine. We both know what the results will be, but it's still scary.

I babble on, feeling like I might literally get on my knees and beg him if he comes back with another reason he shouldn't join me. "She's your daughter. I need you there with me. All of us together." There's a tremor in my voice as I finish out the sentence. "Please."

"Winter, come here." He holds his arms open, and I go to him, breathing in that citrus and spice scent I associate with all feelings of home. With my head to the crook of his neck, he folds his biceps around me and nuzzles down into the side of my cheek. "I will go wherever you want. I will wear whatever you want. I will never turn my phone off again. I will always, always be there for you. For Vivi. You don't need to beg, and you don't need to say please. For as long as I live, for as long as you need me, you'll have me. Okay? Never doubt that."

I nod, but don't say anything. I just squeeze him tighter, relishing the sensation of his strong arms wrapped around me.

"Because I'm your future wife?" I ask, trying to lighten the mood.

"Obviously," he volleys back.

"Did you really call your mom and tell her that?"

He snorts. "Yeah, Tink. When you know, you know."

He trusts himself so thoroughly. Doesn't second-guess himself. No one's ever proved to him he shouldn't.

I love that about him.

"I love you, Theo Dale Silva."

"I love you too, Winter ..."

A wince moves my shoulders. I've been waiting for this to blow back on me. "Don't laugh."

"I would never."

"Okay, it's Peggy."

"Peggy?"

"Shut up." I nuzzle in, biting the sides of my tongue, so I don't laugh.

"Little Winter Peggy has been making fun of Theo Dale for months now. It's just interesting, that's all."

Unable to hold back my laugh, I tip my head and peer up at him. "Theo Dale sounds like somewhere elves live in Middle-earth!"

"Winter Peggy sounds like a farmer Barbie doll that comes with a snowsuit. Summer Peggy comes with a bathing suit and a pair of sunglasses."

Silent laughter racks my body. It's not even that funny, but it's the stress release I needed.

Theo grins at me. "So fucking pretty when you laugh." He kisses the apple of my cheek, then the other, and finishes with my forehead. "Let me go get changed so I can match my little Power Suit Peggy."

And only a few hours later, after a simple swipe of Vivi's inside cheek, Theo and I walk out of that courtroom. Me in my pantsuit, and Theo looking devastating in a stark black suit of his own. He holds my hand and keeps Vivi held tight against his side like the protective papa he is.

I don't even spare Rob a glance as we pass. I keep my chin high and my shoulders back. I don't want to give him the satisfaction of acknowledging his presence.

However, I do glance up at the handsome man I get to call my own.

And as we pass my ex . . .

Theo winks at him.

Now that I've decided it's okay to need Theo as intensely as I do, it's hard to be as mature about letting him walk out that door to go on the road.

All it took was one shy, "You could always come with me?" to seal the deal.

For the next two weeks, I travel with him. So does Vivi. So does Peter. Most of the hotels are not dog-friendly, but I don't ask permission, which means they never tell me not to bring him. We hit Fort Worth, Texas—where I realize Theo isn't nearly as much of a cowboy as I thought—and then San Antonio.

We stroll the River Walk and dine out. He trains hard. I cheer like a lunatic every time he gets on a bull. We make love in the shower once Vivi's down for the night. I fall asleep with Theo's strong arms around me at the end of every single day.

And when we walk up the front steps to our little house on a tree-lined street in Chestnut Springs, we come face to face with the envelope we've been waiting for.

Plus one more. One he doesn't know about.

The paper is cool in the palm of my hand as we head into the house with bags and car seats and strollers. Traveling with a child has given me a whole new appreciation for how blissful it is to travel alone.

And yet, the thought of traveling alone fills me with dread. I'd much rather schlep all our shit around and stay with this little family I've pieced together over the past few months. Vivi turns one in a week. I go back to work a week after that—something I've been trying to pretend doesn't exist.

I've always loved my job. It's always been the place where I can escape real life and throw myself into work I enjoy.

But I don't want to escape my life anymore. I want to set up shop and stay right smack dab in the middle of it. Watching Vivi walk everywhere and learn new words, watching Theo kick ass every weekend.

Vivi is fussing, tired and irritated from the flight, so Theo scoops her up. "I'm going to go put her down for a bit. You open that. I'll be back." He barely looks at me as he gives her kisses and walks down the hallway.

His ass is phenomenal in those jeans.

"Okay," I murmur, pulling out a stool to sit at the kitchen island.

The envelope addressed to me unraveled us in so many ways, but maybe it untangled us so we could braid ourselves back together. Tighter. Maybe this ordeal has brought us the sort of peace we never would have had without it.

My lips curve up because Theo is nervous about this envelope.

Ever since that one comment, he has never questioned me about Vivi's paternity. In his heart, he *knows*, but Rob put a speck of doubt there and he hasn't quite been able to let it go. He also respects me too much to put that question out again though.

Me? I already know what story these papers will tell. They're going to tell me there is no possible way Rob got me pregnant through the walls of our separate rooms. It's going to tell me that the hottest night of my life spent in a hotel with a man I barely knew lines up perfectly with the day Vivi was born.

Perfectly imperfect. That's Theo and me.

Sometimes I wonder if we'd have ended up where we are today if things hadn't played out the way they did. If he'd known about her right away, would I have taken my fresh start? Would I have cut people out of my life who needed cutting? Would I have found the sense of freedom I did in those months I spent living on my own? Or would I have dragged Theo into the maelstrom of my family drama? Would I have felt I went from being under one man's thumb to another? Would Summer and I be where we are now?

So many what-ifs. But it feels like everything worked out exactly the way it was meant to.

"Well, she fell asleep in about ten seconds."

"Figured as much." The sight of him steals my breath like it did all those months ago. Rugged and handsome and sensual. He makes my mouth water and my stomach flip—he makes me feral in a way I've never felt for a man. He woke up a part of me I never knew existed, a little piece of myself I was living without.

"So? Did you open it?"

I tilt my head at him. "Did you really think I would open it without you?" He takes a seat beside me. His knee touches mine, and he moves his foot over to the bottom rung of my stool.

Then he tugs the stool closer so my legs fit between his.

Just like that night in the hotel bar.

"Okay, Tink. Let's open it."

"Them. I have two things here for you."

His dark eyes are lightly hooded as he stares down at the counter, and I decide to put him out of his misery. If he's nervous, I'm excited. This envelope means I can finally deliver that last killing blow to Dr. Robert Valentine.

The other means that Vivi can be his in a way she should have been from the very beginning.

I rip them both open and unfold the sheets. Laying them in front of Theo, side by side. I don't bother reading them. Instead, I put my hand on his back and watch his face. His heavy brows, the stubborn set of his jaw, the straight line down his strong nose.

And the joy in his eyes when he hits the ink that confirms what we already knew.

He wasn't there for Vivi's birth, but he can be here for every moment after because he's her dad.

Then his gaze shifts over, to the papers he wasn't expecting. The ones that detail legal name change from Vivienne Hamilton to Vivienne Loretta Silva. My way of showing Theo that he'll never be an interloper—he's stuck with us for life.

He says nothing, but I watch his throat work. "This . . . this is . . ."

"If you want, we can get another DNA test done to officially match you with—"

He spins and kisses me, his hands tangling in my hair as he claims me with his mouth, brands me with his hands.

We don't talk. There's nothing left to say. We talk with our hands as each piece of our clothing gets discarded. We talk with our lips as he lays me on the couch and hovers over me. We talk with our bodies as we come together achingly slow and the most delicious tension unfurls between us.

It strikes me that perhaps I'm not an easy woman to love, but Theo does it so effortlessly that I feel like I could be. Like I deserve to be.

I come alive beneath his hands. I come apart beneath them too. And he puts me back together every damn time.

We lie here in the afterglow, bodies sticky with perspiration, hearts beating against each other, arms wrapped tight like nothing in the world could pull us apart.

"You ready to throw those flowers out now?" Theo's husky voice pulls me from my thoughts. He glances over at the sideboard, upon which sits the vase containing moldy water and black, wilted roses. "Because now they're more gross than they were in the first place."

I rub my cheek against his toned chest and giggle, feeling lighter than I have in . . . well, maybe ever.

"No. I have a plan for those."

41
Winter

Winter: You ready?
Summer: Very.

I hear the shuffle of three other sets of feet behind me as I walk up the winding brick pathway to the house I used to call home. Now, compared to where I live with Theo, it feels gaudy and overdone. Big and empty. It takes up every square inch of space on the lot. The trees are too small and new, and I can hear the rush of traffic from the nearby freeway.

It's not Chestnut Springs.

It's not home.

When I near the three marble steps that lead to the massive door, I peer over my shoulder. Summer is grinning almost maniacally. Rhett is standing behind her, hands on her shoulders.

But it's Theo who keeps me staring. Like always.

He's leaned up against the side of the garage, arms crossed. Plain white tee stretched over his biceps. Jeans hugging his long legs in a way that makes my mouth water.

Combat boots tugged carelessly over the top.

Laces not tied.

I remember thinking once that the very last thing I needed in my life was a man who didn't tie his laces.

It makes me laugh now, a light little chuckle that bubbles up from somewhere near my heart.

How wrong I was.

I feel like he rolled up and loosened my laces when I didn't realize I was tied up far too tight.

"You're gawking, Tink!" he calls out and I flush. Of course, I'm gawking. Theo Silva was the hottest man I'd ever seen back then, and he still is now.

He winks at me.

I roll my eyes.

And then I turn, march up to the door and ring the doorbell. I know Rob is home because I called the hospital and asked my favorite charge nurse to confirm. It takes him a while to get to the door because the house is obnoxiously large.

When he answers, he's wearing a pink polo shirt and a pair of white shorts. His hair is perfectly coiffed to cover his receding hairline.

I almost recoil at the sight of him, but it's not just physical. Rob has shown his true colors in recent months, and they're ugly.

This man is rotten to his core.

Just like the vase of dead, musty flowers I'm holding.

"Winter." He looks smug until his eyes trail behind me and he notes the audience.

This is a man who thrived on me being isolated, having no one. And here I am, with people who love and support me. Who show up for me even when I'm not at my best.

His grin melts away, like a pretty mask slipping from his face to reveal all the ugliness beneath.

"Hi, Rob." I hold the flowers out to him.

He takes them before glancing down and realizing they're decaying. A dry, curled leaf falls at his feet.

"I really enjoyed these. They were beautiful. Then I went out of town with my family for a bit. Came back and saw them like this, all moldy and rotten. Reminded me of you, so I figured I would hand-deliver them."

"You came here to give me dead flowers?"

I smile. It's a fake, practiced smile, one I use when a patient is pissing me off. "No, I came to deliver the envelope that's taped to the front." I point at the vase. "Right there."

His face scrunches, but he doesn't make a move to touch it.

"Summer and I put a lot of work into our affidavits, so I hope you enjoy them. I know the hospital administration and the medical board will."

A normal person would go white. They'd be terrified. But Rob goes from red to a deep purple. I'm not sure I've ever seen him so angry.

"You wouldn't *dare*."

His voice is pure venom, but he doesn't scare me anymore. I step closer to him, lifting my chin and narrowing my eyes as I pluck a dead petal off one rose and drop it, watching it fall away like all my loyalty to this man.

I thought I loved him once, but I didn't know what love was.

I do now though.

"Oh, but I would." My tone is cool and controlled. It bites. "Because you didn't just come for me this time, you slimy fucking weasel. You came for *my* daughter. You came for the man I *love*. You came for my *family*. You went too damn far this time."

"I'm going to—"

I don't let him get a word in at all. "I haven't fucked you since the day I found out you were a predator. And now *everyone* is going to know it."

I turn and walk away from him, ignoring his curses and threats. The smashing sound of the glass vase does nothing but make me smile. I feel like I tossed a grenade into that depressing house and walked away.

I feel free.

Vivi's birthday party is perfect.

Everyone has pitched in to make turning one a special occasion for her. She looks precious in her sundress, covered in a print of oranges and leaves. The decorations are hysterical. Custom printed—compliments of Willa—with photos of Vivi's favorite thing in the world ... Peter. And the setting at Wishing Well Ranch is perfect, just like the weather. Our end-of-summer heat is warm but not unbearable, and the smell of freshly cut hay permeates the air.

Rhett set up the big white tent on the back field near the main ranch house, and everyone who's here is family, in some way or another.

Loretta. The Eatons. Theo, who keeps trying to carry Vivi around with him, but she went from walking to running pretty damn fast and gets a thrill out of making her dad chase her. His mom gets a kick out of it too. Tells him it's payback for the way he was as a toddler.

She keeps us on our toes.

Willa baked the cake. Summer and Sloane decorated. Cade is manning the barbecue. Jasper is playing a game of field hockey with Luke, who just yelled, "Oh, fuck off!" when he thought he was going to score on Jasper, but didn't. Harvey made a bowl of punch that tastes like fruit juice, but I suspect contains far more alcohol than necessary for a one-year-old's birthday celebration.

Beau has yet to show up.

"Harvey, how much booze is in what I'm drinking right now?"

He grins over at me from where we're leaning against the fence. "Enough to take the edge off for you."

"What edge? I'm relaxed. If you take too much edge off me, I might spill your beans just to get even."

His brows lift as he takes a sip out of his red Solo cup. "What beans?"

I smirk and drink again. "The you and Cordelia beans."

He chokes on his drink, and I slap his back while he thumps a fist on his chest.

"Oof. Okay, well, no one would forgive me for killing you, so maybe I'll just keep that one to myself. Though I'm really not sure how no one has noticed."

Harvey clears his throat and glances around at the group of family and friends. Music plays. Burgers get flipped. Everyone carries on in the most comfortable sort of rhythm. "Same way they never noticed Vivi is a tiny version of her dad. They weren't looking."

I nod, staring at Theo holding his mini-me as they cheer Luke on to get a ball past Jasper.

"I'm not ready to tell them yet," Harvey says after a few beats of silence.

"I was joking."

"It feels off-limits. Her being who she is. But sometimes—"

"Sometimes things just happen, and you don't realize how right they are until you're in the thick of it."

He gives me a grunt and a nod from where we stand, propped against the fence.

I break the tension with, "Is there a geriatric version of the pro-creation prowl?"

This time, he doesn't choke. He tips his head back and *howls*. "Girl, did you really just say that to me?"

"Hey, if you're gonna dish it out, you gotta take it." As we laugh, I hear tires crunching on the gravel driveway behind us.

The black Suburban SUV is one I recognize only because Kip Hamilton has driven the same vehicle for my entire life. Every couple of years he gets a new one, of the same make and model.

"That's what I figured you might need to take the edge off for."

"Hmm." I arch a brow. "You knew he was coming?"

Harvey shrugs. "Summer may have mentioned it to me while setting up. That's why I used two bottles of bourbon in Harvey's Special Drank rather than the usual one."

My nose wrinkles. "Did you just say *Drank*?"

Harvey cackles, clearly living to confuse the hell out of everyone around him. "Yeah, that's what I call it."

I'm shaking my head as I watch my dad step out of his vehicle. And then Theo is there, jogging up the short hill to shake Kip's hand.

Summer sidles up beside me, holding Vivi. "You okay, Win?"

I nod, feeling a splash of nerves roiling in my gut. So, I have some more drank. Hopefully, it will chase them away. I watch Theo and my dad open the back hatch of the SUV and pull out . . .

I gasp.

Because what my dad and Theo are carrying down to the party is something I never thought I'd see again. Something I swore was long gone, sold, or rotting in a landfill.

But within moments, they set it right in front of me, rendering me speechless.

It doesn't just look like the dollhouse from when I was a little girl.

It *is* the dollhouse from when I was a little girl.

Tears spring up out of nowhere, and my hand covers my mouth. In many ways, it's just a dollhouse. But in others, it's so much more.

Harvey's hand lands on my shoulder, and Summer's rubs at my back.

"I hope it's okay that I told him," she whispers.

Theo smiles at me like the cat who caught the canary while my dad is having a hard time meeting my tearful eyes.

"I thought Vivienne might like this."

I sniff, staring at my father, who is proud, and stubborn, and flawed. Today, he looks humbled.

"Years ago, I found it in the back alley when I was taking the trash out. And I put it in storage. I wanted to give it back to you, but I didn't know how." He glances up at me, and I stand here at a loss for words. My dad has made many mistakes but showed up today anyway. He helped me find a lawyer. He left my mom. He's never fought for me before, but he is now.

And I've learned a lot about forgiveness in recent years.

Especially how hard it is to forgive yourself.

"I just wanted you to have it. Consider it a peace offering. I haven't been good enough for you—Theo here gave me a real wake-up call on that—but I want to be. If you ever think you'd like that too, you've got my number."

With a pained smile, he turns to leave. I feel kindred with him somehow. The old version of me was here once too. I glance at my sister, the one who forgave me so wholly that I was able to start fresh.

And Theo, the man who didn't hold the shitty things I'd done over my head as some sort of proof of what kind of person I was. He took me at face value and allowed me to start fresh too.

"Dad." He stops but doesn't turn. "Why don't you stay? Try some of Harvey's drank. It's uh, good for taking the edge off."

Quiet confusion fills the space for a beat.

My dad faces me now, a small tug on the corner of his lips. "Why did you just say *drank*?"

I burst out laughing. The stress, the pressure, the confusion . . .

It all feels more bearable when I'm with my family.

Later that night, when the sun gets low in the sky, Theo curls his hand around mine and walks me to the other side of the ranch house. Our feet crunch on the gravel driveway and the hum of friendly conversation grows quiet as we get further away from everyone.

We left a cake-covered Vivi in Kip's arms. Her grandfather is so taken with her he didn't seem to mind the mess.

"Where are we going?"

"To be alone for a minute."

"Are we sneaking away to fuck?" I whisper, as though anyone could hear us.

Theo chuckles, the rumble in his chest warm and comforting. The press of his black dress shirt slides like silk against my bare arm.

His head turns, his eyes tracing me up and down while his tongue darts out over his lips. "I hadn't planned on it, but you look very fuckable in that red dress, Doctor Hamilton."

"How much farther? My feet are tired from standing in these boots all day." I sound whiny, but I don't care. I don't have to be at my best with Theo.

He'll love me at my worst, and at my whiniest. Today I'm tired, overwhelmed, and feeling a little wrung out.

He turns suddenly, scooping me into his arms as I squeal and reach for his neck. "Heading to that same spot in the pull-through where you dressed me down almost two years ago."

I laugh and let him carry me until we're standing in front of the ranch house.

Right where I shoved my keys between my fingers and lost my shit on him.

Right where it all started.

Theo places me on my feet as I peer around the property. It was cold, dark, and snowy that night. And I was stressed out.

But tonight it's warm and golden. The sky is a pale pink. My feet are killing me, but I'm content.

And when I look back at where Theo was standing—he's now down on one knee.

Holding a little blue velvet box with a stunning teardrop solitaire ring glinting off the rosy sky.

And I freeze.

Theo chuckles. "I know this might feel soon, but hear me out."

I nod woodenly. It doesn't feel soon. It feels like a dream.

"I was in this exact spot when you gave me the best and hottest verbal lashing of my life. You were all wild eyes and fighting words. I thought I'd never seen a more heart-stopping fiery woman in my life. You were ... well ... you were mean. But I appreciated your spunk. That was the night I knew I wanted you."

Fucking tears fill my eyes again.

"That was the night I told my friend I thought I was in love with you. And I had no idea how right I was." He shyly lowers his gaze for a moment. "I was being an obnoxious little shit disturber. I was egging you on because I liked the way you scratched back. I liked *you*."

A tearful giggle ripples out of me. Only Theo Silva could have liked me that night.

"That night, all the best things in this world came into existence. You. Vivi. Us."

A tear spills down my cheek, and I reach up, nodding as I swipe it away. He's right. That night changed the world.

Our world.

"That night I realized I'd never get over you. Time, distance, none of it mattered. That night, I knew there would be no one like you for me. I was so sure of it. I could feel it in my bones. I still do."

I can't keep up with the tears anymore, so I just let them fall. Accepting this isn't some disease I have.

It's happiness.

I drop to my knees, wanting to look into this man's face. The one who never treated me like I needed saving but saved me all the same. I cup his cheek and he presses a kiss into my palm before forging ahead.

"That night we were reckless." His voice cracks. "But god, I'd be reckless with you over and over again if it means ending up here."

That sentiment. This man. It's like there was something missing inside me. Like I wasn't whole, until he came along.

"Yes." I reach for the ring.

"I haven't even asked yet." His corresponding laugh is thick. Tearful too.

"You don't need to. The answer is yes."

He drops the box and slides the ring onto my finger with shaking hands.

We stare at my hand for a moment. Just the two of us.

"Winter Hamilton, will you marry me?"

I smile through the tears. "Would hate to make a liar out of you after how long you've been telling people you're going to marry me."

He winks at me. "When you know, you know."

And this time I don't roll my eyes. I kiss him.

I kiss him until there's nothing else but his lips on mine, his hands in my hair, and his ring on my finger.

Epilogue
Theo

Eight months later ...

"Where's Vivi?"

Winter and I walk out of the dressing room, side by side. It's the final night of the WBRF championships.

The crown jewel I've chased my entire career. The one I've always fallen short of. The one I've clawed my way back from injury to make a run at this year.

"In the stands with your mom and everyone else." She glances down at her clipboard, all business tonight.

"Doctor Hamilton?" one of the guys calls to her from a bench as we walk past. When we turn, he holds his hand up. His thumb is pointing in the wrong direction. "You think I should go to the hospital? Or can we patch this up here?"

"Well, Jude, I think your thumb is broken and you're probably going to need surgery."

"I don't wanna miss the last rides though. Gotta see our boy here take it all." He grins at me like the maniac he is.

Winter sighs, checking her watch. "You fucking bull riders are nuts," she mutters before glancing at me. "I'll be out right away."

I smirk and shoot her a wink. "Sure thing, Doc."

I catch the tail end of her eye roll as she turns back to Jude, speaking in a matter-of-fact way about ligament damage, splints, and painkillers.

Going on the road has been a hell of a lot more enjoyable since Winter took a position as a tour doctor. Sure, it means she's constantly patching up a bunch of dumb bull riders, but all the guys adore her and her no-nonsense approach.

And I love having her and Vivi with me at every event. The entire crew is here in Vegas for the finals, which means Vivi is in the stands. The guys have almost taken her in as one of our own. She hangs out behind the scenes with a bunch of cowboys, so we've all but guaranteed she's going to have a trucker mouth when she grows up. Not to mention a bunch of protective uncle figures.

I already feel bad for whatever boy comes sniffing around her.

I chuckle to myself as I walk down the long corridor, calm and collected, considering what I'm walking into.

The lights hit and the roar of the crowd gets louder the closer I get to the ring. Rhett is there waiting. I think he's more nervous than me.

But I have a good feeling. I have the same feeling I had the night I met Winter.

A knowing. A gut instinct.

Tonight's my night.

"Ready?" He claps me on the back as I approach the paneling.

389

"Yup."

"You realize only one cowboy has sat this bull for the full eight?"

I laugh, because you have to be at least a little nuts to do this for a living. "About to be two."

Rhett nods, his jaw popping. "So you're going to—"

"Rhett." I grip my friend's shoulder. My mentor's shoulder. "I could not have asked for a better coach. Thank you for all you've done. But . . ." I glance out into the stands and try to make sense of the feeling of familiarity that consumes me. "I just want to soak this up tonight."

He nods, slaps my shoulder and steps away, giving me the space I need.

My routine passes in a daze. I get through all my steps. I don't look around for Winter, because I know she's here. I swear it's like I could sense her approach. Without even seeing her, I know where she is, exactly which fence panel she likes to sit on and watch me.

Vivi is here. My mom. My friends. I swear my dad is here too.

And suddenly, this stadium feels an awful lot like home. Like every single person I care about is here to cheer me on. Like after years of doing my own thing I'm not alone at all anymore.

The ride is a montage of pictures that flicker through my vision. The rope. My hand. The gate. A buck. A turn. My mind is blank. All I see is that buckle I'm about to win.

All I know is that the thing I've sworn I was going to get since I was a boy is about to be mine.

All I know is that when I leap off that bull's back and chuck my helmet up into the air, Winter is in my arms before it even hits the ground.

All I know is that this win is only important for a few moments. Because when Winter whispers in my ear, "Hope you're ready to do this dad thing again, because there's another Theo doppelgänger on the way," nothing is more important than *us*.

Reckless
playlist

▶ **Take My Name**
Parmalee
02.37

▶ **To Hell & Back**
Maren Morris
03.15

▶ **Every Little Thing She Does Is Magic**
The Police
04:20

▶ **If I Was a Cowboy**
Miranda Lambert
03.14

▶ **Die From A Broken Heart**
Maddie & Tae
03.08

▶ **Go Around**
Kane Brown
03.22

▶ **GOOD TIME**
Niko Moon
03.34

▶ **Hell of A View**
Eric Church
02.54

▶ **Starting Over**
Chris Stapleton
04:00

Brazillian Stroganoff Recipe

*Shared by Larissa Cambusano, whose
family makes this recipe often*

Ingredients:

- 2 boneless, skinless chicken breasts (cut into very
  small pieces)
- 2 tbsp butter
- 1 tbsp olive oil
- 3 garlic cloves (minced)
- ½ onion (diced)
- 3 tbsp ketchup
- 2 tbsp soy sauce
- 1 tbsp mustard
- 1 cup heavy cream
- Salt to taste (approx. ¼ tsp)

- 4 oz can of sliced mushrooms (optional)
- ¼ cup tomato sauce (optional)

Instructions:

1. Sprinkle salt over cubed chicken and set aside.
2. In a large skillet, melt 1 tbsp of butter over medium-high heat and add the olive oil. Wait until hot and add chicken in a single layer. Don't disturb until it starts to sear. Push it all to one side when it begins to brown.
3. Add 1 tbsp of butter, the onion, and the garlic to the empty side. Sautee until translucent.
4. Add heavy cream, ketchup, mustard, soy sauce, and mushrooms (if using.) Mix everything.
5. Check that chicken is done. If it's not, lower heat, cover pan, and let it cook for a bit longer (until it's no longer pink or a thermometer registers 165 F)
6. Once the chicken is cooked but still soft and moist (don't overcook it or it will be hard and dry), turn off the heat and try it. Correct salt if necessary, and if you like it more acidic, add ¼ cup of tomato sauce.
7. Enjoy it over rice along with some potato sticks.

This engagement was supposed to be for show. This agreement? It has an end date.

He once told me he'd never fall in love.

And yet here I am, head over heels for my fake fiancé.

Keep reading for a sneak peek of

Hopeless . . .

Pre-order today at

PIATKUS

Chapter One
Beau

I thought pissing my brother off and storming away would make me feel something.

I was wrong.

Even acting like a raging dick when I'm supposed to help a family friend move into their new house feels ... bland.

As I walk down the main drag in Chestnut Springs, my fingers curl into my palms, nails digging against skin.

I don't feel that either.

I only feel tired.

But not tired enough to sleep.

A train horn blares and I freeze in place. For years, I've covered the way loud noises startle me, but it's different this time.

You'd expect me to choose either fight or flight, but these days I just *brace*.

Pause.

Wait for any emotion to hit. Fear, anxiety, disappointment.

But these days I feel nothing.

I pivot on the corner of Rosewood and Elm to watch the train puff past. Chugging along. Back and forth. Point A to point B. Load. Unload. Wait overnight. Start over again.

"I am a train," I murmur, as I stare at the wheels crushing against the tracks.

A woman pushes a baby in a stroller past me and shoots me a confused look. Her expression changes to surprise when she recognizes me. I think we went to high school together, but that could be said about anyone in this town who was born within a few years of each other.

"Oh, Beau! Sorry, didn't recognize you for a second there."

Probably because I haven't cut my hair in months.

I don't remember her name, so I plaster on a smile. "Not to worry. I'm blocking the crosswalk, aren't I? Here . . ." My arm stretches out to press the crossing button for her.

The woman I can't remember shoots me a grateful grin, hefting a bag up on her shoulder while trying to keep hold of the stroller overflowing with an unnecessary amount of stuff. "Thanks! Nice to see you out and about. You had all of Chestnut Springs worried for a couple of weeks."

My cheek twitches under the strain of keeping my mouth upturned. Yes, I was JTF2, Canada's elite special ops force. Yes, I knowingly missed our transport out to save a prisoner of war. Yes, I was missing in action for weeks and was in rough shape when they found me.

I'm still in rough shape.

People love to talk about it.

You gave us quite a scare.

Try to catch your ride out next time, eh?

I bet you're loving all this attention,

I know they all mean well, but the way they express their interest bugs me. Like my getting stuck in enemy territory on deployment has a single fucking thing to do with them. Like I scared people on purpose, or just casually decided not to pick up a phone.

"Gotta love the small-town support," is what I say, because *You thought you were worried? Try being me* just makes people uncomfortable.

"Well, you've got it in spades," she replies. With a kind nod, she turns and crosses the street.

I look away, not wanting to follow her but not knowing where I'm going either. The opposite direction, I think.

Which is when my eyes land on The Railspur, the best bar in Chestnut Springs.

It doesn't matter the sky is blue, and the sun is out on a beautiful summer afternoon. It doesn't matter that Rhett and other friends need my help with unloading furniture a couple of blocks away.

At this moment, the town bar looks like a damn good hole to hide in.

And a drink doesn't sound too bad either.

"Gary, if you don't slow down, I'm going to take your keys away."

The ruddy-faced older man scoffs as I pull up a stool a few down from him and turn it so one elbow rests on the bar and I'm facing the door. Western decor fills the space, a wagon wheel chandelier, polished wood floors, and mason jar glassware. It may be just another a small-town bar, but the extensive updates give it an elevated sort of feel.

"Don't know when you got so lippy," he grumbles, dropping his pint glass away from his lips. "You used to barely talk to anyone. Now you're bossing me around like a little tyrant all the time."

Shiny, almost black hair swishes over Bailey Jansen's tanned shoulders. Her back is to us as she bends down to pull glasses out of the small washing machine behind the bar.

"Got comfortable, I guess. And you could use some bossing, old man. Sitting here, harassing me every day."

"I do no such thing. I'm perfectly nice to you. One of the only ones who is, I reckon."

She spins now, white towel in hand, to point at her only customer in the quiet bar. "You are. And I consider you a friend, which is why I tell you every day you drink too damn much."

Her gaze snaps to mine, dark eyes widening in surprise, like she didn't hear me over the country music and hum of the dishwasher.

"If I stop, you'll be out of work. And maybe even a friend."

Gary is talking to her like he hasn't noticed my presence, but she responds to him without looking away from me. "I can live with that, Gar." She pauses, tongue darting out over parted lips.

Full, glossy lips.

"Beau Eaton. Nice to see you."

The man turns, now alerted to my presence. "Well shit, that is Beau Eaton, isn't it? Big fella, aren't you?" Gary slurs and Bailey's free hand darts forward to swipe his keys off the bar.

Gary's eyes close and he groans. "Every fuckin' day."

"Yep. Every fuckin' day." She shoves them into her back pocket and then turns back to the washing machine where glassware has backed up. "Beau, what can I get you? Got anyone joining you? Probably want your favorite couch, yeah?"

I swallow and glance at the couch where my brothers, friends, and I enjoyed many a night out. It feels like a different version of myself sat there. The new Beau sits at the bar with the shy neighbor girl who wears a pair of acid-wash Levi's better than anyone he's ever seen.

"Nah, just me today. I'll have whatever Gary here is having."

"A Buddyz Best for the town hero!" Gary slaps his palm on the bar and I flinch. My eyes freeze on his weathered hand, flush against the polished wood of the bar top. When I lift my gaze, forcing myself to act casual, Bailey's got her brows drawn tight, dark irises boring into my face as though she has me all figured out.

The flat smile I force onto my lips doesn't seem to impress her. In fact, before she turns away to pour me a frothy pint, her head shakes subtly, like she's disappointed.

My gaze trails over her body again, and I rack my brain to remember the last time I saw her. She's always been sweet, shy little Bailey Jansen. Sadly, born into the least respected family in town. Her dad and brothers have dabbled in it all—drugs, prison, theft—and her mom took off years ago.

Worst of all, their land borders ours. I can see it from my house on the ranch, just on the other side of the river where I've put up a barbed wire fence so those assholes know where to turn back around.

But Bailey has always been different. I think I've always felt bad for her, always felt protective of her. The stares, the whispers. I imagine living in a small town where almost every resident has a story about your family must be fucking brutal. So, I've always been nice to her. I like her—have no reason not to.

She's worked at the Railspur for years now, I just . . . can't remember how many. Can't decide if enough years have passed for me to notice the way her tank top lifts today, showing a peek of skin on her flat stomach. Or for me to think about the way her perfectly round breasts would fit so well in my hands.

"How long you been working here, Bailey?" I ask, watching her shoulders go a little tense when I do.

She clears her throat. "Just over four years. Started at eighteen." *Twenty-two.*

Fuck. I'm thirty-five, which means I was a teenager when—I brush the thought away and drop my eyes as she tosses a coaster down in front of me, followed by a pint of golden lager, white foam spilling over the edge.

"Thanks," I grumble as I swipe a hand through my hair.

"Mm-hmm," is all she says.

Bailey is the only person in town who hasn't fallen all over herself to tell me what a hero I am since I got home. She works quietly and I try to keep my eyes from straying to her, wondering why she went from chatting happily to shutting down the moment I sat at her bar.

"MIA for two weeks, huh?" Gary starts in, and I see Bailey roll her eyes as she polishes a pint glass to a clear shine.

"Yup." Oh, good. The only thing anyone talks to me about anymore.

"How was that?"

"Gary!" Bailey's hands fall to her sides and a look of pure shock paints her face.

"What?"

"You can't just ask things like that."

"Why not?"

I can't help it. I chuckle and decide to rescue Bailey from feeling like she needs to save me. "Real warm. Got a nice tan."

The man narrows his eyes, movements a little sloppy. I wonder how long he's been here since it's barely after lunch and he's clearly wrecked. "Heard you got burned. Not the tan I'd be hoping for."

"*Ga-ry.*" Based on the way she enunciates his name, he's truly horrified Bailey.

My palm slides across the bar, drawing her attention. "It's okay. Everyone knows about the burns."

She blinks, eyes suddenly looking a little glassy.

"Really, I'd rather people shoot straight than kiss my ass or tiptoe around me. Why do you think I'm hiding out here in the middle of the day?"

"Because Bailey is the best bartender in town!"

She snorts, lips tipping up as she goes back to polishing a glass. I try to remember if I've ever really seen her smile. I'm not sure I have. She's always busy trying to blend into the background, and I'm only ever here when it's busy. I don't even know if I've ever properly heard her voice, until now. The gentle, melodic tone to it is almost soothing.

I'm sick of people talking to me, but it strikes me that listening to Bailey talk might now be so bad.

The first sip of my beer goes down cold and refreshing. I sigh, feeling a weight come off my shoulders in the presence of the town drunk and the town pariah.

I feel a kindred spirit to them right now, a misfit in my own home.

"Third-degree burns on my feet," I announce, since bluntness seems to be the theme here today. "Skin grafts."

"S'okay. You can find some girl with a weird foot fetish who will love that shit."

"Jesus Christ, Gary. No more booze." Bailey props her hands on the bar and drops her head with a groan.

"So long as your dick is okay." He waves his hand up and down my body. "Face looks fine, wouldn't you say, Bails? You'll be alright, kid. You'll find someone to love ya."

Bailey's gaze wanders over my features curiously, a warm blush painting her cheeks as she softly replies with, "Yeah," and then blinks away.

Her eyes, that one little word, it . . . makes my blood pump faster. It makes me feel something.

My throat bobs as I swallow the dryness in my mouth, trying to push that moment away.

Then I take another sip and swipe a hand over my stubbled chin. "Love is the last thing I need. But this beer is really hitting the spot."

And maybe if I drink enough of it, I'll be able to sleep for more than a few hours tonight.

Chapter Two
Bailey

It's been two weeks since Beau Eaton walked into my bar in the middle of the day. Two weeks since I took one look at him and almost dropped the glass in my hand. He's hard to miss with his broad shoulders and tall, well-built frame, long legs that have him a head above most men who walk through that door. Light brown hair, a little too long, flops over his forehead, the perfect frame for silver-gray eyes. Even looking a little unkempt the way he does right now. Beau Eaton is fucking hot.

And hot is one thing, but Beau is *nice* too. And funny.

A true triple threat—or at least he *was*.

He's never treated me like I'm wearing a scarlet letter on my chest, even when others have. I really only know him from the bar, but he's never held my family's reputation against me. He's always offered kind words, a polite touch on my elbow, and a good tip at the end of the night.

But he's still the town prince, and I'm still the town trash.

I'm the bartender and he's the hero.

He's an Eaton, and I'm a Jansen.

And yet, he's here every damn day since the afternoon he walked in here looking like a caged animal who broke free.

Here every damn day drinking with fucking Gary.

The first day started out sweet enough. He was endearing if I'm being honest. But for the past two weeks, his presence has slowly morphed from light to dark, gathering itself into an ominous storm cloud.

It's getting to where he's making everyone around him uncomfortable. You can feel the electricity in the air, like lightning ready to strike.

I'm feeling fed up with him too. He's reminding me of my dad, or my brothers, and I have sparse patience for that kind of toxicity.

He comes in mid-afternoon and nurses his pint, quietly simmering. I swear I watch his frustration bubble up to a boil right before my eyes. His hand stays clamped around the glass and he takes tight sips from it with white knuckles.

I'm almost positive he's going to shatter it one of these days. He seems too big, too strong, too angry to be squeezing something that fragile so hard.

"So, what'd you do when you spent those two weeks stuck in the desert?"

My teeth clamp at Gary's words. I know he means well, but he's not reading the room right now. Not reading Beau. Must have missed the way he flinched when a booming thunder storm rolled through not thirty minutes ago.

Yeah, Beau looks ready to burst tonight, but Gary hasn't noticed.

"Tried to stay alive," Beau bites out. There's a tremor in his voice, a quality that reminds me of a dog when they growl at you. It's a warning to back away.

And Gary is too drunk to notice.

"They say you missed your flight on purpose to stay behind and save that journalist. That's some real hero complex shit."

Beau just stares at his pint, gazing into the golden liquid. They've already talked about this, but alcohol makes a person repetitive. I know because I've spent years studying drunk people. I'm practically an expert.

"Imagine where your life would be if you hadn't."

My lashes flutter shut, because my gut tells me there was a line, and Gary just stepped right over it.

Or right into it.

Beau's thickly corded arm swipes out, knocking both their glasses onto the bar floor. Beer sprays across the smattering of patrons seated nearby, and if not for the music blaring at this point in the night, I'm certain The Railspur would be dead silent as they watch the altercation unfold.

Beau stands so fast his stool topples behind him with a crash. Gary looks terrified. "Imagine where your life would be if you didn't sit here drinking and embarrassing yourself every fucking day, Gary. Ever think about that?"

His chest heaves, the splatter of liquid making the cotton of his T-shirt stick to his clearly defined pecs. Only someone who grew up in the household I did could be smack dab in the middle of a moment like this and be checking a guy out.

Childhood trauma much?

Beau isn't my dad though, and I'm not worried the way I would be if I were in the house I grew up in.

"Beau," my voice comes out clear, not a single waver to it.

"All alone every damn day, a young girl as your best friend. Seems a little pervert—"

"Beau Eaton, shut your mouth and get your ass outside."

His head swivels, gray eyes latching onto mine like he just noticed my presence. Like he didn't expect little Bailey Jansen to be the one barking at him.

He straightens, but I don't care how tall he is.

He doesn't scare me.

Not even when he's like this.

I point to the emergency exit that leads to the patio, and my hand doesn't shake at all. I'm not nervous. I'm pissed off.

Beau turns stiffly, striding around the end of the bar, past the server station and straight out into the fading light. If I didn't know how many drinks he's had, I wouldn't notice the slight stagger in his steps, or the way he leans on the door just a little heavier than necessary.

Before I cut through the small wooden push gate to follow, I glance back at Gary.

"Too far?" he asks, averting his gaze.

My lips flatten against each other. "Yeah, Gary. Too far."

He swipes a hand through his thinning hair and drops his head, hand tapping over the keys he laid on the bar the minute he sat down. "I'll catch a cab."

I respond with a firm nod before shoving out the door onto the darkened patio. The summer storm drove away all the people seated here, their forgotten glasses now partially filled with rainwater.

I can still smell the storm. And Beau. Pine mingles with something deeper, more sensual. Tobacco maybe, like a cigar.

He's slumped against the outer brick facade of the train station turned bar. As I approach, he shoves his fists into the pockets of his jeans, chin dropped almost to his chest, eyes fixed on the sneakers he's always sporting.

They feel out of place for him, too white and shiny, too pristine.

"You can't pull that shit in my bar," I say.

He scoffs, still refusing to meet my gaze. "*Your* bar, huh?"

"Yes, Beau. *My* bar. My place. The only place in this town where people don't treat me like shit. I bust my ass working here. I bust my ass trying to make customers like me. And behind that wood is *my* bubble. Gary isn't perverted, he's fucking lonely. And he's one of the few people who is consistently kind to me. So, if you think you're gonna waltz into *my* bar acting like some sort of untouchable asshole and scaring all *my* regulars away with your antics, you've got another thing coming."

Now his eyes are on me, a little unsteady, but narrowed. "Untouchable asshole?"

"Yes." I cross my arms, like they might give me some protection from him. He looks a little wild tonight, a little dangerous, not like the happy-go-lucky guy we all thought we knew before his last deployment.

Silvery light plays off his features, tan skin and luminous eyes almost glowing as he stares me down. The only thing that moves between us is his chest rising and falling in time with mine.

But I don't look away. I'm so over men trying to intimidate me. And it feels wrong on him, so I don't let him have it.

After our stare down moves from heated moment into awkward territory, he looks away, jaw flexing.

"Did I embarrass myself?" His voice is all gravel and rumbles over my skin.

"You did. But the good news is your last name is Eaton, so everyone will forgive you and go back to kissing your feet the minute you walk in there and flash them a smile."

"Bailey, what the fuck? Did you really just say that to me?"

"Yes." My head tilts. "Because it's true. All I had to do was to be born into my family and everyone looks at me like they're waiting for that part of my genetics to rear its ugly head. Like I'll go from hardworking and polite to a hillbilly criminal mastermind in the blink of an eye just because my last name is Jansen." His brow furrows deeper the longer I talk. "So, yeah. I think you're gonna be fine, even though you embarrassed yourself."

"That's not true."

"What part?"

"People thinking that about you."

"Ha!" The laugh lurches from my throat, sharp and lacking any humor. "That is adorably naive," I say, shaking my head in disbelief.

"Well, I don't think that about you."

I swallow now, eyes flitting away. It's true that Beau has always been kind to me—to everyone, really. Maybe that's why this new version of him pisses me off so much. "I know." I shoot him a grateful smile. "You're one of the good ones, Beau. That's why you can't keep doing this."

"Doing what?"

"Sitting at my bar and drinking yourself into a sullen stupor every night."

A quiet keening noise escapes him as his head rolls back and forth against the wall, hands coming up out of his pockets to scrub at his face. "It helps me sleep at night."

"What?" I can hear my heart pounding in my ears. Somehow, that's not the response I expected.

It's painfully honest.

"The alcohol. It helps me fall asleep. I go home to the ranch and crash. I haven't been sleeping well these days."

My stomach drops at his admission.

"You telling me you drive like this?" My finger waves up and down him, catching on the bulge of keys in his front pocket.

His wide eyes plead with me, desperate and forlorn. I feel monumentally stupid for assuming he was too good of a guy to get behind a wheel in this state.

"Beau." I step forward, right up to him. He tenses, but I'm too pissed off to have many boundaries right now. And I've always felt more at ease around him than most people. He's always had a way of making me feel like that, which is why I don't think twice about shoving my hand into the front pocket of his jeans and wrapping my fingers around his keys.

His body is entirely stiff. I can feel his muscles coil, but he makes no move to stop me. The jangle of metal between us has me looking up into his eyes for a sign I've taken things too far.

I angle my face up to his, I only see those moonlit eyes and the way his Adam's apple bobs as he swallows.

I'm caught in his thrall for a moment.

"I'll make you a chamomile tea," I say, breaking the tense silence between us. "Helps with sleep."

He nods and drops his head. The tension between us evaporates as he follows me back into the bar, gaze trained on the floor to avoid the prying eyes staring at him after his outburst.

I can tell he's ashamed. And he should be, but I'm not going to pile onto his punishment. Instead, I prepare him a steaming mug of tea, wipe up the beer he spilled, and carry on with my night like he isn't here.

I refill the tea.

He drinks the tea.

We don't talk, but he watches me. I see him spinning the mug between his broad palms. I feel the outline of his keys in the back pocket of my jeans.

Pete, our cook, walks out of the back at 10 p.m. "You all good out here, Bails? Kitchen's closed."

I scan the bar. It's busy, but not unmanageable. We're only open for two more hours on a Monday night anyway. "Yup. All good here," I reply, giving him a brief thumbs up.

Pete returns the motion and heads out the front doors.

It's when I check Beau's tea again that he stops me. "So, he leaves and you're here alone for the rest of the night?"

I shrug as I take his mug to add water. "Yeah. I'm a shift manager now, so if it was busier I'd have kept a server on, but I cut her early."

He rests his forearms on the bar, pads of his long fingers pressed together like he needs something to do with them. "But you're alone? You shut down alone?"

Steam rises as hot water pours from the dispenser.

"Correct." I slide the mug across the bar top until it bumps into the tips of his fingers as I try to remember how many refills I've done since the tea is looking awfully watery.

I crouch down and rummage through the box of tea on the bottom shelf. The Railspur is not a big tea place, but I find another bag of chamomile and drop it into the mug.

When I tie the string around the handle, Beau doesn't move his palms from around the cup, like he's desperate to soak up the heat.

"That's not safe for you. What if something happens?"

My fingertips brush against his hand as I complete the knot.

I peek up now, lifting one eyebrow. "Like some guy pitching a fit and knocking beer all over the place?"

He glares at me, and I try to keep from smirking at him.

With a nonchalant shrug, I answer the question. "I deal with it."

The only thing Beau gives me in response is a hard stare and a grunt.

But he doesn't leave. He drinks tea at my bar all night long. For hours, he sits there, keeping watch. And when I kick everyone out at midnight and shut things down, he stays behind, silently guarding me.

"Are you sober?" I ask as he walks me through the darkened parking lot to my car.

"I've been drinking fucking chamomile tea for four hours. I've never been more sober or hydrated in my life."

I suck in a deep breath and pull his keys from my back pocket, holding them out to him on a flat palm. "Don't pull that shit on me again, Beau."

His throat works as he reaches forward and swipes the keys from me. "You're not how I remember you, Bailey."

I let myself smirk now, because, of course, we all change. I couldn't stay that frozen, terrified little girl forever.

I wanted to change.

"You're not how I remember you either, Beau."

His eyes shift back and forth between mine, like he's searching for something in them. "What nights do you work?"

I snort, looking down to pull my own keys from my purse. "What nights don't I work?"

"Okay, what nights do you work *alone*?"

"Sunday through Tuesday," I reply, zipping my bag.

Beau nods and says a terse, "Okay," before spinning on his heel and giving me his back, looking every bit the military hero he is. Head held high, shoulders perfectly straight.

Regal, like the prince everyone treats him as.

He must have missed the memo though. Because this man seems to think he's some sort of knight in shining armor.

One who starts pulling up a stool every Sunday through Tuesday to drink chamomile tea until midnight, so I don't have to close by myself.

Acknowledgments

I'm not sure I've ever written a character I relate more to than Winter. Motherhood is a wild ride, and while I've had the most incredible supportive husband with me from the start, I still had days where I wanted to hide in a closet and cry. Single moms: you are the real heroes. Seriously, standing ovation to you.

With that said, this book didn't come about without the support of some seriously amazing people in my life. Major thank-yous going out to . . .

Mr. Silver, I'll always thank you first because you get up and make me a coffee every dang morning before I even get out of bed at 5 a.m. so that I can stumble into my office and write. I don't even really know if I'd be able to do it without that daily ritual. You are my rock, and most favorite barista.

Shoutout to my son whose current favorite joke is calling me *Elsie Shrimp*. It's not that funny if I think about it, and yet it makes me giggle every time, so it deserves to be immortalized. You're only seven and make me laugh every day, and there's something incredibly special about that.

My parents, who are always my biggest supporters. Thank you

for the love and cheerleading, even when I disappear into weird writer headspace and don't communicate for days.

Catherine Cowles . . . these stress boners are for you! I promised I'd work that into a book, and goddamnit, I *delivered*. You're an incredible mentor, and even better friend. I am so grateful for you. And if anyone is wondering, I send Catherine a disturbing number of voice memos on a daily basis and one of them involved telling her about how my dog gets stress boners.

Kandi and Lena, my Spicy Sprint Sluts, you make writing these books easier. And a whole lot less lonely. Waking up to your texts is *always* a highlight.

My assistant, Krista, who pretty much runs my life. No one looks better in fishnets than you. Also, you're my daddy.

To Echo Grayce, my incredibly talented cover designer, who didn't get annoyed at me when I changed and tweaked a million things on these covers—thank you! They are truly stunning.

Paula, my editor extraordinaire. My professional back-patter. My fellow butter-lover. Don't ever leave me. Because *I'd find yoouuu*.

My developmental editor, Júlia. Your insights are next level, and pretending you had the wrong number when you sent me graphic voice memos breaking down the sex scenes in this book brought me great joy and was truly a highlight in this production process. Thank you for tolerating me.

To my proofreader, beta reader, and—gosh, what don't you do? Leticia, this book is so much better for having had your hands on it. Thank you.

To my beta girlies who never fail to crack me up as they read. Trinity, Josette, Amy, you are all so wonderful, thank you for gifting me with your time and opinions. I so appreciate you all.

Saluting my agent, Kimberly Brower, who has done so much for these books and this series. I'm very lucky to have you. Thank you for all your hard work.

Rebekah West, my editor at Piatkus, I so enjoyed working on this book with you. Thank you for believing in me so hard. I am endlessly flattered by all your support.

Finally, to my ARC readers and street team members ... I don't even know where to start. You make a bigger difference than you'll ever realize. Every post makes me smile, every review has an impact. I don't care how many followers any of you have, you're all wonderful and deserving and I appreciate each and every one of you more than you know. Thank you for helping me build this career.

Can't get enough of Elsie Silver?

Go back to the start and re-read
Rhett and Summer's story today!

'Elsie Silver's writing is a true revelation!'
Ali Hazelwood

Available now at

The Elsie Silver Saloon

Come hang out in The Saloon on Facebook and interact with Elsie! Early announcements, exclusive excerpts, bonus giveaways, and general book boyfriend chit chat all happens here.

Take me to The Saloon!